Nicole Helm grew up with her nose in a book and the dream of one day becoming a writer. Luckily, after a few failed career choices, she gets to follow that dream—writing down-to-earth contemporary romance and romantic suspense. From farmers to cowboys, Midwest to *the* West, Nicole writes stories about people finding themselves and finding love in the process. She lives in Missouri with her husband and two sons, and dreams of someday owning a barn.

Carla Cassidy is an award-winning, *New York Times* bestselling author who has written over 170 books, including 150 for Mills & Boon. She has won the Centennial Award from Romance Writers of America. Most recently she won the 2019 Write Touch Readers' Award for her Mills & Boon Heroes title *Desperate Strangers*. Carla believes the only thing better than curling up with a good book is sitting down at the computer with a good story to write.

COLD CASE KIDNAPPING

NICOLE HELM

UNSOLVED BAYOU MURDER

CARLA CASSIDY

MILLS & BOON

First Published in Great Britain 2023
by Mills & Boon, an imprint of HarperCollins*Publishers* Ltd
1 London Bridge Street, London, SE1 9GF

www.harpercollins.co.uk

HarperCollins*Publishers*
Macken House, 39/40 Mayor Street Upper,
Dublin 1, D01 C9W8, Ireland

Cold Case Kidnapping © 2023 Nicole Helm
Unsolved Bayou Murder © 2023 Carla Bracale

ISBN: 978-0-263-30752-8

1223

This book is produced from independently certified FSC™ paper to ensure responsible forest management.

For more information visit: www.harpercollins.co.uk/green

Printed and Bound in the UK using 100% Renewable Electricity at CPI Group (UK) Ltd, Croydon, CR0 4YY

COLD CASE
KIDNAPPING

NICOLE HELM

For the reluctant heroes.

Chapter One

Grant Hudson had been well versed in fear since the age of sixteen when his parents vanished—seemingly into thin air, never to be seen or heard from again. So, as an adult, he'd made fear and uncertainty his life. First, in the military with the Marines and now as a cold case investigator with his siblings.

Privately investigating cold cases didn't involve the same kind of danger he'd seen in Middle Eastern deserts, but the uncertainty, the puzzles and never knowing which step to take was just as much a part of his current life as it had been in the Marines.

And if he focused on seemingly unsolvable cases all day, he didn't have time to think about the nightmares that plagued him.

"Your ten o'clock appointment is here."

Grant looked up from his coffee. His sister was dressed for ranch work but held a file folder that likely had all the information about his new case.

Hudson Sibling Solutions, HSS, was a family affair. The brainchild of his oldest brother, Jack, and a well-oiled machine in which all six Hudson siblings played a part, just as they all played a part in running the Hudson Ranch that had been in their family for five generations.

They had solved more cases than they hadn't, and Grant considered that a great success. Usually the answers weren't happy endings, but in some strange way, it helped ease the unknowns in their own parents' case.

Grant glanced at the clock as he finished off his coffee. "It's only nine forty-five."

"She's prompt," Mary agreed, handing him the file. "She's in the living room whenever you're ready."

But "whenever you're ready" wasn't part and parcel with what HSS offered.

They didn't make people wait. They didn't shunt people off to small offices and cramped spaces. Usually people trying to get answers on a cold case had spent enough time in police stations, detective offices and all manner of uncomfortable rooms answering the same questions over and over again.

The Hudsons knew that better than anyone—particularly Jack, who'd been the last person to see their parents alive and had been the only legal adult in the family at the time of their disappearance. Jack had been adamant when they began the family investigation business that they offer a different experience for those left behind.

So they met their clients in the homey living room of the Hudson ranch house. They didn't make people wait if they could help it. They treated their clients like guests... The kind of hospitality their mother would have been proud of.

Grant had made himself familiar with today's case prior to this morning, but he skimmed the file Mary had handed off. A missing person, not out of the ordinary for Hudson Sibling Solutions. Dahlia Easton had reported her sister, Rose, missing about thirteen months ago, after her sister had disappeared on a trip to Texas.

Dahlia Easton herself was a librarian from Minnesota. Dahlia was convinced she'd found evidence that placed Rose near Sunrise, Wyoming—which had led her to the HSS.

Ms. Easton hadn't divulged that evidence yet, instead insisting on an in-person meeting to do such. It was Grant's turn to take the lead, so he walked through the hallway that still housed all the framed art his mother had hung once upon a time—various Wyoming landscapes—to the living room.

A redhead sat on the couch, head down and focused on the phone she held. Her long hair curtained her face, and she didn't look up as Grant entered.

He stepped farther into the room and cleared this throat. "Ms. Easton."

The woman looked up from her phone and blinked at him. She didn't move. She sat there as he held out his hand waiting for her to shake it or greet him in some way.

It was a strange thing to see a pretty woman seated on the couch he'd once crowded onto with all his siblings to watch Disney movies. Stranger still to feel the gut kick of attraction.

It made him incredibly uncomfortable when he rarely allowed himself discomfort. He should be thrilled his body could still react to a pretty woman in a perfectly normal way, but he found nothing but a vague sense of unease filling him as she sat there, eyes wide, studying him.

Her hair was a dark red, her eyes a deep tranquil blue on a heart-shaped face that might have been more arresting if she didn't have dark circles under her eyes and her clothes didn't seem to hang off a too-skinny frame. Like many of the clients who came to HSS for help, she wore the physical toll of what she'd been through in obvious ways…enough for even a stranger to notice.

He set those impressions and his own discomfort aside and smiled welcomingly. "Ms. Easton, I'm Grant Hudson. I'll be taking the lead on your case on behalf of HSS. While all six of us work in different facets of investigation, I'll be your point person." He finally dropped his hand since she clearly wasn't going to shake it. "May I?" he said pointing to the armchair situated across from the couch. His father had fallen asleep in that very chair every single movie night.

"You look like a cowboy," she said, her voice sounding raspy from overuse or lack of sleep, presumably.

The corner of his mouth quirked up, a lick of amusement working through him. He supposed a cowboy was quite a sight for someone from Minnesota. "Well, I suppose in a way I am."

"Right. Wyoming. Of course." She shook her head. "I'm sorry. I'm out of sorts."

"No apologies necessary." He settled himself on the chair. She didn't look so much out of sorts as she did exhausted. He set the file down on the coffee table in between them.

"I have all the information Mary collected from you."

"Mary's the woman I talked to on the phone and emailed. I thought she'd…"

"Mary handles the administrative side of things, but I'll be taking the lead on actually investigating. I can get Mary to sit in if you'd feel more comfortable with a woman present?"

"No, it isn't that. I just…" She shook her head. "This is fine."

Grant nodded, then decided what this woman needed

was to get some sleep and a good meal in her. "Have you had breakfast?"

"Um." Her eyebrows drew together. "I don't understand what you're…"

"I'd like you to recount everything you know, so we might be here a while. Just making sure you're up for it."

"Oh, I'm not much for breakfast."

He'd figured as much. He pulled his phone out of his pocket and sent a quick text to Mary. He wouldn't push the subject, but he wasn't about to let Dahlia keel over either. He slid the phone back in his pocket.

"I've got your file here. All about your sister's trip to Texas. The credit card reports, cell phone records. Everything you gave us. But you said you had reason to believe she ended up here in Wyoming."

"Yes," Dahlia agreed, putting her own phone into a bag that sat next to her. "Everything the police uncovered happened in Texas," Dahlia said. "But she just…disappeared into thin air, as far as anyone can tell me, but obviously that isn't true. People can't just disappear."

But they did. All the time. There were a lot of ways to make sure a person was never found. More than even Grant could probably fathom, and he could fathom a lot. Which was why he focused on one individual case at a time. "So, there's no evidence she ever left Texas?"

"She took one of those DNA tests, and it matched her with some people in Texas," Dahlia said earnestly, avoiding the direct question. "She was supposed to go to Texas and meet them. She never made it to the people—at least the police there didn't think so. When all the clues dried up, I decided to look at Rose's research. The genealogy stuff that prompted her to take the DNA test. I researched everything she had, and it led me to a secret offshoot of the Texas family that wound up in Truth, Wyoming."

Grant tried not to frown. Because, no, there wasn't proof Rose Easton had left Texas, and also because no one in Sunrise particularly cared to think about Truth, Wyoming. "Ah" was all he said.

"It's a cult."

"It was a cult," Grant replied. "The Feds wiped them out before I was born." Still, people tried to stir up all the Order of Truth nonsense every few years. But there was no evidence that the cult had done anything but die out after the federal raid in 1978.

"Doesn't everything gone come around back again?" Dahlia asked, nervous energy pumping off her. "And if this line of our family was involved then, doesn't it mean they could be involved now?"

Grant studied the woman. She looked tired and brittle. It didn't diminish her beauty, just gave it a fragile hue. Fragile didn't cut it in these types of situations, but here she was. Still standing. Still searching.

She was resting all her hopes on the wrong thing if she was looking into the Order of Truth, but she believed it. She was clearly holding on to this tiny thread for dear life. So Grant smiled kindly. "Let's see your evidence."

HE DIDN'T BELIEVE HER. No different than any of the police officers and detectives back home or in Texas. Once Dahlia uttered the word *cult*—especially one that had been famously wiped out—people stopped listening.

Grant Hudson was no different, except he was placating

her by asking for her evidence. Dahlia didn't know if that was more insulting than waving her off or not. Honestly, she was too tired to figure out how she felt about much of anything.

She'd driven almost eighteen hours from Minneapolis to Sunrise in two days and had barely slept last night in the nice little cabin she'd rented. She was too anxious and tangled up about this strange connection. Too amped at the thought of *hope* after so long.

"I think you probably have all the evidence you care about," Dahlia said, trying to keep her tone even. "I know investigators are obsessed with facts, but facts haven't helped me. Sometimes you have to tie some ideas together to find the facts."

Grant studied her. It had been a silly thing to say, that he looked like a cowboy, but it was simply true. It wasn't just the drawl, it was something about the way he walked. There were the cowboy boots of course, and the Western decor all around them, but something in the square jaw or slightly crooked nose made her think of the Wild West. The way he hadn't fully smiled, but his mouth had *curved* in a slow move that had left her scrambling for words.

"We are investigators, and we do have to work in the truth," Grant said, still using that kind veneer to his words, though Dahlia sensed an irritation simmering below them. "But I think you'll find we're not like the police departments you've dealt with. I'll admit, I think the cult is the wrong tree to bark up, but if you give me reason to change my mind, I'll bark away."

The tall slender woman who'd let her in the house entered the room pushing a cart. She wore adorable cowboy boots with colorful flowers on them and Dahlia had no doubt when she spoke, it would be tinged with that same smooth Western drawl Grant had.

It was easy to see the two were related even if Grant was tall and broad and...*built*.

There was something in the eyes, in the way they moved. Dahlia didn't have the words for it, just that they functioned like a unit. One that had been in each other's pockets their whole lives.

People had never been able to tell that about her and Rose, aside from being named for flowers. It took getting to know them, together, to see the way they had learned how to deal with each other and their parents. The rhythm of being a sibling.

Dahlia had been turned into an only child now, and she didn't know how to function in that space. Not with her parents, who had given up on Rose when the police had. Not with her friends, all of whom were more Rose's friends than hers and who wanted to be involved in a tragedy and their grief more than they wanted answers.

Only Dahlia couldn't let it go. Couldn't hold on to her old life in this new world where her sister didn't exist.

Not dead. Not gone. She didn't *exist*.

"I told you I'm not a breakfast eater," Dahlia said sharply and unkindly. She might have felt bad about that, felt her grandmother's disapproval from half a country away, but she was tired of caring what everyone else felt.

Grant apparently felt unbothered by her snap. "So consider it lunch." He looked at his sister. "Thanks, Mary."

She nodded, smiled at Dahlia, then left. Grant immediately took a plate and began to arrange things on it. Dahlia figured he'd shove it at her, and she had all sorts of reasons to tell him to shove it down his own throat.

Instead, he set it next to the file folder. Picking a grape and popping it into his own mouth before pouring himself some coffee.

Dahlia knew she'd lost too much weight. She understood she didn't sleep well enough, and her health was suffering because of it. She'd seen a therapist to help her come to terms with Rose's disappearance.

But no amount of self-awareness or therapy could stop her from this driving need to find the truth.

She didn't know if Rose was still alive. She was prepared—or tried to prepare herself—for the ugly truths that could be awaiting her. Namely, that Rose was dead and had been all this time. Her sweet, vibrant sister. Murdered and discarded.

It wasn't just possible, it was likely, and yet Dahlia had to know. She couldn't rest, not really, until she had the truth.

And if you never find it?

She simply didn't know. So she'd keep going until something changed.

Grant continued to eat as he flipped through papers that were presumably the reports and information she'd emailed to Mary.

Dahlia wasn't hungry, but she hadn't been for probably the entire past year. Still, food was fuel, and this food was free. She could hardly sidestep that when her entire life savings was being poured into hiring Hudson Sibling Solutions and staying in Wyoming until the mystery was solved.

She finally forced herself to pick a few pieces of fruit and a hard-boiled egg and put them on a plate. She'd been guzzling coffee for days, so she went for the bottle of water instead.

"Tell me why you decided to come all the way out here." He said it silky smooth, and whether it was the drawl or his demeanor, he made it sound like a gentle request.

She knew it was an order though. And she knew he'd ignore it like everyone else had. It was too big of a leap to take, and yet...

"Rose found out our great-grandfather was married before he married our great-grandmother. And he had a son from this first marriage. A man named Eugene Green."

Grant's expression didn't move, but something in the air around them did. Likely because he knew Eugene Green to be the founder of the Order of Truth.

"That's not exactly a close relation, is it? Something like a half great-great-uncle. If that."

"If that," Dahlia agreed. Her stomach turned, but still she forced herself to eat a grape. Drink some of the water. "But it was in Rose's notes."

Grant flipped through the papers again. "What notes?"

Dahlia moved for her bag and pulled out the thick binder she'd been carting around. "After the police decided it was a cold case, they returned her computer to me. I printed off everything she'd collected about our family history. *That's* what took her to Texas. She had a binder just like this. With more originals, but she scanned and labeled everything. So I recreated it. The Wyoming branch and Texas branch of the family are one and the same. It connects."

Grant eyed the binder. "Ms. Easton..."

"I know. You don't believe me. No one does. That's okay." She hadn't come all this way just for someone to believe her.

"And you can hardly look through it all. But there is this." She pulled out the piece of paper she'd been keeping in the front pocket of the binder. "The picture on the top is from security footage of the gas station in Texas where Rose was last spotted. That's Rose," she said pointing to her sister. "No one can identify the man with her, but he looks an awfully lot like the picture on the bottom. A picture of Eugene Green from my sister's notes."

Grant didn't even flick a glance at the picture. "Eugene Green is dead."

"Yes, but not everyone who might look like him is."

Grant seemed to consider this, but then people—law enforcements, investigators, even friends—always did. At first. "Can I keep this?"

Dahlia nodded. She had digital copies of everything. She wasn't taking any chances. If HSS took all her information and lost it, discarded it or ignored it, she'd always have her own copies to keep her going.

"Did you have anything else that might tie Rose to Truth or Wyoming?" Grant asked.

No, she hadn't come here thinking HSS would believe her, but she'd…hoped. She couldn't seem to stop herself from hoping. "No, not exactly."

"Can I ask why you couldn't have told us this over the phone?"

Dahlia looked at the picture. Every police officer she'd talked to about it told her she was grasping at straws. That the Order of Truth was gone, and all the Greens had long since left the Truth area. That the man in the picture wasn't *with* Rose. He was just getting gas at the pump next to her.

"I'm not sure I could explain it in a way that would make any sense to you, but I needed to come here."

Grant nodded. "Well, I'll look into this. Is there anything else?"

Dahlia shoved her binder, sans security picture, back in her bag and then stood. He was dismissing her now that he understood her evidence was circumstantial—according to the police.

She was disappointed. She could admit that to herself. She'd expected or hoped for a miracle. Even as she'd told herself they wouldn't care any more than anyone else had, there'd been a seed of hope this family solving cold cases might believe her.

She should end this. The Hudsons weren't going to do any more than the police had, and she was going to run out of money eventually. "If you don't have anything new in a week, I suppose that will be that."

His eyebrows rose as he stood. "A week isn't much time to solve a cold case."

"I don't need it solved. I just need some forward movement to prove I'm paying for something tangible. If you can prove to me the Order of Truth has nothing to do with this—irrefutably—that'll be enough."

He seemed to consider this, then gave her a nod. "You're staying at the Meadowlark Cabin?" Grant asked as he motioned her to follow him.

Dahlia nodded as she retraced her footsteps through the big stone-floored foyer to the large front door with its stained glass sidelights. Mountains and stars.

"How long are you planning on staying?"

Dahlia looked away from the glass mountains to Grant's austere face. "As long as it takes."

Again, his expression didn't quite move, but she got the distinct feeling he didn't approve. Still, he said nothing, just opened the front door.

"I'll be in touch," he said.

She forced herself to smile and shake his outstretched hand.

Just because he'd be in touch didn't mean she was going to go hole herself in her room at her rented cabin in Sunrise. No.

She planned on doing some investigating of her own. She'd come here hoping the Hudsons could help, sure, but she'd known what she really needed to do.

Help herself.

Chapter Two

"Did you know about this?"

Mary looked down from where she was situated on her horse. She adjusted the reins in her hands and then studied the paper Grant held. Mary frowned. "Is that Eugene Green?"

"Your new client seems to think he's involved."

Her frown deepened. "Did you mention that he died like fifty years ago?"

"I did. I also mentioned the Feds wiped out the Order of Truth in the seventies. You're supposed to do a better job of weeding out the pointless cases."

Mary's frown turned into a blank look she'd perfected. People who didn't know her might consider it a nonreaction, but Grant was her brother. He knew better. And he knew he'd pay for it later. But his irritation with cult nonsense overrode self-preservation at the moment.

"Did she seem *pointless* to you?" Mary asked, her voice calm if icy.

"Not until she pulled out this picture."

"So she's misdirected. Following the wrong lead. People do that kind of thing. Even us." Mary's horse puffed out a breath, energy pumping off the large animal. It was ready for a run, for some work.

But Mary kept the horse still, waiting for Grant to respond in some way.

There were a million dead ends when it came to investigating cold cases. A lot of retracing steps and looking at the same evidence over and over again, trying to find a different angle or shed a new light. And, yes, sometimes an investigator went down the wrong path. More than once.

Even him.

Still, Grant wanted nothing to do with Truth. He'd never found the cult stories interesting the way some people did. Maybe it was the family connection, even if it didn't connect to him. Because like Dahlia and Rose Easton, he had broken branches of a family tree too.

Grant had always felt in line with his mother's track of thinking on the matter. Best not to dwell on it. Best to leave it alone.

Besides, the ghost town of Truth had never done anything except give him a bad feeling—one he now recognized as the same bad feeling he'd gotten in the Marines before something had gone FUBAR.

But their client thought Truth had something to do with her case, and unless Grant's people skills were rusty, he was willing to bet Dahlia Easton wouldn't let that angle go without some proof. So, he had to prove to her she was on the wrong path, and then maybe he could help her find the right one.

"I'm taking one of the dogs," Grant muttered.

"Better clear it with Cash," Mary replied, and she didn't smile exactly, but Grant could read the smug satisfaction all the same. "And make sure to use the business credit card for gas."

Grant rolled his eyes. "I'm not Palmer."

"You're all men, and men are constantly forgetting important details. At least the men I know."

Before he could respond to that, Mary urged her horse forward, and it more than willingly obliged, leaving Grant standing in a cloud of dust.

Grant considered the horse stables. He could take one over. Cash's dog barn was on the other side of the property, as was the cabin where he lived with his eleven-year-old. Izzy would be at school, which meant Cash would likely be training his dogs. Cash trained all sorts of dogs, search and rescue, detection, even some service dogs.

But if Grant took a horse over, he'd have to come back and deal with the aftercare. He wanted this trip done with ASAP. So he got his truck and drove the dusty path from the main part of the ranch to Cash's little corner of it.

It was a sunny fall day, warm enough, but the air would go cold the minute the sun started dipping toward the horizon. The sky was a dark blue, and the land of the Hudson Ranch stretched out around him in rolling hills and long plains that led to those timeless craggy mountains in the distance. No matter what he'd seen out there in the world, Sunrise and this ranch had always been home to the most beautiful sky in the whole world.

He'd always known he'd come back here. The military had been a side trip. To get out of Jack's hair. Assuage some of the restlessness inside of him. See the world. Fight for his country. *Do* something outside of Sunrise and everyone who knew him and defined him by his tragedy.

But he'd always known when that side trip was over, he'd be back here. Working the same land his great-great-great-grandfather had.

Grant came to a stop next to the dog barn, a squat red building where Cash housed all his dogs. Cash himself stood outside in front of a line of dogs. If he'd been in the mood for it, Grant might have found some amusement in how much the sight reminded him of soldiers standing at attention awaiting their orders.

Grant parked and got out, then walked toward his brother as Cash made a hand signal. The dogs all sat in unison. Another hand movement, they all laid down.

Only once Cash was satisfied every dog had its stomach on the ground did he turn to Grant. "What's up?"

"I need a dog for a job. Few hours tops. Nothing special. More company than anything." Grant had no desire to head out to that eerie place alone.

Cash nodded, studied his pack. "Willie." He gave a sharp whistle, and a brown-and-white shepherd got up and trotted over to them. "Don't feed him scraps."

"You're always telling me that."

"Yeah, and you're always ignoring me."

Grant chuckled. True enough. He planned to continue to do so. Who could resist those soulful canine eyes just begging for a treat?

Cash made some more of his hand gestures and different sounding whistles, and Willie bounded up into Grant's truck.

"This about the Easton missing person case?" Cash asked, closing the truck door behind the dog.

"Yeah. How'd you know that? I thought you were keeping your nose out of cases."

"I try, but between Anna and Palmer's big mouths I end up knowing far more than I want to." Cash glanced back at the house. Though Grant knew Izzy was at school, he also knew that's who his brother was thinking about.

Cash would have taken a more active role in cases if he wasn't worried about his daughter's safety or his own as a single father. Which was why, even though he tried to keep his nose out of things, he'd inevitably ask...

"So, what was the Wyoming connection?"

"Tenuous at best," Grant replied. He didn't want to get into it, but no doubt Cash would hear about it one way or another. The only way to prove it didn't bother him was to be the one to tell him. "She thinks it connects to Truth."

It was Cash's turn to chuckle. "Isn't it funny how the one of us the most afraid of Truth got picked for lead investigator on a case that connects to it?"

"The case doesn't connect to Truth. The Easton woman just thinks it does. I'm headed there to prove to her she's wrong." He knew he should leave it at that, but Cash always knew how to needle him into giving up more information than he cared to. "I'm hardly afraid."

"Fifteen-year-old Grant sure was."

"Yeah, well unless you and Palmer have concocted yet another plan to attempt to scare the—"

"Oh, it wasn't an attempt. We scared the living daylights out of you."

Grant rolled his eyes. "I went to war, Cash. I'm not afraid of Truth, Wyoming. Or you and Palmer for that matter," Grant muttered, adjusting his cowboy hat on his head. He got into his truck, ignoring his brother's mocking laughter.

Truth be told—a fact he'd never admit to his brothers—

he'd rather be back in the Marines than spend the next few days in Truth, but he'd learned a long time ago, a man didn't always get what he'd rather.

TRUTH, WYOMING, was a ghost town. Dahlia wasn't surprised. Everything she'd read about it told her that after the federal raid had ended in three dead FBI agents, ten dead cult members and the rest of the adults jailed for life, no one had wanted anything to do with the town except the occasional tourist to gawk at the scene of tragedy.

But no one stayed. No one built inappropriate tourist attractions. It had been the site of something gruesome that no one understood. A fascination, surely, but not one to spend more than a few hours in.

So, no, Dahlia wasn't surprised the buildings were empty or that here on the rock cropping she'd climbed to look down at the town, the land stretched out, gray and brown and deserted and what she figured most would find unappealing.

What did surprise her was the way the ethereal beauty of the area struck her someplace deep inside. It was nothing like home. No green, no sparkling lakes, no fall colors. The land stretched out in all directions, the same grayish color, routinely interrupted by strange rock formations—some skinny and jagged reaching for the sky. Some big fat columns of earth. But it didn't feel like some alien planet. It felt alive and vibrant.

It felt...*right*. As if she belonged down there, walking the length of the abandoned street. She didn't understand the feeling at all. It made her want to cry. Inexplicably.

You're just exhausted, she told herself as she climbed back down the rock. What had she expected to find here? Signs of her sister? Or any civilization? She was exhausted and it was affecting her decision making.

But she walked down what had once been Main Street, and she knew she should feel out of place. Creeped out, maybe, but there was only a thrumming curiosity that had her poking her head into doors. She didn't know what she was looking for or what she was hoping to prove. She was just following instinct…or her gut…or something.

The same something that had pushed her to leave her life behind and come here to begin with. Everything had frozen in place once Rose had disappeared. Dahlia didn't know how to unfreeze it without figuring out…something. *Something.*

She walked into a building that had clearly once been a restaurant of some kind. A few tables were still scattered around the main room, a counter ran along the far wall, with an empty display case that looked like it might have once been filled with baked goods.

Dust and grime stuck to every surface. No one had been here lately. That was clear. Even if they had, why would they leave evidence of it? And what would she do if she found it?

She should have gone back to her rental cabin and slept. This was a waste of time. She should be searching the Green family and their connection to hers, not some Wyoming ghost town.

Maybe her parents were right. She couldn't think straight. She should commit herself until she could again. But Dahlia knew she hadn't had any sort of mental break. Maybe she had let emotions affect her decision-making, but she…

She had to see this through. The right way though. Taking care of herself had to start being a priority.

She stepped out of the abandoned building and then

stopped abruptly. A shudder moved through her. That odd peace she didn't understand evaporated. Replaced by the feeling of being watched.

She swallowed at the bubble of fear. Her eyes darted from side to side as she stood rooted to the spot. She didn't see anything out of the ordinary. She held her breath and listened, trying to discern something beyond the gentle rustle of the wind.

A faint high-pitched sound cut the silence, then was hushed by a quiet command. Dahlia told herself to move, but fear kept her frozen in the doorway. *Run! Hide! Scream!*

She did none of those things. She couldn't. Apparently in a flight-or-fight response situation, Dahlia went with neither.

A soft yip—like from a dog—echoed through the air, and then a large brown-and-white dog appeared around a corner. Relief coursed through her. She nearly sagged against the doorway behind her. Just a dog. Just a—

"Willie. Sit."

It was a man's voice. Sharp and commanding. And the dog immediately plopped its butt on the dusty ground a few yards away. She didn't see the man, but something about actually hearing a voice, or maybe the dog itself, prompted Dahlia into action. She scurried back into the building, crouching behind the wall so that no one could see her from outside.

She pressed her back against the wall. She tried to hold her breath but realized belatedly that wouldn't be sustainable.

How would she know when the man was gone? Would the dog sniff her out? Why was she acting like she needed to hide when she had just as much right to be here as anyone else? As far as she could tell, the land was public property and...

She heard the dog, the faint panting noises, the padding of paws closer and closer and closer until...

"Closing your eyes doesn't stop the bad guy from coming, Ms. Easton."

Dahlia blinked her eyes open and looked up at the tall shadow of a man who stood in the doorway. She hadn't realized she'd screwed her eyes shut in some childish instinct.

Embarrassment washed over her more than fear when she recognized the man.

She frowned at Grant Hudson's disapproving face. "What are you doing here?"

"Shouldn't that be my line?"

She hadn't expected...this. At all. He'd been so dismissive. "You're investigating."

"I said I would."

"I didn't think you'd actually look into Truth."

"You said you needed proof it didn't connect." He held out a hand, and it took Dahlia quite a few ticking seconds to realize he was offering to help her to her feet. She found she didn't want to slide her hand in his but couldn't say why. So she went against instinct and took it.

Firm and callused, he grasped her hand and leveraged her to her feet. The minute she was upright and steady, he immediately let her hand go. He strode back out to the street without another word.

Dahlia didn't know what else to do but follow, like the dog.

"Is this proof enough?" he asked, waving to the empty town around them.

Dahlia followed the path of his hand with her gaze. Even knowing she hadn't been watched but instead was running into the investigator she hired, something had changed. She didn't feel that sense of belonging anymore. Only foreboding.

"Proof that she isn't in Truth right this moment. But that's about it."

Grant sighed. "Ms. Easton, you should understand—"

"I know. I'm very well aware she could be dead." People didn't seem to understand that hope didn't mean she was ignoring the very real possibility her sister had been murdered. That thought plagued her, haunted her, just as much as that tiny sliver of hope that Rose was alive somewhere did. That's why she needed the truth.

The dog made another whining noise. Grant looked down at the animal with a faint line of confusion on his brow. "Go," he offered.

The dog took off down the empty street, and Grant followed him, so Dahlia followed Grant. The dog led them down an alley between two buildings that had been enveloped by some kind of winding vine. It was a narrow alley, and even with the bright sunshine overhead the area was shadowed and dark. Dahlia shivered at the cooler temperature here, looking over her shoulder as goose bumps popped up along her arms.

When she looked forward again, Grant had stopped and was frowning in the same direction she'd been looking. But he shook his head and pressed forward through the alley.

Once on the other side, Dahlia was surprised and confused to find a kind of walled courtyard. Thick, tall stone walls were built along the perimeter—the alley apparently the only way in or out. There was no roof, only the bright blue sky, and there was nothing of note in the courtyard. Just a square of dusty ground and a few patches of grass or brush.

But the dog continued yapping, and as Grant strode over to the corner where it stood, Dahlia's unease intensified. She moved slowly toward where Grant was crouched. He was staring at a small piece of something on the ground.

"What is it?"

"Casing," he replied somewhat absently.

"What does that mean?"

"Someone shot a gun here. And not that long ago." Grant studied the small object, frowning. "Could have been some-one target-shooting. It could be a lot of things." He stood, but there was something...off. He held himself differently now. The frown on his face was more serious.

"So, why do you look so...perplexed?"

He looked up, studying their surroundings with a cold detachment that made her aware she was alone with a vir-tual stranger in a very isolated landscape. Stuck in this little courtyard, as no doubt Grant could block off the one exit before she could make it out.

When his eyes met hers, they were dark and not at all comforting. "Let's get you back to town."

Chapter Three

Something wasn't right. Grant didn't believe it had anything to do with Truth. But it definitely had something to do with the woman driving in front of him.

Grant glanced in his rearview mirror. He'd half expected someone to follow them out of Truth. Half expected *something* to happen, though he couldn't have said what.

He wished he'd had time to investigate, but instinct told him to get Dahlia out of there, and he was still enough of a soldier to follow his instincts.

She hadn't argued. Oh, she'd looked at him a bit like he might be the Devil sent to take her to hell, but she'd done as he said. Walked back to her car, gotten in, then waited for him to bring his truck around so he could follow her back to Sunrise.

He glanced at the rearview again. He couldn't shake the feeling someone had been watching them. He hadn't seen any evidence of that. It was just a feeling.

But added to the lone shell casing, they needed to do a full-blown search of Truth. Much as he was loath to admit it.

It could be unrelated. People went to Truth sometimes. High school kids went out on a dare. Yahoos driven by stories on the internet went out to do whatever rituals they thought might make something happen. That casing could mean anything.

But there'd been a mark on the wall—mostly scrubbed off—that made Grant suspicious *something* was going on in Truth even if it had nothing to do with the missing Easton sister. *Or* the cult.

But he had to get Dahlia tucked away before he could deal with that. She pulled her car off the highway. Surprisingly not a rental, but a compact sedan registered to Dahlia Easton of Minneapolis, Minnesota.

He'd called Zadie, an old family friend now with the sheriff's department, to get him that information. Taking her own car rather than flying or even renting for a few weeks spoke of something longer than a brief trip to check things out.

But Dahlia herself wasn't the case. The missing sister was. And now, for Grant, the case included figuring out what was going on in Truth.

It was a short drive off the highway to the cabin Dahlia was renting. Just inside Sunrise's borders, it was secluded— a pretty little cabin in a pretty little spot.

But she'd do better somewhere with a little bit more foot traffic. Grant didn't believe anywhere was don't-lock-your-doors safe, but Sunrise was about as close as a person could get. She should be closer to people who would, if nothing else, notice if something fishy went on. Then the gossip chain would let the Hudsons know before anything bad happened.

Dahlia got out of her car, and she gripped her bag so hard her knuckles were white. She stayed close to her car as Grant got out of his truck. "You didn't have to follow me here."

She wasn't comfortable with him, and he understood. He

wished he could give her more space, but something was off. The safety of a client came before their comfort.

Still, Grant whistled for Willie to get out of the car. She seemed to relax a little bit around the dog.

"I'm just going to have a look around," he said, trying to sound casual as Willie ambled over to sit next to her.

She looked at the dog. Then him. "Look around what?"

"The cabin."

She shook her head. "Why on earth would you do that?"

"Ms. Easton, did you get the sense you were all alone when you were in Truth?"

"Yes. Yes, it was peaceful actually. Until you came along." She lifted her chin. She might be exhausted, maybe even a little fragile, but she had some fighting spirit in there.

"And what happened when I came along?"

She shook her head. "I don't know. I guess I just…felt your presence or whatever. Not in a woo-woo way. I heard the dog. I…" She trailed off, frowning, but she didn't continue.

He didn't know who might be following her. Who might be hanging around Truth. But he knew there was something off, and he had to wonder if it was something she'd brought with her from Minnesota.

"Would anyone have followed you here? To Sunrise?"

"From Minnesota?"

"Maybe you hired a private investigator? Or there's a family member worried about you? Anyone who might not have wanted you to come here alone."

She blinked, shaking her head. But he knew that was a knee-jerk response. She really needed to consider the possibilities. Maybe she would after he was gone. "I'm just going to do a quick perimeter check. You stay put."

"I—"

He didn't give her a chance to argue. He strode off, the stay-put order being not just for her but Willie as well.

He didn't expect to find anything. Once he got Dahlia situated, he'd head back to Truth, maybe with Palmer and Anna, and go over the things he'd seen, but he had to make sure all was good here first.

He walked around the side of the cabin. The backyard was a small patch of green. Trees created a kind of frame, and Ursula—the lady who kept the cabin—had colorful blooms in pots all over the back porch.

He studied the windows. There were blinds on them, but they weren't drawn. Right now it was too sunny to get a good look inside, but at night with the lights on, anyone would be able to see what Dahlia was doing.

Grant studied the small backyard, walked the perimeter of it and almost passed the small indentation in the scrubby grass. But then there was another one, where grass met a dusty patch of dirt. And then another—this one, clearly a footprint. Too big to be Dahlia's, or Ursula's for that matter.

Lawn care? Ursula's son? Grant studied each footprint, following its progress toward the house, crossing every potential culprit off the list. Ursula's son lived in Houston and hadn't visited since Christmas. God knew she told everyone who listened that little complaint. Ursula didn't hire out lawn services. She believed in handling things at her rental properties herself.

Grant came to a stop at the cabin. The footprints led right up to the structure on the side. There was a window right in front of him, and if he shaded his eyes to look inside, he could tell it was a bedroom.

Dahlia's bedroom.

Dread curled in his gut. Much like back in Truth, it could be a lot of things. Some Peeping Tom, a burglar, either potentially unrelated to Dahlia.

But they were problems, related or not.

Unfortunately, Grant was struggling to believe all this didn't connect. The timing was too suspect. Everything too… centered around her.

He finished his perimeter check, debating whether to tell Dahlia about the prints. Maybe he could just convince her to go home. Not mention…anything.

A frustrating line of thought. It wasn't his job to protect her feelings or assuage her fears. It was his job to get answers.

He made it back around to the front. She sat on the porch stair scratching Willie behind his ears. She looked up at Grant as he approached, her enjoyment of the dog going cold as their eyes met.

She stood.

Grant thought there was probably a gentle way to put it, but he didn't have it in him to find out. Not when her hair glittered in the sun, and those blue eyes looked at him with such distrust, made worse by the dark circles under her eyes.

"There are footprints leading up to that back window that looks into your bedroom."

"Footprints," she echoed.

"Not yours."

Her eyebrows furrowed, and she looked back at the cabin, then the world around them. "It could be the…the owner. The cleaning service. It could be…"

Grant wished he could agree, but he knew everyone who

would have been walking around the cabin, and none of them had a size twelve military-style boot.

"Dahlia, I think you might be in danger."

GRANT'S WORDS DIDN'T make sense. Not when applied to her. So Dahlia laughed. It seemed the only possible reaction. "I'm not in any danger."

"Someone is watching you. If you don't think it could be someone looking out for you, it's someone who wants something else from you."

"I wasn't being followed. No one followed me."

"You're certain?"

But of course she wasn't. Not when he'd introduced the possibility she was in danger. Something had happened to Rose. Didn't that mean something could happen to her? All because Rose had started digging into the past. And then Dahlia had in order to find Rose. "How can I be certain of anything?"

Something on his face...softened. She certainly wouldn't call his expression kind or his demeanor gentle, but her words seemed to affect him. Some way.

"I don't think it's safe for you to stay here until we figure this out."

Dahlia looked behind her at the pretty little cabin. *Someone is watching you.* "Where would I go?" she said, though she hadn't precisely meant to say it out loud—certainly not as a question geared toward him.

"Why don't you grab your things and come to the ranch for a bit? We'll figure everything out."

"But...you're strangers."

He nodded. "Ones you hired to find your sister."

"Yes, to solve a cold case. Not to…protect me or whatever this is."

Any hint of that earlier softness hardened again. "Ms. Easton—"

"Oh, don't drawl 'Ms. Easton' at me. My name is Dahlia. I don't understand why you think I'm in danger. I don't understand—" she flung her arms up in the air "—any of this."

"Neither do I. That's why I think it'd be smart if you came to the ranch so we can go over your case piece by piece. Determine if there's a real threat."

"What's the other option?"

"Coincidence."

Dahlia huffed out a breath. "None of this feels like a coincidence."

"No, it doesn't. I believe that's my point. Still, we can't be sure until we investigate. Now, if you'd rather stay here—alone, unprotected and isolated—it's a free country. If you'd like to use the full services of HSS, you can pack up your things and follow me back to the ranch."

"I don't care for ultimatums."

"I don't care for interfering clients, but here we are."

When she glared at him, he winced a little. She wasn't sure why. Surely, he was being honest. He didn't seem like the kind of man who felt bad about a little honesty.

But he let out a sigh. "I apologize. You're free to do as you wish, Ms. Easton—*Dahlia*. I'm inviting you to the Hudson Ranch while we analyze the potential threat to you, but if you don't feel comfortable, you certainly can make your own decisions."

His businesslike voice meant to appease her was far worse than him calling her an interfering client.

"You could also go home. Trust us to—"

"No." Going home wasn't an option. Not until she had answers.

"Somehow I figured," he muttered, clearly disapproving of that response. "So? Stay or go?"

She needed more time to think. She needed sleep. She needed...help. That was why she'd come here. That was why she was planning on spending every last cent on finding Rose. Grant had been dismissive of her belief there was a cult connection, but he'd gone to Truth. Right away. He'd investigated.

It was more than anyone else had done.

"I just..." She shook her head and swallowed the words back down. Grant wasn't her friend or her confidant. He was her employee. A partner at best. He didn't need to hear about the emotional circles her brain was running in. "It shouldn't take me too long to pack."

He nodded firmly. "Good. I'll wait in the truck."

She nodded, grateful he wasn't trying to enter the cabin. He'd give her space, if not the opportunity to really figure this out.

She stepped inside the cabin. She hadn't had time to appreciate or enjoy it. Now it was tainted by the knowledge someone had been... In Grant's theory, someone had been watching her through her bedroom window.

She stepped into said bedroom and looked at the big window that overlooked the backyard. Pretty. Peaceful. And someone had allegedly been standing right there. Watching her.

And she'd been clueless. She shuddered against the bolt of fear and unease, then turned to grab her things.

"I can't believe I'm doing this," she muttered to herself. It was insanity. A scam. Maybe she was about to meet her end just as Rose had. Because she was pretty sure on the Hudson Ranch she *could* just disappear. Still, she shoved the few belongings she'd taken out back into her suitcase.

Maybe she *should* go home. Maybe—

Grant was there—suddenly, silently. Like he could simply will himself to appear in her doorway without making any noise.

"Stay here. Lock the door. And whatever you do, don't open it up for anyone." Before she could say anything, he was gone, practically like he'd vanished. But not before she'd watched a gun appear in his hand like magic.

She stood there, suitcase in hand, and then the dog from before padded into the room. He plopped himself right in front of her like he was some kind of guard dog.

It was now clear in a way it hadn't been this whole time.

Dahlia had no idea what she'd gotten herself into.

Chapter Four

Grant moved back outside, hand on his weapon as he scanned the world around the little cabin.

Someone was out there. Not just *had* been out there, but was there right now. Watching. Maybe waiting.

He wasn't about to leave—with or without Dahlia—knowing someone might follow. Maybe Dahlia wasn't in immediate danger, because someone had been watching her for some time and nothing had happened, but there were no good reasons for being watched.

Grant took a second to look back at the cabin, grateful Dahlia hadn't followed and Willie had obeyed the order to stay put. Then Grant moved forward. He'd had that watched feeling when he'd been waiting in the truck, but that wouldn't have been enough for him to act.

Sometimes a soldier didn't fully leave behind that watched feeling. But he'd seen the flash of something in his rearview mirror. Just at the curve of the road. He wasn't going to go straight for it though. He was more tactical than that.

He didn't follow the length of the road, he moved through the yard, using the truck as a kind of cover, hoping to move around enough to get a different angle at the road and see beyond the curve without who or whatever he'd seen knowing.

He held his gun and moved silently and quickly, eyes trained on where he'd first seen the flash of something. As he moved up the slight rise of land at the edge of the yard, he saw it again.

A figure darting too quickly out of sight to tell much about. It could have been a man or a woman. No sense of coloring. Just a shadow—human—then gone.

Grant ran after it, determined to get some clue as to who was watching his client. He pushed away thoughts of strange twists of fate bringing him a case that connected to Truth and all he struggled to forget. He let the mechanics of the all-out run block all those thoughts. There was only one target: whoever was watching them.

But the figure had too much of a head start, and as he came to the curve of the road, he knew going any farther would leave Dahlia alone and too far out of his reach to help if someone else was involved or the runner doubled back.

Grant came to a stop, scanning the landscape. He scowled, and after one last look around and another minute to return his breathing to normal, he turned and walked back to the cabin. He kept his instincts honed to the world around him, but he knew in his gut whoever had been there was long gone.

It ate him up that he couldn't follow, but he'd need to get Ms. Easton somewhere safe first.

There was more to this whole thing than that woman had let on. Well, he'd give her the benefit of the doubt. Maybe she didn't know what she'd gotten herself into. Sometimes that happened, especially with cold cases that weren't quite as cold as people thought.

It did not ease his frustration any. He returned to the cabin, tested the door. She'd followed his instructions and locked it. At least she could follow directions sometimes.

He knocked and waited for her to answer. When she pulled the door open, Willie was still right next to her.

Grant crouched and gave the dog a scratch behind the ears. "Good dog," he murmured, then stood and studied Ms. Easton.

She was looking a little rough around the edges. He had enough sisters to know not to say that out loud. "I saw someone, probably whoever's been watching you, but unfortunately they were too far away to pursue safely. I think it's all the more reason for you to come stay at the ranch."

"Why would someone be watching me?"

He'd also worked with enough clients to know not to give them—particularly the nervous ones—all the possibilities. "Hard to say. We'll figure it out. Let's head on back to the ranch. Why don't I drive you?"

"I have a car." She gestured helplessly at it.

"I know. Let's just leave it here for the time being. A little misdirection."

"Misdirection," she echoed.

She was in some kind of shock maybe. He moved around her and grabbed the suitcase she'd had clutched in her hands when he'd first come in. "Come on," he said, gesturing her forward and then striding through the front door as if he had no doubt she'd follow.

But he did actually have a few doubts. He made it to the truck before he allowed himself to look over his shoulder.

She was following, Willie at her side, but clearly not convinced this was the best course of action.

He got in the driver's seat and texted his sisters to get a room ready and be around so they could help Dahlia feel more comfortable about her stay. When she finally got into the passenger seat, Willie jumping over her lap and then scrambling into the back, Grant weighed his words.

"We're going to let the police and Ursula know that someone was poking around the cabin, watching through the windows. And everyone at Hudson Ranch will be on the lookout for anyone following you. We'll get to the bottom of it in no time."

Grant started the truck and pushed it into Drive.

"This sounds like a lot more than investigating a cold case."

"Cold cases sometimes warm up, Ms. Easton." While he wanted to write it off as some kind of Peeping Tom, the facts just didn't add up. "And when they do, we protect whoever is in the cross fire."

IT WAS PROBABLY supposed to be comforting, but Dahlia couldn't relax sitting in the passenger seat of Grant's truck. He kept those dark eyes trained on the road and his mouth in a firm, tense line.

Dahlia glanced behind her at the dog, who sat in the backseat panting happily.

If this was the *cross fire*, as Grant had so helpfully put it, she supposed it wasn't all bad. And she supposed if the cold case was warm, that meant—had to mean—they were on to something with Truth.

He retraced the route she'd taken this morning. From her

cabin to the sprawling Wyoming ranch. She hadn't known real people lived like this. The Hudsons had to be loaded. She didn't know anything about ranching, but the sheer size of their operation had to cost a bundle. And while she knew she was paying for the Hudsons' services, she didn't think even that would fund all this. Even if they had a hundred cold cases they were solving for a fee.

Grant pulled the truck to a stop in front of the house.

"What about talking to the police?" she asked. Something about the house was so…inviting. Comforting. She had a hard time trusting it.

"Yeah, we'll take care of all of that at dinner." Grant got out of the truck, the dog bounding after him. Dahlia had no choice but to follow.

Grant was carrying her suitcase toward the house, and the dog ran off into the fields barking happily, and Dahlia could only scurry after Grant's long-legged strides.

"At dinner?"

"My oldest brother. He's Sunrise's sheriff. We'll tell him all about it at dinner. Just a forewarning though, whatever my brothers say about me and Truth, it isn't true."

She just stared at him. *Me and Truth.* Like he had some kind of deep dark secret about the place she was *sure* connected to her sister's disappearance.

He laughed, and that was something of a surprise in and of itself. Thus far, he'd been stern or overly polite. Not *amused.*

"I'm sorry," he said, and seemed genuinely apologetic. "Not in some scary I-was-in-a-cult way. Truth's been a ghost town since we were born. I think you can imagine what teenage boys do in ghost towns, but if you can't, they spend a lot of time trying to scare the tar out of each other."

"Oh."

He opened the front door and gestured her in. She hesitated, because surely everything she was doing was silly. She could hear her father's voice in her head: *Everything too good to be true usually is.*

But Grant was inside with her things. He handed the suitcase off to Mary, who was apparently waiting for their arrival.

"I know the Meadowlark Cabin is so cute and a great place to relax," she said, reaching forward and taking Dahlia's arm. "But we've got a nice room for you, a private bathroom, and you'll be safe and sound until everyone can get to the bottom of everything."

And then Dahlia was being firmly maneuvered deeper into the gorgeous house. She glanced back at Grant, who was standing there still looking like that stern cowboy.

But he'd investigated. He'd warned her about someone watching her. And he'd laughed when telling her about teenage shenanigans.

Mary led her up a staircase. "This is sort of the guest wing," she explained. "So, you'll have privacy for the most part in this hallway, and there's an en suite bath in your room."

Before Dahlia could protest once again, Mary kept right on. "I know it likely feels strange to come stay at a stranger's house. But I just want you to know this isn't out of the ordinary for us. We've put up clients before. Sometimes it's easier to accomplish things if people are on the premises."

But this wasn't about accomplishing things. It was, allegedly, about keeping her safe.

Mary opened a door and gestured Dahlia inside. The room

was spacious and beautiful. The walls a buttery yellow with floral prints. There were lace curtains over the big windows. The bed had that Western quality of somehow looking both feminine and inviting and big and sturdy.

"If there's anything I can do to put you at ease, if you want to have someone join you—your parents, a friend? There's no extra charge for that. There's a lock on the door, a phone in the room. Bathroom is through there with any toiletry you might need, but if not, ask. Think of it as a bed-and-breakfast."

"I'm not paying you for a bed-and-breakfast."

Mary smiled kindly. "You're paying us for a service. This is part of the service if it needs to be. Unpack. Relax. I'll come get you for dinner."

There was nothing to say. Mary was already gone, leaving Dahlia alone in this...truly perfect room.

She stepped to the window and pulled the lace curtain back, looking out over the ranch. Everything about it was beautiful. The grassland, the mountains in the distance, the buildings and fences that dotted the landscape looking both old and impeccable at the same time.

Rose would love it because it was generations and roots and legacy. She would be throwing herself into these people, what they knew and how they all connected.

But Dahlia wasn't her sister. She couldn't get past how wrong this all felt. No matter how genuine Mary seemed or how capable Grant *was*. She didn't belong in their home.

Someone *had* been watching her though, she couldn't deny that or be okay with it. She'd felt it at times and brushed it off. It irritated her that Grant didn't believe the connections she'd found, even as she understood why he'd be skeptical, but he *had* protected her and listened to her even when he didn't believe her.

She supposed there was something noble in what the Hudsons were doing, trying to solve cold cases. She'd picked them for not just their proximity to Truth but because the story on their website had been about their own parents' cold case.

Dahlia wanted to believe they cared because of that connection even if her own cynicism held her back sometimes, but this seemed too good to be true.

And her father had always warned her about that.

She sighed and stepped away from the window. She didn't unpack. She just…sat down on the bed and tried to get a handle on her roiling emotions.

The next thing she knew, someone was knocking at the door. She'd fallen asleep, clearly, though she didn't remember lying down. Drowsily, she got back up and realized outside the sun was starting to set.

Mary was at the door with that kind smile on her face. "Hungry?" she asked.

Dahlia didn't have a chance to respond before Mary was leading her out of the room, back down the stairs, through the living room she'd initially met Grant in and then to a whole new wing of the house.

She heard voices—raucous but pleasant—before she entered the room. Mary led her into the spacious dining room dominated by a long table and *lots* of people. The chairs at the table were nearly all full. Grant and three carbon copies of him, a woman who was currently arguing loudly with one of them and then a girl not more than ten or eleven who was feeding scraps to the three dogs patiently waiting under the table.

The table itself had a huge family-style meal, bowls and platters overflowing with food. It looked like Christmas or some big family celebration, but Dahlia could tell by the way they acted, it was just the norm for them.

Mary gave her arm a little tug and then gestured her to a seat. "Dahlia, this is everyone," she said, as the voices around the table quieted. "We've got the brothers Jack, Cash, Palmer, and you know Grant. My sister Anna. Cash's daughter Izzy. Don't bother trying to remember all the dogs' names. Half of them look alike, and they're all running around constantly. Now, you sit right here and help yourself."

Dahlia was already overwhelmed, and she wasn't sure she'd caught any of those names. None of this felt...right. She cleared her throat and did not sit down. "I do appreciate this. I really do. But I shouldn't be interrupting your family dinner. I'm not paying for room and board. I'm—"

"We charge for work. That's honest," Jack said, with a firm nod. "We don't charge for hospitality—not when we've got plenty to spare. Now, sit and eat up. You need it."

Dahlia didn't know how to argue with that, particularly coming from a stony-faced man who looked even more like a cowboy out of an old Western than Grant did, complete with shiny star badge pinned to his shirt.

Dahlia slowly sank into the seat. Grant himself put a heaping pile of mashed potatoes on her plate before passing them along to Mary next to her.

He gave her a reassuring nod. "I'd advise you listen. No one argues with Jack's hard head and wins."

So Dahlia did just that.

Chapter Five

Grant hadn't slept well. He'd gone over Dahlia Easton's case again and again, adding his own experiences, and felt no closer to a lead than he had when the Peeping Tom, or whoever was watching her, got away.

He wanted to prove that Eugene Green and Truth had nothing to do with her sister's disappearance, but no matter how little he *thought* they connected, he hadn't found a way to prove they didn't.

And that bothered him.

Still, he was up at dawn with his brothers to handle the necessary ranch chores. Some things they hired out, but the brothers always met in the mornings to handle a few jobs like all the Hudsons had since they'd arrived in Sunrise over a hundred years ago.

He met them at the stables, same as every morning since they'd been kids. But only Palmer and Cash were there.

"Where's Jack?"

"Went in early," Palmer said, pulling his hat lower on his head against the rising sun. He looked like he'd been out late last night, probably drinking, but Grant said nothing about that, as he was already in a terrible mood.

"Said he was going to take pictures of those footprints and write up a report. Have one of his deputies check around, see if anyone's seen anything suspicious," Cash added.

"That's good." Grant envied him. It was an actionable step to take. Take a report. Collect evidence. *Do* something instead of read the same reports over and over again.

"She's a looker," Palmer offered.

Grant could have pretended he didn't know who his brother was talking about, but he didn't see the point. "She's a client," Grant replied irritably. And sure, pretty as a spring day. But she was barking up all kinds of wrong trees.

Case in point: Eugene Green. "Cash, you looked at the file?"

Cash nodded in assent as they all got up on the horses. They didn't have to talk about what they were doing today. Jack kept a strict calendar and schedule, and he always made sure everyone knew what their role for the day was.

"What do you make of this attempt at a Eugene Green connection?"

"Well." Cash took his time responding as their horses walked side by side through the cool, pretty morning. "The security picture she's got is grainy at best, but you can't discount some similarities to Eugene Green."

"The guy was a lunatic. He could have had kids all over the country," Palmer added.

"Ones that wouldn't necessarily know a thing about him," Cash pointed out.

"It could also be a coincidence," Grant said. "Reaching."

"Could," Cash replied, and once again let silence settle over them. Because Cash was never in a hurry. He took his time to draw any conclusions. "But it's not the only connection to Eugene Green. The missing sister was all up in these DNA tests and whatever."

"Can't those things be wrong?" Palmer asked.

"Anything can be wrong. But it could just as easily be right." Cash looked over at Grant and shrugged. "I know you want to. I get why. But we can't discount the facts."

"I'll take over this one if you want." Palmer flashed a grin. "I'd take Red *very* seriously."

Grant didn't know why that comment set his teeth on edge. His brother was forever saying things like that and making his way through the female population of Sunrise and just about every surrounding area. And somehow, he hadn't ticked off the wrong woman yet.

"Take her over to Mrs. Riley this morning. She'd know all about the Green family tree and all that. More than any DNA ancestry site or just about anyone else. I know you don't *want* it to connect to Truth, but we all know how cold cases like this go. Any little connection can lead you to a bigger one."

It was a solid idea and an honest lecture. Grant didn't care for either from his little brother. "Maybe *you* should take over the case?"

Cash looked wistful for a fraction of a second before he was shaking his head and nudging his horse in the other direction. "Gotta get Izzy off to school. Then I'll be working with the dogs. Call if you need anything."

"Dumb thing to say," Palmer muttered once Cash was out of earshot.

"Well, he should take some cases. He can't *never* leave the ranch just because he's got a daughter."

"His choice," Palmer replied.

Because when push came to shove, the two younger brothers tended to stick together. And Grant didn't have Jack here to be on *his* side, though no doubt Jack would be.

So Grant worked with Palmer in mostly silence until breakfast time, then broke off and headed back to the house. Cash's suggestion was a good one. He'd take Dahlia over to the library today and maybe stop by the sheriff's department and check on things.

It wasn't going to connect to Eugene Green. It probably wasn't going to connect to anything. But for all of Dahlia Easton's more...fragile tendencies, she was determined to see this through. Stubborn, no doubt.

So, if nothing else, he had to *disprove* a theory that was going to lead her on a wild-goose chase. And maybe Cash was right and they could find some bigger more plausible thread to tug.

He couldn't help but think of the way she'd clearly been so lost and overwhelmed at dinner last night. He couldn't blame her—the Hudson clan could be overwhelming even when you were one of them—but he knew in part it was hard for her, because they were a family, and she was missing a piece of hers.

But so were they. And had been since their parents had gone missing all those years ago. He should have said something about it, should have made the connection to her so she might have felt some...sliver of comfort.

But he'd just filled up her plate and watched to make sure she ate and then let Mary handle things from there.

He was the investigator, and his job was to find answers. Even knowing there might never be any answers to give.

He got to the stables and took care of his horse before walking back to the house. He saw a figure sitting on the side porch and realized that flash of red meant it wasn't his family or a ranch hand but the woman in question.

He walked toward her, though there was an odd, errant bolt of a thought that told him he should turn around. Go anywhere but forward. But that made absolutely no sense, so he walked forward. To the porch, to Dahlia.

She sat on the little rocking chair his grandmother had liked to do her knitting on in the summer. In the here and now, Dahlia had a mug of coffee cupped between her hands. Her red hair whipped around in the breeze, and she watched him approach with careful eyes.

She looked exactly right there, like she'd been born to sit on his porch and wait for him to arrive. Which was the strangest damn thought he'd ever had, perhaps, in his entire life and left him completely mute.

She didn't say anything either. For a lot longer than made sense. Eventually she broke the silence.

"I expected a *howdy* maybe."

His mouth quirked. "Fresh out." His voice sounded gruffer than it should have, so he cleared his throat. "The library in town has all sorts of things on Truth, as does the geneal-ogy society, which has an office in the library. Why don't we eat breakfast and head over? We'll stop by the sheriff's department, see if they've found anything about the guy watching you."

She didn't say anything to that, just kept watching him with those careful eyes. Wary.

He didn't have any right to be frustrated, but it bothered him all the same. For reasons he couldn't begin to sort out. "It must be hard to trust perfect strangers, even if you are paying them. Doesn't hurt my feelings. But I do know things would be easier if you'd give us a chance."

"I'm here, aren't I?"

"You are. And just about always looking for the rattlesnake to strike." He could understand it and still be frustrated by it. Apparently that was going to be his predominant feeling around Dahlia.

But the breeze teased the red waves of her hair, and her blue eyes held his in an eerie silence that settled over him like a touch.

Okay, maybe not the *predominant feeling.*

Then she blinked and gave a little nod. "You're not the enemy is what you're getting at, and treating you like one probably doesn't move the needle any closer to finding answers."

"That's a good way of putting it."

"I've been looking for help for a year. Someone, anyone to take me or Rose seriously. Even my parents don't."

He thought she might break at the mention of her parents. She looked on the cusp of tears and Grant wanted to back away from *that*. She straightened her shoulders though. Blinked back the tears.

"I've been fighting *everyone* for answers. Even the people who've helped... It only lasts for so long. At a certain point, you can only depend on yourself."

He hadn't expected her words to cut him off at the knees, but they did. Because he knew that feeling. Was so well acquainted with it, it had helped build HSS—the fact that, eventually, he and his siblings hadn't had anyone else to lean on. They'd learned that when faced with something difficult, they could only trust themselves.

But he had his siblings. He had family and roots, and Dahlia Easton didn't seem to have much of anything.

"At a certain point, I hope you feel like you can depend on us, but even if you never feel that way, we'll see this through. That's a promise."

She looked down at her coffee. He wasn't sure it was disagreement or just feeling overwhelmed, but she didn't lift her gaze again when she spoke. "When do we go to this library?"

DAHLIA HADN'T WANTED to eat breakfast. She'd slept better last night than she had since she'd left Minnesota, but her stomach still roiled and made it hard to feel like eating—even if last night's dinner had been delicious.

Still, much like last night, somehow Grant maneuvered her into eating a small plate of eggs and toast. And, though she didn't plan on admitting out loud to anyone, it did make her feel sturdier. More like she was capable of surviving this strange new world she found herself in.

Maybe—she could admit in the privacy of her own head—she hadn't been taking care of herself very well. Maybe she needed to if she was going to actually get to the bottom of Rose's disappearance.

Then she'd had to go out with Grant and climb into his big intimidating truck, this time without her dog friend as company. She did have Rose's binder replicas though, and she clutched them too hard as Grant drove them into town.

"Do you think your library will have something my sister didn't?"

"It's possible. Not everything's on the internet, especially when it comes to a small town like Sunrise, and it seems as though Rose didn't make a connection to Wyoming until she got to Texas, right?"

"As far as I know."

"So, she didn't make it here. Which means there might be records or clues into the family connection that might lead us to an answer."

He didn't believe it was Truth or Eugene Green. She kept telling herself it didn't matter. People believing her hadn't mattered this whole time, so why should it start now?

But she found herself wanting to explain to him until he agreed with her. Luckily, she'd learned when to keep her mouth shut, even when she didn't want to. Maybe her parents had taught her something worthwhile after all.

He didn't try to fill the silence as he drove—off the sprawling Hudson Ranch and toward the town of Sunrise.

It was beautiful. The whole area—ranch or driving or even the cute little western town. Dahlia had always planned on visiting the West at some point. Make it out to Yellowstone or even Colorado, but school and then work had taken up most of her time, and when she finally went on vacations, it was always with Rose, who preferred cities or old museums on the East Coast.

But there was something so open and vast about Wyoming. Sunrise was just a postage stamp of a town that clustered around the main thoroughfare. And in the distance, craggy peaks that felt intimidating or awe-inspiring depending on the moment.

Grant pulled his truck into a parking spot in front of a squat stone building that didn't look like much, except old. But as they got up and walked to the door, Dahlia noted the little details that made it special. Impressive little cornices shaped like books. Tiny books carved into the wood frame around the door. She followed Grant inside. Small, definitely, but...warm. Inviting. So much more so than the new, more industrial-like building her library was housed in back home.

The woman behind the desk looked up, then straightened a little as if she recognized Grant. When she flashed him a smile, Dahlia was *sure* she recognized him.

"Hi there, Freya," he offered somewhat absently, like he didn't notice the woman brighten the minute she laid eyes on him.

"Morning, Grant." Her eyes flicked to Dahlia, and the smile dimmed a little. But she held firm. "Here for work?"

Grant nodded, then gestured at Dahlia. "This is Ms. Easton."

"Hi," Freya offered, and though she was definitely speculating about some things based on the way she gave Dahlia a once-over, Dahlia didn't feel any animosity. Exactly.

"Is Mrs. Riley in?"

"Just like always," Freya said, trying to share a conspiratorial eye roll with Grant, but Dahlia watched him miss it, as he was already looking deeper into the library, presumably for Mrs. Riley.

"Thanks," he said, not giving poor Freya a second look. Dahlia moved to follow Grant, but something about Freya's crestfallen expression made her stop.

"I love what you've done with this place. It's so inviting. I'm a librarian in Minnesota, and everything is so...bureaucratic. I can't make any choices about decor without like three people writing off on it."

"Oh well. Probably a little bigger than this, huh?" Freya sounded wistful again.

"But not nearly as special."

The corner of Freya's mouth tugged up, and she looked around as if seeing the library with new eyes. "Thanks. It really is cozy, isn't it?"

"I love it." She smiled and then followed Grant, who was waiting by a door with a somewhat impatient frown on his face.

Once she approached, he knocked on the door.

Dahlia felt like she should probably keep her mouth shut, but Grant seemed totally ignorant. "She likes you."

He frowned at her, then over at Freya. "She dated my brother."

Well, that did change things, Dahlia supposed. She glanced back at Freya. "Well, regardless of what she *did*, she's currently very into *you*."

Grant grunted and said nothing more as the door opened to an older woman. She looked at Grant, then Dahlia.

"Your turn, huh?" the woman said to Grant.

He nodded. "Mrs. Riley, this is Dahlia Easton. Ms. Easton, this is Mrs. Riley. She runs the historical society, the genealogical society and knows just about everything about the history of Sunrise."

Mrs. Riley eyed Dahlia with some suspicion. Dahlia wondered if this was the small-town distrust of outsiders she'd read about but never experienced.

"Come on in then." She waved them into the cramped room. Shelves lined two walls filled with labeled binders and boxes. She had a little table in the middle of the room— also filled with stacks of folders, books and binders. Then the two chairs in the room were filled with stacks as well.

"So, what are you wanting to know?"

"I'd like to ask for your discretion before we show you anything," Grant said.

Mrs. Riley grinned, a flash of a woman with *some* sense of humor. "You can ask."

Grant sighed but didn't argue with her. "Ms. Easton's sister was tracing her family tree when she disappeared over a year ago. Ms. Easton found some…loose connections to Sunrise and—"

"Not to Sunrise," Dahlia interrupted. "To Truth. To the Greens."

Grant closed his eyes as if in pain. Mrs. Riley's bland expression went into a furious scowl, but Dahlia paid no heed. She took her binder, opened it to the page that had led her here and handed it to Mrs. Riley.

The woman looked at the page, then back at Dahlia, eyes narrowed as she pointed to the section on the Greens. "How'd you find out about this?"

"Wait. *You* know about this Texas connection?" Grant asked Mrs. Riley.

"Of course I do," the woman replied with a sniff. "I made sure I knew every last inch of that family so they could never hurt mine again." Then her gaze turned to Dahlia, and it was *cold.* "Guess you're one of them."

"It's a loose connection at best," Dahlia replied, but that didn't win her any favors.

"*Loose* wouldn't matter to the Greens." Mrs. Riley tapped her bright pink fingernails on the book. "The cult was big into blood ties and rituals. He'd have known his tree backward and forward. He'd have known about *you.* Which is why I asked, how'd you know about this?"

"I didn't. My sister did research and took a DNA test."
And disappeared.

"Eugene Green is dead, Mrs. Riley. We all know that,"
Grant said, as if he said it firmly enough, this woman would
simply have to accept it.

Mrs. Riley huffed. "Maybe. Maybe not. There're rumors,
and some of them connect to Texas."

Grant muttered something that sounded like "God save
me from conspiracy theories," but Mrs. Riley didn't seem
to catch it.

She turned away from the binder Dahlia held out. "I don't
need any Greens hanging around *my* office."

"You're not—" But Grant didn't finish the sentence. Mrs.
Riley folded her arms across her chest and just glared.

It wasn't exactly a dead end, Dahlia assured herself as she
followed Grant out of the small office. If Mrs. Riley knew
about conspiracy theories that connected to an alive Eugene
Green in Texas, there was a chance someone else in town
knew about it.

She waved at Freya as they passed, and Grant gave the
woman an absent nod at best before they stepped back into
the pretty fall morning.

"I'm sorry about that. I did *not* see that coming, but I
should have."

"It's not a big deal."

"It is to me. It isn't right to hold people accountable for
some random offshoot of a family you didn't even know
about." He sounded strangely vehement. Like he'd…maybe
dealt with similar before.

"It isn't right my sister is gone," Dahlia said gently. "The
world doesn't work on what's right."

He grunted, clearly not loving that answer. What must it be like to be a man who went through life thinking he could make everything right simply through sheer force of will?

"The sheriff's department is just down the street. How about a walk?"

Dahlia thought he made the suggestion for himself. He was a contained man, but frustrated energy pumped off him. So she agreed and fell into step beside him as they walked down the sidewalk.

She still clutched the binder to her chest. She looked down at it, then at the frustrated man next to her.

"It isn't about me. Mrs. Riley being upset. It's about her... life. I don't know what the Greens did to her, I don't need to know in order to understand."

"That's very generous of you," Grant replied. He looked down at her, and something in his expression softened. "You want it to be a lead, but they're just stories. And Mrs. Riley is going to tell *everyone*, so it's going to be all stories and conspiracy theories. I think there's one about aliens? It's going to get ridiculous, and I just want you to understand these aren't leads. If there was any truth to all the stories that fly around about Truth and the Greens, the authorities would have found that out a long time ago. It's not hope. Trust me, I have been there, and all it does is prolong the pain."

She wanted to bristle, but she heard a world of experience in his words. He had been there, she knew, because they had the story of their parents' disappearance on their website. They promised dedication and hard work because they knew what not having answers felt like.

Still felt like.

"How does it not eat you alive?" she asked, her voice a

mere whisper. She knew she shouldn't ask. It wasn't polite, and what's more, she was almost certain she'd hate the answer.

"It's always eating you alive," Grant replied softly. "You just have to do other things while it does."

Which was *dire* and not at all hopeful. "Forever?"

"If it's forever." He glanced at her. All dark-eyed intensity. But also…a pain under it all. She supposed it drove him—all of them. She'd only been missing her sister a year. They'd been missing their parents for over a decade.

"So, you still have hope for your parents?" she asked, *had* to. Because it seemed hope was the source of the pain, but Dahlia knew it was also the source of everything that kept *her* going. Did that die at some point? Would she be left with…nothing?

"I wish I didn't," he said, looking away, jaw clenched. Unknown years of pain in every syllable of those words.

"That's not a no."

He stopped in front of a door and hesitated, which didn't seem to fit the man at all. But in the end, he didn't respond to her. He gestured at the door that read *Sunrise Sheriff's Department.*

"Come on. Let's go talk to my brother."

Chapter Six

Jack had found the footprints at the rental cabin, and he had a deputy working on questioning anyone who might have been around the Meadowlark Cabin while Dahlia had been there. There were no clear answers on who might be watching her. Unfortunately, it wasn't looking good they'd find any, unless they caught the watcher in the act in the future.

Grant didn't like it. The idea she might be in danger and the idea the woman who was stirring up Truth talk would be under his roof for the foreseeable future.

But she'd answered Jack's questions carefully and concisely. She'd asked a few of her own about what she should be doing to keep herself safe.

She seemed to be in better shape than she had yesterday, and he didn't know why that gave him some odd sense of satisfaction. Like he'd had anything to do with it, even if he *had* all but tricked her into eating breakfast this morning.

After Jack was satisfied, Grant drove Dahlia back to the ranch in silence. He'd give her credit, she didn't seem to mind the silence. It settled over them easily enough. He supposed they were both lost in their own thoughts, worries. Hopes.

He scowled at the road in front of him. He didn't allow

himself to think much on *hope*. He focused on reality. Facts. Probability.

In all *likelihood*, his parents were long dead. If they weren't, it still wasn't a *good* story. But no matter how his brain told him those things, over and over again since he'd been a teenager, his heart still wanted a different outcome.

Which was damn foolish.

He pulled the truck in front of the house. He wasn't sure what to do with Dahlia. Usually when he investigated a case, the person looking for answers wasn't his responsibility to cart around.

Maybe he'd dump her on Mary while he tried to figure out what the next step would be to get ahead of all the Truth gossip.

When Dahlia got out of the car, Grant heard the yip of a dog. Willie came racing around the corner and zoomed straight for Dahlia. Jumping and yapping happily as if they were long-lost loves.

Dahlia knelt and accepted the dog's excited kisses while she rubbed him down. "There's my hero."

Something uncomfortable and unacceptable tangled low in his gut as she smiled at the dog. For a second, her worries had lifted, and he wished with an intensity the situation didn't warrant he could give her that kind of happiness long term.

But some cold cases were never solved, as he well knew. *That's not a no.*

He *knew* his parents were dead. Knew it.

Palmer appeared on the porch. "Good. You're home. I've got something to show you." He glanced at Dahlia. "You and Willie can come too, Ms. Easton."

Her smile faded as she stood. "I suppose that means it's about me."

Palmer shrugged apologetically, then waved them to follow. Not through the house but around it, back where Willie had run from. Grant walked toward the fence that wrapped around the front and back yards—more for decoration and land demarcation rather than keeping the animals in one place or the usual functional ranch fences.

As they walked, Willie kept right next to Dahlia. She seemed to relax around the dog, so Grant made a mental note to see if Cash would let Willie stick around the main house until they figured out if Dahlia was safe.

"Are you the brother the librarian dated?" Dahlia asked as they walked.

Palmer looked back at Grant with raised eyebrows. "Freya? Yeah, we went out a few times a few years ago."

Dahlia frowned at him, as if she objected to his term *date* when explained in that way. But she didn't know Palmer. A few dates *was* about as close to a relationship as he ever got.

"So, it was nothing serious for Grant to worry about," Dahlia continued.

"Grant?" Palmer laughed. "She's always had a thing for Grant. Long before she went out with me, but he doesn't date local women." Palmer grinned at him over Dahlia's head. "Or much at all. Everyone knows that. Including Freya."

"I'm glad we can discuss everyone's private life so openly, but I'd prefer to focus on the case." Grant didn't shove his hands into his pockets like he wanted or hunch his shoulders. He remained passive. Blank.

Palmer jerked a thumb in Grant's direction but leaned

down to stage-whisper conspiratorially to Dahlia. "All work, no play, this one."

Grant didn't like the serious bolt of anger and frustration that shot through him when Palmer was just being Palmer. Trying to get a rise out of him. It wasn't anything Grant hadn't heard before.

Dahlia smiled a little at Palmer's quip, but she didn't quite jump in as Palmer likely hoped or Grant expected.

"I suppose it's important work," she said instead.

Palmer rolled his eyes but stopped at the fence line around the front yard. "Found some footprints. Not any of ours and shouldn't be a ranch hand's." He glanced at Dahlia and tried to smile reassuringly. "Doesn't mean they're not, of course."

Grant wanted to swear, but he held it in. All the tension that had gone out of her shoulders at Willie's arrival was back.

"I don't really understand this," she said, looking at the clear set of footprints in the mud.

"Did you call Jack?" Grant asked.

Palmer nodded. "Took some pictures and sent them over. Deputies are all tied up, but they'll be by eventually. Haven't told Cash yet. He's going to flip."

"Why?" Dahlia asked, directing the question at him rather than Palmer.

"Cash...worries," Grant said, trying for diplomacy. "Izzy likes to wander."

"The daughter," Dahlia said, chewing on her bottom lip. "Should I not stay here? I don't want to bring trouble to your door. That isn't—"

"We can handle it," Grant assured her. "You've got the sheriff living on the premises, along with trained investigative professionals. We have a great security system, which Palmer can assure you is some of the best."

"I make sure of it. Plus, this guy here is a war hero."

Dahlia's eyes widened as she turned to him again. "War hero?"

Grant tried not to react to the term. He hated it. He hadn't done anything special—except survive when a lot of men hadn't. "I was a Marine. Doesn't make me a war hero."

"That's not what the paper said when he came home."

"Can we focus on the task at hand?" Grant said, failing at keeping the snap out of his tone. "Dahlia, I'd like you to go inside. I'm going to look around and see what else I can find."

She frowned at that, then looked down at Willie sitting next to her. "I'd like to look too. I feel like..." She struggled over whatever she wanted her next words to be. "I just want to know what I should keep an eye out for. Does that make sense?"

Grant exchanged a look with Palmer. He didn't really want Dahlia tagging along, but it was hard to refuse someone who wanted to learn in order to protect themselves.

"I'll go break the news to Cash before he hears it through the grapevine. Text if you find anything else. Jack will call Mary when they've got a deputy on the way, but it won't hurt to have it checked out before they get there."

"All right. Tell Cash we're keeping Willie with us for the time being."

"Will do." With that, Palmer left, and Grant had to decide how best to handle a woman and a dog when he'd much prefer to search alone.

"Grant, I really don't understand why someone would be watching me."

"Neither do I, which is why we're going to get to the bottom of it. We're going to see how far we can follow these footprints." He looked the way the footprints were pointing. There was no clear glimpse *into* the house from here, but that didn't mean they hadn't searched for other places. "Now, make sure you follow me. We don't want a bunch of extra prints. We want the police to know exactly what they're looking at."

Dahlia nodded solemnly. "What about Willie?"

"Willie knows how to follow orders."

"Oh."

Grant studied the footprints, then hopped the fence a good few feet away so he wouldn't disturb them. Willie wriggled under the bottom rung, but Dahlia stood there looking unsure.

She was dressed in jeans and tennis shoes and a winter coat, and the fence was low and easy to climb over, so he wasn't sure what held her back. "Do you need help?"

"No." But she looked so unsure as she awkwardly maneuvered over the fence. Grant took a step toward her as if to steady her. But she got on the other side without tripping or toppling over.

She offered him a rueful smile. "I'm not very athletic." She steadied herself on the fence instead of his outstretched hand. "I can follow directions though."

He thought about yesterday when she'd gone off to Truth by herself. He supposed he hadn't directed her *not* to, but it didn't exactly speak to compliance.

Still, he gestured her forward, because she definitely deserved to know what to be on the lookout for when she was the target.

DAHLIA FOLLOWED GRANT, though her tennis shoes weren't holding up very well against the mud they tramped through. But it was a fairly good landscape to see footprints in.

Or so said Grant. He pointed to little marks, indentations and holes and actual outlines she could see. There were paw prints and other signs of animal activity. He explained each of them to her patiently and as if it were important information to know.

She supposed for him it was. So she listened and filed away what she could. But she'd never been an outdoorsy person. She preferred books and being able to control the temperature of the room she was in.

They walked and walked, and every once in a while, Grant would stop, crouch, study another print. When they were human, or he thought they were, he pulled out his phone and took a picture.

Willie followed along, right beside her, never darting off, though sometimes he would stop, sniff and let out a faint *woof.*

Dahlia had always wanted a dog, but her father and Rose had been allergic, and then when she'd finally moved out at Rose's insistence, her apartment hadn't allowed pets. She should think about getting one in the future, but she couldn't seem to see a future anymore.

There was just finding Rose or finding out what had happened to her. Everything else was…not important.

So she walked with Grant. In silence. Dahlia didn't usually mind that, but the conversation with Palmer had given little glimpses into Grant the man. Which she supposed was none of her business, but she was staying under their roof for the time being. They were helping her.

Why not know more?

"So, Jack is law enforcement, Cash handles the dogs, and Palmer is the security. Mary does all the administrative work, but what do you and your other sister specialize in?"

"Anna is a private investigator. She likes the flexibility of going off and working for herself when she needs to."

He did not answer in regard to himself. When she slid in a little mud, he immediately reached out and grabbed her arm, helping her stay upright. Once she was, he immediately dropped it and kept on walking.

"And you?" she pressed. It wasn't usual for her to press, but something about this man's tight-lipped nature made her want to.

He shrugged, knelt and studied another print. "I fill in where needed."

"Jack of all trades?"

"Guess so. They all started this when I was still deployed, and they weren't sure when I'd be coming home. This is animal," he said, standing again and then moving forward.

There was something about the way he said *deployed*, devoid of just enough emotion to make her curious. He didn't sound bitter or resentful, but there was a tenseness to him when he or Palmer spoke of his military career.

She thought military made perfect sense. He was so... large. So self-possessed. It wasn't hard at all to imagine him in military camo holding one of those big intimidating weapons. If that was what Marines did. She didn't know.

But Palmer had called him a war hero.

"Where were you dep—"

"Look, it's not interesting. The military is the military. I didn't do anything special. I'm not a hero. I joined the Marines at eighteen. I did my time, went on a few deployments, did as I was told, watched out for my brothers and when my final time was up, I came home. Beginning and end of story."

Dahlia didn't argue with him, though she inexplicably wanted to. She couldn't imagine being any kind of soldier, away from home, in this weird system of guns and violence and war. So it *was* kind of interesting…intriguing. Courageous.

But she could also imagine why he might not want to talk about it. So she bit her tongue and kept following Grant, Willie happily trotting beside her.

The next time Grant crouched at a print, even Dahlia could see it was a footprint. They were more toward the back of the house now. If she put her feet where the prints were, she'd be looking at the back window.

She studied the house, trying not to let the fear take over like it had yesterday. But that was the window to the room she was staying in. Not that whoever stood here would be able to see in, but after yesterday, everything about this felt ominous and terrible.

"Both of these full prints are very similar to the one outside the cabin yesterday," Grant said, taking pictures from different angles. "Which leads me to believe it's the same person."

Dahlia nodded. Same person. Someone was…stalking her, basically. And as she wasn't interesting and hadn't made any enemies in her life, there seemed to be only one logical conclusion.

"If someone…" She struggled with the next word, emotionally and being able to say it past all that emotion. "If someone murdered Rose, they wouldn't want people poking around her disappearance, would they?"

She thought she might surprise him with the question, but he only looked grim. Like it had already crossed his mind. Like he already believed it.

A shudder of worry went through her. Her parents had warned her she was getting in over her head. Were they right?

"It's only one theory," Grant said gently, but she knew just by the fact he was *being* gentle, it was the most logical one.

"Even if it's true, even if she's dead, I can't give up. I have to find out what happened."

"Even if it puts you in danger?"

Dahlia looked from the footprint to the mountains in the distance. Such a pretty place, and someone out there was watching her. But they hadn't done anything to hurt her.

The *yet* seemed to hang in the air around her.

"I can't live with myself if I go back home. If I put it all away. I just can't." She met Grant's direct brown gaze. Maybe he didn't understand or couldn't, but maybe she didn't need anyone to understand except herself. "I'd rather risk something than try to live under the weight of not doing anything."

For a moment they stood there staring at each other in a grave silence. Then, finally, he nodded. "Let's go inside and update Jack and talk to Palmer about increasing some security measures."

Chapter Seven

Grant made sure Dahlia got back to her room, Willie in tow, then had his usual afternoon meeting with his siblings.

They discussed increased security, which wasn't the first time. Cold cases were often just that, cold, and came with no immediate danger, but they'd found themselves in a few questionable situations before, which had led Mary to develop a coding system, just like security threat levels.

Today, they moved the ranch's security level from green to yellow.

Of course, this meant that Cash was missing from the HSS meeting, as he likely wouldn't let Izzy out of their remote cabin for the foreseeable future. Mary and Anna thought it was a travesty, but Grant figured none of the rest of them were parents, so they didn't really get a say in how Cash decided to keep his child safe.

"It has to be an out-of-towner," Jack said, clearly frustrated neither he nor his deputies had come up with any leads yet. "Maybe someone followed her."

Grant had gone through the same reasonings. Tried to convince himself this had nothing to do with Sunrise or, worse, Truth.

But there was absolutely no evidence to the contrary.

"Someone had been at Truth. Before she got here. That shell casing I found wasn't old, but it wasn't brand new."

"Kids," Jack scoffed.

"I want to believe that too."

"Look, if *Grant* is willing to consider the possibility of Truth being involved, I'd say that's some damning evidence right there," Anna put in.

"I'm not saying Truth is actually involved." Though Grant realized with every passing step in this investigation, he had a harder time dismissing it out of hand. "I'm saying someone has been hanging out in Truth lately. I'm saying Dahlia's being followed only after making the connection to her family history and Truth."

Grant looked at his older brother, whose expression gave nothing away.

Jack had taken care of them since the moment their parents had disappeared. He'd kept the ranch going, made sure they did their homework and were fed and became responsible adults. Even though Grant had been sixteen himself, in a lot of ways, Jack had stepped into the role of father despite the small two-year age difference between them.

Grant had done everything he could to earn Jack's approval, and it was hard now not to wither under his older brother's stare. But these were facts.

"My deputies will keep asking questions," Jack said. "If she feels comfortable, I think it's best if she stays here until we get to the bottom of it."

"I agree," Grant said with a nod. "I think she will too, depending on how long it takes. But she's pretty determined to get to the bottom of what happened to her sister, even if it's bad news."

For a moment they were all silent because they knew that even when you were determined, even when you never gave up, sometimes answers never materialized.

"I could post a deputy out here tonight. Be on the lookout for someone."

"If Palmer and Anna are good with it, I think we should just take turns in house. We'll have a better sense of who should be coming and going anyway."

"It's a big ranch."

"It is. But we all know nothing is getting by Cash as long as Izzy is there. We've got the cameras at the entry points. We stay up and watch them, maybe we can catch this guy."

"He's not setting the cameras off with movement," Palmer said. "I can change from motion-induced to twenty-four seven surveillance, but we'll have to up the security budget for the month."

"All in favor?" Jack asked, because he ran the business like a democracy even when he'd rather be dictator.

But wouldn't they all?

Everyone raised their hands, and Mary noted down the agreement so she could handle the funds. They tackled some other admin details, but Dahlia was their sole client right now, and with an active threat against her, it was hard to think about much else.

They ended the meeting and parted ways to go handle their individual jobs or chores. Grant *wanted* to throw himself into ranch work, but instead he settled in the big armchair in the office and went through Dahlia's binder all over again.

Eugene Green. Grant didn't for a second believe conspiracy theories. The man was dead, and the picture Dahlia had that *resembled* Eugene Green was grainy and fuzzy at best.

But she didn't think it *was* Eugene Green. She had said it could be someone that *looked* like him.

Grant flipped to the family tree again. Dahlia's family was an offshoot of what appeared to be a very normal branch that hadn't ever settled in Wyoming but had gone down to Texas. Before Dahlia had been born, her father had gone to college in the Midwest and married a native Minnesotan, which is how she and her sister had ended up there.

He looked at the picture again. The woman identified as Rose Easton was just as grainy as the man, and the picture was black and white. There was a resemblance, he supposed, somewhere around the mouth and nose, between the woman and Dahlia. The resemblance between this man and Eugene Green as a young man easier to see.

But nothing about it was concrete, and Grant preferred to deal in concretes.

How was he going to find one?

He had to put it aside for dinner. One of the strictest family rules was everyone made it to dinner unless they had a *really* good excuse. Dahlia was already there when he entered the dining room. She still looked uncomfortable, but Willie was curled up behind her chair, and she was listening to Anna talk animatedly at her.

He took the seat next to her, and she offered a small smile as Anna continued to chatter and Mary brought out the food. It was the same kind of dinner as last night, except Cash, Izzy and a lot of the other dogs were missing. Dahlia was still quiet, but who could blame her with Anna and Palmer dominating the conversation like they usually did.

When they were done with dinner, he felt like he should say something to her about the fact that following the Eugene Green theory might lead them in the opposite direction, about the plans to keep her safe, so she could sleep tonight.

But in the end, she seemed content to talk to Mary and pet Willie, so Grant escaped the dining room with Palmer and went to their little security center—a small room on the first floor that had once been a porch before the house had been added on to in the fifties. It housed any of Palmer's security equipment, the guns they kept registered in their name locked in their respective safes and a computer.

Palmer booted it up. "I've changed all the cameras to run twenty-four seven like we discussed. It'll record everything, and I've armed the system on the house, but if we're worried the peeper might turn dangerous, we should keep physical watch."

Grant nodded in agreement. "Until we figure it out. Mary's always around, and I'll stick close to Dahlia."

"Yeah, I just bet you will."

Grant didn't rise to the bait. It wasn't worth it. "If her sister was murdered, this could be more dangerous than we originally thought."

"Always that possibility in a cold case. We're ready for it. I'll take the first shift," Palmer said. "Anna's second. You're the early bird, so you get third."

"All right. But come get me if anything is funny."

"Feeling territorial?"

Grant sighed. "How long are you going to try to get a rise out of me using that tactic?"

"Long as I think it might be true. I mean, she was interested in Freya's interest in you."

"I'm pretty sure that was to clear the way with Freya like some sort of ill-fated matchmaker."

"Nothing wrong with Freya."

"Nothing wrong with minding your own business either."

"Go get some shut-eye, bud."

Grant knew it was in his best interest to do just that. If Palmer took a four-hour shift, then Anna took a four, it would put him waking up at 4:00 a.m. Not much earlier than he usually got up, but he'd do better tomorrow if he got a good night's sleep and didn't stay up looking over every detail of the case he already knew by heart.

So, though he *wanted* to, he left his materials where they were in Mary's office, went to his room, got ready for bed and turned off every facet of his mind that wanted to think about Dahlia Easton and her case.

A trick he'd learned in the military that served him well. Still, sometime later, he awoke with a start, the taste of sand and blood in his mouth. An old dream he hadn't had in a long while making his heart pound like he'd just run a marathon. He sat up in bed in the pitch-black and focused on getting his breathing back to even.

It was a mix of things—no one terrible memory from his service. A blend of them. A firefight here, a sniper there, sometimes his Marine brothers, sometimes his family members.

And this time a certain redhead who he certainly didn't want in his dreams, let alone as pale and bloody and very clearly dead as she had been.

It was hard—harder than it should have been—to get his

breath back, so he slapped on his bedside light and did what he'd had to do almost every night when he'd first come home.

Focus on the little watermark on the ceiling. Count. Disassociate. Until his heart beat the way it should. Until his lungs moved easily—inhale, exhale—no hitch, no gulping for breath.

Just home and the reality that his days of war were behind him. He glanced at his clock: 3:15 a.m. Well, there was no point going back to bed for forty-five minutes when it'd likely take him that long to fall asleep after the nightmare.

So he got up, got dressed and went to find Anna in the security room. She was in the rolling chair, feet propped up on the table. She sipped a Coke while she watched the screens and clearly had earbuds in, so she didn't hear his approach.

Still, when he tapped on her shoulder, she didn't jump or startle at all. She just looked up at him, then swiveled around to face him as she pulled one of the buds out of her ear.

She frowned at him. "You're early—and looking a little ghostly," Anna said, studying him with way too perceptive hazel eyes. She looked almost exactly like their mother and acted *nothing* like her. She was the baby of the family, so Grant couldn't say how purposeful that was. She'd only been eight when Mom and Dad had disappeared, and sometimes Grant wondered how much of either of them she fully remembered.

"I'm fine," Grant muttered. He'd gotten a handle on the physical effects of the dream, but the emotional ones lingered.

"Haven't looked that way since—"

"I said I'm *fine*." He looked at the monitors Anna had been studying. "Nothing, huh?"

She paused as if deciding whether or not to argue, then swiveled back to look at the screens. "Not a thing. If he knows we're looking..."

"I think he'd have to be local to know we're looking."

"You were the one who told Jack he *could* be local. Besides, *he* could also be a *she*. You don't know."

Grant resisted rolling his eyes at his sister. Sure, it was possible, but it was a big boot print to be looking for a woman. He almost pointed that out, but something...moved. Grant's eyes narrowed. "Did you see that?"

"A shadow," Anna confirmed, leaning forward.

"That's way too close to where I saw a footprint this afternoon. The one that looked into Dahlia's room." He didn't like it, so he was already reaching for his gun.

"You can't go out there alone."

"Can. Will. Wake up Palmer. And get Dahlia out of that room."

"Don't you think—"

It would take too long. It would all take too long. "Get her out of that room," he repeated, then ran for the back door.

Chapter Eight

Dahlia was roused from sleep by a pounding on her door and the sound of a dog whining. Once she finally woke up enough to understand the noise—and how it couldn't mean anything good—she threw back the covers and rushed to the door.

She wasn't sure why she expected it to be Grant or why something in her chest sank when it was Anna instead.

"Hey, sorry to wake you," Anna said, reaching down to pet Willie. She was calm and even smiled, so maybe this wasn't...terrible.

"I... It's fine. What time is it?" But Anna had taken her arm and was pulling her forward and out of the room, Willie padding after them. Which didn't seem good at all when it was still dark everywhere.

"We might have caught our friend, but if he knows you're in this room, we just want to go above and beyond careful and get you into an interior room. If you're the target."

Target?

Why was she a target for anything?

But she knew there was only one answer to that, and

it meant Rose was dead. So she pushed the thought away. Had to.

Anna pulled her down the hall, and Dahlia felt like she had no choice but to go. It was only when she was halfway down the corridor that she realized she was in her pajamas. Shorts and a baggy tee, fine enough, but not wearing a *bra* underneath. The floors were cold on her bare feet, and everything made her shiver.

Anna, on the other hand, was dressed like it was the middle of the day. Jeans, sweater, cowboy boots.

"Um." Dahlia hugged herself as the chill sank deeper.

Anna looked back. "Oh man, you're cold. I'll get you a sweatshirt or something. Let's just get you into our wing first."

Our wing?

It was a big house. Sprawling, really, and maybe like the wings had been added on over the years as the family expanded.

They crossed through the living room, where a big window overlooked the front yard. It was still only dark out there, but Dahlia saw the flash of red and blue lights.

"The police are here."

"Yeah. Hopefully they're arresting the jerk." Anna looked back at her and then offered another smile. "Don't worry. It's all probably harmless. We're just being super cautious with the active part of this case."

Active? As though Rose missing *wasn't* active. Which made Dahlia's stomach twist into more knots.

They went through the dining room and then up a new set of stairs and down another hallway. Mary stepped out of a door in this hallway, also dressed as if it were the middle of the day, though her outfit was a little bit more *business* than Anna's ranch wear. Slacks, a button-down shirt and a cardigan.

Dahlia felt more and more out of place.

"Oh, I'm sure you're freezing," Mary said immediately. "I'll grab you a robe."

"She needs socks too," Anna piped in before pulling Dahlia into yet another room. This one was small and shaped oddly, all weird angles and stained glass windows. The furniture was old, definitely antique, and Anna nudged her to sit down in one of the fuzzy chairs. Willie flopped down right at her feet.

Mary quickly appeared and handed Dahlia a soft robe and big fuzzy socks. "You just put those on and warm up. The police have already arrived, so it won't be long before we know more."

It was then Dahlia noted the gun at Anna's hip. The way Mary had closed and locked the door. They could act calm and cheerful, but this was serious. And somehow Dahlia felt...at fault for it all. Surely they'd been living completely normal lives before she'd hired them.

"I'm sorry this is happening. I... If I'd known it would cause so much trouble..." She trailed off, because what would she have done? Certainly not stopped looking for Rose and answers.

"Ms. Easton—Dahlia, this is what we do," Mary said. "We have processes in place to deal with this kind of thing because it's always the risk you run when you take on a case—cold or otherwise. We're all well trained to deal with threats. So, please, don't feel responsible for actions that aren't your own."

"Yeah, this is a piece of cake," Anna added.

The room fell into silence, and Dahlia had to look at the sisters. There wasn't much resemblance. Anna was more on the fair side, everything about her dress and demeanor screamed *tomboy*. Mary had darker hair and eyes and seemed all around more...prim.

It reminded her of her own sister. They each took after a different parent in looks and definitely had different personalities. Rose was so outgoing, so ready to try new things and dive into new experiences.

It still didn't make sense to Dahlia that she was the one doing *all* this. Rose was the tenacious one. Dahlia swallowed at the lump in her throat and focused on the stained glass window of a mountain with a big star at the top.

She wasn't sure how much time passed, but she put on the robe, the socks and warmed up a little.

Eventually there was a tap at the door, and Mary unlocked and opened it. Dahlia could hear Grant's voice, though he hadn't stepped in the room far enough for her to see him.

"The police arrested the guy. Jack will question him. For now, everyone can probably go back to sleep. There is just one...slight oddity to the whole thing. He's a kid."

"A *kid*?" Anna repeated.

"If I had to guess? I'd say not a day over sixteen." He stepped farther into the room, and Dahlia leapt to her feet, heart slamming into her ribcage.

"You're bleeding."

"Oh." Grant lifted a hand to his mouth and pulled it back, examining the blood. "Was a little shocked to find a kid, so he got a lucky shot in." Then Grant shrugged like it was nothing.

And his sisters kept throwing out questions like it didn't matter.

"But he wasn't armed?" Anna asked.

"Had a gun on him, but he didn't pull it. Can't say I know what to think about the whole thing. The police will do some investigating, make sure his prints match the others, and he's the only one, but—"

"You're *bleeding*," Dahlia interrupted, because she was still standing here, heart beating too hard, staring at the smudge of blood at the corner of his mouth. Didn't anyone, least of all *him*, care?

All three sets of eyes looked at her with varying amounts of consideration.

Then Mary smiled kindly. "I'll get something to clean it up." She stepped out of the room, Anna at her heels.

"Yeah, I'll help you."

So, it was just her and Grant alone in this strange room. In this strange new version of her life.

"I've had a lot worse than a busted lip from some kid," he offered, as if *that* were some kind of comfort. "You really don't need to worry about it."

Dahlia turned away from him, because no matter what he said, she just hated the sight of blood. Hated knowing—no matter how Anna or Mary acted—that this was about her.

She stared hard at that mountain of stained glass.

"Dahlia," Grant said, and it wasn't the way he usually spoke. All stiff orders and frustration. There was a note of softness he only usually deployed at those family dinners. He was also closer than he had been. "I can't tell you not to be afraid, but I can assure you that HSS will do everything to get to the bottom of this while keeping you safe."

She swallowed. She felt like spun glass. Like every time she got her footing in this terrible situation, some earthquake came along. She didn't want to be weak. She didn't want to cry.

She just wanted to find her sister. She cleared her throat, calling on every last piece of strength within her. "It's very disorienting. I guess I just need to find my footing." *Again*.

"You're doing just fine." He gave her shoulder a little squeeze. Friendly. Reassuring. But when he released her, his hand moved down her shoulder blade. It was a casual move, just the way a hand would fall off a shoulder as someone pulled it away.

But it twisted through her like something else and made her breath hitch.

He cleared his throat and created distance between them—almost as if he felt it too.

Clearly she was delusional. Sleep deprived. "I'm very tired."

"I'm sure you are. We'll keep an eye on the security cameras until we know for sure this kid acted alone, but you're fine to go back to your room and sleep."

She nodded as Anna and Mary came back in with a little first aid kit, smiling over something they'd said to each other in the hallway.

"You want me to take you back to your room? All the hallways are confusing till you get used to it," Anna said.

"Sure. Thanks." Anna stepped back into the hall, and Dahlia followed, Willie always at her heels, but she found herself looking back at Grant, who was standing there letting Mary dab away the blood on his face.

He looked so…strong. Like some Western movie hero. A tiny bit beat up, but noble and true and right. *You're doing just fine.* It was the strangest thing. How easy it was to believe when *he* said it. Because he looked like he knew. Like all his convictions *had* to be right, or the world would crumble into dust.

But he didn't believe her about Truth or the Greens. Because he didn't want to, not because there wasn't evidence.

So he wasn't her friend. He wasn't her protector. He wasn't anything, except a man she paid to help.

But the way he'd touched her shoulder kept her awake for the rest of the night.

Chapter Nine

Grant never did get much sleep after that. What he wanted to do was head down to the sheriff's department immediately, but Jack would want everything on the up and up, which meant no HSS interference until later.

It worried Grant that the perpetrator was a minor. That parents or the juvenile detention center—when they didn't have a local one of those—would complicate getting answers.

But he did his chores, ate his breakfast and waited for Dahlia to emerge from her room. Once she did, he'd take her down to the police station and figure out if there was anything to go on.

The phone in his pocket began to ring as he walked back to the house from his second round of morning chores. The caller ID showed the library's number, and Grant hoped it would be Mrs. Riley with some information or lead now that she'd realized her reaction to the Green connection had been overboard.

"Hudson," Grant answered.

"Hi, Grant. It's Freya."

Grant winced. Good Lord, this was not what he needed. "Hi, Freya."

"I thought I should call you. I know you were working with that redhead yesterday, and Mrs. Riley wasn't very helpful."

"No, she wasn't." Grant stepped into the house, stamping his boots on mats meant to pick up all the ranch mud.

"Well, she was complaining to Mr. Durst about it this morning. About the Greens. Mr. Durst obviously pointed out that they're all dead and so on. But…"

"But?"

"I shouldn't stick my nose in this, I know, but the redhead was really nice. And I wanted to help. And…"

"What is it Freya?"

"Mrs. Riley said something about how she's connected to the Greens? Dahlia, right?"

"Very loosely, it seems. A century ago or something. All that genealogy stuff. You know how that goes. Turns out everyone's related half the time."

"Well, yes, but Mrs. Riley was talking about how the red-headed Greens were always the bad ones. She seemed so… angry, and it was just kind of weird. Even Mr. Durst told her she was being ridiculous."

Redheaded Greens? Eugene Green had been bald and so had the man in that picture with Dahlia's sister. But there were other Greens. He didn't want to remember all the pictures of Truth in its heyday.

"Thanks, Freya. It's good to know that's what people are saying. Can you do me a favor?"

"Anything."

He winced at the fervor in her tone. "If the gossip mill

starts winding up, will you do what you can to stop it? Or at least correct it. No one needs Mrs. Riley stirring people up into thinking this is some kind of direct connection to the Greens or Truth."

"Sure, Grant. I can do that."

"Thanks, I appreciate it."

"No problem. Anytime. Really."

"I'll see you around, Freya. Bye." He pressed End, feeling the way he always did. Uncomfortable, guilty. There was nothing wrong with Freya. She was a sweet woman. And, okay, he could admit he'd known she was going out with Palmer to see if *he'd* pay attention, but he just…wasn't interested.

He was complicated. And there was no point in throwing those complications out for everyone in town to know when they already talked about his family plenty.

Once his boots were clean, he left the mud room and went into the kitchen. Dahlia stood there alone, except for Willie at her feet, staring out the window over the sink. She held a mug of coffee but didn't seem to hear him enter.

The sunlight streamed in, making her red hair glow, like a flame. And then there were those blue eyes, lost and hurting, and he wanted to…

What the hell is wrong with you?

He should be thinking about Mrs. Riley assuming this was some kind of bad Green mark on her. The way Mrs. Riley spread gossip around town, everyone would believe it by the end of the day. Freya would try to turn the tide, but people loved a story.

He should know.

As if she finally sensed him there, she turned to look at

him. She didn't register any surprise or discomfort at him just standing there *staring* at her.

"Do you know any more?" Dahlia asked without any kind of greeting.

"Not really. We can head down to the station whenever you want, confer with Jack."

She nodded. "I'd like to do that right away."

"Of course. But have you eaten anything?"

She looked down at the coffee, then made a face. "I really… I'm not a breakfast person. And it feels strange to…"

She trailed off as he began to open the pantry. He wasn't going to force a full meal on her, but he wasn't about to take her to the police station without something in her stomach. He found the variety pack of granola bars Anna loved so much and held out the box to her. "Pick one."

She hesitated.

He shook the box. "You feel better when you eat, don't you?"

She huffed out an irritated breath but then took one. "Happy?"

"I will be once you eat it."

This time she scrunched up her nose, but she opened the bar and took a bite. But she kept…staring at him.

It took him a few uncomfortable seconds to realize there was a *reason* her eyes kept drifting to his mouth. And they were none of the ones he'd been imagining.

It was because that's where he'd been bleeding last night. It wasn't even really swollen. There was just the little cut on his lip where the kid's elbow had knocked it into his tooth.

"I guess you're doing okay, then," she said after a few bites of granola bar.

"It was really nothing."

She nodded. "I just don't know how to make sense of it all. People don't get hit in my world. There aren't disappearances and stalkers and all this."

He didn't say the obvious. It *was* her world now, whether it made sense or not.

He also didn't say what he should tell her—that the town was going to look at her like the Devil now that Mrs. Riley undoubtedly shared a bunch of wrongheaded rumors. And unfortunately for Dahlia, her red hair wasn't any different than a big red A in this instance.

But maybe once they got to the bottom of whoever was watching her, she'd have enough answers to head back to Minnesota, and it wouldn't matter.

Why that thought settled so uncomfortably in his chest wasn't worth thinking about. "You want to grab anything before we head into town?"

She shook her head. "No, I'm ready."

DAHLIA FELT OKAY. More sturdy than not. She hadn't slept well, but whoever had been watching her had been caught, and it was both a relief and maybe a lead.

She desperately wanted a lead.

But when Grant pulled up in front of the sheriff's department, dread pooled in her stomach. Whoever had been watching her—a *teenager*—was in here.

"Jack will likely ask you a few questions. Hopefully he'll be able to give us some information to go on, but even if he doesn't, just the fact this guy is in custody is a new lead to follow."

Dahlia knew Grant was trying to assure her, so she attempted to smile and nod and feel reassured.

But she just kept thinking about how her sister was probably dead, and this *child,* essentially, might know something or be involved. There might be answers here, and for this entire year, the quest for them had driven her. Even knowing Rose might be—probably was—dead.

Faced with the possibility of confirmation...

"Dahlia," Grant said, with that rare gentleness that made her want to cry. "There's a reason my family specializes in cold cases. It's because they're unique. The way they drag out to the point where answers start to feel like as much of a curse as not knowing. We get it. So we can sit here as long as you need, or I can go in alone."

"It's just... I guess I never fully understood that an answer doesn't really change anything, does it?" She looked out the windshield, desperately trying to hold it all together. "If she's...gone, she's still gone. Whether I know or not."

Grant nodded along. "But you want to know. Or you would have given up a long time ago, Dahlia. A lot of people do."

She let out a shaky breath. He was right. Her parents had given up. Her and Rose's friends. Everyone had said *enough*, and she hadn't been able to. She sucked in a steadying breath. "Okay. I'm ready."

They both got out of the truck, and Grant met her at the front. He put his hand on her back and guided her inside. It was a friendly offer of support. Made all the more poignant by the fact everyone had...stopped offering that. Everyone wanted her to give up. Either be sad or get over it. Not stay mired in the what-ifs.

But Grant and his family understood. Dahlia hadn't realized how much she needed that. How much she missed feeling like someone…cared.

Of course, it was their job, and she was paying them, so it wasn't real care. But it still felt like a weight lifted.

He opened the door, and his hand stayed on her back as they entered. It was a small office, and the woman behind the desk looked up. She obviously knew Grant, but something odd flickered in her gaze when she took in Dahlia.

Still, she smiled and greeted Grant. "Your brother's back in the holding room."

Grant nodded and led Dahlia past the front desk. Jack was standing in a hallway and didn't greet them when he saw them, just nodded his head in a *follow me* gesture. So they did. Back to a little room with a big window. Jack pointed at the teenager inside, sitting next to a woman in a black suit.

"Do you know him?"

Dahlia swallowed and looked through the mirrored window. She studied the teen's face, desperate for any kind of recognition. And found none. "No."

Jack nodded as if that's what he'd expected. "Let's go into my office and have a chat."

He led them to the same small room she'd been in yesterday answering his questions. The same fat black cat slinked off the desk when Jack shooed it.

Jack Hudson did not seem like the type of man to care for a cat, but Dahlia hadn't asked questions then and didn't plan to now.

"Who is he?" she asked.

"His name is Kory Smithfield. Sixteen years old. A year and a half ago, he was reported missing by his parents in Austin, Texas."

Dahlia thought her knees might buckle, but she stiffened them and steadied herself by holding on to the back of a chair. She was afraid if she sat on it she'd never get back up. "Texas."

Jack nodded, his expression nothing but stoic. "We asked him some questions, talked to his parents. They can't come get him, and I didn't get the impression they were that interested in having him home at this point. We're going to have to send him to the juvenile center in Cody, at which point, finding answers is going to get complicated."

"Where's he been living since he went missing?" Grant asked.

"He wouldn't say. Pretended like he didn't run away, but it's clearly him. He also refused to admit he was following or watching Ms. Easton. Which is fine. We have proof. I'd like to bring Dahlia in to talk to him, but we'll need a lawyer present to make that aboveboard, and the parents weren't paying."

"So, what? It's a dead end?" Dahlia asked. Even though... Texas. If he was connected with Texas and had somehow wound up here in Wyoming...

He wasn't the man in the security footage with Rose, so maybe she was making too big of a leap to think it connected.

But it had to, didn't it?

"Not exactly." Jack paused, as if grappling with something significant. His cool gaze moved from Dahlia to his brother. "Grant, he has a tattoo."

She felt Grant stiffen next to her. Neither brother said anything, but their reaction made her think of her research, of all the things she'd read about the cult she was somehow connected to.

"He has an Order of Truth tattoo?" Dahlia demanded.

Grant scowled but said nothing. Jack didn't confirm, but *obviously* that's what it was.

"It connects. He *connects*. You can't deny it. You can't keep denying it. He was watching me. He has an Order of Truth *tattoo*. You have to let me talk to him. You have to let me ask him some questions. You *have*—"

"The only thing I *have* to do is follow the letter of the law," Jack replied stiffly. "I let you go in there, and the entire stalking case against you goes up in smoke."

"I don't care!"

"Dahlia."

She whirled on Grant. "I don't. I don't! He has something to do with my sister's disappearance. Maybe he killed her, and I don't care if he's sixteen or sixty. I will find out what happened to my sister. I *will*."

"Take a breath," he said gently.

But boy, that was the *wrong* thing to say. "Take a breath? This is the first hint of a lead I've had, and you're trying to stand in my way when I hired you all to *help*." She was not going to cry. She wasn't.

Grant put his hand on her shoulder. It should have infuriated her, but there was something about the heavy weight of a big hand and the serious way he looked at her. None of the dismissiveness she was used to from men and law enforcement.

He didn't say anything to her though, instead he moved that serious gaze to his brother. "We don't want to impact any potential case, but surely there's *some* way she can ask this kid a few questions. Or you could on her behalf."

"I've asked him plenty. He's not talking."

"Jack."

Dahlia didn't think Jack would relent. He was like a mountain. Absolutely no give. She expected that from Grant as well, but whatever passed between the brothers—something Dahlia didn't see or understand—had Jack blowing out a breath.

"I have to move him to a cell until we can transport him. Which means I'll have to walk him down the hallway. And there's no reason you couldn't…also be in the hallway."

What was she going to do with a hallway passing? She almost argued some more, but Grant looked back at her with a nod like *This is as good as it's going to get.*

Her mind scrambled for some idea as Jack moved back out of his office and to the holding room she'd looked into.

The teen still sat there looking calm. Maybe a little irritated, but not nervous. Not worried.

Dahlia couldn't imagine running away from home and then being picked up by the police and not being sad and scared.

"Stay here," Jack ordered. "Whatever you ask, whatever he says, it's completely inadmissible in a court of law. So just keep that in mind."

Grant's hand was on her back again, like he'd keep her there if necessary. Still, she didn't know what to say. What to ask. *Where is my sister? Why are you watching me?*

Jack went into the room, said something to the kid before he got to his feet. He was handcuffed, then Jack pulled him out of the room. Dahlia couldn't seem to find words, because the boy laughed and smiled like this was just a fun game.

"I didn't even know sheriffs were real. Sounds fake to me," the boy was saying. "Not good enough to be a real cop?"

Jack said nothing, but he met Dahlia's gaze over the teen's head. Which made the boy look over at her.

He looked at her, and while she saw nothing that made her feel like she knew him, there was something about the way he stared at her that made her feel...exposed. Like he knew exactly who *she* was.

Then he smiled at her, and her blood ran completely cold. She couldn't force *any* words out of her mouth.

He tried to lean forward, but Jack jerked him into place. Still, Dahlia heard exactly what the boy whispered.

"You'll be with your sister soon."

Chapter Ten

Grant didn't think the move through. He simply reacted. He reached out, meaning to get a hand on the kid, but Jack was faster, stepping between them. "He's going to a cell," Jack said icily.

When that little bastard had *threatened* Dahlia. Grant looked down at Dahlia. She'd gone white as a sheet, and no wonder.

"Dahlia." But he didn't know what to say.

She raised her blue eyes to his, looking a bit like a shell-shocked victim. "You heard him, right? You heard what he said."

Grant nodded. He wanted to say something reassuring, but he came up empty. The kid had mentioned Dahlia's sister without prompting. He had an Order of Truth tattoo.

Damn it.

"What do we do if we can't ask him questions? How do we get answers if Jack is all 'letter of the law' about this?" Dahlia demanded. Some of her color was coming back, so that was good.

But they weren't going to get anywhere with Jack. Not when he thought he had a good case against the kid. Not when everything about this was going to stir up everything… *everything.* "I have my ways. Come on."

He got her out of the station before Jack was finished with the kid. Jack would no doubt want to lecture them on what they could and couldn't do.

Typically Jack's work as sheriff didn't interfere with the cases HSS worked because even amongst the suspicious missing persons, many of them committed suicide or died accidentally. The few murder cases they'd found and worked on had involved mostly dead people, so there was nothing active to put Jack in a complicated position with his job.

But this? Dahlia's sister's cold case disappearance now intersected with a current stalking case. That tied to the Order of Truth.

Damn. Damn. Damn.

This wasn't even about him being wrong. He could deal with that. What he couldn't—or didn't want to—deal with was the way this would, yet again, tear up his hometown. A town that had perhaps only in the past ten years started healing from what happened at Truth.

And it would bring up *everything* with his parents' disappearance once more. Grant didn't just dread it. He wasn't sure how he was going to *stand* it.

He unlocked his truck and waited for Dahlia to climb in. She was clutching her hands together, looking like she was about ready to jump out of her skin.

"We've got his name. Where he came from. The tattoo. It's a lot to go on," Grant offered, hoping to relax her some. He pulled out of the station parking lot with the thought of heading home. He and his siblings would all start researching Kory Smithfield ASAP.

And going down those old traumatic roads that led to the Order of Truth.

"What about that casing we found in Truth?" Dahlia asked.

"Jack's got that too, so he'll see if it matches the gun the kid had." But that was another thing that bothered Grant. When he'd wrestled that kid to the ground, the kid had tried to get away. But he hadn't tried to use his gun on Grant. He hadn't been a particularly adept fighter either. He hadn't wanted to be caught, but there'd been no thirst for violence in his reaction.

And yet, the smile he'd given Dahlia, the whispered words, they were *chilling*. As was the thought of that boy with that gun trailing around after Dahlia, watching her.

"The casing could tell us…something, right?"

He wouldn't say what he was thinking. Because unfortunately, without a body, even a murder weapon didn't mean much. But he tried to smile reassuringly at Dahlia. "It's definitely a lead of some kind."

"Wait. Stop," Dahlia said, reaching across and placing her hand on his over the steering wheel. She pointed at the library out his window as he slowed to a stop in the middle of Main Street. "I think we should go see Mrs. Riley. She said she made sure she knew all about the Greens. She might know if Eugene had sons, nephews, someone who looked like him. Maybe they aren't in Truth, but they're somewhere if that boy had a tattoo."

Grant hesitated. It was strange how much he wanted to protect her from the truth. Mostly he didn't mind being a little abrasively straightforward. But he supposed most of the people he dealt with were his siblings and ranch hands, so it suited the circumstances.

Dahlia was… Well, he didn't know how to explain it. She was soft, but she was strong. She was always on the verge of breaking apart but somehow always pulled it back together. And she was doing something he couldn't do anything but respect.

Finding answers for her family, no matter what it took.

So he didn't want to tell her Mrs. Riley wouldn't see her or answer her questions. That she'd likely already spread it around town that Dahlia was the next coming of cults and Greens and Truth nonsense. And the arrest of Kory Smithfield was only going to exacerbate the problem.

But apparently he didn't have to tell Dahlia any of that.

"I know she won't want to speak with me," Dahlia said earnestly, and her hand was still over his on the steering wheel. "But you could go talk to her. I could just…wait somewhere. Here in the truck or hang out in the library. I could go over to the general store if you think she'll see me and not talk. You go in and ask her questions, and I'll stay out of sight."

Grant wondered if even he could get through to Mrs. Riley since she knew Dahlia was his client, but he'd try. *After* he got her somewhere safe. "I'll take you back to the ranch and—"

"We don't have time for that."

They did have time—there was always time—but she had her first real lead in over a year. He understood why she wouldn't want to have patience now when, finally, it felt like something might move forward.

But she very clearly hadn't accepted the situation yet,

or at least the implications as they connected to *her*. If she thought he was going to leave her alone for a second, she was *sorely* mistaken.

"Dahlia." He didn't want to be the one to put the thought in her head, though it was hard for him to understand how she hadn't arrived at the same conclusion yet. "What he said to you back there was a *threat*. Which means the possibility there is still someone out there who might want to cause you harm is high. You're not going to be out of my sight unless you're safe inside the ranch house until we know who else might be after you. And why."

IT WASN'T THAT Dahlia didn't understand what Grant was saying. Once he said it out loud, she went back over the whole experience and sort of…processed the situation. She'd been so focused on the sister part—the confirmation that boy knew something about Rose—she hadn't even fully grasped that her seeing Rose soon was…probably a death threat.

Rose was dead.

And she was sitting in some strange cowboy's truck in the middle of small-town Wyoming, thinking he could help her find answers.

Dahlia let out a slow breath and carefully sucked it in. She felt like she was on the verge of breaking into a million pieces, but she simply wouldn't let herself.

You're not going to be out of my sight unless you're safe inside the ranch house until we know who else might be after you. And why.

He wanted to help. He wanted, for whatever reason, to help keep her safe. He was worried. She knew it was business, not personal, but to be worried about her when it had nothing to do with her mental state felt…oddly like a huge weight had been lifted off her shoulders.

"But I agree with you," he continued when she didn't say anything. "Mrs. Riley might have more answers about the Greens still around and that might be a lead. I'm going to take you back to the ranch though."

Dahlia looked out of the passenger side window at the pretty little town and the sunny fall afternoon as Grant began to drive again. She had hired the Hudsons to look into this. Investigate. Find the connections. And here Grant was doing just that, all the while protecting her from a potential threat.

Going back to the ranch was what she should do. She was hardly going to *ignore* a death threat, but going through her binders in that beautiful room just made her feel like screaming. Which was ridiculous, because aside from a scenery change, that was about what she'd been doing for the past year. And now there was a *lead*. She should want to pore over everything again.

She turned to Grant, studying his profile while he drove. He was no different than Jack. An immovable mountain made up of certainty and strength of purpose. She wished she could emulate it.

Or get through to it. "Grant…" But she didn't have any experience laying out her feelings for people. She hated to ask for anything, hated to be seen as a burden. She *liked* being self-sufficient. She didn't mind being the one everyone forgot about, because that meant no one was paying too close attention to her.

Because when they did, they tended to think her strange or, since Rose disappeared, unhinged.

Grant spared her a glance, then his gaze dropped to where

she realized she still had her hand rested atop his on the steering wheel.

She pulled it back and dropped it in her lap like it wasn't her own appendage. There was just something…comforting about him. She didn't know why. He was abrupt sometimes. She knew he tried to be gentle, but he wasn't especially *good* at it, even if she did appreciate the attempt.

"I know it's hard to sit around and wait. Or worry," Grant said. Because for all his inability to be gentle, he *did* have understanding. True understanding. In a way no one else in her life seemed to. Which was a comfort, Dahlia supposed.

"It's all I've done for a year, and now there's *finally* this… piece. I don't know how to fit it in, but it's a piece. He said, 'your sister.' He *knows* about Rose. I can't go back to the ranch and sit in that room and stew just because…"

"Just because he *threatened* you? That's not a *just* because in my world, Dahlia. It's a big damn *because*."

Dahlia sighed and looked away out the window as the landscape passed. Mountains and fall colors. Such a pretty place, and her sister had likely been murdered. For some reason, that runaway teenager thought she would be next.

She thought about the cranky woman at the library who'd immediately taken against her. That woman had said… "Mrs. Riley told us they would know about me. That they knew their tree backward and forward, and a loose connection wouldn't matter, it was still a connection. But if Eugene Green has been dead fifty years, who was she talking about in the here and now when she said, 'they?'"

Grant frowned at the road ahead of them. He clearly didn't like the connection to Truth or the Greens, but he was no longer trying to talk her out of it. "Listen, Mrs. Riley is…

difficult. Her father joined the cult when she was a teenager. Her mom left her dad because she saw it for what it was, but the dad took some of the kids in there with them, and then… Well, her brother was one of the people who helped bring in the Feds. He always told her their father had tried to escape, but once you're initiated into the Order, you can't leave. Not alive anyway."

Dahlia listened to that reasoning. It explained some of the woman's animosity, she supposed.

"They all died. Her father, her brothers—the ones who were involved, the ones who tried to bring it down. The remaining Rileys have always… Well, they're bitter. Understandably."

"But they're also *knowledgeable*, Grant."

His jaw tightened, but he didn't argue with her. "We just have to be careful about how we approach her. It's a lot of trauma. All this happened before I was born, but for my entire childhood, it was such a…sore subject for everyone. It affected the whole town, generations of families. All of whom lost people."

He didn't say it, but she heard it all the same. *Just like you.*

He sighed before he continued. "And the thing is, this kid and his tattoo… It doesn't just stir up old, bad memories for people here. It means someone out there is still…" He shook his head. "I can't believe I'm saying this, but it means everything we thought *ended* back in 1978 didn't actually end. And that's going to hurt a lot of people."

"They've already been hurt. And so has my sister. Just because time has passed doesn't mean the hurt isn't still there. Surely you of all people know that."

"People want it to be over," Grant said stiffly.

"But it's *not*."

He spared her a glance, and she thought he was going to argue with her further, but instead he reached across the space between them abruptly. He pushed her head down, enough so that she let out a little yelp of pain. "Stay down," he ordered.

A second before something exploded.

Chapter Eleven

Grant kept one hand pushing Dahlia's head down away from the windows and one hand with a death grip on the steering wheel as the truck jerked beneath them.

Someone had shot out his tire. It was better than shooting Dahlia's *head*, but it still wasn't good.

He was halfway between town and the ranch, a stretch of highway that didn't see much traffic that wasn't a member of his family. Which meant this was very carefully planned and not good for either him or Dahlia.

He couldn't drive well on the flat tire, particularly in his best approximation of a crouch in the hopes that any other shots that went off didn't actually hit him or Dahlia. He had a gun, but it was locked in the glove compartment, and if he couldn't drive his way out of this, he supposed he'd have to shoot his way out.

Something uncomfortable and a lot like dread curled in his gut. He hadn't had much luck shooting since he'd come back from the Marines. The few times he'd sucked it up and forced himself to target practice, all his former accuracy and skill seemed to be completely and utterly gone.

So he'd stopped trying.

But now someone was shooting *at* him and Dahlia, and he was going to have to be able to do something about it. Whether his brain wanted to cooperate or not.

The truck was screeching metal now, tire rim against concrete at a bad angle that meant the whole thing could flip if he wasn't careful. Driving much longer like this was almost as dangerous as getting shot at.

So he slammed on the brakes, and Dahlia let out a little yelp as the seat belt kept her from slamming into the dash. He ripped the keys out of the ignition. "Keep your head down," he ordered, releasing her head and shoving the key into the hole on the glove compartment. He unlocked it, then scanned the world around them as he pulled his gun out.

He spotted the shooter in the rearview mirror—up on a ridge and working his way down it. But as far as Grant was concerned, that was the least of his problems. There were three other men moving out from various protected areas—moving to circle them.

He didn't have much time. And if there were any more men hiding, they were probably in for a world of hurt.

But he didn't let his mind go down that road. He could only deal with the threat in front of him. He turned to Dahlia. "You're going to stay in the truck. Call 911. I'm going to take care of it."

"Take care of what?" she demanded, though she was definitely shaken, crouching there low enough her head wasn't visible in any of the windows.

But it was then a few things dawned on him. One, the shooter on the ridge hadn't shot again, though he could have. Two, the three men who were currently moving to surround the truck didn't appear to have weapons—not visible or drawn anyway.

Which meant this wasn't simply an attempt to murder Dahlia, or anyone looking into Rose's disappearance.

It was something else.

"Just stay put," Grant said, and then he had to trust she would. He opened the door, keeping the shooter behind him in sight. He waited to see if the man would lift the gun and aim it at him, but he simply kept moving down the ridge and toward the road.

Grant turned his attention back to the much closer men. Even if they didn't have visible guns, he didn't like the idea of them surrounding the truck. Even if they didn't want to kill anyone, nothing they wanted could be *good*.

"I think you fellas have the wrong people," he called out to the man closest—the one coming for the front of the truck, while the other two spread out to the east and the west respectively. He eyed the open door's side view mirror and saw the other man still climbing down the rock he'd been perched atop.

None of the men responded to him. They just kept advancing. Grant adjusted the grip on his gun, trying to focus on the goal rather than the anxiety clutching at his chest. He had to keep Dahlia safe.

Had to.

"Come any closer, and I'm going to have to start shooting," Grant warned. He aimed at the man in front. "We've called the cops, so why don't you all turn around? Go back where you came from."

They seemed wholly unafraid, though they didn't keep

moving forward. The man in front studied Grant. "Is it true? Do you have her?"

Grant squeezed his hand in an attempt to keep it from going numb like the rest of his body seemed to be doing. "Who?" Grant said, and the three men answered in succession.

"The true one."

"The answer."

"Our promised."

Grant had seen a lot of terrible things. He'd been scared and freaked out more times than he liked to count. But this was possibly one of the creepiest damn things he'd ever encountered.

"That's not going to work for me. I warned you about taking another step."

But the man in front took one. So Grant got off a shot— aiming for a few feet in front of the forward-moving man. The shot went shorter and way wider than he'd anticipated.

He cursed under his breath. *Not now. Now when it matters.*

The men did stop advancing. They didn't turn around and run away or anything, but they stopped taking steps.

"Give us the woman," the man he'd shot at said in an authoritative tone. "And you'll be rewarded."

But there was something...familiar about him. The voice or the way the man in front stood. Grant moved toward him, gun still held and pointed at him. But the man didn't move or even eye the gun warily. He stood, chin held high, eyes on the truck as if he were trying to catch a glimpse of Dahlia.

Not going to happen.

It was when Grant got close enough to see the man's ear that it finally dawned on him who it was. "Lyle?"

"Lyle's dead," the man said flatly. But it *was* Lyle Stuart. He'd been one of Jack's buddies in high school, but once Mom and Dad disappeared, Jack had cut ties because Lyle made trouble wherever he went. And Lyle was *always* recognizable because he was missing half his ear from a dog attack when he'd been a kid.

Lyle had left Sunrise years ago. Grant couldn't remember where he was supposed to have gone, but he did remember it was not long after Mom and Dad disappeared. Jack had said it was a good riddance type situation.

Now, all these years later, here Lyle was. Older, definitely having lived some hard years, but Lyle Stuart. Part of this damn cult that had somehow been revived.

And they wanted Dahlia.

"I've got some bad news for you, Lyle. Dead or alive, you're not getting her."

DAHLIA FOLLOWED INSTRUCTIONS for a while. She'd called 911, though it had been hard to give the dispatcher enough information. She didn't know enough about the area to give first responders an idea of where they were. The dispatcher kept asking her questions she didn't know the answers to.

"Jack Hudson will know where we are," she'd finally said. "The sheriff in Sunrise, Wyoming."

"Sunrise, Wyoming," the dispatcher repeated. "Stay on the line, miss."

Dahlia did, but she wasn't really paying attention to what the dispatcher said, because a loud *bang* exploded through the air. Dahlia dropped the phone and looked up over the dash, eyes frantically searching the area.

There was a man in front of the truck and two other men

on either side of the truck. Grant was moving toward the man in front, but no one seemed hurt. Or scared. While her heart was racing and her palms were sweating.

Phone forgotten, everything forgotten except someone *shooting*, she watched as Grant stopped in front of the man who now stood in the middle of the road as if he were blocking the truck, when the truck was leaning at such an angle, she didn't have any reason to believe it *could* go.

It was almost like they were squared off. They were a good ten feet apart if not more, and they were talking, though she couldn't hear what they were saying. Grant had his gun pointed at the man, but the expressions on their faces weren't antagonistic, exactly.

More wary. Waiting. Considering.

She looked out the passenger window, then the opening left by Grant leaving the driver's side door open. The other two men were watching the exchange, though sometimes they would turn their gaze to the truck, and Dahlia would duck down—not sure why she felt like she didn't want them to even see her when they no doubt knew she was in the car.

She twisted in her seat, still crouched, and carefully poked her head up—inch by inch—until she could see out the back. A man stood there as well, gun pointed at Grant's back.

Dahlia did *not* like that.

But no one was immediately shooting. Still, she couldn't understand why Grant wasn't looking back, wasn't worried about the man with the gun. Surely he knew that man was there.

"Lord of Truth," the man in front of Grant yelled, raising his hands up to the sky. "Help us."

The two other men on either side of the truck began to do

the same. They just kept shouting those words over and over, looking up at the sky like something might drop down and save them. Dahlia looked back at the man with the gun. He was moving again toward the truck. Toward her.

She knew this was about her just by the way the man looked at her through the back window of the truck. He was zeroed in on her, while the other men shouted about truth and help.

She wanted to cover her ears. It was only the voices of three men, but the repetitive words were so loud and alarming.

She heard the back door of the truck creak open, and she no longer saw the gunman in the windows. She looked wildly for Grant, but he was no longer standing off with the man in front, who was still chanting at the sky in time with the other men.

Maybe it was him. She looked back at the door, and a gun barrel appeared. "Get out of the truck," an unfamiliar voice said, though the face was hidden behind the door itself.

She didn't have anything to use as a weapon. Didn't know what to do except…refuse. "No," she replied as she looked around wildly. There had to be something she could use as defense, but as she looked to the right of her, she noticed one of the other men advancing toward the door.

It was locked, but that didn't make her feel safe, particularly since he was still yelling words about truth and help. She didn't *see* a gun, but that didn't mean he didn't have one.

Maybe this was what happened to Rose.

She looked back at the gun pointed at her. It was beyond surreal. Maybe it was not being able to see the man behind it, or how little experience she had with guns, but it was almost impossible to believe it could kill her.

But maybe it killed Rose. Could she convince this man to keep her alive and take her to wherever he'd taken Rose? Maybe she'd die, but maybe she'd know?

Before she could act on that irrational thought, the gun disappeared. She heard a distinctive male grunt and then a clattering sound. She scrambled over to the driver's side to see through the windows.

Grant was grappling with the gunman. He took an elbow to the stomach but barely even winced as he pivoted and jabbed his fist up, hitting the man squarely in the jaw. The man stumbled back and into the truck on a grunt. Meanwhile the shouts from the other men continued to echo outside.

She thought maybe she heard sirens beyond all that noise and prayed help was on the way, because she didn't have the slightest idea what to do.

The gun. Guns. The man had been holding a gun and so had Grant, but where were they now? She peeked her head out of the doorway and saw them both on the ground. One right by the gunman's boot and the other a few yards away, almost in the ditch next to the roadway.

She didn't know how to use a gun, but if she got them both, she could give them to Grant. And none of these screaming men could get them.

She slid out of the truck and onto shaking legs, but she focused on the guns. She crept toward the one by the ditch because she didn't want to get in the way of Grant's grappling. Grant landed another punch, but the man refused to go down.

Dahlia took another shaking step toward the gun. She

could do this. She could help. But she heard movement next to her, and when she turned, one of the yelling men was too close. No longer yelling. Just staring at her and *smiling*.

She wanted to bolt. Just start running and screaming in the opposite direction, but she was only two steps maybe away from the gun. She took another step, but he reached out.

She jumped away, but he never stopped smiling or advancing. He didn't lunge. He didn't speak. Just kept moving for her, arms outstretched.

"Don't move another muscle."

Dahlia froze in time with the man, because it was Grant's voice, low and lethal. When she got it through her head he was talking to the man—not her—she looked over at him.

He had a gun—not the one she'd been going for but presumably the original gunman's, who was crawling on the ground, gasping for breath as blood leaked out of his mouth.

Sirens sounded, and two police cars appeared on the rise. The man next to her and the other shouting man ran. Back from wherever they'd come, still shouting about truth and gifts.

Dahlia took a few halting steps after them. They might know who killed Rose. They might have answers.

"Dahlia."

She looked at Grant and realized he, too, was bleeding. Like…badly. The entire bottom of his shirt was slowly becoming soaked with blood, and it was his *own*. It was then she saw in the hand that didn't hold a gun, he held a knife. Covered in blood.

Her stomach threatened to roil. "Grant," she said, not knowing what else to say. He'd been *stabbed*. She moved haltingly for him, but she had no idea how to fix a stab wound.

The police were coming. She could hear them shouting now as they approached, guns drawn. She looked around, but the man who'd been crawling was gone. *Gone.*

And Grant was bleeding and… She had to do something. Something. But Jack ran over.

"About damn time," Grant muttered.

"He's hurt. He's… He needs an ambulance," Dahlia babbled at Jack, whose face went from worried to a blank kind of coolness Dahlia couldn't believe. Grant was his *brother.*

He started talking into a com unit. Barking out orders as he put his hand on Grant's shoulder.

His face betrayed nothing, but there was a slight shake to his hand as he placed it there.

"The men. They…they tried to… You have to follow them."

Jack's gaze turned to hers. It cooled even more. "We'll handle it."

"I'm fine," Grant said, but he didn't sound himself, and he still hadn't moved. The gun was still pointed where the man had been. He still held the dripping knife. He still bled.

But another officer came running. He held a little white box Dahlia assumed was a first aid kit.

"Why don't you get out of the way," Jack said to her. "Take a seat in one of the cruisers. We'll have questions for you once we take care of Grant."

Dahlia wanted to argue. To *help.* But Jack moved in such a way that he blocked her view of Grant, and he spoke with the other officer in quiet tones she couldn't make out.

Dismissed. No, ordered away. Jack clearly blamed *her* for what had happened, and was he wrong? She'd cowered in that truck, and then even when she'd finally attempted to do something, Grant—bleeding—had been the one to stop the man from getting her.

She backed away from Jack. From Grant. She blinked a few times as she shakily moved for the cruisers still flashing lights though the sirens were off. The men who'd stopped Grant's truck, all gone.

Had any officers followed those men? Maybe she should just run after them. They wanted her. Why not go see why? Better than…this horrible feeling of uselessness and guilt.

But another person arrived, this time in a truck just like Grant's. Mary and Anna got out, and while Anna made a beeline for Jack and Grant, Mary came right for Dahlia.

"Are you okay?" She reached out and took Dahlia by the elbows so that she had to focus on Mary rather than Jack blocking her from Grant or the men who'd run off into the rocks and ridges.

"Grant…"

"They'll take him to the hospital, and I'll take you home. He's fine. Standing on his own two feet, right?" She slid her arm around Dahlia's waist and began leading Dahlia to the truck. Dahlia watched over her shoulder, but between Jack, Anna and the other deputy, she couldn't actually see Grant.

She turned her attention to where the men had gone. "The police…"

"They'll see if they can find who tried to hurt you and get answers," Mary said, giving her a reassuring squeeze and delivering her to the passenger side of the truck.

"But they didn't try to hurt me," Dahlia said, turning to look at Mary. That man had been close, but even when he'd tried to take her arm, it hadn't been violent. He'd been *smiling*. Grant was the one they'd fought. The one they'd hurt.

Mary looked back at her for a long minute. "Dahlia, maybe they didn't physically hurt you, but that doesn't mean they didn't hurt you in other ways." She opened the passenger door. "Get in now. We'll sort it all out back at the ranch."

She didn't want to leave Grant. Or this place that felt like maybe it had answers to Rose's disappearance.

But Mary smiled and squeezed her elbows again. "Dahlia, we're going to help. But there's nothing more to be done in the middle of the road."

We're going to help. They hadn't given up. They'd found something, and Grant had protected her. This was more forward movement than she'd had the entire thirteen months Rose had been gone. She should be happy, excited that there were real leads to follow.

So why did she just want to cry. She swallowed at the lump in her throat. "Are you sure he's okay?" she asked on a whisper.

"If he wasn't, I'd be over there. Go on now. Get in the truck."

So Dahlia finally did.

Chapter Twelve

"I'm fine," Grant said to his older brother. Perhaps for the three hundredth time. He didn't know why he was saying it. It wouldn't ever get through Jack's hard head. He glanced in the rearview mirror at his sister sitting in the back as the cruiser sped toward the hospital with lights and sirens going. He wouldn't get through her hard head either.

A very annoying Hudson trait.

"You were stabbed," Jack said through gritted teeth, every part of his body so tense Grant was pretty sure if he reached out and poked Jack, he'd shatter into a million pieces.

Tempting. But the throbbing pain in his stomach kept him from doing much moving. "Yeah, better than shot," he muttered. He adjusted in the chair, then hissed out a breath. It still pissed him off that guy had managed to stick him with that knife, but his focus *had* been on the gun and getting it away from being pointed at Dahlia. But this was a flesh wound at most.

"They wanted to kidnap her." Grant stared hard at the road that would lead them to the hospital. Where he'd get poked and prodded and stitched up and no doubt sent home in a few hours' time. He felt a little sick at the prospect of *hospitals*. But that was hardly the only thing bothering him. "They were chanting all this crazy stuff about *truth*. Lyle Stuart—and I *know* it was Lyle—said, and I quote, 'Lyle's dead.' This is real cult stuff. And they want Dahlia. They called her 'the answer.' 'The promised' or something. She's the target, and *she's* in danger."

"Yeah, and you're the one bleeding through your bandage."

Grant didn't even bother to look down at said bandage. Paying more attention to all the ways he hurt wasn't going to help. "Did you send any deputies after them?"

Jack flicked a glance at him, his hands flexing on the steering wheel. "I only had one to spare."

Grant stared open-mouthed at Jack for a good minute before speaking again. "Damn it all to hell, Jack. What were you thinking?"

"That I didn't want you or any of my deputies to die?"

"I'm not about to die from a flesh wound. And furthermore—"

"Furthermore, Deputy Brink tracked them for a bit. I've instructed her to put together a search party. They'll comb the area and get some leads. We're certainly not going to let any Order of Truth copycats wreak havoc on our town."

Grant would have preferred to have been part of that search party rather than on his way to any hospital, but at least Jack had sent a team.

Then his brother went and ruined that *at least*. "I think we should back off this."

Grant looked back at Anna, even though it hurt, because if he reacted to his brother's flat-out *absurdity*, it wouldn't be pretty. "Please tell me he's kidding."

Anna looked at Jack, then Grant, as if deciding which side to take. Because Anna was never scared of taking a side. Or making up her own. But she kept her gaze on Jack. "So, what you're suggesting is we back off. Let that woman get taken by some unhinged cult, or copycat cult, and probably be killed just like her sister?"

"That is *not* what I'm suggesting," Jack replied darkly. He pulled to a stop at the ER entrance and switched off his sirens and lights. "We'll discuss it later."

Grant wanted to argue, but he also wanted his infuriating stab wound stitched up so he could stop bleeding through bandages. He didn't want to end up worse for the wear because of how much blood he'd lost.

So he got out of the car before Anna could help him, which made Jack growl. Grant didn't feel the least bit chagrined. His brother was being an overbearing jerk.

Not unusual.

Anna came up behind him and linked arms with him. "He's just shaken because you're hurt. It feels like a failure, so he'll be grumpy, but you know as well as I do he's not going to let that poor woman dance in the wind. Besides, Chloe's the one he put in charge of the search team, and you know she'll be thorough."

Chloe Brink was a fine cop, but... "I should be out there."

Anna shook her head. "Like hell you should."

They walked into the hospital and talked to the ER attendant, and then after what felt like hours, Grant was through all the rigmarole of being admitted and waiting for someone to come stitch him up.

The entire time, he replayed the moments in his head. What he could have, or should have, done differently. What all this meant for Dahlia. "They wanted her," he muttered to Anna.

She looked up from her phone. "Yeah, but they stabbed you."

"Which proves just how dangerous they are."

Anna shrugged.

The doctor came in and stitched him up, telling him how lucky he was and how he needed to take it easy and—*blah, blah, blah*. As if sensing an unresponsive patient, the doctor handed Anna the recovery instructions and the prescription for pain medication Grant had no plans on taking.

Then Anna started talking about horses with the doctor, the young man clearly flirting with her. She laid on the charm and flirted right back. Once the doctor *finally* left, saying they could too, Grant glared at his sister.

"Really? I've been *stabbed* and you're flirting with the doctor?"

"He was cute," Anna said with a grin.

They walked back out of the hospital. Everything in him kind of throbbed, but he'd rather feel the pain than be all zapped out on painkillers.

Been there, done that, no repeat performance, thanks.

Jack was in the parking lot pacing next to his cruiser, his phone to his ear.

"Uh-oh," Anna muttered. "Bad Jack vibes."

"Are there good Jack vibes?"

"Good point," she said with a laugh.

Jack ended his phone call as they approached. He studied Grant in silence for a few moments before he seemed satisfied Grant wasn't going to just keel over. "So?"

"Doctor says he'll be fine," Anna said because Grant

knew Jack wouldn't believe *his* recounting of what the doctor said. "Needs to rest, but it didn't hit anything important."

Jack nodded. "That's good news. Unfortunately I have some of the bad kind."

"Of course you do," Anna said.

"The man who stabbed you? They caught up with him pretty easily...because he was dead."

"Dead?"

"Shot in the head."

Grant was...stunned. "I didn't..."

"No, but someone did. And left him there while they disappeared. Seemingly into thin air."

Grant had to bite his tongue to keep from telling his brother he should have handled things differently. It wasn't fair. Jack had more to worry about than getting to the bottom of this—the safety of his citizens and deputies chief among them.

But Grant should have gone after them himself, stab wound be damned.

"This situation is too dangerous," Jack said, relying heavily on the "I may be your brother, but I was also your father more or less" tone that Grant hated. *Hated*. It was that tone that had sent him to the Marines, at least partially. "We're turning it *all* over to law enforcement. The case. The woman. Beginning and end of story."

Grant didn't say anything to Jack, because it was pointless. Like talking to a brick wall or worse.

But like hell this was the end.

DAHLIA REALLY COULDN'T get over the kindness of Mary. Not only did the woman make her lunch and insist she eat, but she also seemed to understand what Dahlia needed even when Dahlia couldn't articulate it.

She didn't insist Dahlia rest. Instead she brightly suggested Dahlia help with some of Mary's administrative tasks. They were simple—filing mostly—but it helped ease some of that useless feeling and kept her mind engaged enough not to fall apart, but not so engaged she actually had to *think*.

When the phone rang, Dahlia jerked in surprise. She'd been reliving those moments on the road over and over again, trying to work out what she should have done differently as she'd filed the stack of papers Mary had given her.

Mary answered the phone, and Dahlia shamelessly listened in. At first Mary sounded businesslike, then relieved. "Okay. Yes. Yes." There was a flicker of something. Her cheerful demeanor slipping for just a moment. "All right. I'll tell her. Uh-huh. See you soon."

Mary smiled brightly as she hung up the phone and turned to Dahlia at the filing cabinet. "Grant's all stitched up and on his way home. Good to go. He'll be back in the saddle in no time."

But there was something else. Something bad. Dahlia sucked in a breath, bracing herself for… She didn't know what.

"Unfortunately, the deputies couldn't find the men who stopped you guys."

"Oh."

"At least right away." Mary reached out and put a gentle hand on her arm. "I'm sure they'll discover clues to help them search, and this is a concrete crime for them to investigate."

Still, Dahlia got the feeling there was more to it, and Mary was purposefully keeping it from her. She wished she knew Mary better so she could demand whatever information. But at the end of the day, Mary wasn't her friend. She was just part of the organization Dahlia was paying to help find her sister.

And now things were…complicated. Because there was an *active* crime, and the police were involved, and she was somehow…a target in all this.

She wasn't going to ask what Mary was keeping to herself. It didn't feel right in the moment. But that didn't mean she couldn't start…being active. Making some of her own decisions.

Since Grant had found her poking around Truth, the Hudsons had taken over, and she'd let them. She couldn't let that continue. Not with Grant hurt. Not knowing she was some kind of bizarre cult target for whatever reason.

So, she focused on what she knew how to do. What she *could* do. "Mary, do you have anything about the Order of Truth? When I was doing my research, I focused on Eugene Green and his family more than the cult itself. Maybe I need to learn more about this cult."

Mary hesitated, which seemed a rare thing for the woman who was always very composed. "I'm not sure…"

"I can't just sit around. I…" She couldn't explain what she felt to Mary, or she'd end up crying. "I have to do something. And the only thing I'm any good at is research."

Mary nodded as if she understood not just what Dahlia was saying but, on a deeper level, what it meant. "Jack and Grant never wanted anything about the cult around. It was a leftover reaction from my parents. We weren't allowed to talk about it growing up or even joke about it. You see—" Mary waved it away "—it has always been a very sore subject in our house, and Jack and Grant were the oldest, so they took it to heart the most."

Dahlia understood there was more to that story but also that it was none of her business. "I guess I could just do some internet searching," Dahlia said, thinking aloud.

"Oh, don't do that. There's so much bad information. People love to sensationalize a cult. Just...stay here for a second."

Mary disappeared and Dahlia waited, then went ahead and finished filing. It gave her hands something to do. It gave her mind some sense of accomplishment.

When Mary returned, it was with a stack of books. "I'm not sure how Anna's going to feel about this, but I wanted to get them to you before Jack and Grant get back. Maybe it's part and parcel with being the youngest and how little she remembers of my parents, but Anna's always been obsessed with the cult business against the rest of our wishes. These are all hers. If she kept these, they have better information than you'll find on the internet. I promise."

She handed the books off, and Dahlia took them. The top title was *Order of Truth: Fact and Fiction*.

"Take them to your room. Keep them out of sight if you think Grant might be in there. I'll let Anna know you have them, and if she has an issue with that, we'll figure it out."

"Thank you," Dahlia said, even though what she really wanted to say was *Why would Grant be in my room?* "I think I'll go do some reading then. Can you..." She trailed off. She'd see Grant at dinner, and Mary had assured her he was fine multiple times, but still, she just...wanted to see for herself. But for some reason the comment about Grant and her room made this all feel…awkward. "If you ever need more help with things, it makes me feel useful."

Especially since, at most, she could afford maybe another week of their services and their generosity. She needed answers and she needed them quick. So she moved through the maze of a house to her room.

When she got there, she shut the door behind her and looked through the titles. When she'd been researching before coming to Sunrise, it had been all about Eugene Green and how he connected to her, to Texas, to Truth. So, she'd learned some things about the Order of Truth, but not really the inner workings, the beliefs and all that. It hadn't seemed pertinent. Because everything was about genealogy and blood connections.

But the men had been…chanting, reaching for the sky. It had to be some kind of…ritual? Or something related to the cult. She flipped through indexes, trying to determine what kind of information she wanted.

Not the raid or the murders. She wasn't ready to delve into all that. But what did the group believe? What was *their* truth?

Lord of Truth! Help us! They'd shouted.

So, who was this Lord? She found a chapter in one of the books titled "Lord of Truth" and began to read. It didn't seem to be based on any religion she was familiar with. It was a mix of things—nature and signs, but mostly the bottom line seemed to be Eugene Green himself.

He was the Lord of Truth. Only Eugene and his descendants knew the truth.

Dahlia felt a cold chill run through her at the word *descendants*. She wasn't a direct descendent of Eugene Green and neither was Rose, so it made no sense that these men wanted her.

But Mrs. Riley had said they would know their tree. They would know about her.

But maybe that was only part of it. Maybe it was *Rose* knowing about them.

A knock sounded at the door and Dahlia jumped a foot. She looked around a little wildly and realized she'd been reading for some time now. The light outside was dim instead of bright afternoon.

"Dahlia?"

It was Grant's voice. She wanted to throw open the door, see for herself he was all right. But Mary's warning about Grant not seeing the books had her grabbing them all and shoving them frantically under the bed. "Just a minute!"

It was ridiculous. Like she was a child sneaking Harry Potter again when her parents didn't approve. But she supposed as much as she wanted it to be different because she was an adult, it wasn't, because this was Grant and his family's house.

Not hers.

She tried to steady her uneven breathing and the odd nerves that moved through her. She wanted to *see* he was all right, and she didn't want to face what had happened.

But it was time she stopped being such a coward.

She opened the door and tried to manage her best approximation of a smile. He stood there looking just as he had this morning. Maybe he was a little pale, but he stood on his own two feet and didn't seem to hold himself any differently.

He was fine and whole.

"I just wanted to make sure you're all right," he said, his eyes warm and kind.

"Me? You're the one who was hurt." She wanted to reach out and touch him. Assure herself he was as real and sturdy as he seemed. But there was all this space between them, and it felt like some kind of wall.

"I'm sorry," he offered stiffly.

But she couldn't fathom what he was apologizing for.

"For what?"

"They got away. Now Jack's got a crime to investigate, and he will—him and his department—do an excellent job."

"I wish I found that convincing."

He pulled a face. "I wish I could feel more convincing, but the truth is their hands are tied by the law in a way mine aren't. I won't be giving up on this, Dahlia. I want you to know that. I won't rest until we find who's after you. And I am not bound to the laws Jack is."

He said it so earnestly. Like it was a vow or a promise. Like her safety was important to him personally. Like he'd protect her.

"I'm not sure anyone has ever…" She trailed off, because it was a foolish thing to say, to feel. She was *paying* him, and she couldn't keep doing it for much longer. So she needed to figure out how to protect herself. "Grant, I need you to do something for me."

"What?"

"I need you to teach me to fight."

Chapter Thirteen

Grant found himself at a loss for words. She looked a little healthier than she had when she'd first come to them, but she was still on the frail side. She was a librarian and tended toward skittish. She'd told him herself she wasn't athletic. He just…couldn't picture her throwing a punch.

But anyone could learn—that or how to shoot a gun. Anna had always taken to shooting and fighting, but it had been Mary's natural inclination to avoid those things, and still she'd learned. Grant considered her marksmanship a personal triumph. He had taught her, after all.

Before you lost the ability.

"I can see what you're thinking," Dahlia said, sounding *almost* peeved. "And you aren't wrong. I'm weak. I don't know the first thing about protecting myself, except to walk with my keys between my fingers in a dark parking lot, but that's just it. I spent my whole life avoiding the dark parking lot. The sketchy situation. I can't avoid this. And I *hate* what happened today. Not just because you were hurt but because I just sat there and let it happen. I hate the fact I hid and didn't know what to do. I was *weak*."

"You went for the gun. You didn't hide. The fact that

you're here, still standing, after all you've been through, isn't weakness."

But she was having none of it. "I did hide for a while, and I only went to the gun to keep it from them. I don't know what to do with a gun. And if they're going to keep coming after me, I should know how to fight or shoot or something."

"I'm going to be here." He had to resist the urge to take her by the shoulders. To press all of his assurances into her like he could tattoo them on her. "We're all going to be here protecting you."

"Not forever," she replied, clearly troubled.

He didn't know why it bothered him that she was already thinking ahead to that. He didn't know why he wanted to... just protect her. When his sisters had been growing up, he'd been all about giving them the skills to protect themselves.

Nothing about his reaction to Dahlia ever made any sense. But she *was* speaking logically, even if something deep inside him rebelled at the thought. "We can do that. Teach you some self-defense."

She let out a breath as if she'd been afraid he'd refuse the request. "Thank you." Then she took a step forward, hesitated. But seemed to sort of gather herself, or her courage, and reach out. She put a hand on his arm and looked him right in the eye. "I'm so sorry you were hurt."

It was such a genuine flat-out apology—something that had not existed in his life as a Hudson or in his life as a Marine. He could only stare back at her. What did someone *say* to that? Who just came out and apologized with no equivocations or attempts to pick a fight?

She cleared her throat and let her hand drop, which felt

like a loss. For a moment it was like he was reconnected to some old pieces of himself he'd thought he'd lost.

Which was a particularly ridiculous thought. "I've survived worse."

Her eyebrows drew together, and he forgot that people who weren't military or his family didn't always have that same dark sense of humor or slightly warped way of looking at things.

"Were you hurt in the military?"

Grant shrugged. "Here and there. Nothing major. Never sent me home over it."

This did not assuage her concern or smooth out the furrow in her brow. "Is that why you don't like talking about it?"

There was something about her blue eyes, the way she looked at him that felt like looking *into* him. He'd swear she was hypnotizing him if he believed in such things.

"I survived my injuries. No, I don't see the need to recount them, but they don't weigh on me. They are what they are."

"Then what does weigh on you?"

If anyone else had asked that question, he would have tensed. He would have barked out a rebuff as a response or said nothing at all. *Anyone* else.

But it was Dahlia, and she was just…different. And open. She had no preconceived opinions about him. No opinions on his military experience or what he wore to the tenth grade homecoming. She apologized and stumbled in the mud and loved dogs. She had her own demons, and somehow…that made him want to share his own.

"I was lucky. Not everyone was. Not just…making it home in one piece but being able to bear the weight of what you see."

Her hand rubbed up and down his elbow for a second. Comfort, or an attempt at it. "I'm not sure I'm bearing the weight of anything very well lately," she said, her voice quiet. Sad.

He couldn't help himself. He lifted his own hand and rested it over hers on his elbow. He smoothed his thumb over the top of her hand. "Not all weights are meant to be borne easily. Certainly not loss and grief. Those are the weights you have to learn to carry in whatever ways you can. You've come this far, Dahlia. And I am intimately acquainted with the strength you need to push forward when everyone tells you to let it go. Jack and the family... We may not have gotten our answers, but we stuck it out a lot longer than anyone else. We exhausted every option. I'm proud of that, and it made the weight easier to carry eventually."

Her hand was small and warm, the skin soft where his thumb brushed. For a moment her eyes dropped to their joined hands, and he saw the little hitch in her breath and felt something he really wasn't allowed to feel when it came to a client.

Maybe it wasn't a Hudson rule, but it damn well should be.

She looked up then, pinning him with that blue gaze. "I know you said you're not a war hero, but why do people *think* you're one?"

It was enough of an uncomfortable and unwanted topic that he managed to pull his hand away instead of getting lost deeper in this moment that was feeling more and more dangerous.

"Why are we having this conversation?" he asked. "We'll be late for dinner."

"Right." She looked away and attempted to smile as her

hand dropped off his arm, but it faltered. "Sorry. I'm not usually nosy."

"So, why are you now?"

"I...don't know."

"Can I be nosy for a second?"

She sucked in a breath and let it out like she was preparing herself. When she looked at him again, she had her pleasant but distant smile on. "Sure."

He shouldn't ask. He should keep his big mouth shut. It was one hundred percent none of his business. She was a client, and regardless of her answer, it changed nothing. And still the words came out anyway. "There's no one waiting for you back home?"

"Well, my parents, but they're not really waiting for me."

"That's...not what I meant."

Confusion lined her face, but then she seemed to clue in. If the blush creeping into her cheeks was anything to go by.

"Oh. No. There's...no one."

Grant should maybe laugh it off or say something about needing to know for safety reasons or something ridiculous. But he didn't. "Ready for dinner?" he asked instead.

And she nodded and followed him out of the room.

DAHLIA HAD GONE through dinner wondering if Grant had used some sort of...distraction tactic on her. Flirt with the mess of a woman wanting to learn to fight, and she'll forget all about it.

Or something.

But the next morning at breakfast, Anna and Palmer were waiting for her. "Grant said you wanted to learn some self-defense." So he'd listened. And done something about her request.

"Oh, well, yes." She tried not to look around the kitchen and into the big dining room and failed. "Is he around?"

"I sent him back to bed. He looked *terrible*." As if realizing this was the wrong thing to say to the woman who felt slightly responsible for his *stab* wound, Anna quickly continued on. "That was at like five this morning. He's refusing to take the pain meds, so he just didn't sleep well. I bet he'll be back down any minute for some breakfast. Everything else is just fine on the Grant front."

"That seems generous, Anna," Palmer said, clearly teasing as he earned himself a glare from his sister. Then a hard jab to the stomach that had Palmer doubling over a little.

"The element of surprise is your first lesson," Anna said, back to smiling. "That and eat a solid breakfast." They all turned as they heard a noise—Grant entering the kitchen.

Dahlia didn't think he looked terrible, but he hadn't shaved or combed his hair, so he did look a little dangerously disheveled. It made her stomach do little flips. She didn't even *know* this man, not really, and her silly immature reaction to him was really starting to be a problem.

"How's it going, champ?" Palmer greeted.

"Just fantastic," Grant grumbled. But he looked over at Dahlia and managed a smile, if a little gruff around the edges. "Morning."

"Good morning," she replied. "I could make—"

"Mary already made you two plates," Anna interrupted, pulling the refrigerator door open. "She said you're both on the 'on the mend' diet. Lots of protein and liquids."

"I'm not injured," Dahlia protested.

"No, but you're *way* too skinny, and Mary loves to mother. She's on horse duty this morning, but she instructed me by threat of pain and suffering to warm up your meals and make sure you eat." Anna popped one plate into the microwave as she said this. "Go on into the dining room. I live to serve."

Palmer gave an exaggerated laugh. "That's a new one."

Still, Grant and Palmer moved into the dining room, so Dahlia felt like she had to as well. She took a seat in the chair that seemed to be *hers*, while Palmer and Grant spoke of some ranch thing and sipped their coffee.

Anna entered soon enough, carrying two plates she set in front of Dahlia and Grant. "Eat up or face the wrath of Mary, a surprisingly alarming force if provoked."

Dahlia tried to smile. Her appetite hadn't returned any on its own, but the food was always so delicious once she started, she'd manage to eat the whole meal. Maybe she was learning to feed her body even when it seemed to not want to be fed.

"We'll go over some basic protection moves and how to use a gun," Palmer said, as if this were a normal thing to discuss over breakfast. So casual. "Anna and I will show you the self-defense moves since Grant has to rest, but he'll teach you how to shoot."

"Maybe she'd do better with a female teacher," Grant offered, shifting in his chair, then wincing. Dahlia wished there was anything she could do to take the pain away.

"Or someone more on par with a beginner's skills," Palmer said, clearly teasing Anna.

But Anna didn't seem interested in rising to the bait. "Grant's the best shot, by far. And he's the most patient out of any of us, but Mary or I can do it if you want."

"Hey, I can be patient," Palmer replied.

"Yeah, getting out of bed maybe," Anna grumbled.

"I don't really..." Dahlia swallowed. She wanted their help so badly, had even asked Grant for it, but it seemed like too much. "I appreciate—"

"Dahlia," Grant interrupted. "You need to stop thinking you're some kind of burden to us."

She looked at him, arrested by how simply he cut to the heart of the matter when she wasn't sure she'd even realized that was the clearest verbalization of her thoughts.

"But..." She'd always felt...a bit like a burden to everyone. And she'd worked very hard to shrink herself down, shut herself out, so no one thought she took up too much space or asked for too much.

Rose's disappearance had been an odd turning point in her life, giving her a courage and determination she'd never had. So maybe it required a change in how she looked at the world around her.

Not a burden but a person who took an opportunity when it was offered.

"This whole thing is to help people," Anna said, gesturing around the house. "Because we've been there. So, no burdens."

"It has to be a business," Palmer continued. "Realistically. But that doesn't mean it isn't more than that too."

"There's a reason we keep a running ranch along with it," Grant added. "That's about money and legacy. This is about...us."

"Trust me, the three of us? We don't offer *anything* out of the goodness of our hearts," Anna said.

Dahlia found herself glancing at Grant. He didn't argue

with Anna, but Dahlia felt like he should have. He'd been *stabbed* in an effort to keep her safe. *That* was goodness.

"Eat," Grant told her gently. And she didn't know what else to do but that.

Chapter Fourteen

The days passed with very little forward movement. They kept Dahlia on the ranch, watched over by someone or cameras or a dog at all times. In the mornings, Grant or one of his siblings worked on her with either self-defense or shooting.

Jack's sheriff's department found nothing. It frustrated Grant, but when he was being fair, he realized that whatever kind of copycat group this was had been avoiding detection for some time, so just because law enforcement *knew* of them didn't mean it would make them easy to find.

If the group had really found Rose Easton and murdered her, as seemed likely, they'd spent over a year keeping everything under wraps—from law enforcement, private investigators and Dahlia herself.

Much as he didn't *want* to, Grant knew he needed to go back to Truth and poke around. The police had done it multiple times, but Grant just got the feeling there was something more there. And if not…well, at least it felt like *doing* something.

Because teaching Dahlia how to shoot was slow torture in the "this woman is very off-limits to me right now" department. And the very uncomfortable realization that the man he'd been before he'd been deployed would not have cared and done something about it anyway.

He found her with Anna in the little gym they had in one of the outbuildings. They were both breathing a little heavily, likely having been at self-defense practice for a half hour or so.

He didn't dare show up sooner, because watching her learn to punch and block and break holds should *not* have affected him in any way, but it did.

"Dead Eye is here," Anna announced cheerfully when she caught sight of him. "Just in time. I've got a few calls to take." Anna walked over to him, lowered her voice as she passed. "I'm going to be scarce for a few days, FYI."

"Am I the only one you're telling?"

"You and Mary," she replied, then flashed him a grin. "Don't go telling big brother on me. I know a guy who knows a guy. Might be able to get me some info. Might not. I'll be back by the weekend."

He resisted the urge to lecture Anna on being careful. He couldn't say they were alike in many ways, but while Jack, Palmer *and* Cash all wanted to lock her up in a room and pretend like she was still a little girl, Grant understood the restlessness. The need to get out there and take some risks.

But he was still himself and a man and a big brother. "Be careful."

"I was born careful," she replied. Which was a flat-out lie, but there was no use in arguing the point with her. He let her go instead. Just like all his siblings had let him go once upon a time.

When she was gone, he turned to Dahlia. She was standing a little uncertainly on one of the mats. Her gaze was on the gun in his hand, but she raised her eyes and forced a smile.

"I really appreciate—" At his scowl, she waved him off, but she smiled, and this one was genuine, not forced. She had the sweetest smile, not saccharine or anything. Just sort of like they were rare and special when she doled one out.

"It's not a *thank you* this time. Promise," she said. She gave the gun another sideways glance. She'd learned the safety rules and shot it a few times, but she didn't care for the noise or impact.

Dahlia approached him, and he got the impression she was trying to choose the right words to say. She was always so careful with her words, and he had to wonder what had made her that way.

"I appreciate you teaching me how to use it." Then her shoulders drooped and she let out a really long sigh. "I just really hate it."

It was his turn to smile. "Yeah, I can tell."

She wrinkled her nose. "I know I'm a weakling."

"Hardly. Mary's not a fan either. She learned because it's a necessity out here, and it helped put Jack's mind at ease, but she's no fan. Cash won't touch guns around Izzy. They aren't toys. It's okay to be uneasy about them. Better than liking them *too* much."

She nodded. "I appreciate that. So, we could be done with this side of things since I could at least hold one and point it at somebody if I had to?" she asked hopefully.

"And we'll work really hard to make sure you don't have to," Grant said firmly. He'd make it his mission.

Her smile was back, though it wobbled a bit. "Um. The thing is. We've settled in. We've regrouped. I've got…very minimal self-defense skills, sure, but I have to *do* something. I'm running out of money, and before you tell me yet again the money doesn't matter, try to understand it matters to *me*."

He didn't *like* that it did, but he could understand it anyway. Pride and that need to feel like she had some control over her life. Still, he didn't need to dwell on the fact if she ran out of money, she'd leave.

"I was thinking about heading out to Truth this afternoon," he offered instead, though he hadn't really planned on telling her.

But he could admit, here in the privacy of his own mind, he wanted to spend time with her. Even if it was torture. It was the kind that reminded him not everything had broken irreparably in the Middle East.

"Jack won't approve, which means if you want to come, it'd just be us. And Willie. And we'll probably have to lie to my siblings. At least some of them. So you could tag along, as long as none of that bothers you."

She chewed on her bottom lip, and since he didn't want to look at *that* and let his mind wander, he looked at the curls around her temple that had fallen out of the hair tie she had most of her hair pulled back in.

"Well…" she began, not meeting his gaze "…speaking of lying."

Grant didn't need to feign surprise. "*You've* been lying?"

She looked up at him through her lashes. "It's not so much lying as omitting some facts you may not care for." She tried for a reassuring smile. "It's just, those chants really bothered me, and it pointed out a small hole in my research."

"What kind of hole?"

"I'd researched the Greens, how they connected to my

family and what the cult *was*, sure, but not really the actual beliefs or rituals."

Grant usually had a good poker face, but nope, not when it came to the Order of Truth. "You've been researching the cult." It sat in his gut like a weight.

Dahlia looked pained. "Mary mentioned you wouldn't like that."

It frustrated him. That Dahlia looked guilty when she had every right to do whatever the hell she wanted. That his sister was going around discussing anything to do with the cult or his feelings on it with *anyone*. "Oh, Mary did, did she? And who else knows this is what you've been up to?"

"Well—" she blew out a breath "—I am sorry. Anna knows too, but that's it. We've kind of been discussing it, and I just—I *am* sorry. I know it bothers you, but I kept thinking that if maybe I understood…what they thought, what they did, it would give us some clue as to where they were or…" She reached out, just a light finger brush against the sleeve of his coat. "I *am* sorry."

"You don't owe me any apologies for doing what you think is best." Not that he could agree, even if she *was* right. His father had always warned him Truth was dangerous. Because it wasn't just about murderers and religious zealotry. It was about taking advantage of people desperate for something to believe in. Something to belong to.

He didn't think Dahlia was desperate, but she was alone. The few things she'd said about her family didn't paint a close picture. She was here in a place where she didn't really know anyone, trying to find her sister's *murderer*. It wasn't that he thought she was susceptible for falling for a cult. It was just all so dangerous and she had so very little support.

"I don't want you to be mad at me," she said when the silence between them stretched out.

"I'm not," he said, automatically. Being mad at her didn't have anything to do with what he was feeling. He hesitated to tell her the truth. "It's dangerous business. I know you don't need me to tell you that. It's just, I'm not even sure I can explain it. Truth has always been a shadow in this town, a boogeyman of sorts. I don't know anyone whose family wasn't affected, even if it was generations ago. My own parents included, and it was just...we were raised with the belief you don't go poking into Truth. It's an open wound." He sighed. "Anna, of course, loves poking at an open wound."

Her mouth curved very little, as if she agreed with his assessment of Anna, but she sobered quickly. "I don't want to poke at anything. I just want to find out what happened to my sister."

"I know. That's why even if I'm uncomfortable, I can't be angry with you."

"So, if you're all frowny and gruff, it's discomfort, not disapproval."

"Frowny and gruff? I think you've been spending too much time with my sisters."

She smiled a little, some of the gravity leaving her expression. He wished it would lighten any of the weight inside of him.

"It's a dangerous situation in a lot of ways. Particularly if we're wading into a murder investigation. Even if I understand, even if I even think it's a necessary step, poking into the Order of Truth is dangerous. And tricky. I worry about you."

Her eyes widened a little. "No one ever worries about me."

"Well, you can't say that, because I do."

She looked up at him, expression perfectly serious, but searching too. He didn't know what she was searching for. Didn't know if he wanted to give whatever it was if he could.

"Do you worry about everyone you help solve cold cases for?" she asked after a long pause, her voice quieter. More hushed.

He shook his head. "No." He could elaborate on that. Explain how his cases were rarely murders or dangerous, and never had to do with psychotic cults. But he didn't.

So they simply stood staring at each other. There was more he should say or a subject to change or something. His gaze certainly shouldn't drop to her mouth, and his body *definitely* shouldn't lean forward like she was some magnetic force he was pulled to.

But she didn't step back. She didn't break his gaze or do anything to *stop* him. He could have kissed her, easy enough. But the moment stretched too long, got too big in his head. And a loud, sharp bark interrupted any forward progress he'd thought of making.

Willie ran in, tail wagging, so it wasn't any kind of warning bark. Just an excited one. Grant looked at his watch. Had to, instead of risking a glance at her. Noon.

Grant cleared her throat. "That's the lunchtime signal."

"Right. Sure. So, lunch and then we'll go out to Truth… without telling anyone?"

Grant nodded. And felt, not at all for the first time, that he'd never get used to the man he'd become after leaving the military and returning home.

DAHLIA FOLLOWED GRANT INSIDE, and they ate lunch with Mary and Palmer. Then Grant encouraged her to grab a bag and any of her notes she thought might be helpful, and then they headed out to his truck to drive to Truth, Willie at her heels.

It was a strange and probably terrible thing that she was thinking more about the way Grant had looked at her in the gym than she was about her notes and what she might want to investigate once they got to Truth.

She should be thinking about Rose. About murder and danger and wondering why knowing Rose was dead didn't bring her any sense of closure.

But she thought about the way Grant's eyes had moved to her mouth. The way he'd seemed…closer. The way no matter how she told herself she was probably hallucinating, it had seemed like he'd at least *considered* kissing her.

She was a terrible person. At least, that's what she kept trying to convince herself. But somewhere on the quiet drive over to Truth, she had the realization the voice in her head arguing with the trajectory of her thoughts sounded an awful lot like her mother.

Grant had said he *worried* about her, which was hard to fathom when her whole life she'd been told no one really *had* to worry about her. She was a good girl, who followed the rules and would never dream of stepping out of line. So what was there to worry about?

Rose had been the wild one. *And look where that got her.*

Again, her mother's voice. Not her own. If she had a friend in the exact position she was, would she be telling her friend she was a terrible person for thinking about more than just her sister? Or would she remind that friend that tragedy or not, she was still alive.

And for the first time in a long time, the thought felt like an optimistic one.

It wasn't just Grant and the possibility that he might inexplicably be interested in her. It was his whole family. The way they treated her more like family than her own did.

He was *worried* about her safety. She wanted to play it off like…it was just his noble heart. All that military stuff and wanting to help and protect people.

But it felt different, Grant's worry, than anything the rest of his family did. Even if they were nice and compassionate, the way Grant looked at her *was* different.

And your sister is dead.

But you are alive.

She snuck a look at Grant. His gaze was on the road ahead, and he looked so serious. There was a way his siblings treated him, and the kind of indulgent look he gave them when they did, that made her think he hadn't always been quite so stoic. Like maybe the military had hardened him.

But he was hardly all tough outer exterior. There was a softness underneath it all. Or maybe that wasn't the right word. Something hidden.

Willie stuck his head between the front two seats, pushing his nose against her shoulder until she twisted around to give his ears a scratch. "I've always wanted a dog," she said absently.

"Why don't you get one?"

"Oh, both my father and Rose are—were allergic. Then when I was on my own, my apartment didn't allow pets."

He seemed to think that over. "I don't want to tell you

what to do, but at some point you've got to realize you're the adult and get to make the choices in your life for you, not other people. And I only say that because it was a strange realization I had when I got out of the military."

"I don't think you can compare leaving home and going to *war*."

He shrugged. "Depends, I guess, on how much your childhood felt like a war zone. Metaphorically."

She wanted to keep arguing with him, but it was the word *metaphorically* that kept the words lodged in her throat. Metaphorically, it had been a bit like a war. Her parents forever throwing volleys at Rose, and Rose forever hurling them right back. And Dahlia somewhere in the middle just trying to hide.

Grant didn't say any more, but he pulled his truck off the highway and onto the country road that led to Truth. Dahlia watched the landscape, and even though she knew the men that had stopped them in the road, the men who'd killed Rose could be out there, she felt that same strange sense of peace as they came up on the ghost town.

She knew she was supposed to be appalled because of what had happened here, but... "It's such a pretty place."

He pulled the truck to a stop, and she could *feel* his disapproval, even if he didn't say it out loud.

"I know you can't look past what you know happened here, but there's something peaceful about it."

"You don't have to justify your feelings to me, Dahlia. You get to feel what you want. Kinda like you get to make the choices you want."

He started getting out of the truck, but she felt stuck for a moment. He didn't sound mad or dismissive, just like it was obvious. *You get to feel what you want.*

It was…revolutionary. Maybe because she'd led such a small life, but she was used to…defending herself at every turn. To always feeling like the odd man out who had to change what she thought or felt to suit everyone else. To stop all that metaphorical war.

He came around to her side of the truck and opened the door for her. But there was concern in his expression. "You okay?"

She swallowed. Sure, she was fine. Just having her whole worldview upended since the disappearance of her sister. "Yeah." She forced herself to get out of the truck, and Willie jumped out after her.

They stood there, shoulder to shoulder, surveying the abandoned town of Truth. Dahlia felt lost. For so long, the simple act of finding Rose had given her a goal. Something to fight for and toward.

She still wanted to find Rose's killer—she really did—but the confirmation she had to be dead was…disorienting.

And then Grant pointing out all these things she didn't *have* to do. All these old thought patterns and behaviors that didn't suit her.

Who *was* she?

Grant's hand covered hers, his fingers threading through hers. A gesture of support. He gave a little squeeze. Reassurance.

"Come on. Let's go poke around," he said.

Maybe she didn't know who she was anymore, or maybe she'd never known. Maybe she'd always been afraid. But she'd spent the last year doing the unthinkable, leading to this moment where she was holding hands with a handsome cowboy, determined to find answers.

So, she'd figure it out. She'd figure it *all* out.

Chapter Fifteen

Grant didn't know what he was looking for, but that often happened with cold cases—even ones that got a little warm. You had to look and be open for anything.

Even holding hands with your off-limits client.

It was meant to be a comforting gesture, and he felt like it had worked. But it was…more to him. Like reaching out and forging a connection when he'd spent the last year at home struggling to make connections.

She had such strength in her, but she still seemed a little reluctant to use it. He was getting the impression it came from a childhood of shrinking herself into a mold that didn't fit, and he knew…

His parents had been wonderful, but losing them the way they had, had put him and all his siblings in a kind of box. A mold they were expected to fill, and it had chafed, so he'd gone off to war.

And lost who he was.

Not the time. At all. They were here to find clues, not make some kind of large-scale realizations about life.

But he didn't let her hand go. She seemed to need that connection to move forward, and he didn't mind it himself.

It took his mind off the throbbing pain in his side where the damned stab wound never stopped reminding him he'd been hurt.

"Remember that place where we found the bullet thing?" Dahlia asked.

"The casing, yes."

"I was reading, and that was like a holy place where they did rituals and things. Maybe they still do. Maybe that's why a casing was there."

"Do their rituals involve guns? Because even last week on the highway, only one of them had a gun and was using it."

"No. That is something I noticed about a lot of the literature. They don't believe in modern weapons. Though there was a whole section on how Eugene Green stockpiled semi-automatic weapons in a bunker. So, I guess it's your typical 'do what I say, not what I do.'"

Grant nodded grimly, and they walked through the alley and into the enclosed area. It didn't surprise him they did rituals there. It had always given him the creeps, the way the stone seemed to block out everything except the sky. Making you a target.

He didn't particularly want to go back in there, but they *had* found the casing there. So someone had been around. Maybe they'd just been doing target practice, maybe it had been kids, but maybe…there were more clues to be found.

She hesitated at the opening to the enclosed courtyard, which made him feel good about his own pause.

"They chose this place and built these walls because they said it was sacred ground containing some stones that were found here."

Grant looked at the dirt beneath his feet. "They didn't leave the stones?"

"No, they made them a kind of traveling altar for the Truth Prophet. As much as they settled here, there's this sense they always knew they had to be…mobile? Or nomads? Kind of like they needed to cling to this idea of being persecuted."

"Truth Prophet. Who listens to that garbage?"

Dahlia moved forward, and their fingers slid apart. She dropped his hand. "Desperate people do desperate things."

He felt chastised, though he didn't know why. He'd probably seen a lot more people do a lot more desperate things than she ever had. But she moved forward into the walled courtyard. The afternoon sun was high above lighting up the odd shadowed circle of earth and her with it.

The sun gleamed on her red hair. She looked like some kind of goddess. Ancient and powerful. He couldn't paint, couldn't take a picture in focus to save his life, but he somehow wanted to memorialize that moment where she looked… otherworldly and somehow perfectly at home. Here.

Perfect.

She looked away from the walls to him, then frowned. "What is it?" she asked.

"You're beautiful."

She opened her mouth, then closed it, clearly flustered. Part of him thought he should apologize. It wasn't *appropriate*. But it was true, so he didn't know how to pull it back.

She swallowed, visibly, looking up at him with those big blue eyes. Willie wagging his tail between them, as if he were an eager onlooker.

"Well, um. Thanks," she finally said when he couldn't quite come up with the right collection of words.

Grant shrugged. "Just true," he managed. Then he looked around the courtyard. "We found the shell casing right there," he said, pointing. "Was there anything about this place in particular in the books? Like it's special beyond sacred or..."

She shook her head. "Some things were specific, but they were more generic about where things happened. They never named Truth as their town or any of the waterways or mountains they considered sacred, just some of the things they did there. They didn't even specify this place, except that it was a stone circle and sacred because of what was found in the earth. Maybe there's another one somewhere too, but I figured since we knew this one existed, it was probably the one they were talking about."

Grant nodded along. He didn't understand adult people falling for this hocus pocus, sacred and prophets and what have you. Sure, a kid might be predisposed into whatever worship they were brought up in, but people choosing this... It made no sense to him.

Dahlia still stood in the center, squinting up at the sun now. "One thing the books all agreed on was the Truth Prophet is always a Green. They believe in blood and genetic ties. Sort of like the monarchy, but it's more about who's... powerful or connected to the truth, I guess."

He could see that she felt...bad about that. Like somehow she was connected to all this idiocy when she'd never stepped foot here before this month.

"You're not a Green."

She looked over at him. "No, but they want me for some reason." She seemed to grapple with telling him something. He found he didn't want to press. Whatever was on her mind, he wanted her to tell him of her own volition.

You have a real problem.

"They believe in sacrificing people. I think that's what they did here."

The word sacrifice gave him a cold chill, and he could tell it bothered her too. Though even without studying, he knew the Order of Truth believed in human sacrifice. It was part of why they'd been such a story. "None of their so-called sacrifices were done with a bullet."

"No, they weren't," Dahlia agreed. She moved around the courtyard, Willie at her heels. She looked so alone. Like the world was on her shoulders, and Grant knew what that felt like. It didn't matter if people wanted to help you when you felt like there was some wall between you and the people. A wall you didn't know how to tear down or cross or ask for help through.

So, he followed her path around the area, wishing every step didn't cause a spiking pain through his stomach. But it was better than being numb on painkillers. He kept following her path until he was behind her as she studied the ground where they'd found the mysterious casing.

"Dahlia, what's on your mind? Hopefully you know that even if I don't agree, you can tell me. It doesn't change anything." Because he sensed that reluctance in her, and he couldn't help but wonder if she'd been talking to Mary or Anna about it, she would have just said it.

He didn't want to be the reason she didn't speak her mind. Didn't make suggestions.

She turned to face him, chewing on her bottom lip. She looked up at the sun again, then down at Willie. "Rose is blond," she said at length.

"Okay."

"The Greens who are the prophets? They always had red hair. It was a kind of…symbol."

He saw now what she was grappling with. It pained him that she could even think that connected her. "Dahlia, you're not a Green."

"Does it matter if I know I'm not if they think I am? I wasn't into it the way Rose was, but genes are science. It's DNA and chromosomes and… Does me having Green blood change who I am? No. But it makes me someone important to them."

It was why they wanted her. Why they'd been willing to hurt him but not her.

"Grant…" She looked up at him imploringly. Like she needed him to be on her side, and he had a very bad feeling he wouldn't want to be. "I think I need to let them take me."

DAHLIA KNEW HE wouldn't *agree* with the idea, but she hadn't expected him to laugh. She frowned at him as he laughed and laughed.

Then he seemed to get some dust in his nose and sneezed. He winced and kind of doubled over, clearly in pain from the whole thing.

And maybe it served him right for laughing, but she still felt bad. Especially when he let out a quiet string of curses, still bent over.

"Are you okay?" She reached out, hand on his shoulder, one on his jaw, needing to offer some comfort. Maybe it was his own fault for laughing, but she still felt at least partially responsible for his *stab* wound.

He straightened, tilted his head back and breathed deeply, but still winced because that likely hurt too.

"Guess I deserved that," he muttered. Then he reached up and patted her hand that was still on his jaw. But she didn't drop her hand, and then he just sort of left his there.

They stared at each other for the longest time, and she knew this was...secondary. Whatever they were starting to feel for one another didn't belong in a creepy cult, deserted ghost town on the search for her dead sister.

But it was something good in a sea of all that had been bad, and she wanted to cling to it like a life jacket. She could feel what she wanted. She could *do* what she wanted. She wasn't beholden to everyone else.

So when he took her hand off his jaw, she wanted to protest. Until he pulled it toward his mouth. He pressed his lips to her palm, holding her gaze the whole time. She would have said it was offhanded, but it *wasn't*. Because his mouth had touched her skin and that wasn't something friends just *did*. Certainly no friends she'd ever had.

He opened his mouth, and she braced herself for some apology or explanation. But instead of saying something that would make her feel foolish or angry, he closed his mouth.

Instead of excuses or walking away or letting Willie or anything distract him, like what had happened back in the gym, he leaned down and gently placed his mouth to hers.

And it was gentle, but it wasn't timid. It was careful, but he wasn't holding back. There was a sweetness to it and a heat. A deep longing sense of something inside of her clicking into place. Like this moment was exactly where she belonged.

When he eased away, it wasn't so much like an ending, but more like the natural ebb and flow of something. Come together, step apart. *Don't let go.*

And still she had no words, because that kiss was better than anything she'd ever read about. Any movie she'd sighed over. Maybe because it wasn't just fuzzy feelings of "wouldn't that be amazing?" Maybe it was just…reality was better than imagination.

With the right kind of man, anyway.

She looked up at him, not sure she understood the expression on his face. Maybe because it reflected so many things deep under the stoic mask she knew was more habit than who he was.

He was real and human and flawed, and so was she, and… she didn't know how this could happen in the middle of the worst year of her life. But that only seemed to make it more precious.

"Probably not the place for this." He didn't let her go, exactly. He smoothed his hand down her arm, then eased away, but not completely. Not like distance.

"Probably not."

He let out a long careful sigh. "I can't let you be taken, Dahlia. I get it. Why you'd think that'd be a solution. I'm not sure I wouldn't think the same thing in your position. But self-sacrifice isn't the answer here."

"Then what is?"

"I don't know. Sometimes it takes a while to find an answer. But I can't let anything happen to you. Professionally. Personally."

She felt a little flutter of panic because this was not expected. This was not what she'd come here for. Could a kiss change the course of her life? She very much wanted to see if it could. When she never, ever got what she wanted. Not really. "We don't even know each other," she said, her voice little more than a whisper.

"I wish I could agree with you. But you feel right, Dahlia."

It took her breath away. Probably because she knew he didn't say things he didn't mean. Because he wasn't prone to exaggeration or sparing feelings. If there was anything she was sure of when it came to Grant, it was that the truth was as sacred to him as this place had been to the cult that wanted her.

But if they took her, she could find answers. And if they didn't want her dead because of dumb things like bloodlines and red hair, didn't that mean she had some power in the situation?

He lifted her chin with his fingertips, forcing her to look him in the eye. "It isn't an option. I need you to promise me you understand that."

She decided to use his own words against him. "I wish I could agree with you and promise you that."

He frowned, but he didn't drop her chin. He didn't step away, and she realized she'd braced herself for him to do just that. And it wasn't fair. At every turn, Grant had not done what he wanted at the expense of what she wanted. He'd listened, considered, and even when he'd disagreed, it hadn't changed how he treated her, how he looked at her.

How he kissed her.

It was hard to know what to do with that when her agreement with everyone had always been the condition to their love.

"Okay," he said at last, his fingers still gently pressed to her chin. But his eyes darted to the left, and everything about him tensed, though he stood completely still. When he moved, it was a blur and he moved her with him.

He had her pressed up against the wall, the stone cold

against her back, him hard and warm against her front. It might be enjoyable if he wasn't looking at the top of the wall, if their bodies being pressed together was about that kiss earlier and not about him shielding her body with his.

"Grant."

"I heard something," he murmured. "We're definitely not alone. And this place is too open."

She realized he had his gun in one hand while another wrapped around her elbow like he was about to guide her somewhere.

"We'll move carefully out of here." He glanced at Willie, who was standing guard at the entrance. If he sensed anyone, he didn't show it, except in maybe the fact his tail wasn't wagging. But he didn't bark or growl.

"They want me, and not dead, maybe I should be the one protecting you," Dahlia said, worrying over his stab wound.

Grant's expression got even harder. "Just because they want you alive at first doesn't mean they always will. Keep that in mind before you go sacrificing yourself to your sister's memory."

It hurt, she supposed because it poked at a truth, and what she *had* been thinking. That she'd be safe even if it was scary. But maybe Rose had thought that too. Maybe a cult full of psychopaths and sociopaths only had so much use for a person, even if they were a redheaded descendent of a Green.

"I'll apologize for that later," he muttered irritably, taking her elbow. He moved her, always keeping his body sort of wrapped around hers, her back against the wall. Protecting her.

She knew he'd do it to anyone. It was who he was—a protector, a hero. But still, even though it wasn't personal to *her*, it was still something that made her heart stumble. That and even though he'd been harsh, which was just his natural way of things, he admitted the need to apologize.

They reached the opening of the courtyard, and Willie came to attention while Grant looked out, surveying the area presumably for people. "I don't see anyone, but someone is out there."

Dahlia remembered how she'd felt the last time she'd been here. In the end, she'd chalked up that feeling of being watched to the dog and Grant, but maybe there was more. Maybe someone was *always* here.

But they'd looked through the town and found no sign of people, and maybe she wouldn't know what signs to look for, but Grant would.

"Come on," he said, gently moving her out of the courtyard and into the alley, still blocking her as best he could.

They made it to the road when Willie let out a low growl, and Grant turned toward where the dog was focused, but Dahlia felt drawn to look to the right instead. Down the length of the abandoned street.

There was a figure in one of the broken windows. A shadow or…a person. She opened her mouth to tell Grant, but she caught the flash of something familiar. She stood stock still for longer than she could count. Surely it was a dream. A hallucination. She'd finally had that psychotic break her parents were so worried about.

But the figure didn't vanish. It moved from the window to the empty doorway. The figure—the person—appeared as real as anything else. "Rose," she whispered.

Just as Grant whirled around and shot.

Chapter Sixteen

Dahlia's scream echoed in Grant's ears even as he pushed her onto the ground. The man on the ridge disappeared, so Grant didn't think his shot had been in time. But he was ready for a return volley.

Dahlia struggled against him.

"Stay down. Someone could shoot back," he ordered.

"It's her," Dahlia said, still struggling.

Willie trembled next to her—not in fear, but because the dog was eager to track down the threat. But Grant could hardly leave Dahlia here without protection. So Willie had to stay.

Why did you bring her?

More screams echoed in his head, but he knew they weren't real. Or at least real in this moment. Old screams. Old smoke and explosions.

He really did not need this now.

"It's her. I saw her. Grant, I saw her," Dahlia kept saying. But he couldn't get his brain to click in. "Why'd you shoot at her?"

Lincoln is down. Get out of here, Hudson.

He squeezed his eyes shut against the old voices. He hadn't

run. At least there was that. In the moment he could have saved himself, he hadn't. Unfortunately, his attempts to save his superior officer had been in vain.

"Grant?"

"Yeah," he said, or tried to say. It seemed to come out dry and dusty like the desert. But he opened his eyes. Focused on Dahlia. At some point, Dahlia had stopped struggling against his hold but shifted in it so she could look at him.

"What is it?" He could see the concern on her face and knew he had to put the past behind him. But it wrapped around him like a fist, a vision he couldn't shake.

"There was a man on the ridge over there," he said. Because he wasn't about to tell her what was going on in his mind, and he had to focus on the important facts for now. "He ran away, but he could circle around."

"What about Rose?"

He took a deep breath, using all those coping mechanisms the discharge therapist taught him. Breathe. Visualize. Ground himself. But it was hard when he also knew they were in danger. He couldn't compartmentalize the way he should with a gun in his hand, a current threat and old pain. "What about Rose?"

"I saw her. She was in that building." Dahlia pointed down the street.

Grant kept breathing carefully. He stared at the building, trying to ascertain if anything he saw was real or just old fragmented memories.

"I know I saw her. I know I did," Dahlia was saying. So insistent, like she thought he didn't believe her when he couldn't even work up the concentration to believe her or not.

"I thought you shot at her, but…" Dahlia trailed off, he thought. Or maybe he tuned her out.

Then he felt her fingers on his cheek, sort of like before. When he'd kissed her. He *had* kissed her. That had happened. All this was real. *She* was real.

"Grant, what's wrong?"

She looked so concerned, and he knew he had to get it together. They could still be in danger. Just like the highway. They wanted her. And Grant didn't think they particularly cared what happened to him in the process of that. His only saving grace was they didn't seem to be big on the use of guns.

He sucked in one more careful breath and let it out, hoping she'd keep her fingers right there on his face, which helped him do all that grounding he was supposed to do when he had an *episode*.

"You think you saw Rose in that building down there?" he said, hoping his voice sounded as calm to her as it did to him. Not matching what was rioting around inside of him at all.

"I *know* I saw her. At first, I thought I was hallucinating or something, but she moved. From the window to the door. And she was wearing this sweater that I gave her for her birthday a few years ago. It's got all these crazy flowers on it. I found it in a thrift shop, and I knew it was perfect for her."

"Okay. Okay." He tried to give her a reassuring smile. "She was in that building. And there was a man up on that ridge." And he hadn't shot him, because damn if Grant could hit a target these days.

He should have sent Dahlia here with Palmer or Jack or even Anna. Why did he think he could protect her when, very clearly, he couldn't? Couldn't save anyone. Not his parents. Not his sergeant.

Not going to make it, Hudson. Tell the wife I tried.

It had been the worst moment of his life, and this seemed to echo it in all the ways he couldn't allow.

"You have to let me go find her," Dahlia said, her hand still on his face, but she tried to tug her arm out of his grasp.

"It could be a trap," Grant said, not letting her go. She'd take off, and then what? They had to…think this through. Calmly. Rationally. Which meant he had to find his equilibrium. Now.

Her expression turned, and he recognized desperation when he saw it. The need to *do* outweighing common sense. Been there. Done that.

"She could need help," Dahlia insisted, and she sounded so desperate. He could hardly keep holding her here. He didn't want to hurt her. And as much as his instincts shouted at him to get her out of here, were his instincts even any good anymore? Sure, he could shoot at a perceived threat, but he couldn't hit it. He could fight off men and still get stabbed in the process.

Now is not the time for some kind of identity crisis. It wasn't his own voice. He wasn't sure if it sounded more like his father or Sergeant Lincoln, or maybe some imaginary mixture of them both. Regardless of where the thought came from or who it sounded like, he needed to hold on to it.

"We need to get out of here. It isn't safe."

"I can't leave her behind," Dahlia said stubbornly. "Grant, I *know* I saw her. She's alive. She's *here*."

There were tears in her eyes, and if he had to blame his weakness on something, he supposed it was that. On wanting to give Dahlia...the world. "All right. We'll check it out. But you stay behind me. You follow orders. Got it?"

She nodded emphatically.

He should have let her go, moved away from her hand on his face. He should have confronted all the danger around them and come up with a plan. Instead, he pulled her up to standing and pressed his mouth to her forehead. For her comfort. For his.

He just...needed to.

"Promise me. No self-sacrifice," he said, holding her there against him as she leaned into him.

She hesitated, but after a moment, she nodded.

"Out loud, Dahlia."

She let out a hefty sigh and pulled back a little. "Fine. I promise. Can we go find her now?"

It was Grant's turn to sigh. Most of the old visions and voices were gone now. He felt more in charge of the moment and himself. Not that he was particularly sturdy with it.

He turned, keeping his body as a kind of shield between anywhere someone might be and Dahlia. He studied the area. It was too open. Too many places for someone to hide.

He wanted to try to talk her out of it, but if he put himself in her shoes, he knew there'd be no words. If he'd sworn he'd seen his parents down there, wouldn't he do everything no matter the danger to get to them?

"Follow me. Don't look down at the store, watch behind us. Let me know if you see anything, and I mean *anything* that doesn't look right, feel right, whatever. We are basically sitting ducks walking down this street." Once they crossed, they'd be hidden from the ridge, but Grant didn't think whoever had been up there was up there still. And he didn't think they were gone.

"Okay," Dahlia agreed.

Grant turned to the dog. "Willie. Follow." The dog wagged his tail in recognition of the order.

Grant fought down all the bad feelings, all the doubts. It was dangerous. Chances were high it was a trap. But, no, they could hardly just walk away from a potential sighting of her sister.

Dahlia was sure, and he knew what being desperate could do to a person, but…he just believed her. Couldn't help himself. She was sure, and so he'd be sure with her. *For* her.

He started forward, gun drawn, Dahlia far too close at his heels. He fought off the memories of old wars long gone as they moved down the street, as close to cover as he could manage. When they reached the last building, he leaned against the outer wall before crossing in front of the broken window.

"Stay here," he whispered to Dahlia while making the hand signal for stay at Willie. He could tell Dahlia didn't *want* to stay, but he gave her a stern look. "I mean it."

She swallowed but then nodded. Willie stood at the ready right next to her, and Grant had to trust the dog would sound an alarm if something was about to happen to her while he searched the building.

Grant eased into the doorway, gun first, careful to attempt to find cover. But there was none to find, and worse.

It was definitely a trap.

DAHLIA STOOD WITH her back to the building, Willie panting in front of her. But it felt like he was protecting her, somehow. However a dog could.

And all she could do was stand here and think… Rose. She *had* seen her. She kept replaying the moment in her mind. It was the same sweater. Rose's blond hair. Even the way she'd moved from the window to the door had been *Rose*.

Alive.

Dahlia wanted to cry, but her heart was beating so hard against her chest, and the silence made fear freeze any tears.

Too quiet. Too…much. And Grant moving into that building, alone and off-kilter because *she* wanted him to. She wasn't certain he believed her about seeing Rose, but he knew she needed to know. He *cared* about her well-being, about what she wanted.

It was hard to fathom, but when she focused on that, some of the shaky terror settled. She looked around the abandoned town. To her eye, there was absolutely no sign of anyone. Willie sat at her feet, clearly on watch, but not growling or tensed and ready. Just watchful.

Grant disappeared fully inside, and there wasn't a sound. She wasn't sure how he moved that quietly, but he did. She held her breath.

But nothing happened. He didn't return. There were no sounds. Eventually she had to let out her breath even though she'd been hoping to hold it until he returned so she could hear everything that happened.

Willie began to growl, low in his throat. His tail didn't wag. It was straight up. Ears perked, everything about him was like a dog ready to attack, but he didn't leave her side.

Which felt worse somehow, because to her, it meant the danger had to be coming from inside the building. Grant had told her to stay put, but what if…

"Willie," she whispered. She tried to think of any of the commands she'd heard Grant and Cash and the others use on the dogs. There was stay and still and… "Free," she whispered. Cash had said that once when he'd been training a few dogs, and when he'd said free, they'd all relaxed and scattered.

Maybe Willie would know her "free" meant to go wherever he needed to go. God, she hoped so.

Willie immediately headed for the door Grant had disappeared into. But just as he reached the opening, Grant's sharp order pierced the air. "Willie. *Go.*"

The dog seemed as confused as Dahlia felt, because it hesitated there in the doorway.

"Come here, sweetheart," a feminine voice said from inside the building. Willie growled, but Dahlia couldn't heed the warning.

"Rose." She hurried for the opening and then stopped dead in her tracks. It was Rose. Right there. In the sweater Dahlia had given her. But Dahlia couldn't rush forward and envelop her sister in a hug. Cry in relief and joy.

Because Rose was pointing a gun at Grant's head.

"You're here," Rose said, smiling widely at Dahlia. But she didn't sound like herself. Or maybe it was just the gun pointed at Grant. "At last."

"Rose, what are you doing?"

Rose let out a long breath, but she didn't drop the gun. "I have been *waiting*. Just waiting and waiting." Her smile never faltered, but this was not…

It was Rose, but something was wrong. Very, very wrong. "Rose, are you okay?"

"I'm wonderful. I've found the truth, Dahlia. And now

you can too." The smile dimmed a little as her eyes moved to Grant. Who stood stock still, stoic and silent.

Dahlia couldn't imagine what she was thinking, but she didn't like the way Rose was studying him at all.

"Can you put down the gun? He...he's my friend. Please, put down the gun."

Rose pressed her lips together. "He'd have to put his gun down first."

"I'm not pointing it at you," Grant replied. And it was true. The gun in his hand was pointed at the ground. "I don't want to hurt you."

Rose scoffed. "I'm the one with the gun pointed at your head. How could you hurt me?"

"Please, Rose." Dahlia took a halting step forward but stopped because Rose seemed to tighten her grip on the gun. "He helped me find you. Aren't you... Why do you have a gun? It's okay. We can go home now."

"Home? I'm never going home."

Dahlia sucked in a breath. This was all wrong, but she didn't know why. She wanted to cry. Rose was alive. Here and *alive*, and Dahlia wanted nothing else to matter.

But Rose needed to stop pointing that gun at Grant. "I don't understand."

"You haven't found the truth yet," Rose said, and it was almost like the sister she knew. The kind voice but just a *thread* of bossiness. Even though Dahlia was older, she'd always been more timid and introverted. Rose had been the bigger personality, so as they'd gotten older, Rose had taken to telling Dahlia what to do.

Why did everything in the past few weeks seem to come back to her never doing what she wanted? Never standing up for herself? Always bending to make someone else happy or at peace?

It made her angry, and this was definitely the wrong time to be angry since *guns* were being pointed at people she cared about. Dahlia couldn't really believe Rose would kill Grant. Both because Rose wasn't a killer and because Grant, even in the more submissive position, somehow...*seemed* in control.

"Grant, you could—"

He looked at her for the first time since she'd entered, and his eyes were flat and cold. "No."

Dahlia didn't know what to do with either of these people. "What if you *both* put your guns down?"

"No," they said in unison. Willie even growled like he was also saying no.

"What are you going to do? Just point guns at each other all day? This is ridiculous. Rose, you're safe now. We don't have to go home, but we can get you out of here and to help."

"Help? Dahlia, I've found truth. I've found peace, and once you join us, everything will be perfect. I promise. Come with me. Leave *him* behind."

"Rose." Dahlia couldn't understand what was happening. Rose was part of the cult? Brainwashed or...something?

"I have to take you back," Rose continued. "There's no other choice."

Dahlia could tell Grant wanted to speak, but he didn't. She supposed he understood like Dahlia did that Rose wasn't going to listen to either one of them, but Dahlia had the better chance of getting through.

"You're safe now, Rose."

"And so are you." Rose turned her oddly black gaze to

Grant. "I'll let you go, for Dahlia, if you leave. Right now. Don't come back." She looked around him. "You can leave the dog. We'll take good care of him. Won't we, sweetheart?"

Willie still growled.

"His name's Willie," Dahlia managed. She didn't dare look at Grant. "Come here, Willie." She crouched a little and patted her legs, and Willie trotted over. She screwed up the courage to look at Grant.

He had not moved. Not for the door. Not away at all. His expression was impassive, but she saw the flash of emotions in his eyes. Anger and frustration. She tried to beg him with her eyes. *Just leave. I'll get through to her.*

He shook his head infinitesimally, and he was just so… set on something. Determined and honorable somehow. She wanted to reach out and soothe him or beg him or *something*. Because Rose was here, but she wasn't herself, and Dahlia just knew they had to save her somehow.

Grant turned his attention to Rose, everything about him cooling into stoic blankness. But his words were fierce and made Dahlia's heart tremble. "I won't leave Dahlia here with you."

Chapter Seventeen

Grant knew Dahlia wanted him to, and maybe it would have been smart. To go get backup. But he knew someone else was out there. He also knew Dahlia's sister was on something—whether by choice or by force—she was under the influence of some kind of drug.

He couldn't, even for a moment, leave Dahlia alone with her.

They had different coloring, but when staring at both women, it was easy to see they were sisters. The same build, the same mouth, the same too-skinny frame, likely borne of the past year more than anything natural.

But Rose was still his enemy. Until Dahlia was safe.

"I won't leave, but I'll go with you," he said. It was hard. He was not a born actor, but for Dahlia, he'd try. "My maternal grandfather was an elder in the Order of Truth."

Rose looked at him suspiciously. He didn't dare look at Dahlia. He hadn't mentioned it, and he doubted very much Mary or Anna had brought it up. Even with Anna's fascination with the cult, no one was too proud to be the descendent of a Truth elder, especially in Sunrise. It was why his parents had never thought the cult was much of a joke, why his family had always been uncomfortable with Truth and Eugene Green.

His mother had done a lot to make up for being born into the Islay family. Everyone had told him, both before and after his parents' disappearance that it was good she'd married a Hudson—one of the good, upstanding families. That maybe, just maybe, she wasn't tainted by her relations.

But some had wondered, when both his mother and father had disappeared without a trace, if it had been that Islay blood catching up with them.

"My grandmother left the Order when my mom was a child," Grant went on. "And my mother didn't want us to be a part of it, but I've always thought…" Hell, what kind of nonsense was he supposed to spout to get closer? "The truth sounded more like home than the outside world."

Rose's eyes were narrowed as she stared him down. She didn't believe him. He didn't expect her to right away, but he could be patient.

Because he damn well wasn't letting Dahlia just *go* with the woman. Clearly, Rose wasn't well. And no wonder. She'd been a prisoner of the Truth, likely brainwashed and drugged, for a year.

And if she'd chosen it? Well, he'd cross that bridge with Dahlia when they came to it.

"No one escapes the Order alive," she replied.

"They did after the federal raid."

Rose's mouth firmed. "Put down the gun," she said.

"Grant." He wasn't sure what Dahlia wanted from him now, to lay it down or hold on to it. To stay or to go, but he'd made his decision. They'd get into that cult together and burn it down from the inside.

And he'd keep Dahlia safe. If he had to die to do it.

So, very carefully, he crouched and put his gun on the ground. He could hear Dahlia suck in a breath.

They were at Rose's mercy now.

"Can't you put yours down now?" Dahlia asked, and Grant could tell she was trying to be gentle, but nerves assaulted her.

Grant wasn't feeling too free and easy either. One purposeful pull of the trigger, or even a mistake, and he'd be dead.

"You could easily overpower me," Rose said to him.

Grant straightened and held his hands up in a gesture of surrender while also slowly and casually angling his body so the gun wasn't aimed quite so squarely at his head.

"I could, but I'm not going to. I don't hurt women." *Unlike your little cult*, he thought with some bitterness. Because the violence against women and sacrifice of women had been a *big* part of the cult's identity back in the sixties and seventies. They'd railed against the women's movement and had taken out every last frustration on women. It was the human sacrificing and the arms stockpiling that had brought the Feds in, but it had still created decades of trauma for the women involved.

Including his mother.

Grant took a careful breath. He couldn't afford to get angry.

Rose bit her lower lip, looking so much like Dahlia that sympathy waved through him against his will. Maybe he couldn't be angry, but he also couldn't be swayed by her just yet. It was dangerous.

But he also knew, because Sunrise made sure everyone

knew, just what the Order of Truth could do to a person against their will. Particularly a woman. So, it was his job to keep her safe too.

"Rose."

Rose looked over at Dahlia. She frowned a little and brought her free hand to her head. "We need to find Samuel." She didn't lower her gun, but she moved it a pinch, so it didn't feel quite so much like a headshot was imminent.

"What happens when you take us to the cult?" Dahlia asked. One of her hands rested on Willie's head like he was the source of all her calm.

"Dahlia, you don't know how lucky you are." Rose took a step toward her, and Grant had to physically hold himself back from stepping between them. It didn't seem like Rose would hurt Dahlia just for the hell of it, but...

The cult would.

The gun wasn't pointed at Grant anymore as Rose approached Dahlia, but it didn't make him feel any more at ease. Rose stood in front of her sister, gun pointed at the ground.

"Once Samuel gets here, we'll take you to the Lord." Rose reached out and touched Dahlia's hair reverently. "You're the Chosen One."

"I don't... What if I don't want to be?" Dahlia asked. She hesitated, then reached up and took her sister's hand. She drew it away from her hair but then held on.

Rose's expression flickered. "You're *chosen*," she repeated. "The *one*. I thought I could be for a while." She tried to smile, but it faltered. She was also starting to twitch a little. Almost like whatever high she'd been on was starting to wear off.

Grant really wanted to get that gun out of her hand.

He took a step toward her, watching to see if she'd pay attention, but she kept talking to Dahlia as he crept along.

"I can't remember..." Rose shook her head. "It doesn't matter. It's just important that you're here and chosen, so you will be. You'll ascend. You're so lucky."

None of that sounded *lucky*, and Grant would be damned if he let Dahlia be anything in this cult. He was *this* close to being able to get the gun out of Rose's hand when he heard someone's approach. Though it was clearly careful and quiet, Willie sensed it too, growling low in his throat without leaving Dahlia's side.

Grant took a step away from Rose, not sure what they'd be greeted with when whoever it was made an appearance. But he didn't want to look like he was a danger to anyone, and he'd rather position himself between the doorway and Dahlia so she wasn't a target.

She was *clearly* the target.

When the man finally appeared, almost as quiet as a ghost, Grant didn't bother to hide a scowl. "You."

One of the men from the road stood there, and when he recognized Grant, he smirked. He didn't have a gun and didn't reach for one, but a knife was holstered on his hip—much like the one that had stabbed Grant.

"You were only supposed to get the Chosen One, child."

All women in the cult were called child, regardless of age. Grant didn't know how anyone stomached it. But the shakes Rose was beginning to have explained something. She was definitely coming off some kind of drug.

And it didn't quite make sense to him, how a woman

would be so elevated as to be chosen in this cult who had, as far as he knew, always treated women as second-class citizens.

"He's a descendent," Rose said.

This Samuel studied Rose, likely seeing the same things Grant did, regarding her shakes.

"Child, did you eat your breakfast this morning?"

"I was too excited to eat."

His frown deepened, then he turned to Grant. "What kind of descendent?"

Grant didn't want to tell him. He didn't want to be a part of this. He remembered, too clearly, how much any mention of the cult had bothered his mother.

But there was also Dahlia, too much a target of this horror. So he had to swallow his aversion and do whatever it took to save her. "Islay."

Samuel's eyes widened. "An *elder*? I don't believe you."

"Spirit Islay was my grandfather."

"That makes you the son of traitors."

Grant shrugged, and he fought for his next words to come out sounding as gross as they were. "I can't control what the women in my family did."

Samuel nodded thoughtfully. "You'll be tested, but we can use the numbers if you pass. Rose, search him."

Rose shuffled over to him. She took the phone and keys out of his pocket, then his wallet. She rifled through, took the cash and shoved it in a pocket of her dress.

She did not get the knife in his boot. Grant had a bad feeling he was going to need it.

"He's clear," she offered to Samuel.

Samuel nodded. "All right. Let's go before someone comes looking for them. Throw their things in their truck."

Rose scurried off to do just that. Grant watched Samuel. He could overpower the man, but he wasn't sure where it would lead them. And Rose still had her gun, so when she came back...

No, there were too many risks. Still, he inched closer to Dahlia and Willie. Once close enough, he took Dahlia's hand in his. Samuel was paying no mind to that, so Grant gave her hand a reassuring squeeze.

She leaned into him a little bit as they stood there faced with a man who was part of some cult that thought Dahlia was chosen for the color of her hair.

"It'll be all right," he murmured. One way or another, he'd make sure of it.

EVERYTHING WAS SO SURREAL, but Dahlia found holding Grant's hand gave her a certain amount of grounding. Maybe none of this made sense, and maybe her being chosen or not, they were clearly in a lot of danger, but they were in it together. And Grant had gotten her out of danger before.

Of course, he'd gotten stabbed in the process.

She glanced uneasily at the gun Rose still held in her hand when she reentered the store.

"Tie them together," the man named Samuel ordered Rose.

Rose moved to hand Samuel the gun but then seemed to think better of it and looked around for someplace to put it.

Dahlia exchanged a glance with Grant. For whatever reason, it seemed some people in their group wouldn't or maybe even couldn't touch guns. It was something to file away.

Rose took the cord Samuel handed her and moved over to

Grant and Dahlia. She noted their joined hands with a little frown—not of disapproval exactly but of consideration. Rose looked up at Dahlia, but Dahlia couldn't read her sister's expression. When she'd always been able to.

Was it the year of no contact, of thinking she was dead? Or was it whatever this cult had done to Rose? Or worse, was it that Dahlia had never really known her sister at all?

Dahlia let out a shaky breath. There had to be some way to get through to Rose. But it likely wasn't going to be in front of the beady-eyed man standing in the doorway.

Rose wrapped the cord around Dahlia and Grant's wrists, allowing them to still hold hands. She shook as she tied, but the bonds were still strong, and allowed a bit of lead that she handed to Samuel.

So they were like dogs on a leash.

Samuel gave the lead a tug. "Follow along. The Lord will have to decide if you're telling the truth, Blood of Islay. Chosen One, there will be a grand celebration in your honor."

Dahlia couldn't find a way not to react to the words *Chosen One*. It made her shudder and feel sick to her stomach. She'd never wanted to be chosen by much of anyone, but she *really* didn't want to be chosen by monsters.

Samuel pulled the lead, and she and Grant were jerked forward. Out of the building and then down the middle of Main Street, as if they were being paraded through the town, except there was no one there to cheer.

Willie trailed after them. Rose had given him a little water back in the building, so Dahlia felt like he would at least be treated well. God, she hoped so.

She dared to look up at Grant in the fading sunlight. He appeared as stoic as ever, but she worried about his stab wound. She worried about everything he'd said back in the building.

Had he been telling the truth? Or was he trying to trick Rose? Dahlia had the sneaking suspicion everything he'd said had been true, and it was that truth that had made him dismissive and uncomfortable about every mention of Truth from the beginning until this moment.

It explained Anna's interest, Mary's concern. It explained *everything*.

He hadn't wanted to say any of it, but he had so he could stay with her. So he could keep her safe. He'd sacrificed those truths he didn't want to deal with for her.

So she had to find a way to keep him safe too.

They walked and walked, it seemed like in circles. Until the sun fell, the air cooled and she found herself shivering under a vast, amazing array of stars. When Dahlia braved a look at Rose, she was following along, hugging herself and looking sickly in the silvery moonlight.

Dahlia wanted to say something, reach out, *do* something, but Samuel kept dragging them along, and it was clear whether it was out of force or brainwashing or her own choice, Rose had aligned herself with a cult.

Desperate people do desperate things. She'd said that herself, without ever thinking her sister would be the desperate one.

They climbed hills that felt like mountains. Dahlia's mouth was dry as dust, and her head pounded. She'd kill for a drink of water. She looked over at Grant, but with night getting darker and darker with every passing moment, she could only make out the shadow of him in the moonlight.

She worried about his stab wound. She worried about what

would happen when they got wherever they were being led. She worried about everything.

Finally, after what could have only been hours, she started to see flickers of firelight and smell the smoke on the cold air. She was trying desperately to keep her teeth from chattering, but the air got colder and colder.

They got closer and closer, until Dahlia could make out a camp. Lots of little very temporary looking tents set up in a kind of circle around a large RV. Over to the west, a large bonfire was crackling, and many men were sitting around it eating and chatting. To the east, a group of women stood around a kind of cauldron with a much smaller fire. It looked like they were eating as well and cleaning up the remnants of making a meal.

Dahlia's stomach rumbled. Odd to be hungry *now* when emotions had made her incapable of feeling hungry for so long.

But Rose was alive. Maybe Rose wasn't herself. Maybe she was in danger. But she was alive. There was hope.

Or so Dahlia thought. A lot of that hope began to fade when a man approached them. He was dressed in a white robe, and she knew at once he was the man from the security footage. Bald, but a carbon copy of a younger Eugene Green.

"Samuel. My child." He pressed his palms together in front of him, but even in the firelight, Dahlia could see his eyes lock on her. "You've brought me all I desire."

Chapter Eighteen

Grant called upon every last cell of control not to react. He wanted to fly forward and tackle the robed man to the ground. Stop him from ever laying eyes on Dahlia again.

But he didn't. Couldn't. Though some of the cult members clearly didn't carry guns, some did, and he had to find a way to get Dahlia and Rose out of this unharmed.

And bring *all* these people to justice.

The man's eyes turned to him, and his smile turned into a sneer. "Why have you brought *this*?"

"Lord of Truth, this man claims he's of the elder's blood," Samuel said reverently. He handed the lead on the rope to the other man. "Claims blood Islay."

"Islay? Islay are traitors."

"He says the women were traitors," Samuel replied, head bowed.

This leader, his *Lord of Truth*, nodded as if that made sense, just as Samuel had.

"My Lord," Samuel continued. "The child did not eat her breakfast this morning."

"This is a serious infraction, child," the man said to Rose.

"I'm sorry," Rose said, and her voice shook—part of it the

comedown on whatever drug she clearly missed at breakfast and part fear. "I'll atone at once."

She was the main reason he was in this mess, but he couldn't stop the tide of sympathy. Clearly she'd gotten in over her head, even if she'd chosen the cult.

Except Dahlia was the Chosen One somehow. Whatever *that* meant. Even the man before them, this Lord of Truth, looked at her like all the answers in all the world existed in her.

Grant wanted that to be a reason to believe she'd be safe, that she'd have some power in the situation, but he knew too much, had seen too much. His own grandmother and mother had escaped this.

There was no safety in this cult for anyone, but especially for a woman.

As if to prove it, Samuel took Rose off deeper into the camp, and Grant couldn't be sure if it was to help her or hurt her. Dahlia watched her sister go with worry, and Grant could only squeeze Dahlia's hand, a silent promise they would figure this out.

Somehow.

"I will show you to your tent, Chosen One. Blood of Islay, we will have to convene a meeting to decide what to do with you. Come this way."

Before Grant even opened his mouth to protest, Dahlia was doing it for him.

"No," she said firmly, her grasp on his hand tightening even though their wrists were still tied together. "He has to stay with me."

"Chosen One—"

"If I am chosen and promised and all those other things

your men shouted at me when they stopped us on the road a few weeks back, then you…you have to listen to me and do as I say…in this."

She faltered over only a few words. If Grant could have groaned without the man hearing him, he would have. This was hardly the best way to go about it. The man who fancied himself some kind of lord narrowed his eyes, and Grant began to open his mouth, yet again, to stand up for Dahlia. Defend her somehow.

But she did it herself before he could.

"You need me," she said firmly to the man. "You need me to be happy. Until the time."

Time… She seemed so sure, but Grant didn't have a clue what she was talking about.

"Perhaps, but we must test him. We cannot allow just anyone onto our sacred ground."

"You can if the Chosen One wills it."

The man's eyebrows raised. "You've studied us, Chosen One. I'm impressed."

Grant wished what he felt was impressed, but it was only dread and fear that they were getting deeper and deeper into something he couldn't control or escape from safely with Dahlia.

Not just her. Her and Rose, because he knew Dahlia wouldn't leave without her sister. He knew he couldn't ask her to. Rose was a victim here, even if she'd made some dubious choices in how she'd ended up in this mess.

"I presume you wish to share a tent then?"

"Yes," Dahlia said, chin angled upward. Almost regally. She reminded him a little of Mary when she was doling out orders, then figured that's who she was trying to emulate in the moment. If it had been any other situation, he might have smiled.

He'd once had to learn how to be tough too, or tough in a different way than he'd been used to. After his parents had left, he'd had to help Jack run the house. Be the ones the younger kids looked up to. He'd had to never show fury or impatience or any of those other emotions that had been roiling inside of him at sixteen.

So, he'd learned how to be the adult in the situation long before he'd been ready. He'd learned how to be a leader no matter how terrifying that had been.

It wasn't easy, but Dahlia had found some of that leadership, that bravery, despite all the things tumbling around inside of her. He was proud of her.

"All right. Do you know when the time is, my Chosen One?" the Lord asked.

Dahlia swallowed, and though her expression appeared not to change, he felt her hand tremble in his. "No, not exactly."

The man smiled, sending a cold chill down Grant's spine. "Good. It's best when the anticipation is high."

"Pete," the man shouted and clapped his hand. Another skinny man scrambled over. He clearly had a gun tucked into the back of his pants. He didn't wear a robe, and Grant was beginning to think that meant something. The robed men didn't carry weapons. Maybe they were too holy?

"Show them to the Chosen One's tent. Keep them tied until they're inside."

Pete nodded. "Yes, my Lord." Then he was given the lead of the rope and pulled them farther into the center of the camp.

Behind the RV, a large tent was set up—much nicer and bigger than the others. It had its own little fire in front being tended by a woman who didn't look up as the man named Pete led them into the large tent.

He then silently untied the cords from their hands. He bowed to Dahlia, then left.

The tent had a large cot with many blankets, lanterns and decorations. A cooler of food and drinks. Like…the glamping catalogs Mary had shown him one time that had made Jack's lip curl.

But this was a cult. It was beyond creepy. Beyond strange, and Grant knew…there was something he was missing. He turned to face Dahlia. *She* knew more than she wanted him to.

The flap of the tent closed, but Grant was under no illusion they were alone. It was just canvas, and the shadows outside were clear enough. There was a guard posted at the flap door—not robed, so he likely had access to a gun. There was the woman at the fire, who was definitely within hearing distance and was no doubt watching the tent.

"We should probably take turns sleeping," Dahlia offered into the quiet warmth of the tent. She was shivering now.

He couldn't stand it, so he wrapped his arms around her and pulled her close, though it caused a twinge where he'd been stitched up. She leaned into him, the tenseness of her shoulders slowly relaxing as she breathed carefully.

"Explain all this to me," he said, still holding her close.

Her shoulders tensed once again. "Grant…"

"No. No placating. No beating around the bush." He rubbed a hand up and down her back, hoping to warm her or stop her shaking. "Explain it to me. The Chosen One. The time."

She looked so pained, so twisted up, he wished he could comfort her. But he needed the truth first.

"They're going to sacrifice me."

DAHLIA HADN'T TOLD GRANT, or anyone, everything she'd learned in her research of the cult. Maybe she'd even denied it to herself a little bit, but here in the middle of all this… bizarre behavior, she knew it was true.

She would be sacrificed. There was a ritual though, one the cult had to follow to the letter. It hadn't been fully documented in the books, but enough that she knew she was safe until…well, until they decided she wasn't.

But by not telling anyone, she had gotten here. She had found out Rose was alive, and now they just had to save her. And themselves.

"Like hell they are," Grant said with more vehemence than she'd expected. His grip tightened, and she supposed she should feel scared by the threat of violence in his tone, but mostly she felt safe. Protected. Here in the shelter of his arms, she felt like they could really handle this.

But he pulled her away gently with enough of a pull that she had to look at him. Look at the anger and…*hurt* in his eyes.

"Is there anything else you've been keeping to yourself?"

"I didn't know…"

He raised his eyebrows, and the lie died in her throat. It wasn't fair to lie to him when all he'd ever done was try to help. "Yes, I read about the Chosen One and the ritual sacrifice. And, yes, I understood because of how they viewed women and blood…red hair that they might want me for that."

"And you didn't think to *mention* it?"

"I couldn't. I *couldn't*. I knew you'd try to lock me away in some safe room and handle it all yourself. If I had told you, I wouldn't know Rose was alive. We wouldn't be here with the opportunity to stop this. To get Rose *home*."

"Fine. You got what you want. Are you happy?"

It hurt. Because it wasn't just his usual straightforward demeanor. That was betrayal in his tone, lashing out to hurt *her*. But he didn't drop his hands from her shoulders. He didn't release her and step away, so she held on to that.

"No," she said, working to swallow down the tears that threatened. "None of this makes me happy, Grant."

He closed his eyes as if in pain. "I'm sorry," he murmured, then pulled her close again. "Damn it, Dahlia. I *would* have locked you away. This is too dangerous. It's too much of a risk." He blew out a breath that ruffled her hair. She rubbed her palms up and down his back, both assurance and…well, it was a very nice back.

"You really don't know how long it'll be?" he asked, still holding her to him.

"No, that was one of the details that was pretty vague. Only the Lord of Truth knows, I think. Or decides? But they have to keep me happy until that time. Maybe I could ask them to let Rose go?"

He pulled her back again, and this time his hands moved up her shoulders to frame her face. "Dahlia, she'd have to want to go."

Dahlia closed her eyes against the stab of pain the truth

caused. "I know. But…maybe if they told her she could. Maybe she's just afraid. Maybe…"

"She's being drugged," Grant said. "The whole breakfast thing… Too weird to just be breakfast."

"Do you think they're all drugged?"

"It's possible. There was nothing about that in the books you read?"

"No, but they don't speak of the women usually. They're just the servants, more or less, for the men and the truth. The only exception is the Greens, or in this case, the Green bloodline. And only if you're born with red hair." Dahlia didn't know how to feel about that. How Rose must feel about it, drugged or not. A twist of fate, and their situations could be reversed.

"We should get some rest," Grant said, lowering his voice to a whisper, bringing his mouth close to her ear. "They'll have us watched at night. But tomorrow morning, you could say you want a tour. I'll be by your side. We'll figure out where Rose is and map a route out of here."

She had to swallow to focus on the words and not the sensations of his big calloused hands on her face, his breath against her ear. "Do you know where we are?" she asked, attempting her own whisper.

It wasn't about sensations. It was about anyone out there not hearing them.

"I have a general idea. The good news is that even if they covered our tracks, my family isn't going to let us disappear into thin air. They know what we were looking into. They have Kory Smithfield. Anna had some leads."

Dahlia nodded. "You get up earlier than I do. You're injured. You should sleep first."

He frowned at this, but she wasn't about to give up. "They'll likely come wake us up at dawn. Would you rather be the one awake and watching then or the one asleep?"

His frown turned to a scowl.

"It's practical," she insisted, because it *was*. And because if she laid down now, she wouldn't sleep. She'd think about what it felt like in his arms. She'd think about Rose drugged. She'd think about being sacrificed.

That was *quite* the warped combo.

"Can I trust you to wake me up in an hour or two?"

"Of course."

He raised an eyebrow, a clear sign the *of course* was over the top. Which was fair. But she wanted him to truly rest, so she lifted her hand and fitted it over his cheek. "I promise to wake you up. I know I have kept things from you at times, but I don't make promises I don't plan to keep."

He sighed. "It's the 'plan to' that worries me."

She leaned up and gave him a quick friendly peck on the lips. "Good night, Grant."

He grunted, and after a few moments of holding her in place and studying her, he let go and went and lay down on the cot. He fell asleep quickly, and Dahlia set to looking around the tent for something she could use to rebandage his side tomorrow.

She could, of course, demand first aid from one of the cult members, but she wasn't sure she trusted them—not to help him, not to bring suitable bandages.

When that didn't yield anything, she studied the food options, then thought about Rose's discussion about breakfast.

No, she couldn't trust the food or water either.

A noise had her turning to look at Grant. He was asleep—

eyes closed, chest rising and falling, but he muttered something, then turned his head violently to one side as if in pain. She took a step forward as he began to thrash. The groan of pain startled her so much she jumped.

But then she hurried to his side. "Grant. Grant. You're having a dream." Wasn't there something about not waking people up? Or was that sleepwalking? She didn't know. She knew he wouldn't want her to see him like this, but worse, he wouldn't want anyone outside to hear him moaning and muttering.

She nudged his shoulder. "Grant, wake up. It's okay. You're..." Well, he wasn't okay, was he? He was the prisoner of a cult.

He grabbed her suddenly. She bit back a scream, because he simply maneuvered her behind him, like he was shielding her from something. "Stay down," he ordered, but she was pretty sure he was still asleep. Or trapped in some kind of dream anyway.

Dahlia didn't know what to do but wrap her arms around him from where she was wedged behind him and the cot's frame. She pressed her cheek to his back. "Grant, it's okay. Wake up. I'm right here."

Something changed. His breathing was ragged, but she could tell he'd woken up. He kept himself tense. There was no more muttering, ordering or thrashing. He held himself still—too still.

"I'm...sorry," he said, sounding ragged and, worse, mortified.

"Don't be sorry." She stayed exactly where she was. Hugging him, cheek pressed to his back. "You have... PTSD?"

"No. Not like... I have dreams sometimes. Flashbacks.

But they deemed me A-OK and all that. It's just…normal, I guess."

"Of course it is." She hugged him tighter. "You saw terrible things. That doesn't just leave you."

He sucked in a breath and let it slowly out. "Did I hurt you?"

"Don't be silly," she said. "You tried to protect me."

He nodded. "Yeah, doing a real bang-up job," he muttered. But she could tell he was trying to deflect from the dream.

"Grant. What did you dream about?"

He stiffened in her arms and tried to move, but she held tight. Eventually, he put his hand over hers locked at his chest.

"My superior officer was shot. I tried to get him out under heavy fire. Not regulation, but I did it. Or almost. He had a wife and two kids at home. I had no one. But he died, and I survived."

It broke her heart to hear him say it, to know he'd felt it. When she'd seen him with his family. "You had brothers and sisters and a niece who need you very badly."

"You don't understand, Dahlia." This time he pulled her hands off him. He didn't get off the cot like she expected him to though. He turned to face her. Serious. Tired. "They did just fine without me."

"You underestimate yourself. The Hudson machine does not work if you're not one of the cogs in it."

He almost smiled. "Cogs, huh?"

"It's true. You're a unit. You don't function without each other. I'm sure it comes from losing your parents, but I bet if you asked your siblings—any one of them, even Jack— how things ran without you, they'd say not as smoothly, as balanced as *with* you. You're the counterweight. Without you, Jack's too hard, and Cash is too isolated, and Palmer is too—" she struggled for a word "—wild, I suppose. Same with Anna."

"What about Mary?"

Dahlia considered. "Well, probably too internal." She could relate.

"I don't know about all that."

"I think you do. I think you needed it pointed out to you, but I think now that you see it, you can't unsee it." She studied his face and knew it was true. But she also knew… "You haven't told them, have you?"

"I'm sure they know I've had a nightmare or two."

"But you don't talk to anyone about it."

"I just talked to you."

She didn't know much about PTSD. She knew Grant though. Somehow, she understood him. In these few weeks of watching him—with his family, with the dogs, with her. She knew who he was.

She reached out for him, putting her hands on his cheeks, making sure he had to look her in the eye. "It's your turn to promise me something."

"What?" he replied, clearly trying for unmoved, stoic and failing.

"Just talk to someone. It can be a sibling, a friend. It could probably even be a dog."

He was silent for a long stretch of moments. "What about you?"

Her heart melted. Right here in the middle of this mess she just…fell for him. Hook, line and sinker. "It could always be me."

After another long silence, he nodded. Then he got up off the cot and gestured to it. "It's your turn to get some sleep, Dahlia. Dawn will come soon enough."

Since he was right, and they had a cult to outmaneuver tomorrow, she nodded and did as she was told. After all, she knew Grant, and a nod from him was as good as a promise. And he was not a man who went back on promises.

So, she laid down and slept. And when she dreamed, she only dreamed of sunshine and him.

Chapter Nineteen

Grant could let the embarrassment eat him alive, or he could focus on the task at hand. He couldn't do any recon in this tent, but leaving Dahlia sleeping and vulnerable was out of the question.

He looked at his stitches. He'd popped one or two, but they'd stopped bleeding and had scabbed over. He couldn't find anything sterile to use as a bandage, so he'd just have to hope he'd done enough and they'd be out of this soon enough that it wouldn't matter.

His family hadn't known where he and Dahlia had been going, and that's what a person got for sneaking and lying, he supposed. But still, Grant had no doubt they'd started a search by dinnertime, and they'd know to look into Truth. Then, once they found his truck with all his and Dahlia's things in it, they'd be able to track them here.

It would take time though, especially over the dark night-time hours. They were well and truly out in the middle of nowhere at this camp. Oh, the Samuel guy had tried to trick him with the circles and endless walking up and down hills, but Grant knew this stretch of Wyoming better than anyone, aside from his own family. He might not know the exact map pinpoint, but he knew well enough where they were and how to head back to civilization.

What he didn't know was how to convince Rose to come with them. He could outsmart a cult. Between what he knew and what Dahlia knew, and his own skills, Grant had no doubt he could get out of here.

But Dahlia wouldn't leave her sister, so Grant couldn't either.

Grant looked at Dahlia curled up on the cot. She slept peacefully, which was a relief. They'd need their strength and their wits about them. He hated that she was here surrounded by these people who wanted to *sacrifice* her, but they had a bit of a reprieve tonight.

Maybe if she could convince her sister not to eat the breakfast they were so intent on tomorrow, they could convince her to leave once backup showed up.

The problem was, even drugged, Rose shouldn't be okay with Dahlia being *sacrificed*. Even brainwashed, the idea of her sister being killed should be reason enough not to have brought Dahlia here.

Grant didn't like it, but of course he didn't like any of this. So he had to find a way to get them both out of here before any rituals started.

He heard the shuffle of people outside, saw shadows moving, and then the tent opened. Grant didn't pretend not to be awake and watching. He hoped they got the message that he'd protect Dahlia at all costs.

"Good morning," the man who'd brought them here last night boomed, making Dahlia jerk awake and sit up in the cot wide-eyed.

Grant scowled. "Thanks for the wake-up call, Pete."

Pete bowed at the waist. Hell, this place was weird as could be. "You are most welcome, Blood of Islay."

Grant exchanged a look with Dahlia. She was frowning like he was, but she looked sleep tousled and still a little out of it.

"Come. It's time for breakfast, Chosen One."

Dahlia rubbed her eyes then got off the cot. "It's a bit early to eat, isn't it?"

"We eat with the sun. We worship a new day and the opportunity to find truth in the lies." He led them out of the tent. The fire from last night had died, and there didn't seem to be anyone around tending it anymore.

"Where's Willie? Where's my dog?" Dahlia asked, looking around as they walked.

"The children are taking very good care of him."

Dahlia exchanged a glance with Grant. Worry and confusion. Grant could only shrug his shoulders. They hadn't seemed intent on hurting the dog, so he had to hope that might work in their favor.

Pete led them past the RV and smaller tents to a long table. The women all sat at it with the men standing around. There were bowls in front of each woman with some kind of oatmeal mixture. Rose sat at the end of one bench, and Willie was on the ground next to her. His tail began to wag when he saw Dahlia.

"This is your seat, Chosen One," Pete said, pointing to a chair at the head of the table next to Rose.

All the women bowed and murmured chants of "Chosen One." Grant had to fight the urge to pick her up and walk her right the hell out of here—sister and any objections be damned.

But she wanted her sister, and he wanted to take these people down. So he stood where he was and bit his tongue.

"Blood of Islay." He was handed a stick of some kind of jerky. "Your breakfast, brother." Grant studied the jerky, then the women and the men.

He didn't know if it was more or less disturbing the men clearly weren't drugged since it appeared all the women were.

The men all stood around the women, watching as if to make sure every last drop was eaten. Grant wondered if this was an everyday occurrence or if it was happening today because Rose had skipped her meal yesterday, so there were extra precautions in place. He glanced at the man next to him, who'd handed him the jerky.

"Do we always eat standing up?" he asked, attempting to be casual.

The man looked around. "We must protect our children."

Grant tried not to make a face at that. It was just so disturbing. Not one of these women appeared to be under eighteen. He supposed the only saving grace was he hadn't seen any evidence of *actual* children.

The man—the "Lord"—from yesterday stepped forward, taking a place at the opposite end of the table Dahlia sat at. He looked at the women and their bowls of oatmeal. "Children, I am your Lord of Truth. And here, in each bowl, is the truth. Eat so that you too may see a glimmer of the truth I feed you."

Dahlia looked over her shoulder at him, eyes wide, clearly worried that she was going to eat.

Over his dead body.

So, Grant would have to create a diversion.

DAHLIA TRIED NOT to panic, but she was not going to eat this laced oatmeal. She looked back at Grant, who stood there looking stoic somehow. But she knew he wasn't.

She wished she had his ability to turn off panic or anger or whatever feeling he was hiding, but she felt like every emotion chased across her face. Refusal and fear and panic.

Grant gave her a little nod, not a *go ahead* nod, she knew. But more something like *I'll take care of it*.

The Lord of Truth blathered on about the importance of eating every bite, of all the truth you could find with a clean bowl.

It was *insanity*. Dahlia tried not to get hung up on how anyone could fall for this nonsense. *Desperate people do desperate things.*

Had Rose been desperate? Had all these women?

Willie barked, causing Dahlia to jerk in surprise. The sudden movement upended her bowl, but before anyone could move to do anything about it, Willie hopped up next to her *on* the table. Then he began to run up and down it, yipping happily while women jumped up in an effort to grab their bowls or stop the dog.

But he ran, bounced, barked. He didn't growl. He acted like he was playing some kind of entertaining game, and every woman's shriek and every man's order to stop was only part of the game.

Dahlia looked at Grant. He was focused on the dog and made a little noise, almost a whistle and a hand motion. Then Willie dismounted the table, barked like crazy and ran away from camp.

Some of the men took off after the dog. Some of the men

were ordering the women to clean up or eat what had spilled. In the chaos, Dahlia leaned over to her sister.

"There are drugs in there," Dahlia said, feeling a little desperate to shake some sense into Rose. "You should avoid eating it at all costs."

"It helps," Rose said. "It is for our own good. It's the truth."

"No, it's for theirs." Dahlia looked around the table. "Try to remember what you felt like before you came here," Dahlia said—not just to her sister but to all of them who could hear her desperate whisper. Maybe they'd grown up in this horror, but maybe they were like Rose and had been kidnapped into it.

Even if Rose had somehow come to believe in it—which Dahlia found hard to accept of her vibrant, passionate sister—Rose wouldn't have joined this cult without a word, leaving everyone behind to worry about her. Dahlia couldn't believe that.

"Avoid what they give you. Just for a day or two. See how you feel. I promise you. It might be bad at first, but you'll be clearer. You'll find the *real* truth. Not their truth."

"Blasphemy," a woman hissed.

But Dahlia ignored her. She kept her gaze on Rose. Imploring. "Please. Just avoid it as best you can. Let your mind clear."

Rose held her gaze, almost like she was considering what her sister was telling her. Then she smiled, but it was a creepy smile, like the Lord of Truth. "Dahlia, you should try our way. The real truth. It's…transcendent."

Dahlia swallowed, hating what she was about to say, but if she had to play the Order of Truth's game to get her sister out of here, then so be it. "I'm the Chosen One, Rose. Wouldn't I know best?"

Rose blinked at that, then looked down at her spilled oatmeal. When she looked back up at Dahlia, it was with an expression Dahlia remembered from their childhood: stubborn rebellion. She took her spoon and began to scoop up every spilled drop of oatmeal. From the table to her mouth, defiantly eating every last bit.

Dahlia was speechless. She was literally rendered immobile by her sister's behavior.

But then Rose ate Dahlia's too. Dahlia wanted to believe it was some kind of self-sacrifice. She was desperate to believe it. But Rose looked at her defiantly as if to say, *See, I'm right. You're wrong.*

"Rose," Dahlia said, wanting to cry. "Why?"

"You don't understand. You can't understand." She was starting to look angry. Certainly not scared or even relieved Dahlia was here. She just looked *mad*. "You're the Chosen One and you don't even understand," Rose said, sounding a bit like a petulant child.

"I understand. Being chosen means they're going to *kill* me," Dahlia replied in a whisper. Most of the men were making sure the women ate their oatmeal off the table or had gone off to find the dog, but they could start paying attention to *her* at any minute.

"Yes," Rose said. As if it were a good thing. A *right* thing. That they wanted her dead eventually in some ritual sacrifice.

Dahlia could only gape at Rose, who smiled.

"And aren't you lucky?"

Chapter Twenty

Once the breakfast ruckus died down and was cleaned up, Grant and Dahlia were escorted back to their tent. Grant was relieved. Standing around the group of people was just...too much. The thought of his mother growing up in this nightmare was painful and the threat of Dahlia being *sacrificed* too much to bear.

There were murmurs about hunting down the dog, but Grant was convinced Willie had gotten a good enough head start. Willie would go find Cash or someone and lead them back.

He would have sent him last night if he'd gotten the chance, but this was perfect. It had allowed Dahlia to avoid eating the drugged oatmeal. Grant didn't know what diversion he'd manage for lunch, but they'd cross that bridge when they came to it.

Before Pete left them, Dahlia spoke. "I want to see my sister. In here. Alone."

Pete blinked, looked at Grant almost like he was looking for permission, then back at Dahlia. "I don't know…"

"I want to see my sister. Do as you're told by the Chosen

One, or ask your Lord of Truth. I don't care, but I want her brought to me. Here."

Grant had never heard her speak so forcefully. What happened at breakfast was clearly bothering her, and he wanted to comfort her in some way, but he didn't know how. This was a mess of a situation.

Pete scuttled out of the tent, and Grant figured it would be a while before he returned. He didn't seem very…confident. He'd likely go talk to the lord guy first.

Dahlia was pacing, eyebrows furrowed, tension and upset radiating from her. He couldn't let her keep stewing, so he stood in her path. When she stopped abruptly and looked up at him, he held his arms to the sides.

She closed her eyes, her expression crumpling, and she fell into him. He wrapped his arms around her and held her close. She took a deep breath, and her shoulders relaxed. "Grant, she ate both of our bowls," Dahlia said, voice scratchy.

"She was saving you." He wasn't sure it was true, but he hoped it was for Dahlia's sake.

But she shook her head. "I wish I believed that were true." She looked up at him without releasing her grip or making him release his hold on her. A few tears had fallen over. "She wasn't saving me or doing anything selfless. At least, she didn't act like she was. It was like she was…defying me because I told her they were drugged. Or trying to prove something, like she wants to be here? I don't know, but she thinks I'm *lucky* for being the sacrifice. Grant, I'm afraid I just can't reach her."

Grant brushed some of Dahlia's hair out of her face. "We'll keep trying," he promised.

She let her forehead rest against his chest as she took another ragged breath. "I can't leave this place without her."

"I know." He rubbed her back and then...told her something he swore he'd never tell anyone. "My mother once, and only once, told us about escaping the Order. How hard it was, how many tries it took. How many times her mother would be on the verge of giving up. The only thing that kept my grandmother going was not wanting this life for her daughter."

Dahlia looked up at him. Her eyes had filled again, in sympathy as much as worry over her own sister. So he made her a vow he wouldn't break. "We'll keep trying until we get her out. I promise you that."

A few more tears fell, but she didn't sob or cry. She just squeezed her eyes shut, and the tears fell over. "I don't know how I'll ever repay—"

He took her by the chin. "Dahlia. Stop thinking of this as an exchange. I'm here not just because you hired me—in fact, if that was why, we never would have been taken by that Samuel guy. We wouldn't have been in Truth. We'd have listened to Jack and turned it all over to law enforcement weeks ago. I'm here because I care about you."

She opened her eyes. Met his gaze. For a moment, she simply looked at him. When she spoke, it was with the kind of gravity that humbled him. "I care about you too, Grant."

But anything else they might have said or done was interrupted by the flap being lifted and Rose entering the tent.

She studied them standing in each other's arms. Even with tears on Dahlia's face, there was something cool in Rose's expression that Grant didn't trust. So he didn't let Dahlia go. Didn't step away. He wanted to...protect her somehow.

Because Dahlia was probably right, and there was no reaching Rose—at least here, drugged and in the cult. Dahlia knew her sister, and Grant knew how this cult in particular could mess with a person and warp them.

But he also knew Dahlia would never just let Rose stay here, whether Rose wanted to leave or not. Dahlia hadn't given up on Rose when she thought she was dead. Why would she give up on her sister alive and standing right here?

Besides, Grant had vowed to get her out, so he'd find a way.

DAHLIA FELT...GOD, she was so tired of thinking about how she felt. The swings of emotion were such a pendulum, and in the midst of it all, she was in this strange place, and her sister...was a stranger.

"You wanted to see me?" Rose said. She sounded sweet and happy, but there was something about the way she looked at Grant that made Dahlia uncomfortable.

"I wanted to make sure you were okay. Since you ate my meal this morning, you must have ingested twice the amount of drugs meant for any one person."

Rose smiled wide, but her pupils were so dilated her eyes were nearly black. "It was oatmeal, Dahlia. Sustenance. The great gift of truth from the great Lord of Truth. You only have to accept his truth to be free."

Dahlia wanted to press her face into Grant's chest again and just...push all this fanatical talk away. She'd been prepared to deal with Rose being dead. Or even kidnapped. But somehow, being *part* of this cult, saying these things and seeming to believe them...

Dahlia just didn't know what to *do*. How did you get through to someone drugged and brainwashed?

But much like the past thirteen months, she knew she couldn't give up. "Rose, can you tell me how you ended up here?"

"The truth brought me," she said, still smiling.

"I think Dahlia meant something a little bit more concrete," Grant offered. "You disappeared in Texas."

"No, I found the Lord of Truth in Texas," Rose corrected. Dahlia wouldn't call the look she sent Grant *mean* exactly, but it wasn't nice. "We didn't know you were the Chosen One then."

"How did you find that out?" Grant asked, earning another pointed look from Rose.

"Does it matter?"

"It does to me," Dahlia said earnestly.

Rose sighed heavily. She stood in one place, but her eyes darted around, and she occasionally shook a hand this way or that, like she was filled with an energy she couldn't quite control or decide what to do with.

"The Lord didn't like that you were looking for me, of course. I told him no one would care if I disappeared, and you proved me wrong, sister." It was accusation more than anything good. Like Dahlia *should* have forgotten her sister, assumed she was dead and moved on.

"I had to find out what happened to you," Dahlia replied, trying to keep the hurt out of her voice. Rose wasn't herself. She was *drugged*. Dahlia couldn't take anything at face value or be hurt by Rose's words. "How could I let it go? You *disappeared* into thin air. I thought I was searching for your murderer, Rose." She swallowed down the frustration, reminding herself Rose was alive, and that was what was important. "I'll never give up on bringing you home." It was a promise Dahlia had to keep.

Rose shook her head vehemently. "*This* is my home. The Order is my home. I have a place here. A role. Not like *home*. Constantly arguing with our small-minded, simpleton parents."

"Rose…" Dahlia didn't have the words. She knew her parents and Rose had a strained relationship, but this felt bigger. Here in the midst of all this insanity.

"People care about me and for me here," Rose continued. "The Lord took special care of me. I'm a Green. I'm special."

"We *aren't* Greens."

"We are! We have the blood!" She stamped her foot like a child, though Rose's temper had always retreated to childishness if given the chance. "And I was important until *you* came along." Her fingers curled into fists. "I had to bring you. The Lord saw you and then wanted *you*. But you should have stayed in Minnesota. You should have forgotten about me, and then maybe *I* would have been chosen."

Dahlia didn't know how to comprehend this. Being chosen meant being sacrificed. Being special meant ending up *dead* in the Order of Truth. Well, if you were a woman.

Why couldn't Rose see that?

Dahlia looked helplessly at Grant. His expression was one of sympathy. He understood what this group could do to a person's mind, and he didn't judge.

But he also didn't know how to fix it. Change it. Did anyone?

"Don't I mean anything to you, Rose?" Dahlia asked,

trying to keep her voice from shaking. "You're my sister. I love you."

"You're the Chosen One," Rose replied, her smile wild again. Her eyes darting everywhere. "This is the truth. You will meet the Lord in the sky. You will be free. And your ashes will lead us to a deeper truth." Rose moved forward with every word, reaching out much like the men had done by the highway.

But there was something far more menacing in Rose's eyes. Like she might reach out and try to choke the life out of Dahlia.

Grant stepped forward, blocking Dahlia and stopping Rose's forward progress.

Dahlia was shaken to her core. Her sister…wanted her dead.

Your sister who's been traumatized, drugged and brainwashed for a year. She tried to repeat that to herself over and over again, but she still felt dumbstruck, scared, betrayed.

"You could let us escape," Grant said to Rose. "Dahlia could disappear. Then you could be important again."

Dahlia tried to protest. How could he… How could Grant, of all people… How could he think she'd leave Rose here when he'd promised to help? Surely Grant understood that even with the threats, the anger, Dahlia would never leave without her sister.

Outside of the Order, she could find Rose help. She could have her *actual* sister back. She was sure of it. She had to believe it, hold on to that possibility. Just like no matter how hard she'd tried, she'd always held on to the possibility that Rose was alive.

And Rose *was* alive. There had to be a positive ending to this mess.

Rose seemed to consider Grant's proposition, and when Dahlia opened her mouth to find the air to argue, Grant gave her a firm shake of the head.

"Grant—"

He shook his head again. "I made a promise," he said softly. "I intend to keep it."

He'd promised to get Rose out of here. So...this was some sort of trick or plot or something, and she had to go along with it.

"I also made a promise," Rose said loftily. "To bring my Lord the Chosen One. To find the truth through your glorious sacrifice, Dahlia." Rose smiled once more.

Dahlia didn't know how to reconcile the fact that Rose looked almost exactly the same as she had the last time Dahlia had seen her, but there was...nothing on the inside that was the same.

In the silence that followed, Dahlia heard the faint yip of a dog. Willie? Oh, she hoped not. Even though everyone had been kind to the dog, she had a bad feeling this morning's breakfast shenanigans would earn him some kind of punishment.

"Grant?"

His expression was unreadable. But she knew he'd heard it too. Still, he turned to Rose. "Think about letting us go. Or coming with us when we leave."

"You won't be going anywhere, friends," Rose said sweetly. "Except to the Lord in the sky." She wafted out of the tent.

Dahlia collapsed onto the cot. Her legs couldn't keep her

up any longer. She buried her face in her hands, trying to think. She only looked up when she felt Grant's hand on her knee.

He was crouched in front of her at eye level, clearly worried. But before she could say anything, he spoke in a low whisper. "Help is here."

"What?"

"That bark? Willie's alerting. Cash or Palmer or *someone* from my family is here, Dahlia. We have to get out. Now."

Before Dahlia could protest or explain that despite everything, she couldn't leave without her sister, she heard people shouting. Grant ran for the tent flap, so she followed.

When they got out, people were running in the opposite direction. No one was paying much attention to them. But Dahlia heard Willie again. From behind.

She turned with Grant, and there across the open field was Willie. Just standing there. He let out another little yip, and Dahlia saw a flash of light.

Grant grabbed her. "Did you see that light?"

"Yes."

"It's Anna. Run for her. Right now. Don't stop. Don't look back. Just run to right where you saw her, no matter what you hear, no matter what happens. You run."

Her fingers curled into his sweatshirt. "What are you going to do?" she demanded, her heart beating overtime. He wasn't going with her, and she couldn't leave Rose *or* him.

He pried her fingers out of the fabric of his shirt. "I'm going to bring you your sister."

Chapter Twenty-One

Grant ran. He didn't have a gun, but he had the knife in his boot. The biggest challenge he faced was the fact he didn't know where Rose would be. Most of the people running around were too busy shouting orders or following them to pay him much mind.

He hoped it would stay that way. The men were all congregating around a kind of hole in the ground. Grant still ran, but when he looked back at the men, he realized what they were doing.

Pulling guns out of some sort of underground stockpile. *Hell.*

It didn't bode well for him, but he had to find Rose. He went around all the tents, even circled back and searched the RV, but he could not find any of the women, and the longer that went on, the more concerned he became.

He decided to return to where the men had been pulling weapons out of the ground in hopes they'd lead him to the women, but now they were gone too.

Damn cults.

He stilled and listened. Even though it was eerily quiet, at some point, he'd have to hear something to go on.

Old flashbacks threatened. Sand and blood and Sergeant Lincoln. Shouting and gunshots and explosions.

But he kept his eyes focused on the here and now. The grass beneath his feet. The sound of the tents flapping gently in the wind. In his mind, he retraced their path here yesterday. Up and down a few hills he'd thought were meant to distract, but maybe...

He headed east, the way they'd come. As he closed in on a hill, he heard it. The faint murmurs of people. So he climbed the hill carefully and silently.

Once close enough to the rise to peek over, he saw all of them in the distance, the men and women, but...the whole scene made his blood chill.

The women were all on their knees, men lined up behind them. With guns. There was another line of men behind them, all in robes that billowed in the wind. They didn't hold guns or any weapons.

They all faced north, and Grant realized even though he couldn't see them, law enforcement was somewhere over the second rise.

Anna had come in from the south in order to get him and Dahlia out before law enforcement moved forward.

It was too much like that federal raid. Hostages. Stockpiles of arms and insanity. Too many people were going to end up hurt or even dead, and still...as he searched the faces of the women on their knees, he didn't see Rose.

Where the hell was she? Had she escaped?

He wished he could believe that, but after everything that had happened in their tent earlier, he couldn't.

If law enforcement was over that hill, these people were

set up like the first wave to stop them. The first sacrifice. But there would be a second.

If Dahlia was still here, they'd want her.

Had they gone after her?

His heart felt as though it fully stopped at the idea. But he couldn't let that stop *him*. He turned and moved down the hill, focusing on silence. On stealth.

Not on the panic-inducing thought someone might have gotten to Dahlia and his sister.

But as he moved back through the camp, he heard lowered voices and had to slow. Had to use the tents as cover to creep closer and closer. Until he was at the place where the bonfire yesterday had been—a big stone circle.

But there was no fire lit today. At least yet. Because in the center of the stones was a big wooden pole. And the so-called Lord of Truth was tying Rose to it.

But the thing that made him fully stop in his tracks was the sheer volume of explosives littered around the both of them.

Hell.

As if sensing him, the Lord of Truth stopped and looked around. Grant was hidden by a tent, but as he studied the area, he realized it was just the three of them, and while the lord guy had explosives, he didn't seem to have a gun on him. The Lord was in robes. He was too holy to carry a gun.

Grant hoped.

So Grant did the only thing he could since his end goal was to get Rose out of this. For Dahlia. He pulled the knife out of his boot and stepped forward.

The man tightened the knot he was tying around Rose and

the pole but glared at Grant. "I don't know what you think you're going to stop. Violence isn't the answer."

"Says the man tying a woman to a pole surrounded by explosives."

"A sacrifice is good and right. It will bring us the truth, the balance. And a way forward until we are once again re-united with the Chosen One."

"You'll never get your hands on her."

The man shook his head and stepped away from Rose. But that didn't make Grant feel any better, because he didn't think it would take much to set those explosives off. Enough explosives to take all three of them out.

"You brought this evil on us, Blood of Islay."

"Yeah, me. So let Rose…let the child go."

There was a moment in which the man seemed to actually consider it, and Grant used that moment of consideration to inch closer and closer.

The man's gaze turned to the explosives. To Rose. "She's not the Chosen One."

"No, she isn't," Grant agreed. Another step. One or two more, and he could tackle the guy without using the knife. "You should let her go."

"But sacrifice brings truth. We need truth to survive. You've brought the outside world upon us, Blood of Islay, and—"

Grant lunged. The man was so impressed with his own little speech that he didn't seem to see it coming. But he still fought like hell even once Grant got him to the ground.

But he wasn't an adept fighter. His attempts at punches were flailing and weak, the robe tangling his arms so that he couldn't get a good punch in. Grant had him pinned to the ground immobile in less than a minute. All the while, the man kept screaming about truth and sacrifice.

"I built this from the ashes! I am the original Lord's descendent. The true leader. I am the truth! There was nothing, and then I breathed the flame of truth back into it all!"

"You should have let it die." Grant pulled his fist back and focused on a spot that would ideally knock the man out for the time being. He used his full force for the blow, and the man went limp.

Grant blew out a relieved breath, but when he looked over at Rose, he swore and jumped into action.

DAHLIA HAD MADE it to Anna with Willie leading the way, and now they huddled behind a hill and waited.

Just waited.

It was driving Dahlia insane.

"How can you let him just…be out there risking his life?" she finally demanded when Anna looked as if she were having a grand old time relaxing.

Anna looked over at her and uncharacteristically seemed to consider her words. "Do you think Grant would just…be cool with us running in to help?"

Dahlia didn't say anything. She couldn't, because of course not.

"And given the choice, would he want to send someone else into all that in his place?"

Again, Dahlia didn't answer. It was pointless. She didn't know why she was arguing, she just… "I can't stand waiting around feeling purposeless."

"I get it. Trust me, more than you could ever understand. But we rush in there, we mess up the plan and what

they're doing. So we have to be careful and bide our time."
Anna studied her for a long perceptive moment. "Grant's
my brother. I love him more than anything. When you love
someone, you need to let them be who they are. Even when
it hurts. I couldn't stop him from going off to war. I can't
stop him from being the hero. No one can. It's who he is."

It's who he is. Dahlia knew that. It made her heart feel
too vulnerable amid an already too emotional twenty-four
hours, let alone *year*. Because she just...*loved* who he was.
The hero complex mixed with insecurity. The way war had
marked him because he *cared*, and the way he didn't run
away from any of that. The way he was with his family. The
fact he couldn't soften the truth to save his life, but sometimes he wanted to, tried to.

"You might want to get used to it if you plan on sticking
around," Anna added.

Before Dahlia could think of anything to say to that, a
loud boom echoed through the air. The explosion shook the
ground even though it seemed to come from far away.

Anna swore and took off at a run, Willie not far behind
her. Dahlia stood frozen for a moment or two, but then she
ran as hard as she could behind them. Toward where smoke
plumed and shouts seemed to sound everywhere.

She kept sight of Willie even as Anna ran much faster than
her and disappeared into the camp, but Willie, bless that dog,
waited until she caught up and then took off again, leading
her closer and closer to the smoke.

She could hear gunshots, but they were farther off.
Was Grant involved in that? Most of the cult didn't have
guns...unless like the cult from before, they'd stockpiled
them somewhere.

All her thoughts stopped the moment she ran into the smoke and flickering flames of the aftermath of the explosion.

Grant was holding a kicking and screaming Rose, and Anna was trying to jump into the fray. There was shouting and shooting coming from farther off—all of it deafening—but it didn't seem to connect with whatever had happened here.

Dahlia watched as Rose fought off two people who'd done nothing but help and been nothing but kind. At her wit's end with all of it, she stepped forward.

"Stop it!" Dahlia screamed at the top of her lungs. She'd never once screamed like that in her entire life.

Rose stilled, surprisingly, and once she did, Grant took one arm and Anna the other. They were all bleeding now. All breathing hard.

"What on earth are you doing?" Dahlia demanded.

"I was going to be the sacrifice," Rose yelled right back. There were tracks of tears down her sooty cheeks. "I was going to be *chosen*. But he stopped it!" She jerked the arm Grant held, but they'd really immobilized her at this point, so she could only yank and yell in response.

Dahlia looked up at Grant. His face was also covered in black grime. He was bleeding from his lip, his nose and his temple. One of his sleeves was burned. And still he stood there stoic—the hero once again.

All the while, gunshots kept sounding in the distance. Shouting. But no more explosions, thank God.

So Dahlia focused on her sister. She stepped forward, close enough they were eye to eye. Dahlia reached out and touched her sister's cheek. "*I'm* choosing you, Rose. And life. For you."

Rose inhaled shakily, but she neither mounted an argument nor looked particularly happy.

"What do we do now?" Dahlia asked of the Hudson siblings.

"Jack's got a whole team," Anna said. "Deputies from a couple counties, some Feds, coming in from the north. Took us some time last night to track you down, but not too long. We've got an escape route to the south so we don't get caught in the…" Anna trailed off, looking first at Rose, then at Dahlia and then never finished.

Dahlia looked at her sister. Rose was staring off in the distance, her expression mutinous. But then it slowly changed, curving into a smile. Dahlia didn't trust that smile. She turned and looked at where Rose was looking while Anna was busy convincing Grant not to run toward the thick of things.

When Dahlia saw what Rose was smiling at, her heart stopped. A man standing on a hill with the perfect view of the four of them.

Holding a gun.

"Get down!" Dahlia yelled, going on instinct and tackling her sister to the ground.

Chapter Twenty-Two

It happened quickly. Dahlia yelled and dove for Rose at the same time Grant had been turning, because something had rippled up his spine. An old wartime sixth sense he'd been trying to ignore.

But Dahlia had seen it first, reacted first, and because Grant had been ignoring his instincts, he grabbed Anna just a second too late.

The gunshot went off, and his sister jerked and let out a yelp.

Grant didn't freeze. He was too well trained to freeze, but as he jumped into action to make sure they were all behind the RV and out of the shooter's target, as he checked to make sure Anna was okay, the *inside* of him froze. Even as he ordered Dahlia to keep an eye on Rose, even as Anna slapped him away and told him she was fine, he was nothing but ice.

"I'm okay," Anna said, giving him another shove with her good arm. She swore a few times, decidedly *not* proving her point. She was *bleeding*. Shot. His baby sister.

But she looked him in the eye. Fully conscious and dead serious. "It isn't bad, Grant. Look." She held up her arm. The bullet had ripped through her sleeve, and the wound bled, but he'd seen worse.

On *soldiers*. Not his baby sister.

"Your arm is burned to hell from that explosion, so don't give me any grief," Anna said.

He sucked in a breath, forcing those old war memories and deaths into the compartment they belonged in. The pain in his arm and everywhere else just seemed like old, faded memories, but Anna's comment made him understand they were real.

This was real. He was injured. And far too much was at stake. Dahlia was struggling with Rose. Trying to talk sense into her.

He didn't bother to tell Dahlia she was wasting her breath. It didn't matter. Dahlia had to do it. He understood that.

And he had to deal with the shooter. The anxiety about shooting he'd had ever since he'd been home tried to crop up. Anna was an okay shot, but she had a *wound* on her shooting arm. His burns were on his left hand.

And there was no way out if they didn't take down that shooter. And since *the gunman* kept shooting, popping one bullet against the RV after the next, Grant couldn't wait him out, hope for reinforcements and let another person get hurt.

"Give me your gun," Grant said to Anna.

She handed it over without a word. He'd done his level best to keep his shooting issues to himself, so she still thought of him as someone who could do this.

Which meant he had to.

"Don't hurt yourself, but see what you can do to help," he muttered at Anna, jutting his chin toward Rose and Dahlia's physical tussle.

"I've got four brothers. Easy peasy." She grinned at him, but she was pale and in pain and…

This had to end.

Grant took a deep breath, felt the weight of the gun and tried to block out everything else. Rose's shouts, Dahlia and Anna's earnest instructions for her to be quiet. The sound of gunfire farther off where maybe his brothers were getting themselves into a situation that—

No. Nothing else. Just taking out the gunman currently threatening him. So Anna didn't get hurt any more, and Dahlia and Rose remained as unscathed as possible.

It was up to him.

But not…*only* up to him. What he'd lost or forgotten in the military, what Dahlia had reminded him of when he'd told her about his nightmare, being honest the way his military therapist had warned him he needed to be—he was part of a family. A team. A *cog* in something bigger than himself.

Everything didn't fall on his shoulders. If it did, he'd still be in one of those tents somewhere trying to come up with a way to sneak Rose out of here against her will. He had a family, backup.

So, he only needed to take care of this one thing. And he *was* good at shooting. He *was* good at accomplishing things when he didn't let everything else crowd around and feel like only his responsibility.

He moved around the RV, calculating angles and where the shooter might be. That old calmness settled over him. When the shooter popped up the next time to fire toward the RV, Grant shot first.

He watched the man drop the gun and then tumble down the hill. He'd hit exactly where he'd meant to.

He let out a shaky breath he hadn't realized he'd been holding. He'd done it. Just like old times.

When he looked back at the women, Anna was right behind him, Dahlia having Rose somewhat subdued.

"Nice shot," Anna offered. "But you're sweating a little," she added with a grin that only trembled a *little* at the edges.

"Better than bleeding," he muttered. "Come on. Let's get the hell out of here."

GRANT AND ANNA led them away from the camp to the south so they could avoid the standoff to the north. Dahlia had to pull her sister, but Rose had stopped mounting arguments.

Granted, it probably had something to do with Anna's threat if she said one more damn word about the truth and sacrificing, Anna was going to knock her teeth out.

Yes, that hadn't been the kindest way of doing things, but it had certainly worked.

They walked for what seemed like forever, Rose walking slower and slower, her head bowing lower and lower as if each step added a weight to her back. Dahlia kept her arm firmly in Rose's but knew she couldn't reach her sister.

No one spoke, but they finally reached a small area where there were a few people milling about. There was a police cruiser and a truck. Mary rushed forward when they came into view.

"Take Anna to the hospital," Grant instructed, grabbing Anna's arm and nudging her toward Mary.

"I'm *fine*," Anna insisted. "He's the one with burns on his arm."

Mary exchanged a look with Grant over Anna's head. "Everyone else is okay?"

"Everyone here," Grant said. "Give us a few."

Mary nodded, offered Dahlia a kind smile and then took Anna toward the truck while a uniformed deputy walked over to them.

"Hey, Grant," the deputy said to him. "Ma'am," she added, nodding toward Dahlia. But when she spoke, it was to Grant. "Jack's handling up north, but he wanted me to tell you it's pretty much done. Collecting weapons, getting everyone transported. Arguing with the Feds, of course. The women will be taken to a psych eval, the men taken into whatever agencies have room. They'll sort it all out from there."

Grant nodded, then gestured at Rose. "She'll need to go with them. This is Rose Easton. The missing person Hudson Sibling Solutions has been working on."

The deputy nodded. "I can transport her myself, but I'm going to have to cuff her."

Grant looked back at Dahlia apologetically, but she understood. Much as she hated it.

"It's okay."

The deputy stepped forward, handcuffs outstretched. Rose didn't look at her, didn't mount a fight, but once the handcuffs were in place, she looked at Dahlia.

"You'll never stop the truth, Dahlia," she said. "Never."

Dahlia wanted to collapse right there, but Grant slid his arm around her shoulders as she watched her sister be lead away. "I know it seems dire," he murmured gently. "But she'll get the help she needs, and she'll be...more the woman you remember."

More. Not totally. Because no matter what help would do, Rose had been fundamentally changed in there. Just as Dahlia had been fundamentally changed trying to find her sister.

When she turned into Grant's chest, she didn't cry. But she let his gentle hold keep her upright, keep her from thinking in worst-case scenarios. He'd become…her rock. When she'd never once had one of those.

It turned out having someone to lean on was really a good thing. Because she knew, since he'd told her about his nightmare, he'd lean on her when he needed to.

But this was over, more or less, and he wasn't hers to lean on anymore. She closed her eyes and held on then for the last few moments of whatever this had been.

THE NEXT FEW days passed in such a blur. Dahlia didn't remember half of it. There were questions and cleanup and the Hudsons being absolute godsends.

They'd told her about cult detox programs, scholarships to pay for it. They'd driven her everywhere, taken care of everything and never once made her feel like even a second of a burden.

She supposed it was because they'd been raised with an understanding of cults. They'd never found their missing people, but they found answers for others and had learned how to tie up all those loose ends.

Rose was still antagonistic toward Dahlia, but she was settled in a facility not far outside of Sunrise. Dahlia knew that she couldn't keep sponging off the Hudsons, but the thought of going home, of being so far from Rose, and the people who'd become her friends…

It was too much. She didn't *want* to go home. She wanted to stay put.

She just didn't know how on earth she was going to make that happen.

Opportunity came from a surprising place. Dahlia was driving her car down Main after a visit with Rose when she saw Freya on the sidewalk frantically waving at her. Dahlia pulled her car to a stop and rolled down her passenger window as Freya jogged over.

"Freya. Hi. Is everything okay?"

"Hi." Freya smiled. "Sorry to flag you down, but I wasn't sure how to get in touch in a way that I didn't have to—well, anyway." She looked up and around the street, then leaned farther into Dahlia's passenger window. "I'm leaving town."

"Oh. Well." Dahlia didn't really know what to do with this information. "I hope for good reasons?"

"Yes! I got this job at a museum in Denver, and it's a great opportunity, and I've never been anywhere and—well, *anyway*," she said again. "My job is up for grabs. It doesn't pay much, but you seemed so taken with the library I thought I'd let you know. If you're interested, I can put in a good word for you with the library association who decides on hiring. I mean, they'd need a résumé and references and all that." Freya waved it away like it was nothing.

And it was…nothing. Dahlia knew she was qualified for a small-town library position. And it would…give her the means to stay close to Rose while she completed the detox program.

And Grant.

In the days since everything had gone down, he was always there. Making sure she ate, helping her with logistics for Rose's care and dealing with all the legalities for both of them. Bandaged up from wounds he'd gotten helping *her*. Helping *Rose*.

But he'd also been…careful. And brought up her leaving often. Not because he wanted her to go, she didn't think, more like he was preparing for the eventuality.

But this was an opportunity not to have that eventuality. She smiled at Freya. "I would love if you'd put in a good word for me."

"Here." Freya handed a little card across the way. "My email and cell. Send me all your stuff. I'll get it sorted."

Dahlia looked at the card, then up at Freya. "Can I ask… why?"

Freya grinned at her. "You said the exact right thing about the library that day, and I wouldn't want to give the job to someone who didn't understand. Besides, I've been making gooey eyes at Grant almost our whole lives and I've never once seen him look at *anyone* the way he looks at you."

Dahlia felt herself blushing. "Well…"

"Just send it ASAP. You'll be a shoo-in." She stepped back from the car and offered Dahlia a little wave.

On a deep breath, Dahlia pulled away from the curb and drove to the Hudson Ranch. When she pulled up to the house, Grant was waiting for her like he always was.

Willie yipped happily and sat next to her car, tail wagging wildly while she got out. She petted him, murmuring happy greetings to him before moving on to Grant.

"You look happy," he greeted. "It went well?"

"Not really," Dahlia replied, taking the seat next to him on the porch swing. He'd made this a kind of…routine. She would get back from a visit with Rose and he and Willie would be waiting. She could talk or just sit.

He really was such a *good* man. And no matter how she told herself, or maybe it was her mother's voice in her head, that she shouldn't make decisions based on any one person... he'd saved her. And Rose. He *cared.*

He was a good man, and she was in love with him. She didn't want to go back to Minnesota, where her life had been gray and boring. She wanted to stay *here.* With Grant.

She didn't want life to be quite as exciting as it had been the past few weeks, but she wanted a life with people who made her feel like the best version of herself.

"There was no change," Dahlia said, trying to accept the bolt of pain and believe it would ease. "She still hates me and went on about truth and sacrifices."

Grant wound his arm around her shoulder. "No matter what she says, she doesn't hate you."

She didn't reply that her sister wanting her dead for any kind of truth wasn't *love*, but she understood what he meant. Rose had been psychologically traumatized and needed time. She needed healing.

She'd give Rose time and herself a life.

"I can't keep staying here, Grant. It isn't right to use your family this way." She lifted her head from his shoulder. "And don't argue with me. It is *using.*"

He gave her a tight smile. "All right." He studied her face, and none of that tenseness left his expression. "But whenever you come to visit Rose, you have a place to stay. With friends." He gave her shoulder a squeeze.

And Dahlia realized she'd explained it all wrong, so she laughed.

Which caused him to frown.

"Grant, I can't leave her here." She took a deep breath

and used all that bravery she'd found over the past fourteen months. She reached out and touched his cheek. "And I don't *want* to leave you."

He blew out a shaky breath, leaning his forehead to hers. "Thank *God*," he said, making her laugh. He wanted her here. Thank God, indeed.

"Freya is moving to Denver and told me she'd help get me the librarian job."

Grant pulled back a little in surprise. "Freya? Librarian job…here?"

Dahlia nodded. "She said I'd be a shoo-in. It would be a job, so I'd have income. I could find a place of my own in Sunrise. Be close enough to visit Rose and—well, to have a life. Before Rose disappeared, I wasn't really living. I was just existing. Then Rose disappeared and I was only surviving. Now I want a *life*. Here. With friends and Rose and… you."

"Good. Because that's what I want too."

She leaned forward and pressed her mouth to his, not letting herself be afraid or guilty for reveling in the *good* for once.

"I love you, Dahlia," he murmured against her mouth.

It was her turn to let out a shaky "Thank God." She looked into those steady brown eyes and smiled. "I love you too."

So, they sat on the porch talking about the future, the sound of Willie's tail thumping a happy soundtrack to the beginning of a new life.

For both of them.

* * * * *

UNSOLVED
BAYOU MURDER

CARLA CASSIDY

Chapter One

Peyton LaCroix tapped her pencil on her desk and stared outside her office window. From this vantage point she could see up and down the main street of Black Bayou. The little town looked tired, with storefronts that were weathered and old. Heat shimmered up from the sidewalks, not uncommon for mid-July in Louisiana.

Above the buildings and in the distance, tall, bald cypress trees rose up and dripped with Spanish moss. Along with the cypress trees there were also water tupelos and black gum trees. They were a constant reminder of the swamp that half surrounded the small town.

The swamp and the people who lived there had always fascinated Peyton. The dark, murky waters with all the strange vegetation held both a sense of mystery and a faint hint of danger.

She'd found the people who came from the swamp to be proud and passionate, hardworking and generally law-abiding. Except for one. Her pencil lead suddenly snapped.

Her office door flew open and Kylie Bradford entered. "Hey, boss," she said and flopped down in the chair opposite Peyton's desk. "I'm bored."

"That makes two of us," Peyton admitted.

"I'm thinking about going out and committing a crime just so you can defend me."

Peyton laughed. "I'm not *that* bored. However, you would make a good defendant…nothing bad in your background and with your halo of blond hair, blue eyes and angelic features you could definitely charm a jury."

"That's good to know for future purposes," Kylie replied with a grin. "I really came in here to see if you wanted a sandwich or something else to eat. I'm going to run down to Big Larry's for my lunch."

Big Larry's was a sandwich and burger joint a block away from Peyton's office. "I'm really not in the mood for a sandwich, but I would eat a side of his cold pasta salad."

"Then pasta salad it is," Kylie said and stood. Peyton grabbed her purse from under the desk, but Kylie waved her away. "Lunch is on me today. I'll be back in fifteen or twenty minutes."

"Take your time. It's too hot out there to rush," Peyton replied.

When Peyton had opened her law office here in Black Bayou, she'd advertised for an assistant and the twenty-five-year-old, bright and energetic Kylie had answered the ad. She'd hired Kylie and since that time the two had become great friends.

With Kylie gone, Peyton leaned back in her chair and closed her eyes. For the past fifteen years she'd been solely focused on her career as a defense attorney. She had graduated law school early and then had been lucky enough to get a job at a highly respected, busy law firm in Shreveport.

During her last three years there she had worked on several high-profile cases that she'd won.

However, a year ago she'd realized she was beyond exhausted by the long hours and frantic pace her work entailed. She had no life outside of work so she'd made the decision that it was time to come home. She had moved back to Black Bayou and bought a small home and the building where she now had her office.

Her home was a cute two-bedroom that was perfect for just her, but her office building needed tons of work to replace rotting boards and repaint the entire building on the outside. The amount of work needed was the reason she'd gotten a good deal on it. Unfortunately, she hadn't yet pulled together all the energy or the funds to start any of the renovations.

She had a healthy retirement fund but so far hadn't been willing to tap into it for the repairs. She'd much rather make the money with her practice, but things had been slow.

At thirty-three years old she was now half-broke, but glad to have a slower pace. She was also ready to start building a personal life for herself. That started tonight. She had another date with Sam Landry, a respected banker she'd seen several times since returning to Black Bayou.

Kylie returned with lunch, and the afternoon hours crept by. The last case Peyton had worked had wrapped up the week before. A teenage boy from the swamp had been caught spray-painting the side of a building owned by a prominent family, and that family wanted the book thrown at the boy. The district attorney had overcharged the kid, and his distraught parents had come to Peyton for help.

At the bench trial, Peyton had argued passionately for a

reduction of charges. She made a case for probation and community service and thankfully, the judge had agreed with her.

His parents had been thrilled, but Peyton also knew they were not a moneyed family so she'd cut her fees in half, and Kylie had set up a payment plan for them.

It was just after three when Kylie came back through her office door. She shut the door behind her. "There is a totally hot guy out there in the waiting room. I've never seen him before and he wouldn't give me his name but he insists he wants to see you."

"Then by all means send him in," Peyton replied. She didn't care how *hot* the guy was, she was just hoping he needed counsel. She could definitely use the work.

Kylie left the room and a moment later *he* stepped over the door's threshold. A loud roar resounded in Peyton's head as she stared at the man who had been her first love…and her first betrayal.

Fifteen years had passed since she'd last seen Beau Boudreau, a man spawned by the swamp…and perhaps the very devil himself. He'd been twenty-one years old the last time she'd seen him. At that time he'd been darkly handsome with a hint of something wild and magnetic.

The years hadn't changed that. If anything, age had chiseled his features, removing anything boyish that had once clung to him. His shoulders were still broad and his hips were slim. His body exuded a sinewy strength. His long black hair was now cut short, and there was something hard and bitter in the depths of his eyes.

He now gazed at her with dark, hooded eyes as he appeared to take in each and every one of her features.

Her pulse immediately quickened as a flash of memories

flooded her brain, hot and painful memories she'd spent the past fifteen years trying to forget. The flicker of a kerosene lantern...the pain and then the pleasure of Beau. Finally, the utter heartbreak that had left her scarred forever.

"I didn't know you were out." She finally found her voice.

He walked over to the chair before her desk and sat. He exuded a tightly controlled energy that was both compelling and more than a little bit off-putting. "I got out this morning and got to Black Bayou about an hour ago."

"Why are you here, Beau?" She was grateful her voice was cool and calm, not reflecting the hundreds of emotions that roared through her.

His lips curved into a sardonic grin as his heated gaze swept over her. "I know how the last fifteen years have treated me. I was curious to see how they'd treated you and I must say, *ma chérie*, they have treated you very well. You are more beautiful than I thought you would be, even more beautiful than I dreamed about. Did you ever think of me while I was away?"

"No...never," she snapped quickly. His wicked grin let her know he didn't believe her. "What are you really doing here? What do you want, Beau?"

The smile disappeared and once again there was a flash of pain...of something bitter in the depths of his eyes. The emotions were only there a moment and then disappeared as his eyes went as dark and enigmatic as the swamp waters. "I want you to help me reinvestigate the murder that sent me away."

She stared at him in stunned surprise. "Beau, you were convicted and you've now served your sentence. Why stir it all up again?" The last thing she wanted was to go back to that place and time when he'd ripped the very heart…the very soul, out of her.

He leaned forward, his gaze so dark, so intense, it threatened to swallow her up whole. "I was innocent when I was convicted, and I'm innocent as I sit here today. We need to find something that will overturn my conviction, something that will prove my innocence to everyone."

He sat back in the chair. "I need you, Peyton. I don't have much money, but looking at the outside of this building I thought maybe we could barter. I'll do the work on your office in exchange for you helping me to investigate the crime that wrongly put me in prison."

"Beau, this whole thing is absurd," she said.

"It's not absurd. It's a matter of my honor…my reputation. This is about my life, Peyton." The words exploded out of him with a passionate force. He drew in several deep breaths before continuing. "I need this, Peyton. I need you."

"And I need some time to think about all this, Beau," she finally said.

"How much time?"

"I'll let you know my decision sometime tomorrow afternoon."

He stood. "This is important, Peyton. Fifteen years ago a murderer got away with his crime, and that murderer is probably still walking the streets of Black Bayou."

He didn't wait for her reply. He turned and left the office, taking most of the energy in the room with him. Peyton released a shuddery sigh, still shocked by what had just happened.

At that moment Kylie came back into her office and sank

down in the chair Beau had just vacated. "So who was that hunky guy?"

"Beau Boudreau."

Kylie frowned. "Why does that name sound so familiar to me?"

"Fifteen years ago he was charged and convicted in the murder of Lacy Dupree, a young woman who was working as a sex worker out of the motel. Apparently, he just got out of prison earlier today." Once again, a rush of emotions tried to gut Peyton.

"Oh yeah, I remember my mom telling me about it when she was warning me about men. So what does he want from you?"

"He wants me to help him reinvestigate the original crime in order to prove his innocence."

"Hmm... I smell money coming in," Kylie said.

"Well, don't. He wants to barter with me. For my help, he'll do the renovations on this building."

"Is he capable of doing that kind of work?" Kylie asked curiously.

Peyton nodded. "Before his conviction, he and Jack Fontenot were partners in creating a construction company. Beau definitely knows his way around all areas of carpentry." It felt odd, talking about Beau when his name hadn't left her lips for so many years.

"I think I'm going to close up shop early today," she said.

"That's right. You have a hot dinner date to get ready for," Kylie replied.

Peyton laughed. "I'm not sure how hot it's going to be, but I'm definitely ready to call it a day, so you're free to leave as well."

Kylie sprang up from her chair. "Then I'm getting out of here before you change your mind."

Minutes later Kylie was gone, the office door locked, but Peyton remained in her chair as thoughts of Beau swirled around her head.

There had been a time when she'd thought Beau was her future, when she had believed they would be together forever. Her love for him had been fever pitched and all-consuming until the night he'd been arrested for murder.

On that night, after hearing all the ugly details of the crime, her love for him had turned to hatred. She'd recognized him then as not only a heartbreaker, but also the thief of her innocence and the stealer of her dreams.

With his sinful dark eyes and whispered words of love, he'd fooled her completely. She now realized she'd never really recovered from the betrayal.

She finally got up from her chair, grabbed her purse and headed out the front door. She gulped in the hot, sultry air and realized she hadn't drawn a normal breath since Beau had stepped into her office.

She'd told him she'd give him an answer tomorrow, but right now in this moment she didn't know what her answer would be. Could she really go back in time and work with him without losing her very soul?

It would certainly be difficult, especially given the fact that for the past fifteen years in the murder of Lacy Dupree, she'd believed he was guilty as sin.

BEAU RAN THROUGH the swamp, the humid, junglelike air clinging to him like a second skin. *Freedom.* It sang through his veins as the familiar scents of home filled his nose.

Despite the many years away, his feet remembered exactly where to step and when to jump to avoid the alligator-infested water. He'd spent the past fifteen years dreaming of being back here…back home.

He ducked under the Spanish moss that hung from the trees. Insects clicked and whirred, and animals scurried through the thick underbrush as if to protest his presence.

The swamp was in his blood, as was the woman he'd just left. Peyton. All his muscles tightened just thinking about her. And he'd had years to think about her, to remember the scent and taste of her skin, the slide of her nakedness against his and the sweet rapture of making love to her.

She'd been a sweet innocent, something clean and good in his miserable, ugly life. He'd met her when she'd been ten and he'd been thirteen. She'd been sitting on a fallen log deep in the swamp and she was crying.

She'd told him she had run away from home because her parents didn't care about her. All they cared about was the fancy parties they attended. Her plan had been to live in the swamp, but darkness had begun to fall and she was afraid and hopelessly lost.

They had talked for about fifteen minutes and then he had taken her by the hand, led her out of the swamp and walked her home. That had been the beginning of their friendship, a friendship that had blossomed into something deeper… something much hotter as they'd grown up.

For a little over four months they'd been lovers, and memories of those moments when he'd held her in his arms, when his mouth had plied hers with fiery intent, were what had gotten him through the past fifteen years of prison hell.

However, that had been a long time ago and he had no

idea what kind of woman she'd become. The only things he knew about her were that she hadn't married and she'd become a criminal defense attorney. He'd learned those things from the one woman who had believed in his innocence, a person who had written to him regularly while he'd been in the slammer.

Marie Boujoulais had escaped the swamp years ago when she'd opened up the Black Bayou Café. Beau's mother had abandoned him when he'd been five years old, leaving Beau to be raised by his cruel alcoholic father. When Beau was ten, Marie had caught him sneaking into her kitchen to steal food.

Rather than shooing him away, she'd sat him at a table and fed him, forming a bond that had lasted through the years. She was the mother he'd never had, the woman who had civilized the little swamp rat he was quickly becoming without any adult guidance.

He'd go see Marie later this evening. What he wanted now was to be home in the three-room shanty where he'd been living with his father before his life had been ripped away from him.

As he got closer, he quickened his pace. Then he saw it… home. The shanty, which was on poles to elevate it over the dark swamp water, was more weatherworn than it had been when he'd left. His footsteps clattered on the wooden bridge that led to the front door.

"Dad!" he yelled as he walked in. The entire place resonated with a yawning emptiness. Dust covered the tabletops and the top of the small potbellied stove that was used for both heating and cooking. It appeared that nobody had been inside the place for years.

He opened the door of his father's bedroom, half expecting his dad to be passed out among the filthy sheets. But nobody was inside the room.

He then went across the plank floor and opened his bedroom door. The room had been ransacked. Clothes were tossed out of the dresser drawers and the small closet. The bedding had been ripped off and now had a home on the floor.

There was no way he believed this was the work of a thief. He was sure his father was the culprit. If he was to guess, the day his father realized Beau wasn't coming home anytime soon, he went through the room looking for any money or valuables he could find to use to buy him more of the cheap gin he loved.

Thankfully, Beau's tool belt and tools were still in the bottom of his closet. For whatever reason, his father had left those alone.

Beau sank down on the edge of the bed. He didn't care about the state of the room. It could be fixed with just a little bit of work. Despite the mess, this room held most of his memories of Peyton.

For just a moment he allowed those memories free rein. He saw her beautiful features in the flicker from a lantern on his nightstand, felt the heat of her body as their naked limbs tangled together. He closed his eyes. If he breathed just right, he could almost smell the lingering scent of her, one of mysterious flowers with a hint of dark spices and a heady dose of woman.

"Beau?"

The deep voice snapped Beau's eyes open and he got up and left the bedroom. "Hey, man." Jack Fontenot grinned at him and pulled him into a bear hug. "I heard there had been a sighting of you in town, so I took a chance that I'd find you here," he said as the hug ended.

Jack had been a big man with a barrel chest when Beau had been locked up. None of that had changed in the years that had passed. He was clad in a pair of black slacks and a short-sleeved button-up blue shirt that emphasized the bright blue of his eyes. Despite Jack's coming from an affluent family in town, the two had been best friends since the time they were thirteen.

Jack had been fascinated by all things swamp and had spent most of his teenage years hanging out at Beau's place, despite his parents' outrage.

Beau now motioned his friend to a seat on the sofa and then Beau sat in the chair facing him. "I got in earlier today. I thought my father might be here, but he isn't."

Jack looked at him somberly. "Nobody told you?"

"Told me what?" Beau asked.

"He's dead, Beau. He died about three months ago. One of his drinking buddies found him dead in the swamp."

Beau wanted to grieve, but it was difficult to grieve for a man who had either beaten him hundreds of times a week or disappeared for long periods. Still, a hint of grief swept through him...the grief for the father he had never had.

"But you look good and fit," Jack said. "I was afraid that you might come back with a big gut after all the carbs they served you."

"I did a lot of exercising in my cell and in the prison's gym whenever I was allowed. How's the business going?" Fifteen years ago, before he went to prison, he and Jack had started their own construction company. At the time Beau went away, they hadn't filed the actual paperwork to make the company official, but they had been working together for about six months. The company had been Beau's dream of making something of himself.

"Terrific. I now have eight men working for me."

"That's good news. I'll be ready to jump back in within a month or so." Surely, a month would give him and Peyton plenty of time to clear his name. "Maybe we could get together sometime next week and you can show me the books."

Beau certainly didn't expect Jack to share the profits with him when he'd been away, but there should be some money for him as a co-owner of the company. Beau just wanted what was fair.

"Sure, we'll talk business next week," Jack replied. "And speaking of business, I need to get back to it. I just wanted to stop in and welcome you home." The two men stood.

"It's damn good to be home," Beau replied. He walked over to the small desk in the room and found a notepad and a pen. "Why don't you give me your cell phone number. I intend to buy a phone sometime tomorrow, but this way once I have a phone, I can put your number into it."

Jack rattled off his number and Beau wrote it down. Minutes later Beau was once again alone. He sank back down in the chair with the pad and pen still in hand.

There were so many things he needed to do in order to reclaim his life. He'd walked out of prison with only several thousand dollars to his name. He'd earned the money by working in the prison laundry room. With that money he needed to buy a cell phone, groceries and new clothing, among other things. He made himself a list of what he needed to take care of and then stood.

It was already getting late in the day and so he'd take care of most of those things tomorrow. But now he was hungry and there was nothing here to eat. He'd go to the café tonight and see Marie.

By the time he left the cabin, twilight had begun to fall and the moon was a half sliver just peeking over the horizon. Fish slapped in the water at the same time the frogs began to croak their deep-throated rhythm. These were the lullabies of the swamp, the lullabies Beau had missed in the concrete cell that had been his home for the past fifteen years.

It took him only ten minutes after he left the swamp to walk to the café. Instead of going through the front door, he went around back and through the alley until he reached the back door of the establishment.

He wasn't ready to face many people right now. In truth, he had no idea how he would be received as a murderer come home. He'd served his time—no, he'd served *somebody else's time*—but he didn't think that would matter with most people. Certainly, most everyone in town hadn't had a problem believing he'd committed a crime of passion and had strangled a woman in the act of erotic asphyxiation.

After all, he was nothing more than an uneducated, uncivilized swamp rat, abandoned by his own mother and raised by a gin-soaked father.

When he reached the back door, he found two young men standing in the alley. They both wore hairnets and they were smoking cigarettes. "I need to talk to Marie," Beau said. "Can one of you go get her for me?"

"Sure," one of them replied. They both dropped their cigarette butts on the ground and went inside.

"This better be good." Marie's French-accented Creole voice rose above the kitchen clatter.

He stepped into the doorway. Marie's dark eyes widened as if she saw a ghost, then she flew toward him and pulled him tight against her ample bosom.

She finally released him and swiped tears from her eyes. "Beau, I wondered if I would stay alive long enough to see you again."

Beau laughed. "Ah, Marie, you are far too wicked for death to come looking for you."

There was no question that she'd aged. Her black hair was now nearly white and her face sported more wrinkles, but her eyes remained the same. The dark depths held a lifetime of misery, a fierce pride and an ancient wisdom.

She laughed and then quickly sobered. "You look thin. Sit." She pointed to a small wooden table shoved into a corner, out of the way of the kitchen staff. "I know you haven't had a good meal since the last time you ate here."

"You've got that right," he said as he sank down at the table.

She shooed several of the line cooks away from the stove and then grabbed a bowl. She dipped him up a liberal serving of her jambalaya and set it in front of him.

She then returned to another stovetop, grabbed a plate and got him a serving of greens and a big hunk of golden cornbread. She placed that plate before him and then sat across from him.

"I know my father is dead," he said.

"Ah, Beau, I didn't have the heart to tell you in a letter. How did you hear?"

"Jack stopped by my place earlier. He told me."

"I'm so sorry for your loss."

He grinned at her. "We both know his death is no loss to me personally. I grieved for him years ago."

She reached out and patted the back of his hand. "God rest his soul. He was certainly a troubled man." She sat back in her chair. "What are your plans now that you're home?" she asked.

"My main goal is to prove my innocence and find out who really killed Lacy."

Marie stared at him for a long moment. "Maybe it's best to just let the dead stay dead. Maybe it would be better for you to look forward instead of back."

"I can't do that, Marie. I want my good name back." He wanted everyone in town to know that he'd been an innocent man convicted of a crime he hadn't committed.

"You'll be stirring up the devil's dust," Marie said, her dark eyes filled with concern.

"I'll dance with the devil himself to find out who really killed Lacy and framed me for the crime," he replied firmly. "This is something I need to do."

He wanted Peyton to know that he hadn't cheated on her. He needed her to know that he was an innocent man. She'd been a fire in his soul, a lust in his veins.

Each night when he'd been in his bunk alone, it had been thoughts and dreams of their passionate lovemaking and their love for each other that had helped him keep his sanity.

Peyton might not know it yet, but he intended to have her in his bed once again.

Chapter Two

"Surely, you aren't really considering helping that murderer."
Jackson Fortier stared at Peyton, obviously appalled by what
she'd just told him about Beau's visit earlier in the day.

Jackson had been waiting for her on her front porch when
she'd come home from her dinner date with Sam. It wasn't
unusual for her best friend to pop in at the end of a day.

She and Jackson had bonded together as children at the
many parties their parents attended. It was a friendship that
had stood the test of time. It had been Jackson's arms that had
held her years ago as she'd wept about Beau. He had warned
her about getting involved with Beau in the first place.

Jackson's last name held a lot of power. Nothing really got
done in Black Bayou unless the Fortier family approved. He
was a trust-fund baby who now worked as a real estate de-
veloper. Jackson was exceedingly handsome and could be
charming to a fault, but there was no hint of that charm on
his features at the moment.

He sat across from where Peyton sat on the sofa. He
leaned forward, his dark eyes snapping with a simmering
fury. "That man has some nerve coming to you for anything.
Have you forgotten that he stole all your innocence, all the

good you had inside you, and then he trashed it all? He was swamp scum then and now he's a swamp scum ex-con. He's the last man on earth you should get tangled up with again. So please tell me you told him to go to hell."

He leaned back in the chair as Peyton released a deep sigh. "No, I didn't tell him to go to hell."

"So you told him to get the hell out of your office?" Jackson asked.

"Not exactly," she replied. "I told him I'd think about it."

Jackson released a string of curses the likes of which Peyton had never heard from him before. "I can't believe you would even be thinking about helping him. He nearly destroyed you the last time you had any interaction with him."

"If I do decide to help him, it will be strictly business between us."

"Do you really believe you can dance with the devil and not pay a price?" Jackson shook his head.

"He's not the devil," Peyton protested faintly.

"Maybe not, maybe so. What I do know is that man wrapped his necklace around Lacy Dupree's neck and then squeezed the very life out of her."

"He says he's innocent and the killer is still probably out there walking the streets of Black Bayou," she said.

"I've never heard of an ex-con who didn't proclaim his own innocence," he replied with a snort of derision.

Peyton released another deep sigh. "It's getting late, Jackson, and I'm exhausted."

"Of course." He stood and she got up as well. She walked him to the door, where he turned around and gazed at her. "You know I positively adore you, Peyton, and I've always only wanted the very best for you."

"I know that," she replied.

"The best thing you can do for yourself is run as fast and as far as you can away from Beau." He kissed her on the forehead. "Good night, Peyton."

"'Night, Jackson."

Minutes later Peyton was in bed, her mind swirling with everything Jackson had said to her. She knew her friend was right, that she should run as fast and as far as she could from Beau.

But what if he really was an innocent man? A little voice whispered in the back of her head. This was the reason she'd decided to become a criminal defense attorney in the first place…to defend the innocent. So was Beau really an innocent man or was he the monster who had strangled a woman to death?

She finally fell asleep…and into dreams of Beau. In her dream she was in his arms. His bold features were visible in the flicker of a kerosene lantern, and his dark eyes glittered with the hunger of a wild animal.

His hands caressed her nakedness as his mouth plundered hers. Hot…she was on fire and lost in all things Beau. In that moment he owned her—heart, body and soul.

As he entered her, he wrapped his rope necklace with the gold cross around her neck. He pumped into her and as he did, he tightened the necklace around her throat. Faster and faster, he moved against her, into her, and the necklace tightened even more.

"Beau, you're…you're choking me," she finally said with alarm. "Stop…" She reached up to grab the necklace but it was too tight for her to even get her fingers beneath it.

Still, it not only cut into her neck, but also stole her ability to draw a breath. She struggled against him, trying to get free, but he held her tightly in place as he pulled the rope necklace tighter and tighter still.

She couldn't breathe. Her head spun as a blinding dizziness overtook her. She was dying…being strangled to death by the man she loved.

She jerked awake, gasping for air and sobbing. Her heart beat a thousand miles a minute, resounding in her ears like the frantic beat of a Mardi Gras parade drummer gone wild.

She threw off the covers on her bed and got up, the love and then the abject terror of the dream still rocking through her. She went into the adjoining bathroom and flipped on the light, hoping the illumination would chase away the utter darkness of the nightmare.

Half expecting to see a rope imprint around her neck, she stared into the mirror over the sink. Of course, there were no marks on her throat. With a shuddery breath she began to sluice cold water over her face.

Finally, she managed to calm herself down. She went back into her bedroom and sat on the edge of the bed. Had the nightmare been some sort of a warning from the universe? What was she going to tell Beau when he came back in to talk to her? She honestly didn't know.

She finally fell back to sleep, and the next time she awakened it was time to get up and start her day. After showering she stood in front of her closet and pulled out a pair of black slacks and a royal blue blouse that she often got compliments on when she wore it because it perfectly matched her eyes.

At eight forty-five she left her house to drive the five blocks to her office. As she drove, she tried not to think about Beau. She still hadn't made a decision about whether she intended to help him out or not.

With Jackson's warnings and the remnants of the disturbing nightmare still ringing in her head, it was difficult for her to gain any clarity about the matter.

Beau had always been a dark whisper against her skin, a burning flame deep within her. She'd never been able to forget their summer of love…the hot sultry nights when they'd come together with a mindless, wild passion that to date she had never experienced with any other man.

She'd spent what felt like a lifetime hating him. She still hated him for betraying her love with Lacy Dupree. Whether he killed the woman or not, he'd been with her in the motel room where she lived and conducted her business. It had been so difficult to marry the details of the horrible murder to the man she loved.

By nine o'clock she was in her office chair and staring blankly at her computer screen. She started as Kylie opened her door and came in, carrying a coffee cup in hand.

"Morning, boss," she said as she set the coffee on the desk next to Peyton and then sank down in the chair facing the desk.

"Good morning, Kylie." Peyton picked up the cup and took a deep drink of the dark brew. "Mmm, thanks," she said as she returned the cup to her desk.

"Since we don't have anything on the agenda today, I figured I'd work on accounts receivable. We still have a few people who are not honoring the payment plans we set up for them."

"That sounds good to me," Peyton said. "I have some paperwork to do and…" She jumped at the sound of a loud bang outside the building. "What on earth?" She and Kylie both got up, and Kylie followed Peyton to the front door.

Peyton opened the door and there he was. Beau was clad in jeans and a white T-shirt that showcased his broad shoulders and big biceps. He held a hammer in his hand and as he turned to look at her, his sultry lips slid into a sinful smile.

"Beau, what are you doing?" she asked.

"I thought I'd get started on this place. My plan is to work out here in the mornings, giving you time to work on whatever you need to, and then we'll spend the afternoons working together on what we discussed yesterday," he said.

"I haven't even decided if I'm going to help you out or not," she replied.

He dropped the hammer and sauntered closer to her, invading her personal space with his intense masculinity. His warm body heat reached out to caress her. "Oh, you're going to help me," he said confidently, with a touch of amusement.

"And what makes you so sure of that?" She took a step back from him, irritated by his smooth smile. She hated him for the way he had branded her with his touch, spoiled her for any other man who might try to love her, and for leaving an indelible mark on her that she realized now no amount of time could have erased.

"Why am I sure? Because you're curious. Because you've spent many sleepless nights wondering if I was really guilty or not. I think you've spent many nights thinking about me and what we shared. I know I have."

"You're wrong. I never thought about you at all," she replied defiantly…angrily. "The minute I heard about the details of the crime I stopped thinking about you."

He laughed, the low, seductive tone making her heart beat

a little faster. Could he hear the frantic beat of her heart? Was he aware of how deeply she was affected just by talking to him?

"Ah, *chérie*, I've never known you to be a liar before, but I see the pulse at the base of your throat is throbbing. It tells me you aren't speaking the truth right now."

She fought the impulse to reach up and cover her throat. And that made her think about the nightmare she'd had the night before. "Okay, I'll help you."

He raised a dark brow. "You will?" For just a moment she saw a flash of vulnerability in his eyes, a vulnerability that held just a touch of hope. "Why have you decided to help me?"

"You're right, I am curious," she replied. "I'm curious to find out if you were really an innocent man or if you're the cheating, lying son of a bitch I've believed you to be all this time."

He smiled again. His gaze bore into hers and then slid downward, lingering pointedly on the thrust of her breasts before sweeping down the length of her and back up again. "Thank you, Peyton. I look forward to working closely with you."

His words, along with his gaze, held a blatant sexuality that swept a wild wave of heat through her. "I'll see you inside this afternoon," she said stiffly. She turned on her heels and hurried back into the building, half running over Kylie in the process.

She went into her office with Kylie hot on her heels. She sank down behind her desk and Kylie remained standing and looked at her expectantly. "Girl, you've got some explaining to do," Kylie said. "I thought I knew everything there was to know about you, but you missed the part about Beau."

Peyton released a deep sigh. "There isn't that much to tell. When I was eighteen and Beau was twenty-one years old we dated for about four months. Then he was arrested and that was the end of that."

Kylie raised a pale blond eyebrow. "I have a feeling there's way more to the story than that, but I'll get busy on those accounts now."

"Thank you, Kylie."

Alone in her office, Peyton leaned back in her chair and closed her eyes. There was no way to explain to Kylie the overwhelming and abiding love she'd once felt for Beau. There was no way to explain to anyone the white-hot desire, the utterly breathtaking passion of their lovemaking.

There were moments after his arrest that she didn't think she would survive her heartbreak…moments that she could scarcely draw a breath. And now she had invited him back into her life once again.

However, things would be completely different between them this time around. It would be a strictly professional relationship. There was no way she'd let him into her personal life ever again.

He was just a client, and he would never, ever be anything more to her again.

BEAU WORKED ON the front of the building, removing rotten boards until noon, and then he ran home to take a shower. It had felt good to be working again, to know he was going to transform Peyton's building from sad and weathered to something new and inviting.

It was why he'd decided to start the construction company with Jack in the first place. Beau had always enjoyed carpentry and he knew he was good at it and could make a good living at it.

He'd been pleased when he'd broached the idea of a company to Jack, and Jack had immediately gotten on board. Beau was no fool; he knew the Fontenot name would give the company a respectability, a legitimacy, that Beau would never be able to gain on his own.

Beau figured with his hard work and Jack's money and name, there was no way the business wouldn't be successful. From what Jack had told him in their brief conversation, the company had, indeed, become very successful.

However, the construction business wasn't what was on Beau's mind as he made his way back to Peyton's office. He'd been slightly surprised that she had agreed to help him. He knew she must have hated him when he'd been arrested and the sordid details of the crime had come out.

He'd made love to Peyton early in the evening and they had professed their love for each other. Then the next morning he'd been arrested for having kinky sex and killing a sex worker.

He'd never gotten a chance to plead his case with her; instead, he'd been handed over to an overworked public defender who hadn't stood a chance against the aggressive prosecuting attorney whom everyone knew was prejudiced against swamp people. That, coupled with the physical evidence, had put the nail in Beau's coffin.

There had always been a prejudice between the upper crust in the town and the people who lived in the swamp.

Swamp people were ignorant, gator-chasing lowlifes who'd steal you blind if you let them get too close.

And yet, they were good enough to scrub your toilets or sweep your floors or cook for your family. Beau had grown up with the taint of the swamp on him, making it easy for people to believe him guilty of the murder.

Even the woman he'd loved had believed him guilty, and that had been a stabbing pain in his soul that even now burned deep inside him. It had been a betrayal he'd never forgotten.

Peyton had known him. She'd known him better than any other human being on the face of the earth. He'd opened himself up to her...been vulnerable with her. Even though he'd known that her upper-crust family would never approve of him, she'd made him believe that their love was strong enough to see them through any obstacle.

Yet, when push came to shove, she'd been like all the others, assuming the worst of him before even giving him a chance to talk to her. And there was a small part inside him that still couldn't get over that particular betrayal.

Now he was depending on her help to clear his name. The irony of the situation wasn't lost on him. But as a criminal defense attorney, she was the best person for the job, and probably the only person who would even consider doing this for him.

He made one quick stop before heading back to Peyton's place. By that time, it was well after one. He finally reached her building and pulled open the front door. The reception-ist desk was staffed by the same young blonde who had let him in the day before.

She popped up from her desk with a smile. "We haven't

been officially introduced," she said. "I'm Kylie Bradford, Peyton's assistant, and I know you're Beau Boudreau."

"It's nice to meet you, Kylie," he replied.

"I'll tell her you're here." She walked to the door behind her desk and after giving it a quick knock, she opened the door and announced Beau's arrival, then turned around and once again smiled at Beau. "She's ready for you."

"Thanks." He walked past Kylie and into Peyton's office.

As he'd noticed the day before, the room smelled of her, a soft, feminine scent that instantly stirred his blood. He remembered that fragrance from the past…it smelled like sweet love and hot sex, like flowers and dark spices. For some reason it also prompted a touch of irritation in him because of the memories it stirred.

He tamped it down and smiled at her. "So where do we begin?"

"I've been trying to figure that out. I had Kylie send in a request for the official court files from the case. I should have them in hand in the next day or two. I also need to set up interviews with the Chief of Police who investigated the crime, and Charles Landry, who has since retired as prosecuting attorney."

As she talked, he couldn't help but notice how her blue blouse clung to the outline of her full breasts and matched the amazing color of her eyes.

His gaze took in the soft curve of her jaw and her sensual lips. Her dark, shiny hair was captured at the nape of her neck with a large gold barrette, and Beau's fingers itched to release the dark, silky tresses and allow them to spill through his fingertips.

His body responded, tightening against the crotch of his

jeans. He hated himself for wanting her again and he hated her for abandoning him in his greatest time of need.

"Is Thomas Gravois still the Chief of Police?" he asked, trying to focus on the matter at hand.

"He is… Why?"

"He and Charles Landry are two of the most prejudiced people around," he replied in disgust.

She held his gaze and for just a moment he saw a softness there. But it was there only a moment and then gone as she looked back at her computer screen.

"In any case, I need to speak to them, and these are things I need to do alone. In fact, I can investigate the elements of the crime on my own and without any need for you to be with me." She looked back at him again, and this time her eyes held a steely strength.

Beau laughed. "Ah, Peyton, there is no way I intend to take a backseat in my own life. I've spent the last fifteen years alone and unable to do anything to help myself. We work together on this, and I know where we can start right now."

"Where's that?"

"At the Black Bayou Motel, room seven."

She sucked in a quick breath. "There's no reason to go there. It's been fifteen years since that room was rented by Lacy Dupree. There have probably been a hundred people who have rented that room since then."

He laughed once again. "That fleabag place hasn't seen a hundred renters since it first opened its doors fifty years ago." He sobered. "We need to start at the beginning, and the beginning happened in that motel room."

"I'm sure that room is probably rented right now," she protested.

"It's not. I stopped by there and checked before I came here. Ed Johnson said he'd open up the room for us if we came by this afternoon."

"I just don't think that's necessary." Her reluctance was rife in her tone.

"But it is, Peyton," he said fervently. "I need to go back into that room and see if I can remember anything from that night that would prove I didn't kill Lacy. And I need you there with me so I can explain exactly what happened."

She searched his features as if seeking an out. But this was something he definitely wanted...*needed* to do with her and not all alone. Perhaps he was afraid that Lacy's spirit haunted the room—being Cajun, Beau had a healthy respect for spirits of all kinds.

"When do you want to do this?" she finally asked.

"Why not right now? I'm assuming you have nothing else on your calendar for today, so let's go." He stood. "We can get this step out of the way."

"Are you absolutely sure this is necessary?" Her eyes had darkened.

"Positive." He stepped around her desk and held his hand out to her. For a moment she looked at it like it was a snake that might bite her, but then she slid her hand into his and allowed him to pull her up from the chair.

Her hand was just as he remembered it, small and soft and a perfect fit in his grasp. He only got to enjoy it for a moment before she snatched it away from him. She bent down and grabbed her purse from beneath the chair and then stood back up. "I'm assuming I'm driving."

"Unless you want to walk," he replied. "My to-do list tomorrow includes getting a phone and finding a set of wheels." He'd intended to get a phone today, but he just hadn't taken the time to get it done.

Beau followed Peyton out of her office, where she told Kylie they'd be back later.

Together they walked out into the sultry heat of the afternoon. She led the way to a compact navy blue car and once she unlocked it, he slid into the passenger seat. Peyton got into the driver's seat and once again the scent of her swept over him.

He couldn't think about her and the surprising amount of desire she still evoked in him. He needed to be clearheaded to go back into the motel room where he supposedly had killed a woman. And it hadn't been just any woman; it had been one of his very best friends—although few had known that Lacy and Beau had a relationship of any kind.

The Black Bayou Motel was a dismal place. The low, flat-roofed building was weathered to a dull gray and reflected an air of hopelessness and despair. The people who stayed in the eight-unit motel were mostly drunks, drug addicts and prostitutes who rented the rooms out by the month.

Peyton parked in front of unit seven and Beau got out to walk to the office to get a key. He would never admit it to Peyton, but he was dreading going into that room, where he'd last seen Lacy alive and well. To know that she'd died such a horrible death mere minutes or hours after he'd left her there would forever haunt him.

He knew there were no clues to anything still inside the motel room, but he felt as if he needed to go in there to say a proper goodbye to another woman he had loved and lost, and he hadn't wanted to go in there alone.

Five minutes later he unlocked the door and the two of them walked inside. The room held a double bed covered in a nappy gold spread, a banged-up dresser and a small kitchenette. The air smelled musty and stale.

Beau stood in the middle of the room and closed his eyes for a moment. In his mind's eye he remembered the room the way it had looked when Lacy had lived in it.

She'd hung a variety of colorful scarves to hide the ugly gold curtains at the window, and her perfumes had littered the top of the dresser. Multicolored fairy lights had twinkled on the walls as she'd tried to make something beautiful in the room.

I'm sorry, Lacy, he thought. *I'm so sorry I wasn't here to protect you. If only I'd stayed longer with you that night, maybe then you wouldn't have been killed.*

"Beau?"

Peyton's voice ripped him back from the past.

His eyes snapped open. "Yeah," he replied.

She stood just inside the door and gazed at him curiously. "What are we doing here? Even if by some miracle you could find a piece of evidence to prove your innocence, it would do us no good because of a chain of custody issue."

"I knew we wouldn't find anything here," he replied.

She frowned. "Then why did you bring me here?"

"Ghosts," he said softly. "I needed to come here and I didn't want to come alone," he confessed. "I was afraid her ghost might be here to haunt me."

"There's no such thing as ghosts," Peyton replied, not unkindly.

"Maybe not in the ivory tower where you grew up, but we people from the swamps, we know there are ghosts and monsters and all kinds of darkness. In any case, I brought you here to tell you exactly what happened that night. I've waited fifteen years to tell you."

He couldn't keep away the edge of resentment that bit into his words. The early morning he'd been arrested, he'd been sure that she'd rush to the jail to speak to him, to profess her belief in him and remind him of her undying love for him. But she hadn't come then and she'd never come. And as much as he wanted her back in his bed, that resentment would always remain between them.

Chapter Three

Peyton waited for Beau to continue, even as all her defenses rose to the surface. She wanted to help him, if he truly was an innocent man, but did she really want to hear about his time here in this room with a prostitute? Still, a million times in her thoughts she'd wondered about the moments he'd spent with *her*.

Peyton had been a virgin when she'd slept with Beau for the first time. Maybe he'd needed somebody with more experience as a lover? Lacy would have definitely been a more experienced sexual partner than Peyton had been.

Maybe it was best she heard him out, no matter how painful it might be. She'd spent the past fifteen years wondering about that particular night. The truth was surely less painful than her imaginings.

"Lacy was a swamp kid like me," he said, leaning with his back against the wall next to the bed. "I was about seven and she was nine when we first met. Her dad and mine were drinking buddies and her mother had left them when she was seven. Even though she was a couple of years older than me, she always felt like my younger sister. I was her protector while we were growing up and being dragged along to boozing parties by our fathers."

"Why didn't I know anything about her?" Peyton asked. She'd thought she knew everything there was to know about Beau, and yet he'd never mentioned Lacy's name to her.

"Because Lacy wanted it that way." He raked a hand through his thick, shiny hair and released a deep sigh. "She made me promise that I wouldn't speak of her, that I would never tell anyone about our friendship. She knew that you were from an affluent family, and she also knew you had awakened big ambitions in me." He frowned and she saw a flash of pain in his eyes. He quickly broke eye contact with her.

"She thought she would somehow taint me, that people wouldn't take me seriously if they knew I was friends with a known prostitute."

He stood still for several long moments. However, even standing still he radiated an energy that seemed to pulse in the air around him.

He took several steps toward Peyton and his eyes blazed with a fire that nearly stole her breath away. He reached out and grabbed her hand, his grasp feeling fevered. She could also feel the furnace of his body heat and smell the scent of spicy cologne, the woodsy smell of mysterious swamp and utter maleness.

"Lacy and I were friends, Peyton. But we were never lovers." His hand tightened around hers and the flame in his eyes intensified. "Do you hear me? We were never, ever lovers. That part of me always belonged to you."

"Beau, let go of me," she said and tugged her hand from his.

He immediately stepped back from her. She hated how his nearness still made her half-breathless. He was the only man she'd ever had in her life who affected her on such a visceral, physical level. "So why were you here that night?" she asked, focusing on what was really important.

"Lacy called me and said she needed to borrow a couple hundred bucks from me. She'd never asked to borrow money from me before, so I knew something must be up. So I showed up here that night to bring her the money."

"Did she tell you what she needed it for?" Peyton asked.

He shook his head. "She didn't, but she did tell me she was expecting a big payday and then she intended to disappear from Black Bayou. She also said the money from me would get her out of town in case things went sideways."

"A big payday? Did she tell you the specifics of what that meant?"

"No, she refused to tell me, but I got the feeling she was going to try to blackmail somebody, and I think that somebody is the person who killed her."

"But what about your necklace? Beau, it was around her neck when she was found."

"Don't you remember, Peyton? I'd lost my necklace about a week before her murder. You have to remember that. I was so upset about losing it."

Peyton stared at him. Suddenly, a memory formed in her head, the memory of Beau stalking across the floor of his bedroom, upset about the gold cross that had been lost. The cross had been the first thing he'd bought for himself when he'd worked his first carpentry job. Somehow, the memory had been buried beneath all the heartbreak she'd suffered when he'd been arrested.

"I… I do remember," she now whispered.

"She was alive when I left her that night. Somebody must have found my necklace and used it to kill Lacy and frame me for the murder." The words bit out of him with a simmering rage. "Dammit, somebody stole not only Lacy's life, but also fifteen years of mine, and more than anything I want the bastard in jail." He drew in a deep breath and released it slowly. "Now, let's get the hell out of here."

Minutes later they were on their way back to her office. Beau was silent, but his silence felt charged. Meanwhile, Peyton's head reeled with all the information she'd just learned.

Had he really told her the truth about that night? About his relationship with Lacy? It appalled her that she now remembered him losing his necklace at least a week before it was found as a murder weapon.

She now cast him a surreptitious glance. He stared out the front car window as a muscle knotted and unknotted in his jaw. How difficult had it been for him to go back to that room? No matter what his true relationship had been with Lacy, that had been the place where a poor young woman had died a tragic death.

She pulled up in front of her office and the two of them got out. She'd told Kylie before they left that she could finish making calls on the accounts receivable and then she could take off for the day. She'd obviously finished up and left.

Beau followed Peyton into her office and they took their seats, she behind her desk and he in front of it. "So what happens next?" he asked.

His eyes lingered on her. Dark and enigmatic, there was something there that created a shiver that threatened to walk up her spine. It wasn't a shiver of apprehension; rather, it was of something dark and delicious.

She glanced at her computer screen and frowned. "In the morning I'll see if I can set up interviews with Thomas Gravois and Charles Landry and we'll go from there. I don't think there's anything else we can do today."

"We can have dinner together at the café," he said.

"Oh, I haven't been to the café in years," she replied. After Beau's arrest, she'd been unable to go into the place where she and Beau had often eaten together, a place where they had been so happy.

"Then I'm sure Marie would love to see you again. She always had a soft spot for you. Come with me, Peyton. I'm not asking for anything but that you share a meal with me." A lazy grin of amusement curved his sensual lips. "Or perhaps you're afraid."

"Don't be ridiculous," she scoffed. "Why would I be afraid?"

He leaned forward in his chair. His gaze bored into hers, then traveled down the length of her throat and lingered for a moment on the thrust of her breasts. He then met her gaze once again. "Maybe you're afraid you'll want me again."

A new irritation rose up inside her. "Don't be ridiculous. That's the very last thing I'm afraid of," she replied curtly. "But I see prison didn't knock any of your conceit out of you." He merely laughed, which angered her even more.

"So are you up to the challenge?" he asked, a twinkle in the depths of his dark eyes.

She grabbed her purse and stood. "I'm a criminal defense attorney, Beau. I'm always up for a challenge," she said. "Let's go eat."

She heard his low chuckle as he followed her out of the building. Damn the man for his ability to get under her skin. Damn him for making her remember that it had been a long time since she'd made love with a man.

Minutes later the two of them walked into the busy café. The scents were heady…of frying onions and andouille sausage, of shrimp and burgers and all kinds of vegetables. The café itself had the requisite counter across the front, booths against both walls and a row of tables down the middle.

The walls were a pleasant yellow with hand-painted murals, one of cypress trees laced with Spanish moss and another of the main street of Black Bayou.

She suddenly became aware of all the diners staring at Beau as a charged silence filled the air. As Beau took her by her arm and led her down the aisle toward an empty booth in the very back, several voices filled the air.

Murderer.

Swamp scum.

Go back to the swamp that spawned you.

To Beau's credit, he appeared to ignore the hateful words that followed them as they headed for the empty booth. The only way she knew it bothered him at all was in the subtle increased pressure of his hand on her arm.

They reached the booth and he slid in with his back against the wall while she sat on the opposite side, facing him. His handsome features were taut and the muscle in his jaw tense. She had the ridiculous desire to reach out and take one of his hands into hers. She didn't, instead saying softly, "I'm sorry, Beau."

"Apparently, this will be my new normal until we clear my name," he replied.

At that moment Marie came into the dining room and beelined for their booth. "Hey, Marie. You gonna let that swamp-sucking killer eat in here?" an older man Peyton didn't know asked.

"He did his time, Wally, and his money is as good as yours," she replied. "Why don't you fill your mouth with my good food instead of filling it with such hateful nonsense?" She held the man's gaze until he finally looked down at his plate.

She then continued to their booth and when she got next to Peyton, she pulled her up and into a big hug. Peyton hugged the plump woman back and fought against unexpected tears.

When Peyton had been a teenager and dating Beau, Marie had been the loving mother Peyton hadn't had at home. It had been Marie who had answered questions Peyton had about life and about love. It had been Marie who had given her the loving support that Peyton's parents should have given her.

She and Beau had spent many happy hours at a small table in Marie's kitchen. There had been warmth and laughter and love there.

Once Marie released her, Peyton slid back into her seat. "Ah, Peyton, you've grown up to become such a beautiful woman." Marie smiled warmly. "Of course, I always knew you would. Why have you not come in to see me since you've been back here?"

"I've just been so busy establishing my practice here," Peyton replied. It was a lie. Marie nodded, her eyes filled with a crafty knowing in their dark depths. In truth, this place had held far too many memories for Peyton.

"When I heard you were here, I just wanted to come out and see you," Marie said. "Now that you're here, don't be a stranger in the future." She gave Peyton's shoulder a loving squeeze, then with a warm smile at Beau, Marie turned and headed back toward her kitchen.

Moments later they had ordered and then a few minutes after that their drinks and food had been delivered. Peyton took a sip of her iced tea and then leaned back against the leather booth. She was still trying to process everything he had told her in the motel room.

"What?" he asked as her gaze lingered on him.

"I'm trying to figure out, after all this time, how we prove your innocence. The evidence is all gone. You have no idea who Lacy might have intended to blackmail."

He leaned forward, bringing with him that scent of his that threatened to muddy her senses. "It had to have been somebody prominent in the town, somebody who had money and standing. You know the girls who worked at the motel were this town's dirty little secret. I imagine lots of the married men visited those girls under the cover of night."

Peyton didn't want to believe that, but she suspected it was probably true. After Lacy's murder, most of the girls who had been working in the motel rooms had scattered to the wind, but over the years others had taken their places.

She took a bite of her salad and chewed thoughtfully. "Was Lacy friends with any of the other women? Did she ever mention having a best friend who she might have confided in?" she asked after swallowing.

"I think she was pretty friendly with Angel Marchant," Beau replied.

"Do you know if Angel was questioned at the time of the murder?" Angel had also been working and living in the motel when Lacy had been murdered.

"I don't have a clue," he replied.

"Do you know where Angel is now?"

"No, but if she's in the swamp, I can probably find her," he replied.

"We might need to talk to her. I'll know more after I speak to Chief Gravois some time tomorrow," she replied.

"We," he replied. "After *we* speak to him."

She nodded in agreement. For the next few minutes they ate in silence. Despite the fact that her head was filled with thoughts of what she needed to do and where they needed to go next, she was still acutely aware of Beau.

His energy radiated out to her. With each bite he took, his gaze lingered on her and had the effect of a physical touch. She had only had two other lovers since Beau and neither of them had made her feel as loved…as wanted as she'd once felt in Beau's arms. He'd taken her to sexual pleasures she'd never achieved with anyone else. She'd never felt that emotional connection, that depth of intimacy, with any other man since Beau.

However, none of those things mattered now. Remembering him losing his necklace before the murder had taken place had gone a long way toward her believing he was innocent. But she still wasn't sure she believed he hadn't been one of Lacy's lovers, and that alone would keep her from ever being in Beau's arms again.

By the time they left the café, twilight had fallen. "Do you want me to drop you off someplace?" she asked him once they were back in her car.

"You can just drive to your house and I'll leave from there," he replied.

She shot him a sharp glance. "How do you know where I live?"

He gave her that lazy grin that she found so damned attractive. "I make it my business to know the things that are important to me."

She drove to her house and pulled up in the driveway. They both got out of the car. "Nice place you have here," he said.

She looked at the light gray house with the darker gray shutters and deep maroon front door and then gazed back at him. "Thanks. I like it here. It suits me. So I guess I'll see you in the morning."

"I'll walk you to the door," he replied. She didn't want him to, but knew that a protest from her would only earn him mocking her.

As they walked to the front door, she pulled her house key from her purse. "I might be a little late in the morning," he said when they reached her door. "I need to buy a phone and see about getting a vehicle."

"Beau, you're not on any set timeline as far as I'm concerned." She unlocked her door and then turned back to face him. "We haven't really discussed you working on the building. Certainly, if you intend to follow through with it, then when it comes time to order any supplies, I'll pay for those. That's only fair."

He hesitated a moment, nodded and then took a step closer to her. He stood so close his scent surrounded her and infused her with its wicked wildness.

She stood still and he reached out and gently touched the strands of her hair that had escaped her barrette throughout the day. "I appreciate your help in this mess," he said softly.

Her heart began to beat a frantic rhythm. She knew she needed to turn around and escape into her house, yet she was frozen in place as his fingers slowly trailed down the side of her cheek and across the vulnerable hollow of her throat.

The touch of his fingers elicited a heat deep inside her. Oh, she remembered how easy it had always been to get lost in him, to forget everything but the fire of his touch.

As he leaned even closer to her, her brain finally worked enough so that she moved sideways and batted his hand away from her. He laughed.

"I'll see you tomorrow," she said firmly and opened her front door.

"Peyton."

She turned to look at him once again. His eyes glittered as they swept the length of her. His sensual lips curled into a confident smile. "Just so you know… I do intend to have you in my bed once again."

His words, spoken with such confidence, with such sensual appeal, completely irritated her.

"I'll help you clear your name, Beau…but I will never be in your bed again."

He laughed. "Never say never, *ma chérie*."

Whatever else he intended to say, she didn't stick around to hear him. She stalked into her house and slammed the door behind her.

She leaned against the door and tried to catch the breath she'd lost the moment he had touched her. She'd survived Beau once in her life and in some ways still suffered the consequences. She'd be a fool to allow him back into her life in any kind of a personal way…and she was definitely no fool.

WALKING BACK INTO the Black Bayou Police Department the next afternoon was one of the most difficult things Beau had ever done. The last time he had been here he'd been in handcuffs, confused by the serious charges against him and afraid for the first time in his adult life.

Now, despite the fact that he was free and Peyton was by his side, he still had the aftertaste of that residual fear in the back of his throat and it ticked him off.

Earlier that morning Peyton had set up this meeting with the chief of police, Thomas Gravois. Upon their arrival, the deputy at the front desk had ushered them down a long hallway and into a small conference room and then told them the chief would be with them shortly.

"Remember what I told you," Peyton now said softly to Beau. "I talk, you listen. Don't let him get under your skin. This is my playground, not yours."

"I can't wait to get you into my playground," he replied with a grin. It was much easier to flirt with her than acknowledge the racing emotions inside him.

"Beau, if you aren't going to take this all seriously, then why should I?" Her blue eyes pinned him in place.

He snapped the smile off his face. "Trust me. I'm taking this all very seriously." He'd barely got the words out of his mouth when Thomas Gravois walked into the room and sat at the table, across from Peyton and Beau.

The chief of police was a tall, lean man in good physical shape. He had to be in his midfifties by now. He sported a head full of graying dark hair and sharp blue eyes that radiated intelligence.

Beau knew the man had been dirt-poor before he married his wife, Yvette. Yvette was from a respectable, wealthy family…one of the families who held a strong prejudice against the people who lived in the swamp.

At the time of Beau's arrest, Thomas had been a young man with the fire of needing to prove himself burning in his eyes. "Well, well. Beau Boudreau, you finally got out," Thomas said. "I hope you learned some things in prison and now intend to be a law-abiding citizen in my town."

"I was a law-abiding citizen when you arrested me," Beau replied. He kept his tone calm and measured even though the minute the chief had walked into the room, a sense of wild injustice, of raw bitterness, had risen up inside him.

Thomas looked at Peyton. "You called this meeting and I don't have much time, so what's this all about?"

"I'd like to get a copy of your murder book in the Lacy Dupree case," Peyton said.

"Why? That case was closed years ago," Thomas replied in obvious surprise.

"I believe my client here was innocent when he was convicted of the murder," Peyton said.

Thomas stared at her for a long moment and then sat back in his chair and released a deep laugh. "Your client? Oh, this is rich," he finally said. "He got to you again. Peyton, your parents were embarrassed and heartbroken when you were running around town with Beau years ago and now here you are, at it again."

The mirth on Thomas's face suddenly transformed into a self-righteous anger and he slammed his hands down on the table. "I'll tell you right now, that was a clean investigation. We followed the evidence and all of it led directly to your client."

Beau's muscles bunched. He wanted to reach across the

table and punch the man in the face, not for the way he was speaking about Beau, but rather for the things he'd said to Peyton. However, he knew he had to stay calm for her. If he lost his temper now, he'd ruin everything.

"If you're so sure of your investigation then you shouldn't mind sharing the murder book with me," Peyton replied smoothly.

Beau had never seen Peyton in this capacity before. Clad in a crisp white blouse and a pair of black slacks, she looked cool and professional. She was self-confident and poised and he found this side of her sexy as hell.

Thomas released a deep sigh. "I'll have to have somebody dig it out of the records department," he said begrudgingly. "That file has been put away for a lot of years."

"I'd really appreciate it and I'd like to have it on my desk sometime tomorrow," Peyton said, her voice firm.

"I'll see what I can do. Are we done here? I've got another murder investigation to tend to," Thomas said.

"Another murder?" Peyton asked curiously. She hadn't heard about any other murders in town.

"Babette Pitre was murdered two nights ago. Her body was found in the alley between the post office and town hall. Her throat was ripped out and right now we're in the middle of that investigation."

"Do you have any clues?" Beau asked. He knew the Pitre family and had vague memories of Babette as a little girl.

"Your folk seem to think it's the work of the Honey Island Swamp Monster," Thomas replied to Beau.

Your folk. That spoke volumes to Beau, and a wave of anger rose up inside him toward the man he believed had rushed to judgment in Lacy's murder case. Peyton apparently sensed his rising emotion, for she placed a steadying hand on his arm.

"Then we'll let you get back to your investigation," Peyton said. "But I still expect that murder book on my desk sometime tomorrow." She rose and Beau also got up from his chair. "We appreciate your time, Chief Gravois."

Minutes later they were back in Peyton's car and heading back to her office. "That jerk," Beau finally said, breaking the silence that had momentarily existed between them. "I thought you were going to ask him some questions about his investigation."

"I was, but I realized I can get everything I need to know about the investigation from his murder book. It will hold photographs of the crime scene and all interviews that were conducted and witness statements. It will also have the autopsy and forensic reports."

"Then I look forward to seeing that book," Beau replied. "Maybe someplace in those files will be the information to clear my name and point to the real killer."

"Speaking of killing, who or what is the Honey Island Swamp Monster?" she asked. "I've never heard of it before."

"That's because the creature isn't here around our swamps, but rather supposedly in the Honey Island area. According to the legend, the creature is an abandoned child raised by alligators. 'My folk,'" he said the words sarcastically and then continued, "the Cajuns, call the creature loup-garou, which means werewolf."

"So what does this so-called creature look like?" she asked with a curious glance at him.

"He's about seven feet tall and weighs around four hundred pounds. He's covered in dingy gray hair and has large, amber-colored eyes. He's three-toed and emits a horrendous stench. Now that I think about it, it's very possible Chief Gravois might be a direct descendant of the beast."

Peyton laughed. It was the first real burst of laughter he'd heard from her, and it reminded him of how often they had laughed together in the past. "You are so bad," she finally replied. "I suspect Babette was killed by a monster of the human variety."

"That would be my guess as well," he said.

She pulled up at the curb in front of her office and they got out of the car. They had only gone about three steps when her phone rang. She looked at the caller ID. "I need to take this really quick," she said to Beau. "You can go on inside and I'll catch up with you."

Before Beau could move away, he heard her answer her phone. "Hi, Sam." Her voice was low and pleasant and a swift, unexpected wave of jealousy punched through Beau.

He walked away, wondering who the hell Sam was. On an intelligent level he knew it was none of his business, but on a visceral, emotional level he wanted to know every man she had ever dated, every man who had been her lover since him.

He went into the building and Kylie jumped up from her desk. He motioned her back down with a smile. "Peyton's outside on the phone and will be in shortly. By the way, do you know who Sam is?"

"That would probably be Sam Landry," Kylie replied.

"And who is Sam Landry to Peyton?" he pressed.

"He's a nice man…a very respectable banker and uh…he and Peyton have been dating a little bit."

"Ah, good to know," Beau replied even as that niggle of jealousy swept through him again. "I'll just wait for her inside." He walked on through into her office and sank down in the chair facing the desk.

He'd had fifteen years to think about Peyton; fifteen years of wanting her again. Even though he'd felt betrayed by her and had been angry that she'd so easily believed him guilty of the murder, he'd counted down the days until he would see her again.

For him, life had stopped when he'd been arrested, but he now realized that, of course, life hadn't stopped for her. How serious was her relationship with this Sam?

How many other men had held her in their arms, tasted the sweet honey of her lips? How many other men had watched her eyes flash and darken with unbridled passion?

He sat up straighter in the chair as she came into the room and sat behind the desk. "Sorry about that," she said.

"Did the good, respectable banker ask you out for another date?" he asked, unable to help himself.

She froze and stared at him. Then she shook her head and released a small, dry laugh. "I see my trusty assistant has a big mouth."

"You didn't answer my question." He got up out of the chair and propped his hip on the edge of her desk.

Her cheeks flushed a soft pink. "It's really none of your business, Beau."

"Kylie said you've been dating the good Sam. Is it something serious?" His heart accelerated its beat. Her answer suddenly seemed exceedingly important to him.

"We've only gone out a couple of times," she replied.

"Have you slept with him yet?" he asked.

"Definitely none of your business," she replied sharply.

"I was just wondering if when he kisses you, do you moan

in the back of your throat like you used to do with me? Does he know about that spot just behind your ear? The place where when I used to kiss you there, you'd writhe beneath me and moan my name?"

"Stop," she hissed angrily. "Stop it right now. And get off my desk." He laughed and returned to the chair. Peyton's blue eyes fired with anger, but in the very depths of them he saw something more…the sweet familiar flame of desire.

"You have to stop it, Beau. I can't work with you if you're trying to seduce me all the time."

"But you are so beautifully seducible," he said.

"I mean it, Beau. You have to stop. You're a client and as my client all I need from you is your honesty and your respect. Nothing more."

He sobered. "You have my utter respect, Peyton, and I will always be honest with you." Perhaps this was the way to her heart, instead of the seduction path he'd been on.

Then he wondered why he wanted to get into her heart in the first place. How could he ever love again the woman who, even for a moment, had believed he'd committed a heinous murder?

Chapter Four

Peyton leaned back in her chair and rubbed her tired eyes. A glance at the clock on the wall let her know it was after seven. She should have gone home several hours ago, but the murder book had finally arrived at her office at five, and since that time she had been completely engrossed in it.

She'd sent both Kylie and Beau home a couple of hours earlier. Thankfully, the murder book had arrived after they'd left the office. She found it difficult to concentrate when Beau was around. He was both a pain in her behind and a strange hitch in her heart.

Since he'd walked back into her life, she felt off center and overly emotional. He was forcing her to remember things she'd believed she'd shoved out of her head forever. He was making her feel that old breathless anticipation, the sweet flood of desire she used to feel for him. And she didn't want that. She didn't want him, she told herself over and over again.

She jumped at the sound of a knock on the building door. She got up from her desk and went into the reception area. Peeking out the window, she saw Jackson on the front stoop.

Quickly, she unlocked the door and ushered him inside. "Burning the midnight oil?" he asked.

"It's not exactly midnight, but I got caught up in something and lost track of the time." She ushered him into her office and he sat in the chair opposite her.

"Must be interesting for you to still be here at this time of night," he said. "A new case?"

"Actually, I've been reading the files from Chief Gravois on the Lacy Dupree murder case."

Jackson raised an eyebrow. "Any surprises?"

"A thousand." She sat back in her chair and frowned. "Chief Gravois insisted to me yesterday that it was a clean investigation, but it was practically no investigation at all. You know who the star witness was?"

"Who?"

"Louis Rivet," she replied.

"Really??" Jackson shook his head. "That man hasn't been sober for the last twenty-five years."

"Well, that was the prosecutor's star witness. He testified that Beau left the motel minutes after Lacy's time of death. He was innocent, Jackson. I believe Beau was really an innocent man when he was charged and convicted for the crime."

Jackson looked at her with surprise. "And you're sure about that?"

She thought about her conversation with Beau in the motel room and everything she had just read and seen in the murder book. "I'm positive," she replied. "I think there was a rush to justice, and I suspect Beau probably had an incompetent lawyer, among other things. I'll know more about the counsel that represented him once I get the official trial documents."

"So if he really was innocent, then what happens next?"

"We need to find some new evidence that could overturn his conviction and get him a new trial," she replied.

"Whether he's innocent or not, I hope you aren't allowing him to get back into your head on a personal level." Jackson held her gaze.

"Trust me. I have it all under control." She would never admit to anyone how deeply Beau's touch still affected her, how his sensual smile still had the ability to weaken her knees and heat her blood. "So far we have a good working relationship and that's all it is."

"I've heard that the two of you have been seen around town. Gossip tongues are wagging."

She laughed. "Gossip tongues are always wagging in this town. I've never cared much what they are wagging about."

"A lot of people aren't very happy Beau has come back here."

"Where else would he go? This is his home," she replied.

"Have you heard from Sam since your last date?" Jackson asked, changing the subject.

"He called me yesterday."

"He's a good man. The two of you could make quite a power couple," Jackson observed.

"I do like him but we're taking things slow right now," she replied. "I intend to marry once and once only, so I don't want to make any mistakes. Now, what's going on in *your* love life?"

"I seem to be going through a bit of a dry spell," he said. "The women I ask out bore me. It's as if they're all cut out by the same cookie cutter. They're nice and sophisticated and absolutely boring."

"You've got to keep trying. You know you aren't getting any younger, Jackson."

"Don't remind me," he replied with a wince.

"You just have to find that special someone, Jackson. I know you'd be a wonderful husband and an amazing father."

"And you are only a year younger than me, and you aren't getting any younger, either," Jackson replied. "It's time for you to settle down, get married and have a couple of kids. Sam has told me he adores you. He'd make you a good husband."

"Duly noted," she replied.

"Well, I was just driving by and saw the lights on, but I was on the way to my parents' place for dinner." He stood. "Are you ready to leave? If so, I'll walk you out."

"Actually, I think I'll hang out here a little while longer. I want to finish up making some notes while things are still fresh in my mind," she replied. She got up as well. "But I'll walk you to the front door."

Minutes later Peyton was back at her desk, this time her thoughts filled with Sam Landry. Sam was a pleasantly handsome man. He was tall, with brown hair and hazel eyes. He had a kind face to match his kind personality.

She liked him and enjoyed his company, but so far there had been no real sparks with him. There was nothing even close to what she'd once felt for Beau. Of course, she'd been young and inexperienced when she'd first been with Beau.

But that doesn't explain how he still makes you feel, a little voice whispered inside her head. Memories...surely, that was all that was at play with Beau. She was no longer that young woman who had believed that he had hung the moon and stars.

Maybe she would never experience the feelings she'd once felt for Beau with any other man. Maybe she was a fool to even expect those kinds of fireworks again.

She returned her attention to making notes about what she'd read in the murder book. When she was finished, darkness had fallen outside. She stifled a yawn, locked up the files in her bottom desk drawer and then got ready to leave.

Tomorrow she would read through the files once again, looking for anything she missed the first time around. She also wanted to talk to Beau about seeing if he could find Lacy's friend Angel.

Maybe the woman would know something about who Lacy had intended to blackmail. Peyton believed that person was the real killer, and she would bet that person was still here in town. It ticked her off to know a murderer was still walking the streets freely and believing they'd gotten away with the horrendous crime.

She left the building and locked up. The night air was heavy and thick with heat and humidity. The sidewalks were deserted as she made her way to her car parked on the next block against the curb.

She reached her car and clicked the button on her key chain to unlock it. However, before she could even open the driver's door, she was shoved violently against it from behind.

A hard body held her in place against the hot metal of the car door as her brain worked to process what was happening. A burst of adrenaline filled her. She struggled in an attempt to get free, but he only shoved harder against her.

She knew it was a man. He breathed hard against the back of her neck. She could smell his sour perspiration and her heart beat frantically as fear raced through her. Who was doing this to her and why?

"W-what do you want?" she finally asked with a gasp. She prayed it was just a robbery and not anything else. "I have about a hundred dollars in cash in my purse. Let me go and I'll give it all to you."

"I don't want your damned money. Drop your investigation and let Lacy Dupree rest in peace." The voice was a deep growl that she didn't recognize. "Let sleeping dogs lie. This is a warning to you." He suddenly slammed his fist into the side of her face and then released her.

Pain seared through her cheek, dizzying all her senses. As she slumped against the side of the car, she heard his footsteps running away. She managed to get into the car and quickly locked the doors.

Dear God, what had just happened? She raised a hand to her cheek, the pain still throbbing with a breathless intensity. As the adrenaline that had momentarily filled her ebbed away, tears of residual fear and pain sprang to her eyes.

Who was that man? She should probably call the police and make a report, but she wouldn't be able to tell them anything about the man who had just assaulted her. All she knew for sure was that it had been a male.

It had all happened so fast. Even now she was having trouble processing what had just happened. She should have turned around to see him as he ran away. At least then she would have been able to give law enforcement a description of his general height and weight and maybe even a hair color. But she hadn't done that and so she saw no point in making a report.

She finally pulled herself together enough to start her car, even though she continued to cry. All she wanted to do now was go home and lock all her doors and windows. Despite her fear and her weeping, one thing was very clear: they had only just started the investigation, but they had already made somebody very nervous and angry.

Eventually, she pulled into her driveway and parked. As she got out of her car and made her way to her front door, she kept her gaze shooting all around, afraid that somebody might come out of the night shadows to attack her again.

She only breathed a sigh of relief once she was inside with the door locked. She headed directly to the kitchen, where she placed a few ice cubes into a towel and then held it up to her throbbing cheek.

She walked back into the living room and sank down on the sofa, still shaken by what had just happened to her. Had she just had an encounter with the man who had set Beau up? A shiver walked up her spine at the thought. Had Lacy Dupree's real killer just warned her off the case?

BEAU GRINNED AT the old man standing next to the rusty old black pickup truck in the large parking lot of Vincent's Grocery. The little store stood at the very edge of the swamp and was the place where a lot of the swamp people not only shopped but also parked their vehicles.

Gator Broussard was a legend in the swamps. Nobody knew exactly how old he was, but what Beau did know about the man was that he was a rascally character who had spent his life hunting gators. He was missing three fingers on his left hand, the result of a fight with one of the big beasts.

He was clad in a dingy gray T-shirt, and his worn jeans

were tied around his thin waist with a rope. He carried with him a crooked walking cane that had a knife tied to the end.

Somehow, Gator had heard through the grapevine that Beau needed a vehicle and he'd gotten word to Beau to meet him here. "How have you been, Gator?" Beau now asked.

Gator's dark eyes twinkled. "Can't complain. I reckon I've been better than you've been. How you doing, Beau?"

"I haven't exactly gotten a hero's welcome back here, but I'm getting by."

"You got a raw deal, boy. There's no question in my mind about that. I knew at the time you would never hurt Lacy, but a bunch of the powerful people in this damn town made you take the fall so they could sweep it all under the rug and protect one of their own." Gator punctuated his words by spitting a stream of tobacco juice onto the ground next to him.

"Thanks, Gator, I appreciate it."

Gator nodded, his white hair glittering in the early-morning sun. "Now, I heard you were looking for some wheels." He put his hand on the side of the truck. "This don't look like much, but it runs like a top. They took my license a couple of years ago after I plowed into a parked car and they made me take a test that I flunked. Anyway, it's yours if you want it. I ain't got any use of it anymore."

"I appreciate your offer, Gator, but I'll buy it from you." Beau didn't want to be beholden to anyone. Besides, he knew how hard money was to come by for many of the people who lived in the swamp.

"Okay, I'll take a hundred for it," Gator said.

"No way. I'll give you five for it," Beau replied.

"Two," Gator countered.

Beau laughed. "I'll give you four hundred and that's the

end of it." He pulled out his wallet and counted the bills into Gator's good hand. Gator tucked the money into the front pocket of his saggy, worn jeans.

"What have you heard about Babette Pitre's murder?" Beau asked the old man curiously.

Gator's eyes darkened and his smile disappeared. "Nothing much. Just enough to know it's the same as the last two."

"The last two?"

"Colette Castille and Marcelle Savoie were also murdered." Gator spit another stream of tobacco juice.

"When was this?" Beau asked in stunned surprise.

Gator frowned, his wrinkles attempting to take over his entire face. "Colette was about four months ago and Marcelle was about four or five months before that."

"What does Gravois have to say about it?"

Gator's weathered features screwed up into a deeper frown. "He says as little as possible. That man couldn't find a killer in a maximum-sentence prison," he said in obvious disgust.

"Gravois told me *my folk* believe Babette's murder is the work of the Honey Island Swamp Monster," Beau said.

Gator gazed around with slightly widened eyes as if just speaking of the beast might conjure him up. He finally looked back at Beau. "I don't know what kind of a monster ripped the throat out of those women, but it was definitely a monster."

The two talked for a few minutes longer and then parted ways with Beau having the title and the keys to the pickup. Before meeting Gator, Beau had gone to the cell phone store. He now had a phone and a vehicle and it was past time he got to Peyton's office to get some work in. Eventually he'd need to get to the license bureau and see about getting a new driver's license.

He was pleased that the truck fired right up, and as he drove, he thought about what Gator had told him about the two previous murders. Apparently, somebody was viciously killing young women from the swamp, and it didn't sound like much of anything was being done about it.

Unfortunately, Beau was in no position to do anything about it himself. At the moment he had to stay focused on finding Lacy's killer. Gator had told him where to find Angel Marchant, and Beau was hoping that later today, he and Peyton could go speak to the woman who had been friendly with Lacy before her death. Maybe…just maybe the woman would have some information to help.

He parked down the block from Peyton's office and then walked the rest of the way. He still needed to do a lot of work on the front of the building in order to get it into good enough shape for a new paint job.

However, before he got to that work, he wanted to tell Peyton about Angel. "Hi, Beau," Kylie greeted him when he walked in, but she didn't quite meet his gaze.

"Is she free?" he asked.

"She is. You can go ahead in," Kylie replied.

He walked into the office and Peyton looked up from her computer and half-stood as he came into the room. As usual, she looked beautiful. She was clad in a gray pair of slacks and a purple blouse that perfectly matched the vivid bruise on her cheek, a bruise that instantly tightened all his chest muscles.

"What happened?" he asked as he sank down in the chair facing her.

"Nothing important." She reached up and touched the bruise. Her gaze shifted to the left of him, and he immediately knew she was lying.

"Why don't you tell me what happened and I'll decide if it's important or not," he replied tersely.

"I…uh…just had a bit of an encounter last night when I left here," she said, still not meeting his gaze.

"An encounter with what? A ticked-off boxing kangaroo?"

A small laugh escaped her, followed by a wince. "Please, don't make me laugh." She quickly sobered and released a deep sigh. "I was getting ready to get into my car last night when a man came up behind me and slammed me into the car door. Then he hit me and ran away."

Beau frowned at her as a rich anger punched him in the gut. "And who was this animal who hit you?"

"I don't know, Beau. I didn't see him at all."

"Did he say anything to you?" Beau worked it around in his head. Why would a person just randomly sneak up on her and punch her in the face? There had to be a reason for the assault.

She looked away. "He might have said a few things to me," she finally said, reluctantly.

Beau got out of his chair and walked over to stand close to her. "What did he say, *ma chérie*?" What he wanted to do more than anything was stroke his fingers over her bruised cheek in an effort to magically heal her. What he also wanted to do more than anything was find the person responsible for her dark bruise and do more than just punch him in the face.

She once again met his gaze and raised her chin. "He basically told me to drop the investigation and let Lacy rest in peace."

Beau cursed soundly. So she'd been hurt because of him. "That's it, then. You're officially off the case."

"No, Beau. Don't you see? We've only just begun our investigation and already we've made somebody very nervous," she replied.

"I will not put you in a position for anyone to hurt you again," he said angrily. "I'll take it from here and you're done."

"No, I will not be done," she protested, her eyes snapping with blue fire as her chin rose up another notch. She got up from her chair and stood to face him. "I'm a criminal defense attorney and this isn't my first rodeo. I've had plenty of death threats in my career and this only makes me want to work this case even harder."

He could stand it no longer. He took another step closer to her and reached out and gently touched her cheek. "I would kill a man for hurting you," he said softly.

She didn't reply, but her lips parted slightly as if in open invitation, and her eyes darkened in the way he remembered from long ago. Suddenly, he was thrown back in time, back to when she was his and their passion and love for one another was overpowering.

Before he knew his own intent, he leaned forward and captured her lips with his. Instantly, a fire lit in the depths of his very soul. He'd initially meant the kiss to somehow soothe and comfort her, but as she opened her mouth and returned the kiss, it became one to possess and consume.

Her soft, pillowy lips offered sweet, hot honey that he wanted to drink forever. Unfortunately, all too quickly she gasped and took a step back from him.

"Consider that a moment of weakness on my part," she

said as she sank back down in her chair. "And trust me. It definitely won't happen again." Her chin rose again in a show of defiance.

The kiss had shaken him up more than he wanted to admit, and he could swear he saw a hint of desire still in the depths of her eyes. However, he couldn't allow what had just happened to deter him from the conversation they'd been having beforehand.

"What's important here is that you stay safe, and the only way that will happen is if you completely distance yourself from me and the investigation," he said.

"And I refuse to do that," she replied. "I'll just be smarter from now on with my personal safety. I'm moving forward with the investigation, and you can either be a part of it with me or not."

There was that strong, tough woman that he found so appealing. He'd known her as a young girl and now it was magnificent to see the woman she had become.

"Then I will be at your house and follow you to work each morning, and then I will see you home safely each night," he finally said. "I will be your bodyguard and nobody will ever get close enough to you to hurt you again."

"And how are you going to accomplish that?" she asked.

"As of this morning I am the proud owner of a pickup truck, so I now have the wheels to follow you back and forth each day, or better yet, drive you to and from the office and home."

She held his gaze for a long moment and then slowly nodded. "Okay, I'd appreciate that."

Her reply let him know that she'd been shaken up by the attack more than she'd initially let on. The hot burn of anger once again licked his insides. He sat in the chair facing her. "Did you call Gravois and make a report of the attack?"

"No, I didn't bother. I didn't see the person who hit me so I couldn't give any identifying information to Gravois."

"I don't know what that man does all day, but he should be working overtime." He told her what Gator had said about the other two murders.

"That's terrible. I've kind of been following it on the news, although there hasn't been much talk about the murders in town. I certainly hope the killer is caught soon," she replied. "But we have to stay focused on Lacy's murder."

"Speaking of that, Gator also told me where to find Angel. She's deep in the swamp and has become something of a recluse. But he told me the general area where to find her, so I thought we could do that later this afternoon."

"Good. Maybe she'll have some answers for us," she said with a touch of excitement in her voice.

He got up from his chair. "I'll just head outside now and get some work done and then I'll be back in later this afternoon."

"I'll see you later," she agreed and immediately cast her gaze back at the computer screen.

Minutes later Beau was outside the office and working. As he worked, he thought about the attack on Peyton. Even though there was a core inside him that was still angry with her for not believing him years ago, the idea of anyone putting hands on her made him see red.

This afternoon they would venture into the swamp together, a place they hadn't been together in years, and he couldn't help but wonder what kind of emotions that might evoke in both of them.

Chapter Five

Peyton released a deep sigh once Beau left her office. She'd been foolish to think she could keep the details of the attack on her from Beau. She'd never been able to lie or keep secrets from him in the past.

She'd tossed and turned all night long thinking about the investigation, but not once had it entered her mind to quit. Somewhere out there was the real killer of Lacy, and whoever it was, the investigation had made him nervous enough to attack Peyton and warn her and Beau off.

There was no question she felt safer knowing Beau intended to get her home safely each evening. There was also no question that the attack had shaken her. But she wasn't giving up. The one thing the assault had done for her was positively clear any lingering doubt she'd had about Beau's guilt.

Beau…he was a complicated puzzle in her brain. His touch still had the ability to stoke a fire inside her and take her back to the simpler time when he was the love of her life.

On the surface he still appeared to be the slightly irreverent, slightly cocky man he'd been when he was twenty-one.

Despite spending almost a week with him she still felt as if she hadn't really seen the real man he had become.

He had spent fifteen years in prison. That had to change a person at their very core. It had to have changed Beau in ways she couldn't even begin to imagine. And she wondered why she cared. She was just doing a job with him and that was it. Wasn't it?

Even though she now believed he was innocent of the crime against Lacy, she couldn't go back to that place and time when she'd been a young, innocent girl and he'd owned her heart so completely. Still, as her first lover, he would always have a special place in her heart, she supposed.

She shoved these thoughts aside and pulled up the official trial record from the Lacy Dupree murder case. They had been emailed to her that morning from the county records department and she was eager to read through them and see just how badly Beau had been represented by his public defender.

At noon Kylie brought her a sandwich and she ate as she continued to read and take notes. Beau had left, presumably to shower up and return after working through the heat of the morning.

It was almost two when she was interrupted by Kylie knocking on the door. "Mr. and Mrs. Farineau are here to see you."

Peyton looked at her in surprise. "Did they say why?"

"No clue," Kylie replied. "They wouldn't say."

"Then send them in."

Jason Farineau was part of the old guard in town. He'd made a fortune in investments and was on the city council.

He entered the room like an angry bull, with his timid wife, Irene, trailing after him.

Peyton rose from her chair and shook both their hands. "Whoa, who whooped you in the face?" Jason asked.

Peyton raised a hand to her cheek. "I…uh…hit it on a cabinet door. Now, what can I do for you?" she asked once they were all seated.

Irene immediately pulled a tissue from her purse and began to dab at tear-filled eyes. Jason shot her a look of utter disgust and then looked back at Peyton.

"Yesterday my dear wife was caught shoplifting from Chastain's." His voice held a simmering anger. Chastain's was a high-end shop that sold both clothes and decorative items.

"Obviously, she wasn't thinking straight and this is all a big mistake. She had a damned credit card in her purse to pay for the items, but Chastain is pushing Trevor Mignot to throw the book at her and charge her with felony theft, among other things." Trevor Mignot was the current district attorney.

Jason leaned forward, his nostrils flaring. "I need you to make this all go away."

"I'm going to need a lot more information," Peyton replied and turned her attention to Irene. The woman looked positively terrified, and Peyton wasn't sure if she was more afraid of the charges against her and the possibility of a trial or her husband's wrath.

If the store was pushing for a felony charge, then that meant Irene had taken at least fifteen hundred dollars' worth of merchandise. Still, at the pricey store it wouldn't take too many items to reach that dollar amount.

"I just got confused," she said, tears slowly sliding down her cheeks. "I would never steal on purpose. It was just a big mistake and an accident." She glanced over to her husband and her tears came faster.

The meeting with the couple took approximately two hours. By the time they finally left, Peyton had agreed to represent Irene. When she walked them to the outside door she noticed that a thick layer of gray clouds had moved in, darkening the day with the portent of rain.

She turned back to Kylie and smiled. "I will be representing Irene on a shoplifting charge."

"Shoplifting?" Kylie looked at her in stunned surprise.

"Yeah, needless to say, don't mention this to anyone. She deserves her privacy and Jason just wants it all to go away. And speaking of it all going away, have you seen Beau?"

"Yes, he stopped in when you were with the Farineaus. He ran down to Larry's and said he'd meet you back here."

"Then I guess I'll get to work on the new case until he shows up here," Peyton replied.

"New case… I like the way that sounds, and the Farineaus should be able to pay cold, hard cash for your amazing defense skills," Kylie replied. "No payment plans for them."

Before either of them could say anything more, Beau came in. As always, he seemed to bring with him a simmering energy and a bold masculinity that somehow tapped into something deep inside Peyton. Damn him for still having the power to move her; damn him for still having the power to make her want him.

"I saw the Farineaus leaving here. New case?" he asked.

She nodded. "But it's nothing that will take up too much

of my time." She turned to Kylie. "Get me a copy of the police report concerning the former matter."

"Will do," Kylie replied.

Peyton turned back to Beau. "Now, let's go find Angel and see if she has some answers for us."

"I'll drive," he replied.

She raised an eyebrow. "Do you even remember how to drive?"

"Of course I do. I've got my new set of wheels and I now have a cell phone. We can exchange numbers once we get to Vincent's parking lot."

"Let me just grab my purse," she replied.

Within minutes she was in the passenger seat of his truck. On the outside, the truck was rusted and a bit banged up, but the inside was clean as a whistle and already smelled like Beau.

The closer they got to the swamp, the bigger a ball of anxiety pressed against her chest. She hadn't been back in the swamp since the last time she'd made love with Beau, when she'd still believed in a bright and wonderful future with him. Then the next morning he'd been arrested and her entire world had crashed down around her.

At that time he'd not only been her lover, but he'd also been her very best friend. She'd shared with him all her hopes and dreams and all her fears and disappointments. She'd believed him to be her soul mate. She now cast him a surreptitious glance and then quickly stared back out the front window.

It was still there. The powerful force that had once brought them together as friends and lovers years ago, it was still there…simmering just beneath the surface with intensity and volatility.

She didn't want it to be there. She could pretend that it didn't exist; she could even lie to Beau about it, but she couldn't fool herself. She was still hopelessly attracted to him.

He parked the truck in the big parking lot behind Vincent's Grocery. The small store mostly served the people who lived in the swamp. It was walking distance from the gravel parking to the mouth of several trails that entered into the dark marshland.

They got out of the truck and took a moment to put their phone numbers into each other's phone and then they began to walk up a familiar trail.

As they continued to walk deeper into the tangled growth, what little sunlight there had been nearly disappeared, unable to filter through the trees and brush that surrounded them.

Insects buzzed around them and whirred a cacophony of sound, and from someplace nearby a fish or a gator slapped the water. Other small animals ran through the brush ahead of them, and Peyton made sure she stayed as close to Beau as possible.

He moved through the tangled underbrush with complete confidence, like a sleek wild animal in his own environment. At the moment they were on the path that would eventually lead them to his home, but before they reached it, he veered off on another narrow trail.

"Have you ever been to Angel's place before?" she asked.

"No—when I knew her, her home was in the motel next door to Lacy's room."

"Do you know where we're going?" she asked nervously.

He glanced back and flashed her a smile, his straight white teeth visible despite the lack of any real light. "Not exactly. Let's just hope the directions Gator gave me are good ones."

"Let's hope," she replied faintly.

It became darker, cooler, as they entered the heart of the swamp. Peyton's steps faltered and she slowed as the terrain grew more difficult to maneuver. Beau turned and offered her his hand. Eagerly, she grasped his, grateful for the warmth and strength as they continued on.

Birds cried discordantly from the tops of the trees, as if to protest the human trespassers. The air smelled both of strange flowers and more than a hint of decay. Fear, along with a healthy respect for the surroundings, filled her.

"How much farther is it?" she whispered, afraid of what she might awaken if she spoke too loudly.

"I'm not sure, but it shouldn't be too far now," he replied. "Gator gave me the directions to find it. Do you need to stop and take a rest for a minute or two?"

"No, I'm okay." And she was, as long as his hand continued to hold hers. It reminded her of how they had first met, when she'd been a kid lost in the swamp and he had been the hero who had gotten her safely home. There were times when she believed it had been on that night, at that tender age, when she'd fallen in love with Beau.

A howl filled the air, the chilling sound causing her heart to nearly jump out of her chest. "What was that?" she asked nervously.

"I'm not sure. It sounded like a wolf."

At that moment Beau stopped and pointed ahead to where a small shack stood on stilts. Several kerosene lanterns hung on the small porch area, illuminating a dozen or so macabre dolls that hung from the rafters.

"Wh…what are those?" she asked.

"I don't know," Beau admitted. "But there's one thing I forgot to mention about Angel. According to Gator she's not only a healer, but she's also a witch."

A new icy chill suddenly walked up Peyton's spine.

THE WOLF HOWLED AGAIN and the door to the shack opened. Silhouetted in the light from within was a tall woman who held a rifle in her hands. "Who's there?" she called out.

"Angel, it's Beau. Beau Boudreau and Peyton LaCroix. We'd like to talk to you."

She didn't reply for several long moments. Beau hadn't realized just how much he'd hoped that Lacy had confided in Angel before her death until now, when he wasn't even sure Angel would agree to speak with them.

"Then come in," she finally replied.

As he and Peyton got closer to the shack, he saw that Angel had moved one hand from her rifle to the back of the large red wolf that stood beside her.

Beau's hand felt nearly strangled as Peyton tightened her grip on his. Her fear was palpable, and he had to admit a bit of disquiet raced through him as old legends of monsters and beasts and witches of the swamp filled his head.

They moved forward toward a small bridge that would carry them across the swamp waters and to her porch. Beau led the way, with Peyton nearly walking on the backs of his heels.

Angel disappeared from the doorway. The dolls that hung all around the porch were made of cloth with yarn hair and macabre features. Some had pins thrust into their bodies and faces while others had small knives protruding from their hearts. Were they representative of the people Angel had cursed?

He had no idea if Angel believed he'd killed Lacy or not, but he supposed he was about to find out. They walked into the shack to where Angel now sat in a large, dark brown chair, the wolf on alert by her side.

She gestured to the sofa that faced her chair and Beau and Peyton sat. "Beau Boudreau... I didn't expect to ever see you again."

"I didn't expect to ever see you again, either," he replied. "But fate has brought us together once again."

The last time he'd seen Angel she had been an attractive young woman with long black hair and dark eyes that had held a passion for life.

It had been fifteen years since he'd seen her, and he now wouldn't have been able to pick her out of a crowd. Her dark hair now held a white streak down the middle, and she looked as if she'd aged thirty years or more.

A ropey scar slashed across one of her cheeks, and her eyes now held a combination of what appeared to be weariness and a depth of wisdom.

He looked around the room. A variety of plants hung from the ceiling rafters; some he recognized and some he didn't. The air smelled of flowers and berries, of mysterious concoctions and spices. More dolls also hung in here.

"What's the deal with the dolls?" he asked.

She cast him a sly smile. "Haven't you heard, Beau? I'm the wicked witch of the swamp. Men fear me and women sneak here in the dark to see me for a variety of health issues and other things."

"You didn't answer me about the dolls," he replied.

"Beau, I'm a woman living alone here—other than my faithful companion, Wolf." The animal turned his head to gaze at her adoringly. "Making sure everyone sees me as a powerful witch or a voodoo queen who makes dolls and curses people keeps most folk away from me, and that's the way I like it." She reached up and touched the scar on her cheek.

"As long as people are afraid of me, I am safe here." She touched the back of the wolf once again. She spoke in a language Beau didn't recognize. The wolf responded by lying down with his head on his front paws, but the yellow eyes continued to shoot between Beau and Peyton.

"I would think your friend there would keep most people away," Peyton said with a nod toward the wolf. "Where did you get him?"

"I found him as a newborn pup hidden in a thick bush. I found the bodies of his mother and father some ten feet away. They had been shot." Her eyes flashed darkly. "Damn hunters. Anyway, I brought him back here and I am now his mother and his father and his sister and brother. He would kill for me and I would kill for him. Now, why are the two of you here? It's been many years since I've seen either one of you."

Beau leaned forward in his seat. "First, I'd like to ask you a question. Do you believe I killed Lacy?"

A smile curled her lips. "Trust me. If I believed you murdered my friend, then you wouldn't now be sitting in my home. I know you didn't kill her."

"I'm now trying to figure out who *did* kill her," Beau replied. "Somebody murdered her and framed me, Angel. I want to know who that was, and we were hoping you might somehow be able to help us with that."

"I tried to tell Gravois at the time that you would never harm her, but he didn't even want to talk to me. I knew then that he wasn't really looking for the truth. One swamp person was dead and he got another one thrown in prison. That's all he was interested in."

"I visited her on the night of her murder. She needed to borrow some money from me," Beau said. "I got the impression she had plans to blackmail one of her…uh…clients."

Angel nodded. "She told me, and I told her that the plan would get her killed, but she wouldn't listen to me."

A flutter of hope swept through him. Had Angel known the answer all these years and just couldn't find anyone in local law enforcement to listen to her? "Did she tell you who he was?"

"Did she tell me his name? No. All she told me was that he had money and was in a position in town where he would not want people to know he visited a prostitute on a regular basis."

The hope Beau had felt moments ago left him on a deep sigh. "So you don't have any information that can help us find out who he is."

"I can't give you a name, but I might have something here that will help you." As she stood from her chair, Wolf immediately got to his feet. She spoke a couple of words Beau didn't understand and the wolf sank down once again.

Beau watched as she walked over to one of the hanging dolls, one with wide eyes and a mouth that appeared to be screaming. She yanked it down and then walked over to a small desk just inside the front door and grabbed a pair of scissors. Beau shot a quick glance at Peyton, who appeared anxious, yet obviously curious.

"I'm not sure why I kept this for all these years," Angel said as she used the scissors to cut off the doll's head. She returned to her chair and began to pull out the stuffing. Along with the stuffing, a folded piece of paper fell out.

"I knew Lacy kept some sort of a list of her clients and that she hid it in a heat vent in her room, so a few days after her murder I went in and got it." She unfolded the piece of paper that was now a bit yellowed and frayed with age and then handed it to Beau. "I was afraid if I gave it to Gravois, he would just throw it away. I never knew who to give it to, so I just kept it."

Beau stared down at the paper, which held nothing more than a list of initials and numbers. He looked back at Angel. "These initials are for the men who visited her?"

"Yes," Angel replied.

"Do you think the killer's initials are here?"

"I'm positive of it," Angel said firmly.

"Do you have any idea what the numbers mean?" He asked.

"I don't," she replied.

"Why did you keep this for so long?" he asked her curiously.

"Maybe I held on to it all this time because on some strange level I knew one day you would need it to set justice right." Her eyes flashed darkly once again. "If I was truly a powerful voodoo queen, I would make sure Gravois suffered an accident that would cause him to suffer every day for the rest of his life as he has made so many of us suffer."

Once again, a wave of hope swept through Beau as he held the piece of paper tightly in his fingers. "Thank you for keeping this, Angel. It might help us solve Lacy's murder and let me reclaim my life as an innocent man," Beau said.

"And you are helping him with this?" she asked Peyton.

"I am," Peyton replied.

Angel smiled. "I heard what you did for the Mouton family. It was very kind of you."

"I just did what was right," Peyton replied.

Beau stood and Peyton followed suit. "Well, we'll just get out of here," he said. "Thank you, Angel...both for speaking with us and for potentially handing me the key to finding the killer." Angel remained seated and Beau paused at the door. "If I may ask...who scarred your face?"

Her hand reached up and touched the thick puckered scar. "Needless to say, Lacy's murder shook us all up, but we ladies of the night kept working. But it was as if there was a free-for-all in hurting us. Suzette had her arm broken, and about a week after that a client of mine didn't like something I said to him and he pulled a knife and slashed me."

She dropped her hand back to her side. "The next morning, I left the motel and found this place, which had been abandoned years before. I claimed it as my own and began to study herbal healing from the plants and flowers that are abundant around here." She raised her chin as pride shone from her eyes. "I like helping people with my herbal knowledge and now I have the power to pick and choose who comes into my life, and no man will ever get close enough to hurt me again."

"Are you happy here?" he asked.

"Happy?" She cocked her head and frowned thoughtfully. "I'm not sure, but what I do know is that I'm finally at peace. I'm content here with Wolf and the people I serve here in the swamp. Back then, when I was working out of the motel, I wanted to get up enough money to leave the swamp forever, but now I embrace the swamp, which has truly become my mother and my father, and I am no longer ashamed of who I am."

"I'm glad you've found some peace here, Angel," Peyton said.

Angel nodded and stood. Wolf immediately got to his feet next to her. "Please don't tell anyone you spoke to me and don't tell anyone where you found me. I can't do anything more for you than I already have."

"Again, we appreciate whatever force made you keep that piece of paper," Peyton said.

"I hope you find the killer who destroyed so many lives," Angel replied. A sly smile once again curved her lips. "I will make a special doll just for him and bring a thousand curses on his head."

Beau's blood chilled. Somehow, he believed she would do just that, and he was only grateful he wasn't the man she would curse.

Chapter Six

It was raining when Peyton and Beau left Angel's place. Peyton was eager to check out the piece of paper that Angel had provided to them, but at that moment she was too busy fighting against the torrential rainfall. Within several minutes she was soaked to the skin, but grateful that the rain was warm rather than cold.

Beau held her hand again as they traveled slowly through the unfamiliar terrain. It was inky dark, but thankfully, he had a penlight in his pocket. Even though the small light didn't help them look too far ahead, at least it lit the ground enough for them to know where to step without falling into the swamp waters.

"We'll go to my place and wait out the storm," he said, yelling to be heard above the sound of the rain beating against the leaves overhead and the thick brush.

Peyton nodded. Hopefully, the rain wouldn't fall for too long. Flooding in the swamps was always a danger. When they reached the place where they had to take the right trail to go to Beau's cabin, she had a moment of trepidation. The last time she had been in the cozy four-room shack, she and Beau had made sweet, passionate love.

She shoved her disquiet away. Nothing like what had happened years before between them was going to happen now. They would just wait out the rain and if it didn't stop in the next thirty minutes or so, she'd insist that he lead her on out of the swamp.

About twenty minutes later it was a welcomed relief to step into his front door. Here, it was as if time had stood still. Nothing had really changed since the last time she'd been here.

She walked over to the chair and sank down while he moved to the potbellied stove and began to build a fire. "Hopefully, a nice fire will help to dry us out a bit," he said. "Let me get this started and then I'll hand you a towel."

By the time the fire roared in the stove, Peyton had towel-dried her hair and clothing as best as she could.

"Do you want something to drink? I've got cold water and some soda." Beau walked over to a medium-size wooden box in the kitchen area.

"What is that?" she asked curiously.

"It's my home-made refrigerator. As long as I get bags of ice for it every couple of days, it keeps my meat and other supplies cold. If I somehow forget to buy the ice, I can plug it into my generator for just a little while." He opened the hinged top. "So what will it be?"

"I wouldn't mind a water," she said. He pulled out two bottles of water and then placed the lid back into place on the wooden box.

He handed her a water and then he sank down on the sofa while she remained seated in the chair facing him. They both twisted off their bottle tops and took several drinks of the refreshing water.

"Now I'm ready to see the paper that Angel gave you," she said as she put the lid back on the water bottle.

"Then come and sit next to me." He patted the space next to him on the sofa, set his water on the coffee table and then pulled the piece of paper out of his leather wallet. She got up and moved to sit next to him as he opened up the piece of paper.

Instantly, several things flashed through her brain. The scent of him, so wild and evocative, filled her head. His body heat seemed to reach out and fully embrace her.

She'd made love to him when they'd been so young. What would it be like to make love to him now? She was a far more confident, experienced woman than she had been then. She shoved those dangerous thoughts out of her head as she took the piece of paper from him.

She stared down at the string of initials that lined one side of the page with numbers written beside them. She'd hoped for something more. "I wonder what the numbers mean," she said.

"How many times the particular man visited her? Or perhaps some sort of rating system? We'll probably never know for sure what those numbers mean," he replied.

"Maybe they had something to do with how blackmail-vulnerable the men were."

"Perhaps," he agreed.

"So it looks like what we need to do is set up a spreadsheet and try to match up initials with the men in town." It was going to be a daunting task. "Then once we have the names, we'll have to figure out who Lacy's target was and that's probably our killer." She handed him back the piece of paper.

It was going to be a tough job. There were about seventeen sets of initials that needed to be matched up with seventeen men. It was certainly not going to happen overnight.

"Maybe I can get a list of the names of all the homeowners by going to the property tax records, but that won't give us the name of any renters in town, especially not from fifteen years ago," she said.

"I can't imagine Lacy blackmailing somebody who didn't own property or have their own house. Why don't you keep this until tomorrow?" He returned the paper to her.

She pulled her cell phone out of her pocket. "The first thing I'm going to do is take a picture of this." She aimed and then took two photos of the list. "The next thing I'll do in the morning is make a couple of copies of this," she said as she refolded the paper and put it into the bottom of her purse. "I also want to talk to Louis Rivet. Even though the man is an alcoholic, it was his statement that put you in the motel room minutes before Lacy died, and now knowing her time of death and what you've told me about that night, there is a huge time discrepancy."

"Do you really think he's going to remember something like that now?" Beau raised a dark brow in skepticism.

"Yes...no... I really don't know. I'm just hoping he saw somebody else go into Lacy's room after you left that night. I'll tell you what's really criminal...the fact that your defense attorney didn't even try to punch holes in Louis's memory and didn't bring up that Louis was totally pickled on most nights. I could probably argue to a judge that you had ineffective counsel and get you a new trial."

He frowned. "I don't want to win that way. I want to win

by finding the guilty bastard who murdered Lacy and then framed me to take the fall."

"You realize that might not happen," she said softly.

"It *will* happen, because I won't stop until I have the answers. Now, tell me what you did for the Mouton family."

She blinked at the quick change of topic. "Oh, it was nothing really. Their youngest son had been caught spray-painting a building that Lester Granger owns."

"That old coot? I'm surprised that he's still alive," Beau replied.

"He's not only still alive, but he's also the crankiest old man in town. He wanted to throw the book at the boy but I managed to get him off with probation and some community service. I also cut my fee in half and set them up on a payment plan. I would have done it for free, but I didn't want to hurt their pride."

"That was very kind of you, and you're right in that they would have been highly offended if you'd offered your services for free. That's one thing that can be said about swamp people—we have a lot of pride and they always try to pay their own way."

He turned and stared into the fire. For a moment he appeared haunted. His features were all taut lines and angles, and his eyes were as dark as the devil's heart.

The rain had stopped and the swamp around them had come alive with bellowing frogs and insects that sang their nighttime lullabies.

"You must have missed this place when you were away," Peyton finally said, breaking the silence that had grown between them.

"You have no idea." He turned back to face her. "I grieved

for the sound of the swamp…for the smells and the freedom of home."

"How did you survive? I mean, we've all heard horror stories of the vicious gangs and a variety of groups that provide protection to inmates in prison."

A slow grin curved his lips. "I didn't need a group or a gang affiliation to keep me safe. Somehow, a rumor began that I was a voodoo priest and I lived in the deepest, darkest heart of the swamp with wild animals who did my bidding. In that respect Angel and I have a lot in common. Anyway, the other inmates believed I could cast powerful spells and curses and so for the most part they all left me alone."

He could definitely cast spells. Each time he smiled like that, every time he gazed at her the way he was doing right now, she felt as if he'd placed her in a dizzying spell of desire.

He reached out and unfastened the barrette she had on the nape of her neck. Her hair spilled into his fingers. "It will dry much quicker this way," he murmured.

She wanted to tell him to stop running his fingers through her hair. She needed to demand that he lean back from her and give her some space.

However, as his fingers trailed slowly down the side of her jaw and then across her mouth, she was frozen in place by his sensual onslaught. She fought for control despite her body responding to him.

"Stop it, Beau," she finally managed to gasp as she batted his hand away. "If you want to catch a killer then you have to stay serious."

His eyes glittered wickedly. "Right now I am very serious about seducing you."

"Well, it's not working, so give it up," she snapped. She

grabbed her barrette from his hand. "It sounds like the rain has stopped and now I need to get home."

He laughed that knowing, confident laugh of a man who knew what his touch did to her, a man who enjoyed making her heart beat erratically.

When they left the shanty, she waited for him to go before her as she'd been away long enough that even this part of the swamp wasn't as familiar as it had once been, especially in the dark after a rainstorm.

He reached back and took hold of her hand and for just a moment she was cast back in time, to the first time she'd met him when he'd led her out of the swamp. He'd been her hero in that moment, and for years that followed before fate had stepped in to separate them.

She'd thought she could just help him in his endeavor to clear his name, but the truth of the matter was she was precariously close to being in love with Beau all over again. And she didn't like it. She didn't like it at all.

She understood now that he was not only innocent of murdering Lacy, but he also hadn't betrayed her love on that fateful night. He'd told her that he and Lacy had never been lovers and after all this time he had no reason to lie about it. She'd spent the past fifteen years hating him for something he hadn't done.

However, she was terrified of loving him again. He'd spoken so briefly of his time in prison and yet she knew that time had to have changed him.

Right now there was no question that he desired her, but could he ever love her again, and did she really want him to? She shoved these thoughts aside.

It was possible she held the key to Lacy's murderer in

her purse right now. That was all she needed to focus on. Find the killer and then see if the two of them belonged together or not.

PEYTON WAS SEATED at her desk the next morning despite it being Saturday when Jackson walked in. *"Mon dieu,"* he exclaimed and stopped in front of her desk. "That man has only been back in your life for less than a week and already you've been hurt. Did he do that to you?"

Peyton reached up and touched her cheek. She'd nearly forgotten that the bruise was there. "Of course Beau didn't do this to me. He would never, ever hit a woman," she said indignantly. "I…uh…just hit it on a cabinet door in the dark in the middle of the night."

He stared at her for several long moments and then sat in the chair in front of her. "So what else is new besides you bouncing around off furniture in the dark and working on a Saturday?"

Peyton dropped her hand and hoped the bruise hid her blush. She didn't like to lie to anyone, especially to Jackson. But she didn't want to tell him what had really happened concerning the bruise because she didn't want to hear him go on and on about it.

"I've got another case, which is always a good thing," she said.

"That's what you should be doing, building your business, instead of chasing around and trying to find a killer from fifteen years ago."

"I can multitask and do both," she replied and smiled. "You should know by now that I'm an overachiever."

"You were an overachiever when you were younger because you were desperately trying to please your parents. Since nothing you did was ever going to please the two of them and they wrote you off and moved to New Orleans, you don't have to prove anything to anyone anymore."

Jackson knew how hard she'd worked, how desperate she had been to gain acceptance and love from her parents. It had taken her years to recognize that she was never going to get what she wanted...what she *needed* from them. She'd made peace with the fact that the problem hadn't been her, but rather her cold, distant and society-loving parents.

"I'm not trying to please anyone but myself," she finally replied.

"You're certainly not pleasing anyone in town. There's been a lot of talk about your investigation into Lacy's death. Nobody wants that can of worms reopened."

"Why? Why not open that can of worms? So nobody in this whole town cares about finding out the truth? Nobody cares that the real killer got away with his crime?" She looked at Jackson in disbelief. "You have always talked about the injustices and prejudices that go on in this town against the swamp people. Why would you not want me to help a man who went to prison for fifteen years for a crime he didn't commit? How would anyone be okay with that?"

She paused to draw a quick breath and then continued. "Beau's only crime was that he was from the swamp and was easily disposable so Gravois could write *solved* on his résumé. I've seen the facts, Jackson. I believe in Beau's innocence with all my heart and soul, and I don't give a damn what the gossipers in this town think."

"He wasn't good enough for you then and he's not good

enough for you now," Jackson said with a rise in his tone of voice.

She sat back in her chair and looked at him in surprise. "Jackson, I'm just helping him clear his name."

Jackson gave her a wry smile and shook his head. "I've known you for years, Peyton. I see the way your eyes light up when you mention his name. He's drawing you back in and I just don't want to see you get hurt by him again."

"Don't worry, Jackson. I don't intend to let him hurt me again," she assured him. "I'm much older and wiser this time around."

"Ah, but love can make a person feel young again. It can make a smart woman very foolish."

She laughed. "Oh, Jackson, you are such a cynic. Someday love is going to bite you in the butt and you'll become a foolish man."

"I don't see that happening. I'll probably eventually marry a woman to please my parents. That woman and I will enter into a relationship that financially and socially serves our best interests."

"And that makes me very sad for you," Peyton said to her friend.

Once Jackson left, their conversation played and replayed in Peyton's head. The two had often butted heads over the subject of love.

Jackson didn't believe the emotion existed, while she believed in a fairy-tale kind of love. She didn't want a business arrangement for a marriage; she wanted love to include desire and passion and an overwhelming sense of safety and belonging.

She spent the next couple of hours talking on the phone

to the district attorney to see how strong the charges made against Irene Farineau were, and if there was any wiggle room at all to get the charges dropped as long as full restitution was made to the store.

Unfortunately, he couldn't give her an answer without speaking to Claude Chastain, the owner of the store. The DA promised to get back to her in the next couple of days.

Meanwhile, Irene had already been arraigned and released on her own recognizance. Peyton wished she would have been called to represent Irene at the arraignment, but that had taken place before the couple had reached out to Peyton. All she could do now was try to get the woman a lesser sentence, or best-case scenario, get the charges against her dropped altogether.

It was after one when Beau came into the office. He'd driven her there that morning and had been working on the building until noon, when he always disappeared and then returned smelling clean and clad in different clothes.

He had made her promise the night before that she wouldn't do anything with the note from Angel until he was with her. He hadn't even wanted her to look at it until he was present and they could work at it together.

"Good afternoon," he said as he grabbed the back of the guest chair, carried it around the desk and placed it next to hers. "I saw that Mr. Perfect stopped in to see you."

"Mr. Perfect? You mean Jackson? Why on earth would you call him Mr. Perfect?" She looked at Beau curiously.

"I always thought he'd make you the perfect husband. He's handsome and comes from the right social class. He has a trust fund and knows all the right people. And so, there is your perfect man."

She laughed. "There's only two problems with that—Jackson is a close friend and I'm not in love with him."

"In the last fifteen years, have you been in love?" His gaze held hers with a sudden intensity.

"That's really none of your business," she said. She reached for her purse and pulled out the folded note. "*This* is your business and the first thing I need to do with it is make a couple of physical copies."

She was aware of his gaze following her as she got up and walked to the copier machine in the corner of the room. "I'll give you a copy and I'll keep one for myself. The original I'll take to the bank and have locked into my safety deposit box." She brought the copies back to her desk and sank back down. "I think we should also give Gravois a copy of this."

"Why?" Beau asked, obviously not liking the idea of sharing anything with the chief of police.

"Because I'd rather work with law enforcement whenever we can. Besides, if nothing else, maybe his curiosity will help us solve this…this riddle we've been left with. Now, let's get started. We'll work on it for a couple of hours and then I need to run some errands."

"And I will go with you to run those errands," he said. She started to protest, but he held up a hand to stop her. "Your bruise has not even faded yet and already you've forgotten that you're in danger. I will go with you to run your errands."

"Okay, then let's get started on this puzzle of the initials." She opened up a spreadsheet on her computer. The first set of initials was GM. "Gustave Martin," he immediately said. "Does he still own half of the properties on Main Street?"

"He does, and he's married so he would make perfect blackmail material." As she typed his name into the spreadsheet, Beau leaned close to her. As always, his scent fired something deep in the pit of her. It was the wildness of the swamp coupled with a pure clean maleness that belonged to Beau alone.

He still had the ability to make her feel like that breathless teenage girl who had loved him more than anything else in the world. He still had the capacity to make her feel more emotions than any other man had in her life.

She mentally shook herself and focused on the initials. "There's also George Marcel. He's also married and has family money." She added his name into the computer. "We'll just go down the list and add the names that easily pop up in our heads. Then once I get the property tax records later this afternoon, we can add in anyone we missed."

"Sounds good to me," he replied.

For the next hour they went down the list of initials, filling in names as they came to mind and leaving the ones where names didn't immediately come.

They were more than halfway through the list when they came to the initials JF. "Perfect man Jackson is a JF."

"I can't imagine Jackson murdering anybody under any circumstances," she said, even as she typed his name into the spreadsheet.

"No, but he probably would have framed me to keep me away from you," Beau said wryly.

"Don't be ridiculous," she scoffed.

He laughed. "I'm not being ridiculous. You and I both know Jackson hated the fact that we were together."

"He still wouldn't have done anything like that," she replied. "Who else has those initials?" It took only a minute for her to think of another name. "Jason Farineau. He has money and clout, and I would guess he has little respect for his wife, so I can see him frequenting the women at the motel."

"Then there's Jack… Jack Fontenot," Beau added. "But at the time of the murder Jack wasn't married and our construction company had only just started. In fact, I'm seeing him Monday afternoon for a little business talk."

"He still goes on the list," she replied as she typed in his name.

They worked for another thirty minutes and then called it quits so she could run her errands. The first stop was Gravois's office, where Beau waited in the car while Peyton ran into the police station.

"Where did this come from?" Gravois asked when she handed him a copy of the initials.

"It doesn't matter. What matters is we believe these initials are of the men who saw Lacy around the time of her death. And we believe one of those men is her real killer."

He tossed the paper aside and frowned. "This is garbage. I don't know where you managed to dig that up, but it's not worth anything. Besides, do you really think I'm going to spend my time investigating a crime from fifteen years ago? There's plenty of crime happening right here and now that takes up all my time and energy."

His time and energy seemed to be mostly devoted to sitting at his desk and drinking coffee, she thought wryly. "I just thought you might want to know about this. You know, as one professional to another."

The stroke to his ego in identifying him as a fellow professional puffed out his chest. "I appreciate it, Peyton. I like to know what's going on in my town. Speaking of that… how'd you get that nasty bruise on your cheek?"

"A run-in with a cabinet door in the dark." The lie rolled easily off her tongue this time. There was no point in telling him the truth. He wouldn't be able to solve the crime of her attack without her being able to give him something to go on, and she had nothing. "And now I need to run," she said.

From Gravois's office, they went to city hall to get a list of all the tax-paying property owners in town and then they ended up in the bank, where she locked the original list into her safety deposit box.

"Why don't we head to Marie's and grab some dinner," he suggested once they were finished with all their running.

She looked at her watch, surprised that it was already almost six. The afternoon had flown by and as if to punctuate the point, her stomach growled loudly.

Beau laughed. "Now, that sounds like a woman ready to eat."

"And now that I think about it, I'm definitely hungry."

Kylie would have closed up the office so there was really no reason not to grab dinner before heading home.

"It's Saturday night. Will we even be able to get a booth or a table?" she asked as Beau drove them toward the café.

"Marie will make sure we have a place to sit," he replied confidently.

Sure enough, the place was packed when they walked through the front doors. There were also several couples before them waiting to find an empty seat.

"Come on," Beau said. He grabbed her hand and pulled her back outside. "There's always a table in the kitchen for us."

"That was years ago, Beau. I'm sure things have changed by now," she replied.

He gazed at her with dark, enigmatic eyes. "Some things never change with time." He broke eye contact and led her around the building to the back door. When they walked in, Marie immediately spied them and hurried over to hug them both.

"We came to eat, but the place is packed," Beau said.

"You know you always have a table here," she said and pointed to the small table in the corner of the kitchen. "Sit, and then tell me what you want to eat."

They sat where they had years ago, with Marie beaming at the two of them. "Now, this brings me back to a happy place in life. Seeing you two together in my kitchen brings back all kinds of good memories," Marie said.

They ordered their food and while they waited, Peyton thought about Marie's words. Oh yes, there were wonderful memories here. She and Beau had spent many hours here in Marie's kitchen, enjoying the delicious food and laughing together.

This noisy, heavenly scented kitchen was a location where their love for each other had grown. They had teased each other and had long, meaningful discussions over platters of Marie's food. They had planned their future together, and those had been magical times.

She couldn't allow any of that magic to happen this time. Beau was a part of her past and she had no idea if he fit into her future or not. Aside from helping him clear his name, she wasn't at all sure what he wanted from her. Did he want anything more from her than a quick roll in the hay for old time's sake?

She knew instinctively that she couldn't fall in bed with

him now and walk away unscathed. And the idea of making love to him again only to watch him walk away from her tortured her heart to its very depths.

Chapter Seven

Monday at one-thirty in the afternoon, Beau pulled his truck up to the curb in front of J's Construction Company. If the building front was any indication, the company had definitely done well in the past fifteen years. Painted a steel gray, the front of the business also boasted large black letters announcing the establishment. It appeared clean and classy, and a strong sense of pride filled him.

This had been his baby. Even at the young age of twenty-one, he knew the town had needed a new construction company with good, trustworthy and skilled workers.

He mourned for the time lost in being a part of this, in having the hands-on experiences of taking the company from its infancy to where it was now.

He'd called earlier that morning to make sure Jack would be in the office. Peyton also knew he'd be here this afternoon. He'd driven her to work that morning and just before she went into the building, she told him that she had a date that night with Sam Landry. He'd been positively stunned by the news. For some reason he'd hoped she wouldn't be seeing the banker anymore.

He still didn't know what he really wanted from Peyton—

although he definitely knew he wanted to make love to her one more time, if for no other reason than to get her completely out of his blood.

Knowing she had a date later tonight with Sam had kicked him in the ass. Sam was the antithesis of Beau. He was respectable and came from the same background as Peyton. He was a perfect match for her. Beau tried to shove all these thoughts aside as he walked up to the front door of the construction company.

A touch of anxiety filled his chest. He hoped like hell he could just walk back into the business and start working as soon as he finished up things with Peyton.

He opened the front door and stepped inside. The interior was huge, with samples of flooring and tile hanging on one side of the room. There was an area set up like a kitchen, with choices for color and backsplashes and miscellaneous other things. Finally, there was a huge wall of indoor/outdoor paint colors.

He found Jack seated at a desk in the back of the shop. "Hey, Beau." Jack stood and held out his hand.

Beau grasped Jack's hand firmly as he grinned at the man who had been his very best friend while growing up. "Good to see you again. Have a seat," Jack said once their handshake had ended.

Beau sank down in the chair in front of the desk, while Jack resumed his seat behind it. "The office looks amazing," Beau said. "Bigger and much better than I ever imagined."

"Yeah, it's finally all come together. How have you been adjusting to being back home?" Jack asked.

"I've been working a lot with Peyton. We're investigating Lacy's murder in order to find out the real killer. And speaking of Lacy… Did you ever visit her at the motel for any reason?"

"Never," he said firmly. "The day I have to pay for sex is the day I become celibate," he said with a laugh. "Besides, if you remember, I was dating Cecile Macron back then, and she was more than I could handle. Why would you ask me about seeing Lacy?"

"Just curious, that's all. So are you seeing anyone now?" Beau asked.

"I've been dating Mary Ingram for the last five months. In fact, I'm thinking about proposing to her in the very near future."

"I don't know her, but congratulations."

"She's a niece of Jimmy and Anne Ingram. Her parents were killed in a car crash when she was fifteen years old, and she came to live with them about a year after you got locked up. She's a nice woman who, for some strange reason, seems wild about me," Jack said with a wide grin.

"That's great, man," Beau replied.

"So you and Peyton have hooked up again. How's that going?" Jack asked.

"We haven't hooked up in any kind of a romantic way," Beau said. "We're just working together right now. And speaking of that, I'm here to talk about the business. I certainly don't expect you to pay me for all the time I was gone, but as part-owner, I would think I might be due something."

"Uh…" Jack glanced away from him. "Beau, you aren't a part-owner right now."

Beau looked at him in surprise. "What do you mean?"

Jack looked back at him with a deep frown. "Beau, you've got to look at all this from my position. You had been arrested for murder and convicted to spend years in prison. So I felt it was in my best interest—in the best interest of the company—to distance myself from you, so when I went to file the paperwork for the business, I didn't add you on as an owner."

Beau stared at him, stunned by what his friend had just told him. "So you cut me out even though the business was my idea and we had planned all of it as partners."

Jack's cheeks turned ruddy with color. "Hell, Beau, I didn't even know if I'd ever see you again. I had to do what was best for me. Why do you think I didn't write to you? I'm sorry, man, but that's just the way it is."

Beau stared at him for several long moments. "You believe I'm guilty," he finally said.

Once again Jack's cheeks turned red and he looked away from Beau. "I don't… I didn't know what to believe. All I knew was I couldn't have a business partner who was in prison for murder."

For fifteen years Beau had believed he had a business to come home to. That and thoughts of Peyton were what had kept him sane as he went through the long days and nights of prison life.

He was so shocked by this turn of events, for several long moments he didn't know what to say or how to act. He finally managed to pull himself together. "I'm hoping to clear my name in the next month or two. Once I do that, can we revisit this issue?"

"Sure, we can do that, but I really don't see how you're going to solve a crime that happened so long ago," Jack replied.

"We've gotten a major clue and so we're hoping it will help us find the real killer in the next week or so," Beau replied.

"Really? What's the clue?" Jack asked curiously.

"We're keeping it close to our chests until the time we can name our killer," Beau replied and stood. "So I guess I'll just see you around."

"Beau, I'm sorry for the way things turned out," Jack said.

"Yeah, me, too."

"Once you clear your name then come back to see me and we'll talk about the business again."

Beau didn't reply but rather turned and headed for the door. He felt as if his very guts had just been punched out of him.

He didn't understand why Jack hadn't, at the very least, considered Beau a silent partner and put his name on the paperwork as one of the owners. If he was worried about Beau's name being tied to the business, nobody would have had to know that he was a silent partner. It wasn't like Jack had to flash his paperwork every time he did a job.

It was a deep cut, an ultimate betrayal by the man he'd once considered his very best friend. Jack had been like a brother to Beau, but right now Beau felt like he'd been gutted.

Once outside, he got into his truck but instead of heading directly back toward Peyton's office, he drove aimlessly up and down the streets.

Initially, he'd come up with the idea of a construction company because Black Bayou only had a couple of handymen to take care of the needs of the people. More importantly, it had been something he'd wanted to do in order to make himself more worthy of Peyton.

Peyton's family was wealthy, and he'd wanted to be able to bring something to the table to prove to them that he was more than just a swamp rat. He wanted to prove to them that he could provide for Peyton in a respectable, meaningful way.

When he'd come back here after serving time, he'd been oddly pleased to discover that Peyton was still single. He'd believed he'd walk back into his business and he'd take time to explore his unresolved feelings where she was concerned.

However, while Peyton was helping him, she wasn't really letting him into her life in any meaningful way. Hell, she had a date tonight! And now his business had basically been stolen away from him. At the moment he felt more broken than the day he'd been pronounced guilty in Lacy's murder.

He now realized he had nothing here. Even if he cleared his name, he wasn't sure he was willing to go to Jack and beg and grovel for a piece of the business back. He'd thought he knew what his future held, but now he had no clue. Even if they managed to clear his name, he had no idea going forward what he would do for work.

He drove around for about an hour and then finally found himself parked in front of the Voodoo Lounge. It was a dive bar on the west side of town, a place his father had frequented often.

Being raised by a mean alcoholic father, Beau had sworn he'd never grow up to be a drunk like his old man, but right now a drink called to him to take the edge off the raw emotions that roared through him...myriad emotions he couldn't begin to untangle at the moment.

He walked into the dim premises that smelled of stale beer, perspiration and greasy bar food. There were several men seated at the long bar, not speaking to each other but instead staring down into their drinks.

Beau moved to the far end of the bar, not wanting to interact with anyone. He was not in the mood to make friendly chatter. All he wanted was a scotch on the rocks and a few minutes to process where on earth he was going with his life, with his future.

He ordered from the bartender, a young man he didn't know, and once he had the drink in hand, he took a deep sip of it, welcoming the slide of warmth down his throat and into his stomach.

It felt as if all he'd ever known in his entire life was carpentry and Peyton, and he now realized for the first time since being back in Black Bayou that it didn't matter whether he was innocent or not…he was going to have to rebuild his life from the ground up.

Without carpentry…and without Peyton.

He slammed down the rest of the drink and then ordered another one. He sipped this one slowly, staring down at the scars on the bar top. Initials carved into the wood were next to drink rings and cigarette burns.

What in the hell was he doing here? In a dive bar where losers who had given up on themselves came to die a slow death? Dammit, he wasn't a loser. He was a survivor. He didn't belong here.

He needed to get out of there. He checked the time on his phone and realized it was a few minutes before four. Peyton had wanted to go home by three so he was late getting back to take her home.

He pushed the second drink away and then left the bar. As he drove back to Peyton's office, a slow burn of anger reignited in the pit of his stomach.

It was anger at the utter betrayal by the friend he had trusted more than any other man, and by the woman who had once declared her undying love for him, yet had still believed him capable of killing a woman.

It was slow-burning rage at a life that had seen him tossed into prison for a crime he hadn't committed, of having so much of his life stolen from him.

By the time he pulled up to Peyton's office, his anger still clung to him like a layer of Spanish moss hugging a cypress tree.

When he entered the building there was no sign of Kylie at the front desk. Peyton opened the inner office door and stepped out.

"You're late," she said, her tone holding more than a little bit of irritation.

He stepped closer to her. "Does it really take you this much time to get ready for your big date with Mr. Wonderful Sam?"

She frowned. "Don't be a jerk about it, Beau. Sam is a very nice man and I asked you to be back here to get me home by three today. I texted you several times."

He took another step toward her. "I didn't pay attention to the texts and I'm not being a jerk about Sam. I see how perfect he is for you. He comes from the right background, he's highly respectable... On paper he ticks all the boxes for being the perfect husband for you."

"What on earth gave you the idea I'm looking for a husband?"

"I don't know. I know how much you wanted children and time is a ticking." This time his step forward put him so close to her he could smell her tantalizing scent and see the slight whisper of something in the depths of her eyes. "Don't you remember, *ma chérie*, how we planned for our babies? First, a little boy and then a baby girl? Perhaps you were just pretending to want my children. Maybe you were just pretending the whole time to love me."

Her eyes flared wide and she pushed hard against his chest, moving him back a step. "You've been drinking," she said with surprised accusation.

"Ah, give the lady a stuffed bear," he replied sarcastically and clapped his hands together.

"Beau, what are you trying to do right now? Why do I get the distinct feeling you're trying to pick a fight with me?" Her beautiful eyes searched his features.

Just that quickly his anger seeped out of him, leaving a bad taste in the back of his mouth. He looked away from her and took several more steps back. "Don't worry about it. Let's get you home."

The drive to her place was silence and charged with tension. Once they arrived, she got out of the truck and slammed the door behind her. He headed back to Vincent's and then he headed back into the swamp. As he ran through the thick vegetation, he wondered if he'd been a fool all along to believe he could have a life outside the swamp.

Maybe, like Angel, he was destined to live all alone in his shack, picking up odd jobs here and there to make enough money to sustain him.

He'd definitely been a fool to believe he would get the girl, because his girl was now getting ready for a date with another man.

THAT EVENING WAS Peyton's last date with Sam. At the end of the date, after dinner at the café, she'd told Sam they had no future together and should stop seeing one another.

They had dated enough times now that she knew she had no real physical attraction to him. It wasn't fair for her to keep going on dinner dates with him. It wasn't fair to keep wasting his time when she felt the way she did about him. He was a nice man, but he wasn't her man.

She and Beau had worked every afternoon to make sure they had all the names matched up with the initials. She'd checked the tax records to find names there and as of this morning they had twenty-three men on their list, one of whom was assuredly Lacy's killer.

As she stared down at the names, a banging began from outside. Beau had finished up yanking off all the rotten wood from the front of the building three days ago. The next day she'd arranged for a delivery of some of the new supplies he would need to continue the job, and he'd gotten straight to work.

Beau. For the past week she'd been a bit concerned about him. Since the day he'd come back to the office late after having a drink or two and then taken her home, he'd been unusually quiet and distant.

Gone was the wicked sparkle in his eyes, along with the seductive overtures from him. She'd told herself she hated it when he reached out and touched her hair or stroked his fingers down her cheeks. But the truth of the matter was she missed all those things now.

More importantly, she wanted to know what had happened to change things with him. Was he still reacting to the fact that she'd had a date with Sam? She hadn't told him yet that she'd broken things off with Sam, but he'd known she was seeing the banker from the very beginning of this strange working new relationship of theirs.

So if it wasn't that, then what was it? What had changed in him? And why did she miss him teasing and tormenting her with his sinful words and touch?

She shoved these troubling thoughts aside. On the agenda for today was going to see Louis Rivet, the alcoholic whose testimony had helped to put Beau away.

In the excitement of getting Lacy's note from the grave, she'd nearly forgotten what else needed to be done in order to prove Beau's innocence.

It was a long shot that the man would remember anything meaningful about that night so long ago, but she couldn't leave any stone unturned in their pursuit of the truth.

She spent the morning reading over the paperwork she had generated for the case of Beau's innocence. She checked and double-checked the names on their list of potential suspects. She'd been surprised to discover that several of the men whose initials were on Lacy's list of clients were also "happily" married pillars of society.

Once they spoke with Louis, then they would begin interviewing the men on their list and hopefully, the real killer would somehow give them a sign of their guilt.

They had already written off a few of the men on the list, such as Jack Fontenot, who was Beau's business partner. At the time of Lacy's death, he'd been a young man just talking about starting up a business. Neither Peyton nor Beau saw him as a potential blackmail subject.

She'd wanted to write off Jackson, not wanting to believe her good friend could have had anything to do with the murder. Even though Jackson had been a young man, too, at the time of Lacy's murder, his hefty bank account along with his hatred of Beau gave her pause.

Was it possible Jackson had been seeing Lacy? Was it somehow possible he had found Beau's necklace and had decided to remove Beau from Peyton's life? Her heart told her there was no way Jackson would murder a woman, but her head couldn't write him off completely.

The morning seemed to fly by. The banging outside eventually stopped, she ate a sandwich for lunch, and then around one Beau walked into her office. He smelled of clean male, letting her know he'd taken a shower after working in the heat all morning.

"Are you ready to go?" he asked.

"Yes, I'm ready." She pulled her purse from beneath her desk and stood.

Together they left the inner office and Peyton smiled at Kylie. "We're heading out for a while. You know the drill, keep the doors open and if anyone comes in, have them fill out a contact form. We should be back before five, but if we aren't just close up as usual."

"Got it," Kylie replied with her usual bright smile.

Minutes later they were in Beau's truck and headed toward the motel, where Louis still lived in the unit two doors down from the room where Lacy had once lived and had been murdered.

"I still can't believe Louis was the prosecutor's main witness," she said.

"Gravois would have taken a statement from a sunbathing gator if he thought it would help put me away," Beau replied dryly. "Sometimes I wonder if he knows who the real killer is—if he got a payoff or something in order for him to protect the guilty."

"I would certainly hate to believe that of our law enforcement, especially that the chief of police would actually cover up for a murderer."

"I'd believe anything when it comes to Gravois," he replied darkly.

"Well, let's hope Louis remembers something more from that night than seeing you go into Lacy's room and then leave." What she wanted to do was ask Beau what had changed between them. Why had he been so distant lately?

However, this wasn't the place and there wasn't enough time to have any kind of a real discussion with him as before she knew it, he was pulling into the motel parking lot. There was a part of her that was reluctant to say anything at all and just hoped he resolved whatever was going on in his head.

He parked in front of unit five, where a faded red beat-up fishing chair sat just outside the door. They got out of the car and Beau walked up to the unit. He knocked and they waited a moment but there was no answer. He knocked a little harder with the same response.

"Maybe he isn't here," she said.

"Oh, he's here. No self-respecting drunk is seen out and about this early in the day." He banged on the door with enough force to wake the dead.

"Wha…what's going on?" Louis's voice bellowed from inside.

"Louis, we need to speak with you," Peyton yelled through the door.

"Are you the cops?" Louis asked.

"No, we aren't the cops," Peyton replied and wondered why he would be expecting the police.

"Give me just a minute." It took more like five minutes before Louis's door finally opened. Instantly, the smell of booze filled the air. Louis's short legs were clad in a pair of dirty jeans. His protruding stomach was covered with a filthy white T-shirt, and his gray hair was a grizzly mass that looked like it hadn't seen a comb in years.

At one point in his life, Peyton had heard that Louis was a fine car mechanic. Unfortunately booze had stolen not only his job away from him, but also his home and everything else.

He frowned first at Beau and then at Peyton. "Who are you and what in the hell do you want with me?"

"My name is Peyton LaCroix and I'm a defense attorney. I'm here to talk to you about the murder that took place here fifteen years ago."

Louis's frown deepened. "I don't ever like to think about that. It was the very worst night of my life. It makes me so sad. She was such a nice woman. Sometimes she would bring me a sandwich."

"I know it was sad, Louis, but I really need you to think about that night right now," Peyton replied.

Louis's dark eyes gazed at her slyly. "I always think a little better if I have a bit of cash in my pocket."

Peyton started to open her purse, but Beau stopped her. "No. We don't pay for information," he said firmly to Louis.

Louis glared at Beau for several long moments and then his eyes widened and he released a small gasp. "You're him… I saw you that night going into her room."

"That's right. This is Beau Boudreau. He was a good friend of Lacy's. Do you have any idea what time you saw him go into her room?" Peyton asked.

"Don't you remember?" Louis asked Beau.

"We need *you* to remember," Peyton said.

"Let me think a minute." He unfolded the fishing chair and sank down and as he did, she noticed that his hands held a slight tremor. He'd just awakened and he was probably already in withdrawal.

"I was sitting here that night, enjoying a little cocktail or two and watching the people come and go," he said. He frowned again. "That was a long time ago."

"Yes, I know it was, but I really need you to think about it, Louis," Peyton pressed. "It's important. Was it after dark when Beau came here?"

His bushy eyebrows pulled together in another frown. "I'm thinking it was around sunset."

Beau nodded and Peyton continued, "So did you see anyone else come to her room that night?"

He darted a glance to the left and to the right, and then looked back at Peyton. "They told me not to tell about anyone else coming," Louis replied in a whisper.

Peyton's heart banged against her ribs in an accelerated beat. "Who told you that, Louis? Who told you not to say anything about other people coming to her room?"

"Gravois and that other man, the one who bought me a new suit."

"You mean Charles Landry, the former prosecuting attorney?"

Louis nodded. "That's him. He bought me a nice, new suit and then let me stay with him in his big old mansion for two nights before the trial. It was luxury digs, that's for sure. The bed was so soft I felt like I was sleeping on a cloud."

"Back to my original question," Peyton continued. "Did you see anyone else visit Lacy's room on the night of her murder?"

"She had a couple more visitors that night after Beau left. But don't ask me who they were because it was dark and I didn't really see them clearly. Are we done now?"

"Almost," Peyton replied. "Did Lacy's other visitors that night drive here?"

"They did. You'd be surprised by how many fancy cars used to creep in here under the cover of night," Louis replied.

"Did you recognize what kind of cars the visitors drove in?" Peyton asked.

"Nah, I don't know much about cars. They all look alike to me, especially when it's dark outside. But they were fancy ones."

"I am absolutely outraged by what we just heard," Peyton said a few minutes later as Beau left the motel parking lot. "Gravois and Landry paid a witness to forget what he saw. They bribed him with a new suit and a stay in *luxurious digs*. With that information alone I could get you a new trial, Beau. You go back to trial and I know we could win and clear your name."

"I don't care about a new trial, and I'm not sure I care about any of this anymore."

She shot him a look of surprise. "What are you talking about? Beau, what's wrong?"

"Nothing's wrong. But I was wondering if I could just take you on home now. I know it's early, but I have some other things to take care of and I don't want you getting home from the office under your own steam."

"I guess I could go on home for the day," she agreed. "But we go on as usual tomorrow, right?"

He was silent for a long moment and then released a deep sigh. "I guess," he finally agreed.

"You can't give up on this now, Beau," she said fervently. "I don't know what's going on in that brain of yours right now, but you can't give up on finding out the truth. I really believe we're moving closer and closer to learning the answers that will finally set you free and see a killer behind bars."

By that time, he had pulled up in her driveway. She placed her hand on his arm and felt a simmering tension there. "Promise me, Beau. Promise me that we don't stop digging until we have the answers about who really killed Lacy. She deserves justice."

Once again, he was quiet for several long moments. He finally looked at her, but his eyes were shuttered and revealed nothing of his thoughts. He looked at her for just a moment and then gazed back out the truck window. "Okay, I promise," he replied.

"Then I'll see you in the morning." She got out of the truck and then went into her house, her thoughts deeply troubled. Why was she suddenly fighting harder for Beau's innocence than he was? Dammit, what had changed with him?

The first thing she did was call Kylie and let her know she was going to be out of the office for the rest of the day. Once that was done, she decided to indulge herself with a leisurely bath.

Fifteen minutes later she lowered herself into the tub full of warm water and scented bubbles. Immediately, thoughts of Beau once again filled her head.

Why on earth would he be ready to give up on finding the killer when each day she felt them getting closer to discovering the murderer's identity? Once again she was reminded that she really didn't know this Beau. She'd only known him as a confident, bold young man. This brooding, quiet man was a virtual stranger to her.

She remained in the tub until the water turned cold and all the bubbles were gone and only then did she get out. She dried off and then pulled on a pink sleeveless summer shift.

She ate a salad for dinner and then curled up on the sofa to watch a little television. It felt good to give herself the permission to stop thinking about anything important for a little while and instead just enjoy watching several silly sitcoms.

When it finally got dark outside, she was drowsy and ready to call it a night. She turned off the television and pulled herself up and off the sofa.

Before heading to her bedroom, she walked over to her front window to pull the curtains closed. Normally, she did that as soon as she got home from work, but with her normal schedule being disrupted that day, she'd forgotten to do it.

She now reached out for one side of the gray curtain and pulled it closed. She turned, but before she could walk away a boom sounded from outside. The window glass exploded inward and at the same time a scorching pain seared through her shoulder.

She stumbled backward and fell to the floor. *Wha...what just happened?* For a moment her brain refused to work as pain flamed through her.

She was afraid to stand and so she began to crawl toward the kitchen, where her purse was on the counter. Sobs escaped her...deep sobs of both fear and pain. She needed her cell phone. Oh, God, she needed to call somebody for help.

Shock ripped through her as she tried to process what had just happened to her. As she moved, bright red blood splashed on the floor from the wound in her shoulder.

She finally got to her purse, yanked out her cell phone and called for help. "This is Peyton LaCroix," she said amid sobs to the emergency dispatcher. "Please, I n-need help. I've j-just been shot."

Chapter Eight

Beau sat on his sofa and listened to the bog singing its night-time songs. He felt as if he'd been in a fog ever since speaking with Jack. He wasn't sure it mattered anymore whether he proved his innocence or not. Sure, it would be great to find the real killer, the person who had not only snuffed out Lacy's life but also framed him for the crime. But after speaking with Jack, he'd lost his vision of returning to a productive and meaningful life here.

He'd spent most of his adult life as an inmate. He'd been told when and what to eat, when to go to work and when to sleep. Now without his business to go back to, he felt absolutely rudderless.

As a carpenter on his own he would never be able to compete with the business Jack now had. He still wanted to build something for himself career-wise, but he didn't know where to begin.

And then there was Peyton…

"Yo, Beau." The deep voice came from outside.

Beau jumped up and opened his door. Gator stood just outside. "Hey, Gator. What's going on? Out on one of your nighttime walks?"

"I was, but while I was walking, I figured you'd want to hear what I just now heard through the grapevine," the old man said.

"And what's that?" Beau asked.

"I just heard that your lady friend lawyer got shot tonight."

"Got shot?" Beau stared at Gator for a long moment as his brain whirled to make sense of what he'd just heard. "Shot..." he echoed faintly. "Where... Is she okay?"

"I don't know anything else about it other than she was shot and rushed to the hospital. I figured you needed to know."

Energy flooded through Beau. "Thanks, Gator." Beau turned around and went back inside, where he grabbed the truck keys. He then raced back outside, passing by Gator as Beau raced through the swamp to get to where his truck was parked.

The grapevine in the swamp was usually fairly accurate, but in this case he desperately hoped it was wrong. If the gossip was right, then how badly had she been hurt? Where had she been to get shot in the first place?

A hundred questions raced through his head and his heart was beating a million miles a minute when he finally reached his truck. He jumped inside, fired up the engine and took off for the hospital.

If she wasn't there, then he would know the gossip had been wrong. He prayed she wasn't there and that she was in her home safe and sound.

He tightened his hands on the steering wheel as he sped down the streets. He still couldn't figure out where she'd been if she'd really gotten shot. Had she decided to make a quick run to the grocery store? To another store? Dammit, how could he protect her if she decided to go out and about on her own?

He finally squealed into the hospital lot and pulled into one of the empty parking spaces. He cut the engine, got out of his truck and then raced for the emergency room entrance.

Lydia March manned the desk. He'd known her before he'd gone to prison. They had gone to school together. Her eyes now widened slightly at the sight of him. "Hey, Beau."

"Hi, Lydia. I heard Peyton LaCroix was brought in a little while ago for a gunshot wound. Could you tell the doctor I'm here and would like to know her condition as soon as possible?"

She nodded. "I'll be right back." She disappeared through a door that was marked Authorized Personnel Only.

Beau's heart dropped. He'd hoped that Lydia would look at him like he was out of his mind and tell him Peyton wasn't here. But she hadn't, which meant Peyton was here and she had really been shot.

So how badly had she been hurt? Was she now barely clinging to life? How had this happened? The thought nearly cast him to his knees. He walked over to one of the plastic chairs and collapsed down, his heart still beating a rhythm of anxiety.

Lydia returned to the desk. "Dr. Richards will be with you when he can."

"Thanks," Beau replied.

He remained seated in the chair for what seemed like an eternity. His heart continued to beat an unnatural quickened rhythm as he prayed that she would be okay.

Finally, Dr. Richards came through the door. Beau jumped

up out of his chair to greet the doctor. He had no memory of the dark-haired man who appeared to be about Beau's age.

"She's doing just fine," Dr. Richards said. "She gave me permission to speak to you. She's one lucky lady—the bullet only grazed her shoulder. She heard you were here and she wants to see you. I'll take you back to her."

A wealth of relief shuddered through Beau as he followed the doctor through the door that led into the emergency room treatment area. He turned into the first unit and Beau stepped in behind him.

She sat in the bed, appearing small and fragile. She was clad in a hospital gown and it was obvious her right shoulder wore thick bandages.

The moment she saw Beau she burst into tears. He rushed to her side, wanting to pull her into his arms and hold her there forever, but he was afraid of further hurting her. Instead, he leaned over, kissed her forehead and then took hold of her left hand.

"S...somebody shot me, Beau. Somebody shot me right through my living room window," she said amid her tears. "I... I was getting ready to...to pull my curtains closed and somebody shot me."

"I'm sorry, chérie. I'm so sorry this happened to you, but you're safe now," he said softly. He wanted to hear exactly what happened, but first he looked at the doctor. "What happens next?"

"She's free to go. I've cleaned and dressed the wound and given her some pain medication. I'll write a prescription for some antibiotics and pain pills. If you both just sit tight, I'll take care of that and then send the nurse in."

"Thank you, Doctor," Beau said.

"Yes, thank you for taking such good care of me," Peyton added through her tears.

Once the doctor was gone, Beau pulled a chair up next to the side of Peyton's bed. "It's all my fault," she said and grabbed a tissue from the box on the table next to her. She dabbed at her teary eyes.

"How is this your fault?" he asked.

"I made myself the perfect target." She explained to him how she'd forgotten to pull the curtains shut when she'd first arrived home. "When I decided to close them, I made a perfect target in the window. It…it was stupid of me."

Beau frowned. What bothered him was the fact that somebody had obviously been outside her house just waiting for the exact opportunity to shoot her. And he had a definite feeling this wasn't her fault, but rather it was his.

He should have never pulled her into his desire to catch a killer. After she was attacked next to her car and punched in the face, he should have walked away from her.

Before he could voice his thoughts to her, Thomas Gravois stepped into the room. "Peyton, how are you doing?"

"I'm okay, considering I was just shot," she said with a touch of sarcasm. She grabbed the button to raise the head of the hospital bed a little more. "Thankfully, the bullet just grazed my shoulder."

"Well, that's good. I wish I could tell you we've got the shooter under arrest, but unfortunately, we don't." The lawman pulled a pen and a small notebook out of his back pocket. "I didn't get a chance to talk to you before the ambulance took you away, so now I need to know exactly what happened."

As Peyton relayed the events of the night, Beau's brain

whirled with dozens of thoughts. The fact that if the bullet had hit her an inch or so to the left, then she'd be dead, absolutely horrified him.

Who? Who had sat in a vehicle or stood outside in her yard with the intent of killing her? He didn't have to ask himself the *why*. He suspected whoever it was believed that if Peyton was dead then Beau would be so distraught, he'd be so ripped apart, that he'd stop his quest for the killer. And that was probably what would happen.

He'd be devastated if Peyton died, not because he needed her to help him clear his name. Despite his core of hurt and anger at her for not believing in him years ago, he still cared deeply about her.

He focused back on the conversation between Peyton and Gravois. "We canvassed the area and spoke to your neighbors. Unfortunately, none of them saw a person or a vehicle in front of your place. So they were no help in identifying the shooter," Gravois said.

"That doesn't surprise me," Peyton said. "It was dark outside and there aren't enough streetlights in the area to begin with."

"The good news is we found the slug in the wall opposite the front window. I'll send it off to the lab to see what they can tell me about it."

"Hell, everyone in this town owns a gun. It's going to be damned hard to match the striations and whatever to a gun unless that particular gun was used in another crime," Beau said.

"Do you know anyone who might have an issue with you?" Gravois asked her. "Maybe somebody who was unhappy with your representation in a particular case?"

"I can tell you who did this. It's the same person who punched her in the face," Beau said. "It's Lacy Dupree's murderer. He feels the heat of us getting closer to him and he's getting desperate to somehow halt our investigation."

"When did somebody punch you in the face?" Gravois asked, a deep frown cutting across his forehead. "Is that how you got that bruise that was on your face? You told me you ran into a cabinet door."

"It's not important now," Peyton replied. "I didn't see the person at all so I didn't report it because I knew there was nothing you could do about it."

"Still, you should have made a report. I need to know what's happening in my town."

"Speaking of what's going on in your town, have there been any breaks in the Honey Island Monster murders?" Beau asked.

"We're working on it," Gravois said, his frown cutting even deeper. He looked back at Peyton. "We finished up our investigation in your house so you're free to go home whenever you get released from here. I left an officer there to guard it since it was unlocked and we didn't know if you had a key."

"Actually, I'm being released in just a few minutes," she replied. "And I didn't exactly take the time to grab my house keys."

"Peyton, I want you to know I'm taking this all very seriously and will continue to work the case." Gravois shoved his pen and notepad back into his pocket. "In the meantime, the two of you might want to consider halting your little investigation. You're both just asking for trouble."

"Thanks for the advice," Peyton said. "But somebody

has to investigate to find the real killer, and you've made it abundantly clear that you just want to forget that an innocent man went to prison."

Gravois's nostrils flared with his displeasure at her words. "I have more than enough on my plate right now. I don't have the time or the energy to go back and re-solve a crime that happened fifteen years ago. In the meantime, I'll stay in touch and if anything else happens, don't hesitate to call me."

The minute Gravois left, a nurse came into the room. "Here are your two scripts." She handed the two pieces of paper to Peyton. "And here's clean bandages for your wound. The doctor wants your bandages changed tomorrow. Unfortunately, the pretty shift you wore in didn't survive, so you'll have to wear the hospital gown home. Now, let's get that IV out of you and you can be on your way."

Forty-five minutes later they had picked up her two prescriptions and were pulling up in Peyton's driveway. He got out of the truck and then hurried around to help her out.

A single police officer sat in a car by the curb. He got out of his vehicle and approached them. "The front door was left unlocked so Chief Gravois directed me to sit on the house until you returned here."

"Thank you so much," Peyton said. "I appreciate being able to go back inside and not be afraid that somebody is in there waiting for me."

"Trust me. Nobody is inside, but if it would make you feel better, I could do a quick walk-through."

"Do you mind?"

"Not at all. Why don't you two wait out here for a couple of minutes and I'll check out the premises."

"I hate this," Beau said as the officer disappeared into the house. "I hate that this has happened and I hate that I'm not the man with a gun going in to check things out. But as a felon, I can't own a gun. And I hate like hell that this happened to you." A swift anger filled him, but he tamped it down. Peyton didn't need his anger right now.

He reached out to her and pulled her closer to him, careful not to hurt her shoulder. To his surprise, she came willingly into him. "I own a gun," she said softly.

Before Beau could respond, the police officer came back outside. "All clear," he said.

"Thank you," Peyton said and moved away from Beau.

"No problem. I hope we catch the creep. I'm just sorry this happened to you, Ms. LaCroix, and now I need to be on my way."

A moment later the officer was gone and Beau and Peyton walked into her living room. Glass shards glittered on the floor near the window. Beau stepped over the mess to close the curtains and then he turned to face her.

"Are you ready to stop now and leave things up to me?" he asked.

"Hell no," she replied, and that stubborn chin of hers shot straight up. "This just makes me angrier and even more determined than ever to catch this creep. Among his other crimes, he tried to kill me tonight. I just need to be more careful."

"You aren't safe here anymore, Peyton. Don't you understand that? You can no longer stay here, but I know a place where you'll be perfectly safe. Go change your clothes and pack a bag. I'm taking you to the swamp."

PEYTON STARED AT Beau in utter shock. She immediately wanted to protest the very idea, but despite her bravado, there was no denying that she was still shaken up by what had happened here tonight.

She'd been shot, and there was absolutely no question in her mind that it had been attempted murder. There was also no question in her mind that there was a very strong possibility the person would try to kill her again.

The idea of being someplace where she wouldn't be afraid, where she could just take a little time to rest and to heal and to feel safe, sounded wonderfully appealing. She knew she would have all that at Beau's place.

"Okay, just for a couple of days," she finally said. "I'll go change and pack."

"Do you have anything in your garage that I could use to board up this missing window?" he asked.

"I think there might be some plywood scraps out in the garage," she replied.

"You go pack and I'll see what I can do."

She nodded and then went into her bedroom as he headed for the garage. At least the blinds in her room were pulled tightly closed so nobody could see in.

The pain in her shoulder was beyond intense and the whole night felt like a horrible nightmare. She was exhausted, but knew she wouldn't be able to sleep peacefully here in her own bed, for at least the next night or two.

Thankfully, yesterday morning Irene Farineau's shoplifting case had come to an end when the prosecuting attorney had suddenly decided to drop all the charges against her. Peyton suspected some sort of a cash settlement had taken place behind the scenes. In any case, what that meant for her was that she had nothing pending at the office, so she could take off for a couple of days.

She'd call Kylie in the morning and give her a couple days off. She hoped the young woman wasn't in any danger and Peyton didn't really believe she was. Still, at this very moment all she could really think about was getting someplace to take a pain pill and lie down.

She packed a few things in a backpack and at the last minute tucked her gun inside even though she didn't believe the person they were after, the person who was after her, would venture into the swamp to find them. She certainly didn't believe anyone would come into the swamp and discover Beau was around a gun.

She heard some banging coming from the living room and realized Beau was working to cover the broken window. Finally, she changed into a pair of jeans and, with some pain and difficulty, a T-shirt, and then walked back out into the living room where Beau was once again seated on the sofa and the window was covered with a large sheet of plywood. He jumped up from the sofa and took the backpack from her. "Ready to go?"

"As ready as I can be." She grabbed her purse off the kitchen floor where she'd dropped it after she'd made the call for help. "Thanks for taking care of the window."

"No problem," he replied. "It will work until you make arrangements to have a new window installed."

Together they stepped out of the house. She locked the door and then they returned to Beau's truck. "How are you feeling?" he asked softly once they were on their way.

"Like I'm more than ready for a pain pill and some sleep," she admitted.

"Peyton, I'm so sorry you're in pain. I wish I could take it all away from you. I wish somehow that I could erase this entire night." His soft voice, coupled with the warm gaze he shot her way, unexpectedly pulled tears to her eyes.

She swallowed hard against them and closed her eyes. She leaned her head back and released a deep sigh. It was silly, now that it was all over and she was safe, but a deep fear still swept through her. Maybe it was just because she was in so much pain.

However, there was no question that she felt safer with Beau by her side. "I'll need to call to get the glass in my window replaced," she said. "And I also need to contact my homeowner's insurance."

"None of that needs to be done tonight," Beau replied. "Tonight you just take your medicine and rest."

They drove for several more minutes and she only opened her eyes again when the truck stopped. They were parked in the lot by the little grocery store and ahead was the path that would eventually lead to Beau's place.

He got her bag out of the bed of the truck and strapped it on his back, and she grabbed her purse tightly in one of her hands. "Baby, I wish I could carry you in, but that's just not possible," he said.

"I know... I'll be fine as long as you hold my hand," she replied. There was no way she could navigate the swamp darkness without his help.

He reached out and clasped his hand firmly around hers. "Let's go," he said.

They entered the marsh and he walked slowly, murmuring softly to tell her where to step in order to avoid thick roots or the dark water that shimmered around them in the faint moonlight.

The deeper they went in, the cooler the air around them.

It was always far cooler in the swamp. They passed several other paths that went elsewhere and continued on.

Nobody who didn't know the swamp would be able to find Beau's place. She would bet on the fact that her attacker hadn't come from here, but rather he was a townsman who had plenty to lose if their investigation identified him. And townspeople never, ever ventured into the swamp.

By the time they reached Beau's place, her shoulder throbbed painfully and tears once again filled her eyes. She felt physically and emotionally broken and she hated herself for her weakness.

"Wait here," he said when they finally reached his front door. He went inside the dark structure, and a few moments later he'd turned on two lanterns that gave the main room a soft glow.

He walked back over to where she stood and took her by the hand. "Come… Sit on the sofa and I'll get you one of your pain pills and an antibiotic and some water."

She sank down on the sofa and watched as he pulled a jug of water out of the icebox and poured a liberal amount into a glass. She pulled the prescriptions out of her purse, and he approached with the water glass. "Here, you take this and I'll take those."

They made the exchange and then he shook out one pill from each of the bottles and handed them to her. She swallowed them, set her glass on the coffee table and then released a deep, weary sigh.

"This whole night has been nothing but a nightmare," she said. "I still can't believe somebody was outside my house just waiting for the perfect opportunity to shoot me."

"Yeah, I can't believe it, either." She heard the frustration in his voice. His gaze lingered on her for a long moment. "And thank God that bullet only grazed your shoulder. When I thought about what could have happened it makes me sick."

She gave him a tired smile. "It makes me a little sick, too."

For the next few minutes they discussed the events of the night. "I think you're done for now," he said with a smile to her. "Your pain pill must be working because you not only look drowsy, but you're also slurring your words a little bit."

"I am feeling it," she admitted.

"I'm sure you're ready for some sleep," he said. "You can take the bedroom and I'll sleep out here on the sofa," he said.

"Thank you, Beau. If you don't mind, I am ready to go to bed." She rose and grabbed her purse as he picked up her backpack and carried it into the bedroom.

He went in first and turned on a lantern on the nightstand. "I've only slept on the sheets for two nights, but I'd be glad to change them if you want me to," he said and set the backpack on the foot of the bed.

"That's not necessary. I just need a day or two to heal a bit and then I'll be out of your hair," she replied.

"We'll see about that," he said. "If you need anything just let me know." He walked over to her and gently kissed her on her forehead. "You're safe here, Peyton. I would wrestle a ticked-off gator to keep you safe."

She offered him a faint smile. "Then let's pray that no angry gators come knocking at your door."

"Is there anything else you need?" he asked.

"No, I'm good."

"Good night, Peyton," he said and then pulled the bedroom door closed behind him.

She got her nightgown out of the bag and, with some

painful difficulty, got out of her T-shirt and bra and into the nightwear. She then pulled her jeans off and placed them and the T-shirt across the dresser.

Her phone in her purse would stay charged for another six to ten hours or so and then it would be dead and she had no idea whether there was a way to charge it out here or not. For once in her life, she wouldn't mind it going dead. There was nobody she really needed to talk to, and the downtime was just what she needed.

Finally, she crawled into the double bed. Instantly, she was enveloped by Beau's unique scent. She left the lantern lit and stared at the shadows that danced across the ceiling.

It was here, in this room, in this very bed, that she'd lost her virginity years before. That night the white-hot passion she'd felt for Beau had finally exploded and they had taken their relationship to a new level.

She knew that had been a long time ago. But she'd always felt safe and protected here with Beau, and that was still true tonight.

It didn't take long for the pain in her shoulder to ease to a dull throb and a deep drowsiness to overtake her. She rolled over on her side and turned off the lantern, plunging the room into complete darkness.

The sound of the swamp filled the room…the slap of fish…the croaking of frogs…myriad sounds that created a soft lullaby, and soon she heard nothing at all as sleep claimed her.

Chapter Nine

Beau awoke early the next morning and his first thought was of the woman who slept in his bedroom. She had never spent the night here in the swamp before. Years ago, when they had been young lovers, he'd always walked her out of the swamp and to her home in the middle of the night.

She didn't know it yet, but he intended to keep her here until the danger to her was over. That meant she'd be here until they identified the person who had attacked her, the person he believed was the real murderer of Lacy. That meant she was going to be here longer than a day or two.

He had a feeling that it was far too late for him to try to disassociate from her. She was already in too deep with him and the investigation. The killer would probably still go after her no matter how loud and long Beau denounced their partnership.

The only thing Beau needed to do right now was keep her here, where she would be safe, for as long as possible. While she remained here, he would continue to work the case alone.

He got up from the sofa and built a fire in the stove. Once Peyton was awake, he'd cook some breakfast for them both. With the fire burning, he went to the bedroom door.

All he wanted…all he needed to do was take a quick peek at her to assure himself she was okay. The door creaked slightly as he opened it, but thankfully, the noise didn't awaken her.

She slept on her back with her dark hair fanned out around her head on the pillow. She looked utterly beautiful, yet fragile with the shoulder bandage visible beneath the spaghetti strap of her red nightgown.

His chest swelled and his stomach muscles tightened in silent rage as he thought of the terror she must have felt… the pain she would continue to feel from the gunshot wound.

The man they sought had to be a cold-blooded monster. Beau couldn't help but wonder who else the man had murdered. He prayed that they would be able to identify him and get him off the streets forever. The monster belonged in a jail cell for what he had done to Lacy, but he belonged in the very depths of hell for what he had done to Peyton.

He closed the bedroom door and went back into the living room, where he sank down on the sofa. The main thing he wanted to do was take care of Peyton for the next couple of days. He had no idea what she might want or need, but whatever it was, he would move heaven and earth to get it for her.

She'd taken a bullet for him. The full impact of what had happened seemed to be hitting him right now. He felt sick knowing that he was responsible for that bullet. He would always carry a huge amount of guilt knowing that he was the cause of her pain.

Once she was awake, he'd turn on his gas-powered generator that not only gave him electricity when he needed it, but also pumped water into the outdoor shower located on the back porch. Although she might not be ready for a shower today, and that was just fine.

During the evenings since he'd been back here and after he left Peyton each day, he'd worked on trying to update the cabin as much as his limited money would allow.

His father hadn't cared about having electricity or any other of the simple amenities. He'd been blacked-out drunk most of the time and when he wasn't passed out, he was on the hunt to get enough money to buy the booze to get blacked-out drunk again.

Beau wasn't sure how long he'd been seated on the sofa and lost in his own thoughts when the bedroom door creaked open and Peyton walked out. She wore a lightweight red robe that matched her nightgown beneath. Her hair was tousled around her head and she would have looked utterly gorgeous if not for the draw of pain that darkened her eyes and tensed her features.

He jumped up from the sofa. "I'd say good morning but by the look on your face, not so much. Sit, and I'll get you your medication."

"Thanks. I'm not sure how it's possible, but my shoulder hurts more now than it did last night," she replied as she sank down on the sofa.

"That's what they often say about any kind of wounds… that the worse day is always the second or third day." He shook out the pills and carried them to her with a glass of water.

She took them and then cast him a wan smile. "Thanks again, Beau. For taking good care of me."

"There's nobody else I'd rather be taking care of," he replied. "As for the *good care*, that remains to be seen since you just woke up."

She released a deep sigh and looked around. "It's nice to be here. This was the one place in my whole life where I always felt safe."

"I'm glad you feel that way," he replied. "Now, how about some breakfast? You need to eat something and I've got some bacon and eggs with your name on them."

"Oh, Beau, I don't want you to go to that kind of trouble for me," she protested.

"It's no trouble at all." He moved back to the icebox and pulled out a pound of bacon and a dozen eggs. "I hope you like scrambled because no matter how hard I try to make different kinds of eggs, they somehow always turn out scrambled."

She laughed and then groaned. "Oh, please don't make me laugh."

"I didn't know I said anything funny," he replied in confusion.

"It's just the fact that the Beau Boudreau, who does everything so well, is beaten by a fried egg."

He flashed her a quick grin and then got busy placing bacon strips into the skillet to fry. "Once we're finished eating, I'll douse the fire."

"Right now the warmth feels good," she said.

"It always feels good in the mornings, but before long it will become way too warm in here."

Within thirty minutes they were seated at the little table in the kitchen area and eating breakfast. "Do you have your copy of the list of men's names we drew up?" she asked.

"I do, but we aren't going to talk about any business today.

You need to stay calm and unstressed in order to heal," he replied. "So today you just relax."

She reached for another piece of bacon from the plate in the center of the table. "Then what are we going to talk about today?"

"Oh, I don't know. We used to have a lot of things to talk to each other about." He held her gaze for a long moment.

Her cheeks flushed slightly and then she looked down at her plate. "That was a long time ago, Beau. We were young kids and thought we had our entire futures before us."

"The future for me certainly didn't exactly pan out the way I intended. But what about you? Has life been good to you, Peyton?"

"There have been good moments and bad moments, but mostly life has been fairly good," she replied.

"You are so beautiful and so smart, why haven't you married before now?" He looked at her curiously. Surely, she'd had plenty of men to choose from over the years.

"I just haven't found the right person I want to spend the rest of my life with yet." She picked at the last of her eggs and then shoved the plate aside.

"What about Sam?" he couldn't help but ask.

"Sam is just a nice man to spend a little time with, but he's not my person. In fact, I broke things off with him the last time we went out."

"You did?" He couldn't help the happiness that filled him at her words.

"I did. It wasn't really fair to keep going out to dinner with him knowing I didn't see a future with him. And now I'm stuffed and I think the pain pill has made me feel a little bit drowsy. Would you mind if I took a short nap?"

"Of course, I wouldn't mind. I want you to rest all you can."

"Then I'll just see you in a little while." She rose from the table and disappeared back into the bedroom.

As he washed the dishes, he wondered if her need for a nap was really an escape from answering anything more about her personal life. He couldn't help but feel good that she'd broken things off with Sam.

However, he couldn't help but wonder if some man in the past had broken her heart. Was that why she hadn't married? He knew she'd been in Shreveport for some time. Maybe she'd had a bad relationship while there, one that had put her off romance altogether? Maybe that was why she had moved back to Black Bayou—because she didn't want to be in a place where her heart had been broken. Of course, he really had no right to know those things about her. He was only speculating about it all.

Still, he couldn't help but wonder if they'd still be together if he hadn't gone to prison. Would their love have lasted through the years? He didn't know the answer, but he'd always believed they would love each other through eternity.

Once the dishes were cleaned up, he took a poker and worked on dousing what was left of the fire. It had already warmed up enough in the shanty that it was no longer needed to take the chill out of the air or cook.

Once the fire was completely out, he stepped outside onto the front porch. Through the thick leaves overhead, the bright sun peeked. Still, this deep in the swamp it was always semi-dark. Of all the things he'd endured in prison, it had definitely taken him some time to adjust to the bright lights of prison.

He was about to turn and go back inside when he heard

somebody approaching. All his muscles tensed with fight-or-flight adrenaline. He immediately relaxed as Gator came into view.

"Hey, Beau," Gator said.

"Hi, Gator. Want to come in?" Beau didn't really want any company to disturb Peyton's rest, but in the swamp your door was always open when somebody came visiting. Besides, he owed the old man a big favor for telling him that Peyton had been shot.

"I wouldn't mind coming in to sit a spell," Gator replied.

"Then come on in," Beau said. "But we need to keep our voices down because Peyton is taking a nap."

"Got it," Gator said. He walked in and beelined to the sofa. "So the gossip was true. She got shot?"

"Yes, but thankfully, the bullet only grazed her shoulder. Still, she's in a lot of pain and was traumatized by the whole ordeal."

"No doubt. So you decided to bring her here to heal up?"

"That and to keep her safe from any future harm. Can I get you something to drink?" Beau asked.

"I wouldn't mind a big glass of water," Gator replied as he leaned his walking stick against the coffee table.

Beau got up and poured the old man a glass of water and after handing it to him, he sat in the chair facing Gator. "You think she's still in danger?" Gator asked.

"Not while she's here with me. I think the person who shot her is a town person who wouldn't dare come into the swamp."

"How long do you intend to keep her here?" Gator took a deep swallow of water.

"In a perfect world I'd keep her here until we learn who

really killed Lacy, but in reality, I'm just hoping she'll stay for a week or two at the very least."

"You two have been getting into some pretty deep stuff," Gator said. "Personally, I hope you find the bastard who really killed Lacy."

"That's the only way I think Peyton will be truly safe," Beau replied.

"She's important to you," Gator said with a knowing gleam in his eyes.

"She's an old friend and she took a bullet because of me." Beau wasn't about to try to speak about the complexities of his relationship with Peyton any deeper than that.

"An old friend, huh," Gator replied.

At that moment the bedroom door opened and Peyton stepped out. "Oh... I didn't know you had company," she said, obviously embarrassed as she pulled her robe more tightly around her.

"It's all right, Peyton. This is Gator... Gator, this is Peyton LaCroix." Beau got up from the chair and gestured for Peyton to sit.

"It's nice to meet you," Gator said. "I appreciate what you're doing to help Beau." He offered Peyton a toothless grin. "I will say you are mighty easy on the eyes, Ms. Peyton."

"Now, Gator, don't you go flirting with my girl," Beau said, making Gator and Peyton both laugh.

"It's nice to meet you, too," Peyton replied.

"It was Gator who first told me you'd been shot," Beau said.

She looked at Gator in surprise. "How did you know about the shooting?"

"The swamp grapevine. We here in the swamp know most things that go on in town. We sweep your floors and clean your toilets. We're invisible to the people who employ us and meanwhile, we listen and learn. All I did that night was tell Beau what the grapevine was saying about you."

"Well, I sincerely thank you for that," Peyton replied and then shot a warm smile to Beau. "I don't know what I would have done without him."

Her smile created a warmth deep inside Beau. He realized at that moment that what he was really hoping for was that while she was here with him, they could recapture some of the old magic they used to have.

PEYTON HAD BEEN at Beau's for three full days. He'd cooked for her, made sure she took her medicine on time and had done everything he could to take care of her and keep her entertained.

She'd forgotten how funny he could be but as they played cards and various other games to pass the time, he often had her helpless with laughter. She now remembered how much she found his sense of humor sexy and attractive.

He'd also asked her about her time in Shreveport and what had brought her back to Black Bayou from the big city. She'd told him about her work there and how exhausted she'd become from having no balance in her life. She'd explained to him how she had felt like a hamster running frantically in the wheel with no escape.

He also shared a little bit more about what prison life had been like for him. Her heart had ached as he talked about how those years had been for him.

They had been good, serious conversations, reminiscent

of the ones they used to share in the past. She'd worried that they would have nothing to talk about, but they'd also discussed their childhoods…his pain over the fact that his mother had abandoned him and left him to an abusive drunk, and her pain from feeling like her parents had abandoned her at a very young age. They'd opted for a social life where their daughter was merely a hindrance.

Her shoulder had begun to feel better and she'd even managed to take a shower that morning. Now she was ready to get back to what they'd been doing before she'd been shot. She was ready to catch a killer.

Nighttime had fallen and the room was lit with the lanterns. They had just eaten dinner and now Beau sank down on the sofa and she took the chair facing him.

"I think it's time we get back down to business again," she said. "We need to start interviewing the men on our list."

"It's too soon for you to worry about that," he replied. "Maybe by some chance Gravois will identify who shot you and he'll do the work for us."

She gazed at him with narrowed eyes. "Do you really want to leave this all in the hands of Gravois? Beau, a little over a week ago, you were eager to find the killer. And then suddenly you weren't so interested anymore. Something changed with you. Please, Beau, tell me what happened."

He was silent for several long moments and his eyes were as dark as the swamp waters outside. He finally released a deep sigh. "I just came to realize clearing my name isn't that important to me anymore. It won't change the fact that I have absolutely nothing."

"Nothing? What are you talking about, Beau? It will change everything. It will change the way people treat you and how they think about you. And as far as having nothing, you still have your business. Once your name is cleared, I'm sure you'll have a much bigger role there."

"Yeah, about the business…it's not mine."

She frowned at him in confusion. "What are you talking about? Of course it's part yours. The whole thing was your idea…it was your baby from the very beginning."

"Yeah, well, Jack didn't get the memo. When he filled out all the paperwork, he declined to list me as a part owner," he replied, his voice tinged with bitterness. "He told me we'd revisit the issue when I clear my name, but I know nothing is going to change. He wrote me off fifteen years ago and that's that."

"Oh, Beau." She got up from the chair and joined him on the sofa. "That dirtbag stole it from you," she said indignantly. He didn't look at her, but rather stared at some place just over her shoulder. She knew this must have absolutely devastated him. It was a betrayal by a man Beau had considered his very best friend.

She knew Beau had been the driving force for the construction company. Many evenings she and Beau and Jack had sat in this very room and Beau had shared his plans and dreams for the business with Jack. Jack had the money, but Beau had been the brain, the heart and the very soul of the enterprise.

"Beau, look at me," she said softly. Slowly, he met her gaze. "I know how deeply this must have cut you, and I'm sorry. I'm so very sorry." She pulled him awkwardly into her arms for a long hug.

He remained stiff and unyielding for several long moments and then he finally relaxed against her and wrapped his arms around her. He was careful not to touch her shoulder and they remained locked in each other's embrace for a few quiet minutes.

Familiar scents infused her head, the scent of clean male, the faint scent of the cologne he'd always worn and something wild and exciting. It felt good to be held in his arms once again. She realized now she'd never really wanted any other man's arms around her.

She finally raised her head from the crook of his neck and when she gazed at him, her heart seemed to hitch in her throat. His eyes flamed with desire and just that quickly she knew they were going to make love. Not because he wanted her, but rather because she desperately wanted him.

Just one more time she wanted to experience their passion unleashed. It didn't mean she was in love with him. She told herself it didn't have to mean anything. To that end, she leaned forward and placed her lips over his.

He gasped in surprise, but quickly plied her mouth with fiery intent. Their tongues danced together in sweet familiarity, yet also with a new, thrilling excitement.

The kiss lasted until her heart raced uncontrollably and she was half-breathless. Only then did his mouth leave hers, and he trailed a path of nips and kisses down the curve of her jaw and then on down her throat.

Each point of contact shot a shiver of delight up and down her spine. No man had ever made her feel so wild, so completely unbridled, as Beau did even now. His mouth returned to hers and this time his kiss was both feverish and demanding.

She returned the kiss with all the fervor that was inside

her. She felt as if she were eighteen years old again and Beau was not only her forever friend, but also her forever lover.

This time the kiss was short-lived. Beau pulled back from her and his dark eyes glittered wildly in the flickering light from the lantern. "Peyton, we need to stop this," he said, his voice deeper than usual.

"Why? Why do we need to stop, Beau?" she asked.

"Because I can't keep kissing you like this and not want more from you."

His words only heightened her desire for him. "Beau, I want more from you. I want us to make love," she replied.

His eyes flared wide, but he dropped his arms from around her. "We can't do that. You're still hurt and you obviously aren't thinking straight in this moment."

"Beau Boudreau, you've spent the last couple of weeks trying to seduce me and now that you've succeeded, you're saying no to me?" she asked incredulously. "I'm sure we can make love without hurting my shoulder and trust me. I'm thinking perfectly straight. I want you, Beau… I'll confess I've wanted you ever since the moment you walked back into my office."

He stared at her for another long moment and then he got to his feet, bent down and scooped her up in his arms. He carried her into the bedroom, where he gently placed her in the center of the bed.

While he turned on the lantern on the nightstand, she managed to get out of the tank top she'd worn during the day, leaving her clad in her bra and shorts.

"Are you sure about this?" he asked softly as he remained standing by the side of the bed. "Are you really sure, Peyton?" His gaze searched her features. "Because I can turn around right now and leave the room and we'll just forget about this for now."

"Oh, Beau, I've never been surer of anything in my entire life," she replied. "I want you." She raised her hands and beckoned him toward her. "I've wanted you for the last fifteen years."

Still, he paused by the side of the bed, his eyes glittering darkly.

"Beau? What are you doing?" she asked, suddenly unsure what he was going to do.

"Just give me a couple of moments to look at you," he said, his voice husky with obvious desire.

Peyton had never known how powerful a gaze could be, but as Beau's lingered on her, she felt her body responding. Muscles weakened and her nerves tingled as a sweet heat coiled within her.

"Ah, Peyton, you are so beautiful. I dreamed of this moment with you for the last fifteen years. It was thoughts of you that got me through that dark time."

He leaned over and gently touched her lips with his. Soft and tender, his mouth made love to hers. When he was finished with her lips, he moved to her ear, then down her jawline.

As his mouth caressed her, his fingers worked her bra fastening. Once he'd removed it from her, he then moved down to pull off not only her shorts, but her panties as well. He kissed and licked each inch of skin he exposed, driving her out of her mind with need.

By the time he removed his clothing and joined her on the bed, she was already at a fever pitch. Never had she felt so wonderfully alive. Never had she wanted a man more than she wanted Beau now. However, as he started to position himself above her, she shook her head and gently pushed him to his back.

She wanted to kiss him and to caress him until he was utterly wild with his desire for her. She wanted to hear him moan her name over and over again. She wanted him to never, ever want another woman for the rest of his life.

She began to explore the beauty of his body. Her hands ran across his broad chest, feeling his sleek muscles tighten at her touch. She leaned forward and pressed her lips against his skin. She wanted to smell him, taste him and lose herself completely in him.

"Ah, Peyton," he whispered with a groan.

Still, she continued to kiss and nip down his chest. With a low, deep groan, he rolled her over onto her back, and his fingers moved to the very center of her.

Lightly, they danced over the sensitive skin and she thrust her hips upward to meet him. He applied more pressure and his fingers moved faster…and faster. A fiery tension built up inside her and as it crested and her release shuddered through her, she moaned his name over and over again.

When she was still breathless and gasping, he moved between her hips, hovering above her for a single second before sinking slowly into her.

She wrapped her legs around him as tears sprang to her eyes. Her tears were a mixture of enormous happiness and also a touch of grief…the grief of what might have been and might never be again.

His heart beat the same frantic rhythm as her own as he began to move in and out of her. Slowly at first, he moved in her with a measured pace and created a new, growing tension inside her.

Her breaths quickened as he pumped faster and faster into her. She gasped his name as she spiraled completely out of control and a second powerful climax overtook her.

She gasped his name over and over once again. Then he groaned her name with his own release and together they collapsed side by side as they waited for their breathing to slow to a more normal pace.

Still, Peyton's heart continued to beat an erratic rhythm as she realized the truth of the situation—and the truth was she was still deeply in love with Beau Boudreau.

Chapter Ten

Peyton fell asleep in his arms, but Beau remained wide-awake, listening to her soft breathing and loving the feel of her so intimately close to him. When he'd first arrived back home and reconnected with her, he'd believed all he wanted to do was get Peyton back into his bed. On some level he'd thought that having her once more would get her finally and forever out of his blood.

However, that hadn't happened. He now realized that he was still deeply in love with the young woman he'd once led out of the darkness of the swamp as a child. And he had fallen in love all over again with the woman she'd become.

But he wasn't a lovesick fool. He wasn't blind to reality, and the reality was he was a swamp rat ex-con who had no idea what his future held. Peyton came from a prestigious family. He was sure she was well respected in town; at least she had been before he had gotten involved in her life again.

No, he was no fool. No matter how much he loved her, there was no future for a swamp rat ex-con without a job and a bright and beautiful, respected defense attorney.

His only goal now was to keep her safe from harm. Once he knew she was no longer in danger, he'd disappear from her life once and for all. It was the best thing he could do for her…because he loved her enough to let her go.

He finally fell asleep and into nightmares of Peyton running through the swamp with the Honey Island Swamp Monster chasing after her. Beau raced after them, running as fast as he could in his desperation to get to her before the monster caught her.

Her terrified screams filled the air, echoing through the thick brush and trees and shooting terror through his veins. The swamp, which had always been his friend, now fought against him. Tree limbs reached out to slow him down and thick tubers tried to trip him up.

Spanish moss swept across his face, momentarily blinding him again and again. Her screams now came from farther and farther away and he yelled her name, horrified that he was going to lose her to the monster.

He came awake with a deep gasp and shot straight up in the bed. For a moment he was disoriented as his heart beat a thousand beats a minute, and his breathing was hard and labored.

Thankfully, the lantern was still lit on the nightstand. He gazed next to him where Peyton remained sleeping soundly. Thankfully, he hadn't woken her. He released a shuddery sigh of relief.

It had all just been a nightmare. He rubbed his hands up and down his face. Thank God it had just been a very bad dream. He remained sitting for several minutes and then slid out of the bed. His internal alarm clock let him know it was nearly morning.

Bending down, he grabbed the jeans and boxers he'd worn the day before and then carried them out of the bedroom.

He pulled them on in the living room and then stepped out the front door in an effort to completely shrug off the last vestiges of the horrible dream.

It was still dark out, but he could feel the swamp breathing all around him. Morning birds sang from the treetops, and small animals rustled in the brush. He took several deep breaths of the humid air, the myriad scents mingling together to smell like home.

The swamp might have been his enemy in his nightmares, but in truth it was his family and his friend. It was where he belonged, just like Peyton belonged in town. However, before she could return to her own life, he had to catch a killer. Once he caught the guilty party then Peyton would be safe, and his name would be cleared.

Peyton. Making love to her again had been as wonderful…as earth-shattering…as he remembered. If anything, it had been even better than he remembered. He'd made love to her before when she was a young, innocent woman, but last night she'd been a mature woman who had matched him in his fervor, in his very hunger to intimately connect with her.

With a heavy sigh, he turned and went back inside. It was too warm this morning to make a fire, so breakfast would be croissants and sweet rolls and juice.

Eventually, he wanted to buy a small oven and refrigerator that he could run on the generator, but he didn't have the funds to do anything else to further modernize the place. He also still had no idea now how he was going to make future funds, so he needed to hang on to what he had left.

The idea of crawling back to Jack to ask for a job in the company Beau thought had been part his stuck in his craw.

Eventually, he'd figure something out for himself. If nothing else, Beau was a survivor.

It was about an hour later when Peyton came out of the bedroom. She was clad only in her nightgown and robe and shot him a radiant smile. "Good morning," she said. She waltzed over to him and kissed him soundly on the cheek.

"Whoa, somebody is in a good mood this morning," he replied as she walked over to the sofa and sank down. Her gaze was warm and open and without any defensive shutters to keep him out.

"I'm in a great mood, and why shouldn't I be? My shoulder has pretty much stopped hurting, a handsome hunk of a man made sweet love to me last night and I slept like a baby."

He couldn't look at her any longer. He couldn't stand to see the joyous look in her eyes. He definitely didn't want to talk about what they'd shared the night before. "I didn't light a fire this morning. It's already warm in here, so I figured we could just have juice and croissants for breakfast."

"That's fine with me," she replied, her voice more subdued than it had been moments before.

He got busy plating the croissants and sweet rolls, grabbed a couple of paper towels to use for napkins and carried it all to the coffee table. He then poured two glasses of juice and joined her on the sofa.

For a couple of minutes they ate in silence. Rather than being a comfortable quiet, it was strained and tense. "Well, are we going to talk about the elephant in the room or are we going to just pretend it didn't happen?" she finally asked. Her gaze held his searchingly. "I definitely smell regret in the room."

He stifled a deep sigh. "*Ma chérie*, how could I ever regret making love to you? It was beyond wonderful to have you in my arms once again."

"It was beyond wonderful to be in your arms again," she replied, some of her tense energy dissipating. "And now that I've had breakfast, if you don't mind, I'd like to take a shower."

"No problem," Beau said with an inward sigh of relief. "I'll go start the pump." Apparently, all she'd needed was the affirmation that last night had been wonderful for both of them. He'd been afraid she'd want to talk about a future, and he wasn't ready yet to tell her there was no future for them.

Last night had been beyond wonderful, but it was a one-time thing and it would never happen again. He didn't want to lead her on by making love with her again.

Thirty minutes later she was in the enclosed shower on the back porch and visions of her naked and beneath the spray of water played over and over in his head. *Mon Dieu*, even though he was determined not to be with her again, that didn't stop the raw desire for her that roared through him.

She was in the shower for about fifteen minutes before she raced from the back porch to the bedroom clad only in a towel. Finally, she came back into the living room dressed in a red tank top and a pair of navy blue shorts. She looked refreshed and better than she had in days.

She sank down on the sofa next to him. "It's time for us to get back to work," she said. "I'm feeling fine now and I'm more determined than ever to find the man who killed Lacy and shot me."

"Peyton, I don't want you involved in this anymore," Beau said firmly.

"Well, tough, I *am* involved, and I intend to stay involved," she replied just as firmly. "Now, can I see your copy of the list we made up from the initials? We need to come up with a game plan."

"I just don't think it's a good idea for you to be a part of this anymore," he replied, not moving from his seat on the sofa. "You need to distance yourself from the investigation. It might help keep you safe."

"And it might not." She stared at him for a long moment. "Beau, I can either do this with you or I can do it all alone, but one way or another I'm moving forward with the investigation."

He knew she was telling the truth, and there was no way he intended to allow her to move forward by herself. Reluctantly, he got up, walked to the little desk by the door and then opened the drawer that held the paperwork.

He returned to the sofa and handed it to her. She then spread it out on the top of the coffee table. She stared down at the list of names and then released a deep sigh. "Now that I've had a few days away from this, I realize our initial plan to interview these men is pretty impractical. First of all, it's going to take us forever to speak to each person and secondly, I don't think the killer is suddenly going to just confess to us because we asked him a few questions."

He frowned at her. "Then how are we going to move forward?"

A frown creased her forehead as well. "It would help if Gravois would interview all these men and give the whole thing a real air of legitimacy," she said in obvious frustration. "He's better trained in interviewing suspects than we are. He might be able to see subtle signs of deception."

"I seriously doubt that, but in any case, we both know

Gravois isn't going to lift a single finger to help us out," he replied with his own disgust. Beau expected absolutely nothing from the chief of police. In truth, he wished Gravois would solve the deaths of the young women from the swamp who were supposed to be victims of the Honey Island Swamp Monster.

In the meantime, he and Peyton needed to come up with a plan to catch their own killer and at the moment he had no idea what that might be. They sat stewing in their own thoughts for several long moments.

"I think I've got it," she suddenly said and sat up straighter. Her eyes began to sparkle with the bright light that Beau always loved to see, and a swift new dart of desire pierced through him.

"What?" He tried to focus on what she said and not how the scent of her stirred his senses or how her body heat wafted over him. He mentally shook himself. "Do you have a new plan?" he asked.

"I think I do." A frown of concentration creased her forehead once again as she stared down at the list. "What if we send letters to all the men on the list? The letters would say something like, 'I saw you kill Lacy Dupree. Meet me at such-and-such a place and bring lots of cash to keep my mouth shut forever.'"

She looked back up at him. "If you were an innocent man, would you respond to that note? Would you go to the place to meet a blackmailer?"

He thought for a long moment. "No, I'd probably just toss the letter away and think some kook sent it." He continued to think about the new plan and then he smiled at her. "This just might work," he said as an edge of excitement filled him. "I think the killer would definitely show up."

"We've got nothing to lose by trying this, right?"

"Right," he replied. "At this point we have absolutely nothing to lose."

"Then we need to go to my office. I've got the list of addresses there from the tax records. We can match the addresses with names and then write up the letter and I can make copies. I'll call Kylie to come in and help us address and stamp the envelopes and then we can get them into the mail by the end of the day."

She leaned forward and wrapped her arms around his neck. "I feel it in my heart, Beau. We're going to catch this person, and your name will finally be cleared."

Her voice was a soft whisper against his neck and evoked in him a renewed wild desire to take her into the bedroom and make love to her all over again.

He quickly stood, breaking the embrace that threatened to undo his conviction to never make love to her again. "Then let's get ready to go."

"Give me fifteen minutes or so and I'll be ready," she replied. She got up and headed into the bedroom.

He breathed a sigh of relief as his desire slowly dissipated. Instead, he thought about the plan she'd come up with. Could it work?

Would the killer really respond to the letter and show up at a specific place and time to pay off a blackmailer? Would any innocent men show up out of sheer curiosity? He couldn't imagine anyone doing that, but he supposed it might be possible.

Still, in any case, this might narrow the field to only a

few men—and one of them would surely be Lacy's killer, the man who had framed him and shot Peyton.

God, he wanted the answer to the question that had haunted him for the past fifteen years. Who had killed Lacy Dupree? When he'd lost his necklace, he'd never dreamed somebody would find it and use it to frame him for murder. He'd never dreamed that he'd be locked up in prison for fifteen long years.

An hour later they were in Peyton's office. She sat in her chair behind her desk and he pulled the other chair around to sit right next to her. They began working on matching all the names to the addresses. Thankfully, they had viable addresses for all of them.

They next moved on to crafting the details of the letter. "Where is a good place for us to set up this meet?" she asked.

Beau frowned thoughtfully. "It has to be someplace fairly isolated and yet you and I need places to hide so the perp doesn't initially see us. There also needs to be enough light that we can see who exactly he is."

"Any ideas?" she asked.

"I'm thinking. What time do you think this meeting should take place?" he asked.

She frowned. "I don't know... I was thinking around midnight—what do you think?"

He shrugged. "Midnight sounds fine with me, and how about Vincent's Grocery? The place has security lights all around it and if we tell the man to meet us on the south side, then you and I could step into the cover of the swamp to watch who shows up."

"That sounds perfect," she replied. "What day do we want

to make it? The letters should reach everyone by day after tomorrow at the latest."

"Then let's make the meet for Friday night," Beau replied. That was four days from now. He had a feeling they were going to be the longest days of his and Peyton's lives.

The sound of the outside door opening shot Beau up and out of his chair. He took only a couple of steps and then relaxed as Kylie came into the inner office.

"Oh, boss, I'm so glad to see you," the young woman said as Beau returned to his chair. "How are you feeling? You look really good. Beau must be taking good care of you."

Peyton shot him a warm smile. "He has definitely been taking good care of me."

"She's been an easy patient," Beau said.

"That's good to hear. And you're really doing okay?"

"I promise. I'm doing just fine," Peyton assured her.

"I just can't believe you were shot," Kylie replied.

"Well, I was, and I lived to tell the tale." Peyton smiled at the young woman.

"You said on the phone that you have some envelopes for me to address?" Kylie asked.

"Yes, here's the list of names and addresses, and we want to use the plain envelopes, not my official ones," Peyton instructed. "And wear gloves so no fingerprints are on them."

Kylie took the list from her. "Got it. I'll get right to it." She left the inner office.

"She seems like a good kid," Beau said once she was gone.

"She is, and there are days I wouldn't know what to do without her. She's very bright and a hard worker," Peyton replied. "Now, let's get back to work on this letter."

It took them a half an hour to complete the letter, after

which Peyton made all the copies. By that time Kylie had all the envelopes addressed.

"Kylie, I don't know for sure when our usual office hours will resume, but I'd appreciate it if you continue monitoring the front desk during the day in case somebody needs my representation," Peyton said. "However if you don't feel safe doing that, then we'll just lock the place up for the time being."

"I'm not afraid. I'll be here every day. You can depend on me to hold down the fort while you're gone," Kylie replied. She gestured to the stack of envelopes. "I don't know what the two of you are up to, but I hope it works out the way you want it to."

"So do we," Beau replied.

Beau and Peyton had made the decision not to allow Kylie to see the letters or share with her what they were doing. "Thanks, Kylie. You can go ahead and take off now," Peyton said.

It took them another half hour after Kylie left to stuff and stamp the envelopes. They both wore gloves as well. He was surprised to realize darkness had fallen outside. The project had taken far longer than he'd expected and the hours had flown by.

Peyton placed the envelopes in her purse and then they left the building. Besides the actual post office building, there were three public mail drop boxes around town.

They agreed to divide the letters and drop some into all three. Once it was done, they were both silent on the way back to the swamp.

When they reached Beau's place, Peyton collapsed on the sofa and released a deep sigh. He sank down next to her, the enormity of what they'd just put into place whirling around in his head.

"How are you feeling?" he asked her.

"Nervous...anxious and a little bit excited," she replied. "What about you?"

"Nervous...anxious and a little bit excited," he said, making her laugh.

Her eyes shimmered as she moved closer to him. "Oh, Beau, just think, in a matter of four days it could finally all be over." She moved even closer to him and he couldn't help but draw her into his embrace.

He closed his eyes as he held her, breathing in her unique scent and remembering every moment of their lovemaking. He thought of each moment of laughter they had shared over the past few days and his heart squeezed tight. Four more days and the real murderer would be exposed. Four more days and his name would be cleared of the murder that had sent him away.

He should be deliriously happy that it was all coming to an end. However, in this moment with Peyton in his arms, all he could think about was how in four more days it would be time for Beau to get out of Peyton's life for good.

PEYTON PACED THE small confines of the shanty while Beau sat on the sofa watching her. Two days had passed since they'd sent out the letters. By now the killer had probably received his. Two more nights and hopefully, they would meet the killer face-to-face.

That thought had her filled with a wild energy. This had to work. Their little scheme had to uncover the man who had killed Lacy and framed Beau. If this didn't work, she wouldn't know how to move forward on the case.

For the past two nights Beau had slept in the bed with her, but he hadn't made any move to make love to her again. Despite her yearning for him, she hadn't pressed him on the issue.

However, she did yearn for him. She wanted to feel his lips on hers, taste his desire on his mouth again. She desperately wanted to feel his naked body move against hers as he possessed her completely once again.

They had eaten dinner a little while ago and bedtime would soon be approaching. Maybe he had been hesitant to make love to her again. Maybe he didn't realize the depth of her feelings where he was concerned. Or perhaps it was just the stress and anxiety about how things were going to go down on Friday night.

"Would you please stop the pacing," he now said, his voice a bit terse. "You're making me more stressed out."

She walked over to the sofa and sank down next to him. "With each minute that passes I get more stressed and more anxious for Friday night to be over with."

"I feel the same way," he admitted. "The hours can't go by fast enough. I keep twisting and turning different scenarios in my head, trying to think of ways this plan could fail."

"It's not going to fail," she replied firmly. "It can't fail."

She smiled at him. He looked so hot in a pair of worn jeans and a white T-shirt. His dark, shiny hair had grown slightly shaggy over the past couple of weeks, making him look more like the young man she'd fallen so deeply in love with, the man she was still so deeply in love with.

"It's going to be wonderful to finally know who framed you for the murder," she said.

"I definitely want to know the answer," he replied with a touch of anger in his voice. "I want to know who stole my life away from me. The bastard stole everything good from me. I also want to know who attacked and shot you."

She placed a hand on his arm. "Two more days and we'll have all the answers."

"I hope so."

She leaned closer to him. "And then we'll have to plan to do something wonderful to celebrate our success," she said.

"I don't think I'll be in the mood for much of a celebration," he replied with a frown.

She cuddled even closer against him. "Surely, we could figure out something to do to celebrate," she said in what she hoped was a seductive voice. "Maybe we could start our celebration right here and right now."

To her surprise, he gently pushed away from her and stood. "I think I'll go start the generator so we can charge up our phones."

She frowned as she watched him walk through the kitchen area and then disappear out the back door. Normally, Beau would be the one trying to seduce her back into his bed, but now she found herself trying to seduce him.

Had she somehow disappointed him when they'd made love before? He certainly hadn't acted disappointed in any way during the act. So why wasn't he rushing to take her to bed and make love with her again?

She'd believed they were rebuilding a relationship, a love that had been denied to them by a terrible fate. She could have sworn he was falling back in love with her as she was with him.

Had she been wrong all along? Had his sole purpose been to use her to help him find the killer? To simply have her in his bed one more time for old time's sake? God, she hoped that wasn't the case. The very idea of that being true absolutely crushed her.

The thrum of the generator filled the room. She got up from the sofa and went into Beau's bedroom to grab her cell phone and cord. The one working outlet was in the kitchen. As she plugged in, Beau came back inside.

He went into the bedroom and returned a moment later with his phone. Once he had his plugged in, he sank down in the chair and she returned to the sofa.

"We'll let them charge but sooner or later I need to run to Vincent's and get more gasoline."

She knew the little grocery store had a single gas pump on one side of the building. "Do you want me to go with you when you go?"

"No, that's not necessary. You should be safe here for me to make a quick run," he replied. His voice held a distance and his eyes were shuttered closed.

Now that she thought about it, he'd been fairly distant with her all day long. Was it just because of the stress of the case coming to an end? She would have thought that would make him deliriously happy but while he mouthed the words, she didn't feel any real happiness radiating from him.

Suddenly, her love for him felt too enormous to hold inside. She wanted his name cleared, but more than that she wanted a future with him. She wanted to fulfill the dreams they had once made, dreams of loving each other forever and her having his babies.

Fate had given them a second chance to make those dreams come true—all he had to do was love her like he had years before. She'd really thought she'd felt that emanating from him over the past couple of weeks, but maybe she'd been wrong. Or perhaps all she had to do was tell him how deeply she'd fallen in love with him again... Maybe he just needed to hear her words of love.

"Beau, can we have a serious conversation?" she asked.

"Of course. What's up? Are you suddenly having second thoughts about our plan?" He gazed at her curiously.

"No, nothing like that," she replied. She gazed at him for a long moment, suddenly feeling shy and uncertain. She had no idea how he might react, but the one thing she was certain of was her love for him.

"I just wanted you to know that I'm wildly and desperately in love with you." The words blurted out of her before she even knew for sure how she intended to tell him her feelings.

He appeared to look at her in stunned surprise. Initially, she thought she saw a flash of wild joy in the depths of his eyes but then they once again shuttered darkly against her. "I'm not surprised you think you're in love with me. After all, I took care of you when you were in pain and I'm now doing the best that I can to guard your life."

"Beau, I don't just *think* I'm in love with you. I know I am." She got up from the sofa and crouched in front of where he sat in the chair. "I loved you when I was a young girl, and now I love you with the maturity of the woman I've become. I want to spend the rest of my life with you. I want to have your babies. Beau, I want the future we once promised to

each other. After Friday night we can finally have it all…
We can have all our dreams come true."

His muscles bunched and the knot in his jaw began to
tick. "That future was destroyed."

"But it doesn't have to be destroyed," she protested. "It
was just postponed for fifteen years. We can still have it all,
Beau. We catch the bad guy and clear your name and then
the future is ours."

The knot in his jaw clenched and unclenched. "And what
kind of future do you really think you're going to have with
me?" He got up from the chair, and to her surprise he half
knocked her over as he stood and took several steps away
from her. He turned back to look at her and his eyes blazed
with emotions she couldn't begin to decipher.

"Tell me what you foresee when you think about a future
with me," he said. "Have you considered the fact that I'm an
ex-con swamp rat without a job? Have you thought about the
fact that I don't even know what I'm going to do when this
is all over? I'm trash, Peyton, and you deserve much better."

"Don't say that," she replied and she quickly scrambled
back to her feet. "You are not trash, Beau Boudreau. And
you are not a swamp rat. I'm not worried about you not having a job. You're smart and resourceful, and there's no doubt
in my mind that you'll figure something out."

He raked a hand through his hair and gazed at some point
over her head. "It's not going to work, Peyton," he said.

She took several steps closer to him. "As long as we love
each other, we'll make it work. Look at me, Beau. Look at
me and tell me you don't love me."

His gaze met hers. "It doesn't matter whether I love you

or not." The muscle in his jaw ticked faster. "The truth of the matter is I'm not sure I can ever forgive you."

"Forgive me?" She looked at him in stunned confusion. "Forgive me for what?"

His entire body tensed and there was no mistaking the anger that suddenly emanated from him. "You knew me better than anyone else in the world, Peyton. You knew all there was to know about me, and yet you didn't believe in me."

"Beau, I'm sorry, but after you were convicted, I'll admit I didn't know what to believe," she admitted.

"I'm talking about before that. I'm talking about the minute you heard that I'd been arrested for the murder. You didn't come down to the jail and talk to me. You didn't come to hear what I had to say. I waited and waited in that jail cell for my girl to come and offer me support." His features appeared tortured with a combination of grief and anger.

She stepped toward him and reached out in an effort to touch him, to somehow soothe him. She'd never dreamed he had these kinds of feelings toward her. She'd never realized what a betrayal that had been to him.

He took several steps backward from her. "I needed you, Peyton, but you never came. When it came right down to it, you believed what everyone else believed about me…that I was a cheat and a coldhearted killer." He released a bitter laugh. "And what a stupid murderer I was…to leave my necklace wrapped around Lacy's neck and lead the police right to me. Still, you abandoned me when I needed you most."

Tears sprang to her eyes. "I'm sorry. Beau, I was eighteen years old. When I heard you'd been arrested, I didn't know what to do. I had everyone talking to me…confusing me. I was so young, Beau. I didn't know how to handle what was happening."

Hot tears ran down her cheeks as she realized the depth of his pain. She took several steps toward him, wanting to touch him, to embrace him in an effort to somehow heal this... heal him. "I'm sorry, Beau. I'm so sorry I let you down. In my heart of hearts, I never believed you were guilty. Please forgive me for not being there for you."

He'd apparently held in these feelings about her for the past fifteen years, and she didn't know how to fix this except to plead for his forgiveness. "Beau, please... I love you so much. Please, tell me we can get past this and that you love me, too."

The anger left his features, leaving behind a weary exhaustion. "I'm going to go get some gas. I definitely need some fresh air." He didn't wait for a response, but rather turned on his heel, grabbed his cell phone from the desk and then strode out the front door.

Chapter Eleven

Thick emotion pressed tight against Beau's chest as he shut off the generator and then grabbed the two plastic gas containers off the back porch. He then headed away from the shanty.

He hadn't meant to go there with her. He'd never intended to tell her how badly he'd felt betrayed by her all those years ago. But it had been the best defense against her words of love. Holding that against her would give him a reason to tell her they'd never have a future together.

Now her words of love played and replayed in his head. He'd wanted her to fall back in love with him; he'd wanted her to love him as much as he loved her. But he'd recognized the truth, and the truth of the matter was in this case love just wasn't enough.

He couldn't change who he was...what he was. No matter how much they loved each other, he still had no viable future to offer her. She was far better off without him.

Tears blurred his vision as he walked through the dark paths toward the grocery store. She loved him, and his heart should be singing with happiness.

The moment he'd found out she was still single, and then

when he'd walked into her office and seen her again, his heart had remembered all the wonderful things about her... all the magical moments they had shared together. He'd told himself all he wanted was to get her into his bed, but he'd been lying to himself. He'd wanted her for an eternity.

He'd been a damn fool. He'd not only fooled himself into thinking they could pick up where they'd left off all those years ago, but he'd also toyed with her emotions by allowing her to believe the same thing.

He now needed to embrace all the anger he'd felt when she hadn't come to talk to him, when she hadn't shown her support to him after he'd been arrested. He had to make his anger keep a strong shield around his heart. He needed that shield to keep her out of his life. It was the kindest thing he could do for her.

She would be fine without him. She was smart and beautiful and eventually, she'd find a man worthy of her love. And they would build a wonderful life together.

She had a respectable business to build and Beau would only be a liability in her life. He had to make her see that the dreams they'd had fifteen years ago simply weren't viable in the real world. They had merely been the innocent fantasies of children.

"Yo, Beau." Gator appeared on the path in front of him.

"Hey, Gator," Beau replied. He quickly swallowed hard against all his emotions. The very last thing he wanted was for Gator to see him distraught or teary-eyed.

"I've never known you to make so much noise traveling through the swamp, but just now you definitely sounded like a pissed-off boar crashing around," Gator said.

Beau held up the two gas cans. "I probably was crashing around. I'm just heading to Vincent's to get some gas for my generator."

"How's that pretty woman of yours doing?" Gator asked.

"She's pretty much healed up so she's doing just fine," Beau replied. He wanted to insist to Gator that Peyton wasn't his woman, but he couldn't force the words to his lips right now.

"Any word from Gravois on who shot her?"

"No, nothing. And I'm assuming there's been no break in the swamp women's murders."

"Nothing that I've heard, and you know I hear most things," Gator replied.

"I've never known a man who has murders happening right under his nose and can't catch the guilty person," Beau said in disgust.

"He put you behind bars quick enough," Gator said.

"You got that right. He can solve a crime wrongly if there's a convenient swamp rat to take the fall."

"That's probably what's going to happen with the murders that have taken place. He'll find somebody from the swamp to lock up, but the murders will continue 'cause he'll lock up the wrong person."

"So you think it's a townie killing those women?" Beau asked.

"My gut says so, and my gut usually isn't wrong."

"You probably have that right," Beau replied. "By the way, what are you doing sneaking around out here?"

Gator laughed. "You know I sometimes like sneaking around. I get tired of the four walls and feel the need to be out here in the wild. You know how it is, Beau."

"I do, and now I'd better get moving. I don't want to leave Peyton alone for too long," Beau replied.

"Go on, then," Gator said. "I'll see you later."

Beau continued forward as Gator disappeared into the darkness. At least meeting the old man had forced Beau to pull himself together.

Now all he felt was a deep, burning sadness in knowing that after Friday night he would say goodbye to Peyton forever.

THE MINUTE BEAU LEFT, Peyton collapsed in tears on the sofa. She'd truly believed she and Beau had been working toward a future together. She'd truly believed he was as deeply in love with her as she was with him. And maybe he was...but he couldn't forgive her.

She'd never dreamed that he'd been holding in so much resentment toward her. She didn't know how to fix this. She didn't know how to make right a mistake she'd made fifteen years ago.

At that time, she'd been so young. Her parents had hammered into her Beau's guilt, as had her girlfriends, especially when she'd learned that Beau had been in Lacy's room that night. She'd been confused and hadn't known what to do so in the end, she'd done nothing. And that had been her mistake...her sin.

There was no way to make Beau understand. There was a part of her that didn't understand why she hadn't run to Beau to hear his side of the story, why she hadn't been there to support him through the ordeal. Definitely, her youth had played into it.

She'd only been eighteen years old, and fairly sheltered at

that. She hadn't known anything about crime and what happened when a person was arrested. She hadn't even known she could go to the jail and speak with Beau.

And the payment for that one mistake was that she would never truly have Beau's love again. There would be no future for them as long as he held on to that resentment.

Her grief stabbed straight into her heart, hurting with an agonizing pain she'd never felt before. It was more painful than the day she'd lost him to prison, more painful than a bullet in the shoulder.

Over the past couple of weeks, she'd seen Beau and the man that he had become. She'd actually envisioned building a life with him, building a family with him. She saw them reclaiming the dreams and plans they had made as a young couple in love. But apparently, that wasn't going to happen now.

She'd cried over the demise of those dreams on the day he'd been convicted and sent to prison, and she now cried over the death of them once again.

She had to face reality, and the reality was that apparently, he didn't love her after all. She would've sworn that she'd seen his love for her shining in his eyes. She'd believed she'd felt his love for her in his simplest touch. How had she been so wrong about things? And why hadn't he told her how much he resented her from the very beginning?

She didn't know how long she cried before she finally sat up and wiped her tears away. Maybe she could talk to him again when he came back from getting the gas. There had to be a way for her to make him forgive her. There just had to be a way that they could get beyond this and finally live the future they'd once dreamed about.

She got off the sofa and went to the icebox. She pulled out of it a cold bottle of water. She ran the bottle across her forehead where a headache threatened to blossom, then she opened it and took several drinks. She carried it back to the sofa, where she sank back down and placed the bottle on the coffee table.

Footsteps sounded outside the shanty, and she got up from the sofa and quickly wiped the last of her tears off her cheeks. She drew several deep breaths and prepared herself to beg for Beau's forgiveness…to beg him for his love again. When it came to this, she had no pride. She would beg and plead to get him to forgive her.

A quick knock sounded and then the door opened. Jack Fontenot walked in. "Peyton," he said, sounding surprised. "I didn't expect to see you here."

"Jack," she replied with equal surprise. "Beau's not here right now. He went down to Vincent's to get gas for the generator."

"Actually, I knew Beau wasn't here and I knew you were here. It's actually you I wanted to talk to."

"Me? What do you want to talk to me about?" she asked. And how did he know that Beau wasn't here? An edge of disquiet suddenly swept through her.

"I wanted to talk to you about your investigation into Lacy's murder," he said.

"Okay. Why don't you have a seat." She gestured toward the sofa.

"Thanks, but I'll just stand. I don't intend to be here that long," he replied. "I was just wondering how close you and Beau are to naming the guilty party?"

"Very close," she replied.

"And are you keeping close contact with Gravois about the murderer?" he asked.

"Gravois hasn't been very interested in our investigation," she admitted. "Jack, you should probably come back when Beau is here."

"I told you I don't need to talk to Beau. Aren't you listening to me?" Jack's blue eyes appeared as cold as ice as he took another step toward her.

Her Spidey senses went on high alert and all her muscles tensed. The scent of danger suddenly filled the room and half dizzied her mind. "Well, I'd feel more comfortable to speak to you with Beau here. So I think it's time for you to go, Jack," she said stiffly. She walked around him and toward the front door.

"I can't go until I confess all my sins to you."

"Your sins?" She looked at him in confusion.

"I tried to warn you off the case, Peyton. When I attacked you by your car, I warned you to drop your investigation, but you didn't listen to me," he said.

She gasped. *Jack?* It had been Jack who'd shoved her against her car and smashed her in the face? "You did that to me? But why? Why on earth would you care what we were doing?" And then it hit her. Of course he cared. He cared because he had killed Lacy. Beau's best friend had killed Lacy and framed Beau.

"Bingo," Jack said. "I can see by the look on your face that you get it now." His features twisted into a frightening mask of anger. "That little bitch wanted me to pay her off to keep her mouth shut about all the times I visited her and what we did while I was with her."

His voice rose as he continued, "She wanted me to go to

my parents and get fifty thousand dollars. She threatened to destroy my reputation at a time when we were going forward with the construction company. I'd found Beau's necklace that day at a job we had done and it seemed like the perfect opportunity to kill two birds with one stone. I knew the construction business would be successful, so why share it with anyone?"

"Jack, my God, he was your best friend," Peyton replied, stunned by what the man had just told her and also now terrified about her own safety. They'd considered Jack, but had quickly taken him off their list of potential suspects. He hadn't even received one of their letters.

"Friends come and go, but a successful business and money are what counts in life. Now all I need to do is take care of you, and Beau will be too heartbroken to care about who killed Lacy. He'll drop the investigation in his grief over you."

He pulled from the back of his jeans a handheld three-prong gardening cultivator. "I'll make sure I rip out your throat so Gravois thinks it's the same killer who has been murdering swamp women."

For a brief moment Peyton remained frozen in place, her brain swirling around in an attempt to make sense of things. There was madness in the air…utter madness and death. Then Jack lunged at her. With a scream, she whirled around and ran out the front door.

She raced down the walkway with Jack's footsteps thundering just behind her. Thankfully, darkness had fallen. Surely, she could lose him in the dark. Still, Jack had spent a lot of his youth here in the swamp so he wouldn't be afraid to follow her wherever she went.

Beau, where are you? Her heart screamed his name over and over again. How long before he returned to the cabin? What would he think when he found her gone? Would he come looking for her or would he be relieved that she was no longer there?

All these thoughts raced through her head as she ran for her life. The dark swamp seemed to fight with her as she quickly became disoriented. Branches seemed to grab for her and more than once she tripped and nearly fell. The Spanish moss fluttered across her face over and over again, like a shroud attempting to capture her.

The sound of Jack crashing through the thick vegetation after her filled her with a terror she'd never known. She cried out as she stepped into the swamp water and her foot sank into the muck. She yanked her foot free and continued running.

Her breaths came in panicked, sobbing gasps, causing a painful stitch to stab into her side. He was gaining ground on her. Dear God, he was just behind her and she couldn't run any faster. She was pushing herself as hard as she could. Still, she could hear his panting breaths and imagined she could feel his hot breath on the back of her neck.

Beau. His name now filled her head with the grief of knowing she would never see him again. Jack was going to catch her, and he'd use the gardening tool to rip out her throat. Beau or somebody else would eventually find her dead body and Gravois would write it up as just another Honey Island Swamp Monster attack.

BEAU REACHED VINCENT'S and went inside the small store. There was a limited meat counter, several bins full of vegetables and fruits and rows of canned goods and sundry other items.

Vincent was behind the counter. Beau wouldn't even begin to guess the old man's age, but despite his advanced years, Vincent could be found behind the counter almost every single day. Beau knew he was a widower who lived in a small apartment in the back of the business.

Vincent was neither town nor swamp, but rather a hybrid of both, who easily moved back and forth between the two worlds. Still, all the people who lived in the swamp appreciated the store so close to the wild.

"Hey, Vincent," he greeted him.

"Hi, Beau. How's it going?"

"It's going. How are you doing?"

"The arthritis is kicking my butt lately, but other than that I got no complaints," he replied. "Now, what can I do for you tonight?"

"I need ten gallons of gas." Beau got his wallet out to pay for the purchase.

"Okay, you're all set and the pump is on," Vincent said once he got Beau's money.

"Thanks, Vincent." Beau picked up the gas containers, walked back out the front door and then around to the side of the building where the single pump was located.

As he filled first one of the containers and then the other one, his thoughts returned to Peyton. Somehow, they needed to coexist for two more days and then hopefully the killer would be caught and Peyton could get back to her real life.

Dammit, he shouldn't have allowed his anger to get the best of him. He should have never spoken to her about the resentment that now didn't seem so important in the grand scheme of things. At least, he should have waited until after Friday night to speak to her about it. The last thing he wanted to do was push her out of the shanty before Friday night.

He still had no idea what he intended to do with his future, but he'd eventually figure something out. He just needed time. Once the real killer was caught and Peyton's safety was assured, his brain would be cleared to think about what his next move forward would be.

With both cans filled, he left the grocery store and headed back toward home. The cans were unwieldy enough to keep him at a slow pace as he traversed the small trails that would eventually lead him back to the shanty.

He knew he'd broken Peyton's heart before he'd left. He also knew he was going to have to somehow navigate her emotions so that she'd stay with him for as long as she was in danger.

The next couple of days were probably going to be difficult, but they had to remember that the end goal was to catch a murderer.

He'd only gone a short distance when he first heard it. A high-pitched scream that echoed through the darkness. He stopped in his tracks, unsure if the scream had been from a person or some sort of a wild animal.

The scream sounded again. This time he knew it was a person. It was Peyton. He dropped the gas cans and ran toward where he thought the shriek had come from.

Adrenaline surged through him. His heart beat a frantic rhythm as he crashed through the thickets. "Peyton!" he cried. What was happening? Why was she screaming? Had she tried to leave and somehow fallen into the swamp water? There was no question she was in some sort of danger. "Peyton!" he yelled again.

"Beau!" Her cry came from someplace to his right. He reached a trail and veered off in that direction. Where was she? Oh, God, it was just like the nightmare he'd had where she'd been chased by the Honey Island Swamp Monster and he'd been unable to find her to save her.

He had to find her now. This wasn't a dream where he would wake up with her safe beside him. He continued to run, slapping at branches and leaves that threatened to slow him down. His heart threatened to beat out of his chest as deep gasps exploded out of him.

She screamed again and this time he was closer to her. Her scream not only sounded terrified, but it was also filled with pain. What was happening to her? He surged ahead, silently praying that when he reached her, she would be all right.

There was a break in the darkness as the overhead vegetation thinned and the full moonlight shone down. That was when he saw them... Peyton was on her back and Jack stood over her with some sort of weapon in his hand.

For a moment Beau couldn't make sense of what he saw. Jack? Why was Jack out here attacking Peyton? But the *why* didn't matter. At the moment the big man didn't see Beau. Beau jumped on his back and took him down to the ground.

Peyton sobbed as she crab-walked backward to get out of the way. Beau glanced at her and realized her lower leg was bleeding badly.

"You bastard, what are you doing?" Beau roared in anger as he slammed his fist into Jack's jaw. He reared backward as Jack swung a gardening tool at Beau's face.

Beau dodged the hit and once again smashed his fist into

Jack's face. Jack laughed, the sound maniacal as he spit blood from his split lip. He swung the tool again, this time catching Beau across the chest in a glancing blow.

At the same time, Jack attempted to roll Beau over so that Jack would be on top. But Beau knew if that happened it would give Jack a huge advantage and right now Beau had that advantage.

As the men continued to exchange blows, Beau worried that he wouldn't be able to take control of the situation. He knew if he failed to take Jack out, then Jack would kill Peyton.

"You should have left that bitch's murder alone," Jack now yelled. "If you hadn't gone and stuck your nose in it, then I wouldn't have to kill you both now."

Jack? *Jack* had killed Lacy? He was the one who had framed Beau? In a million years Beau wouldn't have guessed Jack as the guilty party.

"Jack, you were my friend. How in the hell could you frame me for murder?" he asked.

Jack grinned up at him again from beneath where Beau sat on his chest. "You were expendable. You're nothing but swamp scum." He swung the tool again. Beau once again managed to dodge the hit.

The big man suddenly screamed and writhed against the ground. "My leg…oh, God…my leg."

Beau glanced behind him to see what had happened. Gator stood beside Jack's legs, the knife end of his walking stick buried in Jack's calf. "I definitely caught me a big one this time," the old man said with a wide grin.

Chapter Twelve

The next couple of hours flew by in a blur for Peyton. With Jack still immobile on the ground, Beau called Chief Gravois and told the lawman to bring an ambulance and meet him at the edge of the swamp by Vincent's.

She continued to cry uncontrollably, both from the pain where Jack had raked the garden tool down the side of her calf and the residual terror of what she'd just endured.

Beau left Gator in charge of Jack. "Stab him as many times as you need to in order to keep him here," Beau instructed the old man. "I'll be back with the law as soon as possible."

"Don't you worry about me," Gator said. "I've wrestled bigger beasts out here. This one isn't going anywhere."

Then Peyton was in Beau's arms. She buried her face into the crook of his neck and continued to weep as he carried her slowly out of the swamp and to Vincent's parking lot.

He continued to hold her until Gravois's car and an ambulance pulled up. Two paramedics brought a gurney over to where he stood and only then did he release her.

"Gravois, it's Jack. Jack Fontenot killed Lacy and framed Beau and he came out here to kill me," she managed to gasp amid her tears, right before she was loaded into the back of the ambulance.

She was taken to the hospital, where a doctor cleaned up and tended to the wounds on her leg. It took twenty-two stitches to close the deeper lacerations. He also cleaned up various cuts to her arms and legs from her wild dash through the swamp.

Finally, she was given a tetanus shot, pain medicine and then she was taken to a hospital bed. Left alone there, tears once again rose up inside her.

She still couldn't believe it had been Jack all along. He'd killed a young woman and betrayed his best friend, all in the name of money. It was bad enough that he'd pushed Beau out of the company, but this new information must be devastating to Beau.

Had Gravois believed what she'd said? Was Jack now in jail where he belonged? And where was Beau? How badly had he been hurt in the fight with Jack? It had been horrifying to watch the two men exchange blows.

She had so many questions and no answers. Night had completely fallen and the pain meds had begun to work, making her groggy. Would Beau come to see her? She hoped so. She desperately needed to see him, to assure herself he was okay. Surely, he cared enough about her to want to check in on her.

She fought to stay awake, waiting for him to come...needing him to come. Despite her desire to the contrary, she eventually drifted off to sleep.

Morning light drifting into the nearby window awakened her. She stirred and immediately groaned. Not only was her leg screaming in pain, but she felt like she'd been run over by a big truck. Every muscle in her body ached and she knew it was due to her sprint through the swamp.

She had almost escaped Jack the night before. She'd almost thought she was going to be able to outrun him. In the end, he'd lunged at her and caught her on the leg. If Beau had been one minute later in finding her, Jack would have succeeded in his desire to kill her.

Tears pressed hot against her eyes. They weren't tears of pain, but rather because Beau hadn't come to check on her the night before.

They were also tears of fear...maybe he couldn't come to see her. Maybe the beating he'd taken from Jack had put him someplace in this hospital.

When would somebody come in and fill her in on what had happened after she'd been whisked away by the ambulance? When would somebody come in and tell her about Beau's condition?

She'd been awake for about half an hour when a young blonde woman in lavender scrubs came in and introduced herself as Mandy.

Mandy took her vitals but had no information about anything that had happened the night before. Soon after she left Peyton's room, breakfast arrived.

She was grateful for the hot coffee, but only picked at the scrambled eggs. She had no appetite for food, but she was positively starving for information.

Her breakfast tray had just been taken away when Dr. Richards walked in. "First a gunshot wound and now this. You're keeping the emergency room busy," he said with a smile.

"No offense, but I would much prefer that the next time

I see you is a social occasion and not a professional visit," she replied.

"How are you feeling?"

"A little rough," she admitted.

"I wouldn't expect anything different," he replied. "From what little I've heard you went through quite an ordeal last night."

"It was a terrible nightmare. So what happens now?"

"I'd like to keep you until after lunch, give you some more IV antibiotics and pain meds and then if you're feeling like it, we can talk about you going home sometime after lunch. That sound okay to you?"

She nodded. "That sounds fine. But can you answer a question for me?"

"Depends on what the question is," Dr. Richards replied.

"Was Beau Boudreau brought in for any treatment last night?"

"Not that I'm aware of. I can certainly tell you he isn't a patient in the hospital."

Relief fluttered in her heart. If he wasn't a patient here, then he was probably okay and that's all she'd wanted— needed—to know.

"Now, I'll get out of here and let you rest and then I'll be back around noon or so to see how you're doing," Dr. Richards said, and then he was gone. Mandy returned to administer the medicine and then Peyton was once again left alone.

She closed her eyes, and she must have dozed off, for when she opened her eyes again Beau was sitting in the chair next to her bed. He had a black eye and one side of his jaw was darkened with a bruise.

Her heart squeezed tight at the sight of him. "Oh, Beau."

She only managed to get his name out and then a wave of tears overtook her.

"Peyton, don't cry. Are you hurting? Do I need to get the doctor?" he asked in alarm.

"No. I'm n-not crying because I h-hurt. I'm crying because you got hurt," she managed to say through her tears.

He leaned over and took hold of her hand. "I'm okay, Peyton. Besides, I'd fight anyone in the world to keep you safe." He squeezed her hand and then released it.

"Is Jack in jail?" she asked as her tears began to ebb.

"Not yet. He's someplace here in the hospital under armed guard. Gator's walking stick did a bit of damage to Jack's leg."

"Thank God for Gator and his trusty walking stick," she replied. "So tell me everything that happened after I was taken away."

"Jack tried to convince Gravois that we had it all wrong, that he had nothing to do with Lacy's murder. But I pointed out that Jack had come to my cabin with a weapon to kill you. Gravois started asking Jack some difficult questions and Jack finally fell apart and wound up confessing to everything. It's over, Peyton. My name has been cleared and you're free to go back to your life without worrying about any danger."

She searched his features, seeking some softness, some sense that he loved her. She thought she saw it in the very depths of his beautiful dark eyes.

"Beau, please forgive me for the mistakes I made fifteen years ago." Tears filled her eyes once again. "I'm sorry I wasn't there for you when you needed me. But I'm so deeply in love with you, Beau."

He raked a hand through his hair and released a weary sigh. "I'm in love with you, too." Her heart sang with his words. "But Peyton," he continued, "I'm not going to be your future."

"What do you mean?" Her heart immediately took a nose-dive.

"I mean once you're healed up, you need to go back to the life you were living before I interrupted it," he said.

"But I don't want that life," she replied frantically. "I want the future we planned years ago. I want a future of us loving each other and living together. I want to have your babies, Beau. We can have it all now. Remember how you used to tell me I was your swamp princess? I want to be that again."

"I'm swamp, Peyton, and I'll always be swamp and you'll never be. I'd just be a hindrance to you going forward." He stood, his eyes now shuttered. "Forget about the future we once planned together. We were just kids dealing in fantasy and not reality."

"Beau...please," she cried. "I want you... I need you. I've never loved a man the way I love you."

"Eventually, you'll find the right man to love. Just forget about me, Peyton. Please, just forget about me." He didn't give her an opportunity to reply, but instead turned on his heel and left her room.

What had just happened? He'd told her he loved her, but he was walking away from her? Because he was from the swamp? Because he thought he'd be a hindrance in her life going forward?

Tears chased each other down her cheeks. He'd apparently turned all noble on her, and that ticked her off. Damn him for thinking he knew what was best for her.

She cried until she had no more tears left to cry and then she finally managed to pull herself together. Thankfully, she did, for at that moment Gravois walked into her room.

"Peyton, do you feel up to a chat?" he asked. "I need to get an official statement from you, so is this a good time?"

"It's a fine time," she replied. As he took a seat in the chair next to her bed, she raised the head of her bed so she was sitting up straighter.

"Can you start from the beginning and tell me exactly what happened last night?" he asked.

She began from the time Jack had stepped into the shanty. She told him about Jack confessing to killing Lacy and setting up Beau. Then she told him about Jack's desire to kill her in order to stop their investigation.

As she talked about the terrifying run through the swamp, tears once again burned at her eyes. "I finally tripped and that's when he caught me in the leg. Then Beau showed up and the two men fought. If Beau hadn't shown up when he did then there's no question in my mind that I'd be dead. Jack was going to tear out my throat so you'd believe it was another Honey Island killing."

When she was finished, she swiped away the tears that had leaked down to her cheeks—tears of residual fear and immense sadness over her conversation with Beau.

"Peyton, I don't even know where to begin," Gravois said. He gazed at her with sad eyes and a humbleness she'd never seen from him before. "I can't believe I got so many things wrong in my initial investigation into Lacy's death. I not only did a disservice to Beau, but also to the entire town. I would have never guessed that Jack was the guilty party in this and I'm sorry it took you getting hurt for the truth to come out."

"I'm not really the one you need to apologize to. Beau lost fifteen years of his life. He's the one who deserves an apology at the very least."

He nodded. "I'll be speaking to the town council about some sort of a monetary settlement with Beau. It's the very least I can do."

Minutes later Gravois was gone and the smell of food wafting down the hallway and into her room let her know it was lunchtime. Shortly after she was served lunch, Dr. Richards came back into her room with Mandy at his side.

"How are you feeling?" the doctor asked.

"Ready to break out of here," she replied.

"Before I let you go, we're going to take a look at your stitches and change your bandages," he said. "Then if everything looks good, I'll write you a script for antibiotics and some pain meds."

Half an hour later her bandages had been changed, her IV had been removed and she was redressed in the jean shorts and navy blue tank top she'd worn in. She'd also called Jackson for a ride home from the hospital, and she now sat on the edge of her bed to await him.

"Girl, what have you gotten yourself into this time?" he asked minutes later as he swept into her room. "I hadn't heard that you were here, otherwise I would have been here first thing this morning to check up on you. So tell me all."

"Jack Fontenot tried to kill me last night but thankfully I managed to escape with just some stitches in my leg," she replied.

"The town is all abuzz this morning about Jack's guilt in Lacy's murder. I guess you were right about Beau all along."

"Yeah, I'll try not to say 'I told you so' too many times," she replied with a wan smile.

At that moment Mandy came back into the room pushing a wheelchair. "All ready to go?"

"I'm ready." Peyton took a seat in the wheelchair while Jackson ran ahead to move his car up to the curb.

"Do you mind driving me through the pharmacy? I've got two scripts to fill," she asked once she and Jackson were on their way away from the hospital.

"No problem," he replied.

As they waited in the drive-through for her medicine, she filled him in on everything that had happened the night before. However, she didn't say anything about what had occurred earlier that morning with Beau.

"I have one more favor to ask," she said as Jackson pulled away from the drive-through window.

"Anything, my love," Jackson replied with a warm smile.

"I don't want you to drop me off at my house. I need you to drop me off at Vincent's Grocery."

Jackson shot her a sharp glance. "What are you doing, Peyton?"

"I'm not sure," she admitted. "All I know is Beau loves me and I love him. Jackson, he's my happiness and I desperately hope my future is with him. I have to go talk to him."

"For God's sake, you just got out of the hospital. You have a million stitches in your leg. Surely, this can wait."

She shook her head with determination. "No, it can't wait. I need to talk to Beau right now." Her heart beat frantically with her desperate need. Beau didn't get to just walk away from her for her own good.

Jackson sighed. "You know all I've ever wanted for you

was your happiness. Far be it for me to stand in the way of true love." He turned the car and headed in the direction of the little grocery store.

"Thank you, Jackson. I want your support and I need your friendship always."

"And you'll have my friendship always," he returned. "I suppose that means I'll have to make nice with Beau in the future."

"That's a must. Honestly, Jackson, if you just give him a chance you might actually like him."

By that time Jackson had pulled into Vincent's parking lot. He parked the car, shut off the engine and then turned in his seat to gaze at her. "Do you even know your way through the swamp to get to his place?"

"I think I do." She looked toward the swamp and a bit of trepidation swept through her. "I have a general idea of where his shanty is."

"Then let's go," he said and opened his car door.

"You aren't going with me," she protested.

"I can't let you go in there all alone," he replied. "You aren't even sure where you're going."

"And you know the way?" She raised an eyebrow at him.

"Of course I don't, but I can't just let you go off all by yourself when you're obviously hurt," he replied.

"Jackson, I insist I go by myself," she said firmly. "I don't want you with me. Besides, if I get lost, I'll just yell for Beau. If he doesn't come for me, then I have a feeling Gator will find me and lead me home."

Home had become the shanty with Beau. It was where she belonged. She belonged wherever he was, and he belonged with her. She was determined to go into the darkness of the swamp to claim the love of the only man who lit her up inside.

BEAU YANKED THE sheets off his bed and tossed them into a bag to take to the laundromat. The sheets all smelled like Peyton and he refused to spend another night surrounded by her evocative scent.

He pulled out a clean set from the top of his closet and then set about remaking the bed. He'd already packed up her clothes and cosmetics into the backpack she'd initially brought with her when she'd come to heal from her shoulder wound. He'd also packed away her cell phone.

In the next day or two he'd see to it that she got all her items back. He just couldn't face doing that today. The hospital visit he'd shared with her earlier in the day had left him emotionally drained except for a deep grief.

Still, he knew he'd done the right thing in breaking things off with her. He'd already brought enough pain, both physical and emotional, to her life.

The anger he'd felt toward her in betraying him all those years ago was gone. It had died the moment he'd heard her scream when Jack had attacked her. Besides, he couldn't be angry with her for being young and malleable to the forces that had surrounded her.

Still, without that anger he was left only with his deep love for her. And it was that love that had made him leave her. He kept telling himself over and over again that it had been the right thing to do.

He was not only reeling from his breakup with Peyton. His head was still trying to wrap around the fact that it had been Jack who had murdered Lacy and set Beau up to take the fall.

The man had completely fooled Beau. Beau had grown up with Jack. They'd been friends for years, close friends, but Beau hadn't recognized the darkness that apparently lived in the man's soul.

He finished making the bed and then went into the living room and sank down in his chair. He was exhausted. The previous night had been endless, starting with Jack's arrest. After the arrest he'd first gone to the hospital to check on Peyton's condition. The doctor had told him she'd received a number of stitches in her leg but was resting comfortably.

That was all he needed to hear—that she was okay. Then he had driven to the police station to give Gravois an official statement.

It had been nearly dawn by the time he'd gotten home. He'd tried to nap, but sleep had remained elusive. Now sleep tugged at him and with a deep sigh, he surrendered to it.

He immediately fell into dreams of Peyton. Her presence and her laughter here had chased away all the dark memories of growing up with his father and the fact that his mother had abandoned him. In his dream he held her in his arms, and her beautiful blue eyes stared into his. Love. It emanated from her very being and warmed him through to his very soul.

She suddenly vanished. His arms were empty and aching with her absence. He called out her name, needing to find her. Tears burned at his eyes as he realized she was truly gone…gone forever.

"Beau…" Her voice whispered his name.

Where was she? And why was she calling his name. She needed to stay away from him.

"Beau." This time it was louder than a whisper and he suddenly jerked awake. She stood just inside the door. Her leg was wrapped up in bandages and a wrinkle that he recognized as pain etched across her forehead.

"Peyton." He jumped up out of his chair. "What are you doing here?"

"Beau, I... I need a place to heal again," she said and then burst into tears.

He quickly walked over to her and then led her to the sofa, where she collapsed. He couldn't believe she was here. He couldn't believe she'd walked through the swamp all alone with an injured leg to get to him.

She cried for several long moments and then pulled herself together. "Please don't make me leave, Beau. I need to be here with you."

Her eyes begged him and he didn't know what to do or what to say to her. He'd thought he'd said all he needed to say earlier in the day in the hospital room. So why had she come here?

"Peyton, it's obvious you're in pain. Do you have medicine to take?" He was buying time to figure out what he was going to do now that she was here.

She pulled two prescription bottles out of her pocket. "One is an antibiotic and the other is pain medicine. I'm due both."

He took the bottles from her, shook one pill out of each and then got her a glass of water. He carried the pills and the water to her. She took the pills and chased them with a big gulp of water and then set the glass on the coffee table.

"Why did you come here, Peyton? I thought I made it clear to you earlier this morning that we needed to part ways," he finally said.

"You made that decision. I didn't," she replied. "You don't get to just walk out of my life, Beau Boudreau. You don't get

to decide what's good for me or not." Her chin raised defiantly and she struggled up to a sitting position.

He took several steps back from her. "It's the best decision I could make for both of us."

"That's baloney." She struggled up and got to her feet.
"No matter what you say, we were destined to be together
on the first night when you led me out of the swamp. You
love me, Beau. I know you do, and I love you."

Tears slowly seeped from her eyes, breaking his heart all
over again. *Stay strong*, he told himself. He had to stay strong
but it was so damned hard when she was standing right in
front of him with her love for him on full display.

"Peyton, please don't make this more difficult than it already is. Why don't you rest for a little while and then I'll
take you home," he said.

"Don't you get it? This is my home." She moved closer to
him. "Wherever you are is my home. We're a team, Beau.
It doesn't matter that you're swamp and I'm town. It never
mattered. You're my strength, the rock I can depend on to
always have my back. And I'll be your strength whenever
you need me to be."

Her words chipped away at his resolve. As she stepped
even closer to him all his muscles tightened. "Just love me,
Beau. Let me love you and give you babies and let us build
the future we deserve, the one that was stolen from us by
Jack."

She was now so close to him he could smell her, that scent
that always dizzied his senses. "Peyton," he said in protest,
but his voice sounded weak to his own ears.

"You are not any sort of a liability in my life, Beau. You

are my heart and my very soul." She reached up and wound her arms around his neck. He stood stiffly in her embrace.

"You will never meet a woman who will love you as much as I do. For God's sake, do the right thing and give us a chance."

He could stand it no longer. He crashed his lips down to hers, kissing her with all the love he had in his heart for her. When the kiss finally ended, he gazed down into her eyes.

"I love you, Peyton. I love you with all my heart and soul, but I never want to be the reason you don't get business. I don't ever want to affect your life in a negative way."

"If somebody doesn't want to do business with me because my husband grew up in the swamp, then I don't want to do business with them," she said fervently.

"Husband?" He quirked an eyebrow.

"You are going to marry me, Beau Boudreau," she said with that confidence he found so sexy.

He laughed. "Yes, I'm going to marry you."

"And right now we're going to celebrate that we caught a killer and cleared your name."

"And what do you have in mind for a celebration?" he asked, even though he already knew. His entire body lit on fire as she smiled at him seductively.

"You have to be gentle with me," she whispered.

"I promise I can be very gentle." He swept her up in his arms and headed for the bedroom.

She owned his very heart, and he knew she was his future and he was hers. Their love had been interrupted years ago, but now he was positive their future together was bright.

Epilogue

"Come on, Beau, we need to get going," Peyton yelled from the living room into the bedroom.

"I'm coming," he replied as he walked into the room. He flashed her that slightly wicked smile that always melted her insides. He picked up the backpack on the sofa and slung it around his back. "Ready?"

"Ready," she replied. Together they left the shanty to head into town.

It had been a little over two weeks since the truth had come out about Jack's guilt and Beau's innocence. To Peyton and Beau's surprise, Beau had become something of a folk hero among the townspeople, and it had been amazing to watch him gain back his own self-respect.

They now walked through the swamp toward Vincent's parking lot. This time Peyton felt more confident about navigating through the tangled growth. Her leg was healing up nicely, although she would always bear scars from that horrible night.

They had also decided how the logistics of their lives would work. During the week while she worked in her office, they stayed in town in her house. From Friday evening until Monday morning, they stayed in the shanty, the place they jokingly referred to now as their love shack.

"Today I should be able to finish up the painting on the office," he said once they were in his truck.

"It's already looking much nicer," she replied.

"It will look even better when it's painted a steel gray with black lettering. It will look fresh and very professional. People will be committing crimes left and right just for a chance to do business with the new and improved LaCroix Law Firm."

She laughed. "I certainly hope not. There are already enough crimes taking place around here." Her laughter died as she thought of the swamp women who had been so brutally murdered. Gravois still had nobody under arrest for the crimes.

They reached the office and together they got out of his pickup. "I'll just get to work out here and I'll see you around noon so we can have lunch together," he said.

"Before I head inside there's something I wanted to toss out to you," she said.

He grinned at her, that slow, sexy smile that made her knees weaken. "You know I'll catch whatever you throw to me." He drew her into his arms.

"I was just thinking with Jack's arrest, there's an opening for a new construction company in town," she said.

He frowned. "It's not that easy, Peyton. I don't have any start-up money for something like that. Jack was my financial backer initially and after that fiasco I'm not sure who I'd want to be my next backer."

"What about me? I have some money tucked away in my retirement account and I could use it to back you. It would be a great partnership… I provide the money and you run the business."

He stared down into her eyes. "You would do that for me?" he asked softly.

She smiled. "Don't you get it, Beau? I would do anything for you. Besides, I consider you an excellent investment."

"And I would do absolutely anything for you," he replied as his dark eyes loved her and his arms tightened around her. "I love you, Peyton."

"And I love you." She barely got the words out of her mouth before he took her lips with his in a tender kiss that spoke of deep commitment, abiding love and a beautiful future with the slightly wicked, slightly irreverent, man from the swamp.

* * * * *

COMING SOON!

We really hope you enjoyed reading this book.
If you're looking for more romance
be sure to head to the shops when
new books are available on

Thursday 4th January

To see which titles are coming soon, please visit

millsandboon.co.uk/nextmonth

MILLS & BOON